FURY

FUSE #3

E. L. TODD

HARTWICK PUBLISHING

Hartwick Publishing

Fury

Copyright © 2021 by E. L. Todd

All rights reserved.

No part of this book may be reproduced in any form or by any electronic or mechanical means, including information storage and retrieval systems, without written permission from the author, except for the use of brief quotations in a book review.

Mom and Dad,

Thanks For Everything

-Rabbit

"Like a leech, I hold on, as if we belonged

To some precious pure dream

Cast off, you've seen what's beneath

Now fail me."

— CHEVELLE "CLOSURE"

CONTENTS

1. Guilty of Treason — 1
2. His Reign Continues — 7
3. Allies — 15
4. The Hidden Passage — 23
5. The Riverglade King — 35
6. Best Friends — 45
7. Polox — 61
8. The Army Marches — 77
9. Wor-lei — 89
10. Death Will Have to Do — 103
11. Invincibility — 113
12. Suicide Mission — 139
13. The Assassin — 153
14. See The Truth — 175
15. Trust — 187
16. Brothers Riverglade — 199
17. King of Dragons — 213
18. The Black Curse — 233
19. Peony — 257
20. The Burden of the Veil — 273
21. Girl Talk — 299
22. Hatchling — 327
23. Into the Mountain — 355
24. Fazurks — 367
25. Talc — 391
26. The Sacrifice of the Durgin — 405
27. Blood, Flesh, and Bone — 425
28. Unkingly — 449
29. The Queen of Corruption — 469
30. Not a Moment Longer — 479
31. Stunning Scales — 497
32. One Thing in Common — 513

33. Baaaaaahhh	529
34. Just You	563
35. Return to Eden Star	583
Message from the author	605
Finder's Reward	607

1

GUILTY OF TREASON

General Callon stepped before Queen Delwyn, at the base below her throne. With his hands behind his back, he waited for the execution promised to him, still in his battle armor. None of his weapons had been stripped from his possession by the watchmen or the soldiers.

Queen Delwyn stared from her throne, flowers interwoven in her hair, her long dress flapping in the subtle breeze that moved through the open windows. Her beauty matched that of the surrounding forest, but her eyes possessed more cruelty than the tips of blades on the battlefield. "I gave my orders. Yet, here you are...your bow across your back, your sword at your hip." Her eyes glanced over him, seeing the flower medals pinned to his chest, decorated as a war hero.

The queen shifted her gaze to Aldon—the new general. "Unarm him. I won't ask again."

Callon stared at the queen, unsurprised that his position had been revoked and granted to someone new.

General Aldon looked to Callon.

Callon gave a nod.

But General Aldon remained rooted to the spot. He directed his eyes back to the queen, helpless.

Callon turned his gaze back to the queen, seeing a firestorm burning in her eyes. "I've given my life to Eden Star. My family has given their lives to Eden Star. I wish to be executed with honor."

A volcano of rage imploded, rocks of fire shooting across the surface of her face, her green eyes now red-orange with lava. "Leave. Us." Her long nails gripped the edges of her throne, her bracelets of flowers shifting as her tendons tightened underneath.

General Aldon silently excused himself.

So did Melian, her queen's guard.

Silence ensued. Angry silence.

"Was it worth it?" Still and angry, she was a predator perched on the edge of her seat.

"She's my family—"

"And I'm your queen." She rose from her throne, the flowers interwoven in her gown matching the ones in her hair. Her words echoed somehow, even given the open windows with vines crawling inside.

"You're more than my queen. You're my family. And as much as you hate it, she's your family too."

Reptilian eyes emerged, narrowed to slits. "She's an abomination. Nothing more."

His hand gripped his other wrist behind his back, the only physical reaction he was allowed to have. "I stand by my decision and will accept the consequences of my actions. Do what you must."

"Does she live?"

"Yes."

"Then why isn't she here?" She approached the top of the stairs, her bare feet emerging from under her dress.

"She has other obligations."

Her eyes narrowed once more, and then she began her descent, gliding down the stairs like she had invisible wings. "She departed the lands she wanted as home. You went with her. What was so important, Callon?"

"She needed my help—"

"In what regard?"

With her face right in front of his, he held her gaze. "She needed to save someone. But she couldn't do it alone."

"Save who from whom?"

"A friend from an enemy."

Her eyes flicked back and forth between his, growing more furious. Her intelligence was unparalleled, and with her fast mind, she was able to connect the dots that she'd never seen. "You should be ashamed for what you've done."

Rush's face came across his vision, blue eyes full of arrogance, the eyes of an executioner. "I regret my part in it, but I don't regret protecting her. If I hadn't been there, she would have perished."

"If only she had…" The queen stepped away, giving a cold side glare as she moved, her beautiful dress dragging across the floor with a gentle rustle. Her attention turned out the window, seeing the endless evergreen. "Did the empire see you?"

Callon's eyes were focused on her long hair, the flowers interwoven in the blond braids. "Yes."

Her body pivoted, her eyes provoked. "Look what you've cost us—"

"We've been at war with the empire for thousands of years. It's not a new provocation. They slay my wife, my child, and my brother, my king. They're fully aware where we stand. They're fully aware that I would stab King Lux with my sharpened blade if he ever crossed my path. The silence and separation have not dulled my ire—nor my sword."

Her breaths had deepened, along with her anger. "She's banned from Eden Star. Marked as an enemy to the elves."

"She is no enemy—"

"She's provoked the empire. They'll hunt her—and they will not follow her here."

Powerless, he could do nothing to protect his niece, not this time.

She stepped closer, the anger glazing over like a fog that evaporated with the afternoon sun. "I will not claim the life of a Riverglade, so you're spared. But you're no longer the General of Eden Star—as I'm sure you've surmised. Several lifetimes of loyalty do not excuse a single betrayal."

"You're right, Queen Delwyn. Thank you for your mercy."

She turned away and rose up the stairs back to her throne. When he remained, she turned around halfway.

"You will grant Cora sanctuary in Eden Star."

Her intelligent eyes turned into pointed arrows. "I will not—"

"Because if you don't, I will reveal her true lineage to the elves."

Her movements were sudden, facing him quickly and returning to the bottom stair. "How dare you—"

"I'm no longer the general of your army. Now, I'm a mere citizen, so I have no obligation to protect your secrets, secrets that shouldn't be kept from your people. A queen rules with reverence and respect, not self-interest."

Her eyes remained fixed, furious and contained.

"Do not misunderstand my loyalty because it is to you and Eden Star, as always. But she's my *Sor-lei*. And I will do whatever I must to protect her."

2

HIS REIGN CONTINUES

Anastille was blanketed in darkness. A moonless night, the land without a breeze. The midnight black dragon soared across the open skies, invisible to everyone down below, unless their eyes were on the stars.

And for just a brief second, those stars disappeared.

Cora experienced the world with a new perspective, with the flight of a bird, the strength of a mountain, and the agility of a highly intelligent being. Her mind flickered in and out of consciousness as she rested on the journey, but Ashe remained strong, even though he hadn't taken a flight so long in thousands of years.

We approach Eden Star.

Her eyes opened, unable to make out the forest with her eyes. ***You can see it?***

I can feel it.

The expansive wings stilled, bringing in a slow descent to the grass below. Cora could feel the air against the bottom of her wings, feel the earth against her talons once her heavy body collided with the ground with a distinct thud.

It was surreal.

We complete the journey on foot.

I'm not sure how to change back...

Pull the energy to yourself.

Yeah...you're going to have to do better than that.

Draw a deep breath. But that breath is energy.

She closed her eyes and completed the instructions, falling forward and landing flat on the ground the second she was on her feet. The lush grass blanketed her fall just a bit, making her eyes smart at the collision of her nose against solid earth. At least it didn't break. "That was graceful..." She pushed herself up and immediately opened her canteen to drench her parched throat.

You'll improve.

"Need anything before we go?"

A grizzly.

"Then you should hunt now. That won't be an option in Eden Star."

You will hunt, Cora. I just completed a long journey.

She winced at the awkwardness. "I'm sorry, Ashe. I-I don't hunt."

You're half human.

"But I'm full elf...when it comes to this." Before they were fused and they spoke with their minds, she'd felt a distinct connection with the black dragon that was as close as what she had with Flare, but when they were fused into a single person...it was different. Not only could she hear his thoughts, but she could *feel* his thoughts too. All the nuances of emotion were practically words. It was a whole different method of communication. "I'm sorry."

Ashe's disappointment was as hot against her flank as if he were a nearby fire. Silent but present, burning. *Then I will make this quick.*

Her vision blurred and she was on the ground again, but she could still see her human palms against the grass.

Ashe was nearly invisible, his enormous black body blending so well into the night that she wouldn't have known he was there, otherwise. But then he took a step—and his presence was unmistakable. She listened to his wings open and his body leave the ground as he went on his evening hunt.

She sat on the grass and waited for his return.

Cora approached Eden Star, sunrise making the sky lighten from its deep darkness. She felt heavy, like she was the mass of both human and dragon bundled up in the same body. Once she stepped into the tree line, she felt it.

Home.

The birds greeting the sun with their morning song, buzzing around the canopy. Bees and other pollinators were visible in the spots of sunlight, going from one flower to the next. There was heavy uncertainty that came with her return to Eden Star, but the soothing calmness of the forest made her forget that.

Eden Star. It's exactly as I remember.

"You've been inside the forest?"

Many times. How will the elves greet you?

"Honestly, I'm not sure…"

Anger. Heavy anger. His emotions were so crisp and sharp that sometimes they didn't need words to communicate at all.

"If my uncle is here, we'll be fine."

If? Where else would he be?

She didn't even want to think about it.

She continued on her way into the forest, knowing the guards would intercept her eventually. They probably watched her that very moment, their bows drawn from invisible places in the trees.

We aren't alone.

She looked over her shoulder, seeing an elf clad in the same armor that Callon wore. Black with a green cape, flower medals pressed to his chest, a powerful sword at his side. He watched her from a distance, walking at her pace.

She halted.

The elf approached her, regal and still, his expression hard, eyes lifeless. He halted too.

I don't remember elves greeting one another with such silent hostility.

Well...I'm not very popular here.

The elf spoke. "I'm General Aldon. Callon has asked me to escort you straight to his home upon your arrival."

Oh no. He's lost his position...because of me.

But he lives.

Cora followed General Aldon through the trees and grass, the sounds of the forest becoming louder as they approached the heart. Soon, the trees thinned out, revealing the pathway through the market, the homes in the trees, the wagon with fruit picked from the fields.

Elves were up at first light—and their eyes were immediately on her.

You're not respected or revered among your people.

Like I said...not very popular.

Then the queen won't listen to you.

Not right now. Cora ignored the stares, her eyes straight ahead or on Aldon's back.

Minutes passed before Ashe spoke. *I believe that will change.*

Well…thanks.

You changed me.

But you aren't a bitch.

A what?

Never mind.

Aldon approached the base of the tree, Callon's home high in the branches, hummingbirds sticking their tongues into the flowers right outside his kitchen window. Aldon stopped at the stairs and regarded her.

Excited to see Callon's face, but also terrified that their relationship had changed, she eyed the stairs.

"I'm to relieve you of your weapons." Aldon extended a single palm, ready to take the sword at her hip, made of dragon scales.

In the eyes of the elves, you're an enemy.

Not them. Just that bitch I mentioned earlier.

Aldon's hand remained hanging in the air between them.

She didn't know what else to do except untie her sword from her belt.

Your sword is made of dragon scales. She can't see it.

What else am I supposed to do?

"General Aldon." Callon emerged around the tree, walking gracefully down the vines that made loose stairs, and reached the earth below their feet. In a green tunic and brown pants, he was dressed as the others, but he still carried the command of a general. He didn't need weapons or armor to pull it off.

General Aldon turned to him, giving him a nod as a respectful greeting.

"Her weapons don't need to be relieved."

General Aldon held his stare.

Her heart tightened in her chest. Her throat suddenly went hot. The sight of Callon made every breath deep and slow.

I feel your love.

Callon gave him a nod in dismissal. "If Queen Delwyn wishes to contest it, she can speak to me herself."

General Aldon took his leave.

General Callon's reign continues.

He walked away, leaving the two of them alone at the base of the tree.

Callon turned his dark green eyes on Cora, examining her with his typical hard expression. The only indication of his emotion was his change in breathing, which had suddenly grown heavy. "I'm glad you're home, *Sor-lei*."

She moved into his body and embraced him, her pack still on her back, her cheek against his chest. "I'm so sorry...."

His arms circled her shoulders and gave her a tight squeeze. "Come. Just about to have breakfast."

3

ALLIES

THEY SAT TOGETHER at his dining table near the window, colorful butterflies passing across the opening, branches with flowers wrapping around the walls and entering the home. Small birds would come close, their chirps the soundtrack of the forest.

Hot bowls of slow-roasted oats were on the table, filled with a mixture of strawberries, blueberries, and crumbled walnuts. A sprinkle of brown sugar was placed on top, along with a dollop of maple syrup.

Callon kept his eyes down on his food most of the time, eating with exaggerated slowness, his spoon sitting inside the bowl for a while before he scooped up his next bite. When he chewed, his eyes lifted to hers.

She hadn't eaten anything fresh or good in a while, so she devoured her bowl then refilled it with the leftovers from the pot on the stove. Even without conversation, it somehow felt as if no time had passed, as if she'd never left Eden Star in the first place. "How are you?"

"Better now that you're home."

"I didn't mean to make you worry."

"Under the circumstances, it was impossible not to."

"Rush would never hurt me—"

"Let's not speak of him." His eyes immediately went back to his bowl as he swirled his spoon around.

Cora gave a wince at his sharp coldness. "I'm so sorry… You really have no idea." His disappointment was a worse pain than the physical agony she endured at the hands of the Steward of Easton. Emotional pain was far worse than physical…as she recently learned.

"Even if I'd known whom you were saving, I would have done it anyway. Even if I'd known it would cost me the position I've held for thousands of years, it wouldn't have changed anything. So, don't be sorry." His eyes remained out the window, watching the birds sit on the nearby branch.

"It's hard not to be…"

"A man's duty is to his family." His eyes shifted back to hers. "Everything else…comes second. It was also time for me to step down. General Aldon is the person I recommended for the position—and Queen Delwyn was wise to listen."

"It seems like you're the one still in charge."

He watched her without reaction, his fingers still on the edge of his spoon. "As I said before, I've been in the position a long time."

They disobey a queen's orders in favor of his. That means he's earned the unquestionable loyalty of his people—more than their own queen has. I liked him when he served under King Valnor. I like him still. He's a good man. Loves you like a hatchling.

I know he does. "I'm surprised Queen Delwyn has allowed me to come back at all."

Callon dropped his gaze back to his bowl, scooping up a bite that was now cold.

It's because of him.

How do you know?

It's been a long time since I've been among the elves, but I do remember one thing. It's not about the words they speak—but those they don't speak.

"How did you convince her?"

"I didn't." He took a bite, a long and slow bite. "I blackmailed her. Not out of desire, but necessity. When she questioned me about our whereabouts, I spoke the truth, a veiled truth. She is my queen, and I respect her and serve her without reservation."

"How did you blackmail her?"

"Threatened to tell the elves who you really are."

Queen Delwyn is corrupt, it seems.

I think it's more complicated than that.

Nothing is complicated unless we make it complicated.

"That probably pissed her off."

His eyes went back to his bowl. "I had no other choice. If I were still her general, it would have been different…but I'm not anymore."

"Then that was stupid on her part."

He scooped another bite of oats onto his spoon. "She responded emotionally. Not strategically."

Not a good quality in a leader.

Have you met Queen Delwyn?

No.

"So…what does she know exactly?"

Instead of taking the bite he took so long to prepare, he left it in his bowl. He seemed to be finished because he abandoned his food this time. Elbows rested on the table, and his arms folded on top. "That you went to save someone from the empire. I joined you to keep you alive. That's it."

"So, she doesn't know about—"

"No."

"Well, thank you for keeping it quiet."

His eyes flicked away out the window.

If he hadn't deceived his queen, you would have been exiled from Eden Star—even he couldn't prevent that.

I know.

"Queen Delwyn asked if I'd been seen, and I couldn't lie. The empire knows that we're allies now. The battles have been on hiatus, but we still remain at war. That hiatus may end now."

He's right.

"Shit..."

Callon's eyes narrowed.

"Sorry," she said quickly.

"They've been searching for you, but now they know exactly where to continue their search. As a firsthand witness to your abilities, I'm unsurprised that finding you is their priority."

"But the forest can't be breached...right?"

"Nothing is guaranteed."

They gave me sanctuary...and now I give them war. "I shouldn't have come here." The consequences of her actions were heavier now that this place wasn't just a mythical forest. It was her home now. Images of the forest burning came into her eyes, the tree houses crumbling to the ground, the throne on fire.

"This is your home. So, yes, you should have come here."

Her eyes moved back to his.

"Whether it's one or all, we protect our own. We will protect you."

"I don't want to be protected. I want the forest to be safe."

"Like you said before, King Lux would have come eventually. He might just come sooner now. That's the only difference."

"Not if I leave Eden Star and they follow me…"

He gave a slight shake of his head. "You'd buy us time. But nothing more."

The guilt consumed her. Drowned her.

He continued to stare at her. "I will do my best to prepare you for what's to come. And when it arrives, you will have my sword, shield, and bow to get you where you need to be."

Your very own general.

"Thank you, *Tor-lei*."

His eyes dropped to his rejected food.

"I hate to ask for more, but…"

His eyes returned, serious and focused.

"Would it be possible to convince Queen Delwyn to march on King Lux first?"

He absorbed the question before he gave a shake of his head. "It's possible. But not probable. Until the war is brought to our borders, we won't engage. We've lost enough battles to know that it's hopeless. In this regard, I'm in agreement with her decision. Too many men. Too many dragons."

"What if we had allies?"

Callon stared at her differently now, his eyes narrowed like tips of arrows. "*Sor-lei*, what happened after I left you?"

Don't tell him.

We can trust him—

I said, don't.

"I have some powerful allies now. That's all I can say."

4

THE HIDDEN PASSAGE

HER TREE HOUSE was exactly as she left it.

The only difference was the dishes that she left in the sink. Instead of sitting there covered in mold, they'd been washed and set out to dry on the counter.

Callon.

Her sword leaned against the wall at her bedside, and her bow and quiver of arrows were left on the counter. Her old clothes still hung in the closet, so after a bath, she donned something more comfortable and sat up in bed.

The night darkened, the birds quieted, and soon it was just the crickets and occasional crack of a branch from a heavy owl. Arms folded over her chest, she stared into the darkness, seeing the moonlight shine off the canopy. *We need to tell him.*

No.

You just said you liked him.

I do. Doesn't mean I trust him. He hates dragons, like all elves.

Well, he saved Flare from the Steward of Easton.

For you.

Doesn't matter why he did it.

It matters greatly.

So, what's the plan here? My entire purpose in bringing you is so you can speak to Queen Delwyn and negotiate an alliance.

That was before I realized you are unanimously disliked and the queen is corrupt.

Corrupt is a harsh word...

She denies her people truth. That's the definition of corruption.

Doesn't matter because we need her.

Not if she'll betray me. Could save her people by sacrificing mine.

She wouldn't do that—

Every elf they've lost is a consequence of my ill decision. Wouldn't hesitate—if it were me.

She'd never forget the look on Callon's face when he saw the red scales and long tail of a dragon. He'd been so livid, he'd almost chosen to stay behind. That feeling of detest must be mirrored throughout society. **Callon is loyal to his people—but he's more loyal to me. Any secret I confide in him is safe.**

Ashe turned quiet.

We need to tell him, Ashe. He can't help us if he doesn't know.

He hates dragons like the rest.

He does. But he'll change his mind...and then change the minds of everyone else.

"Rise."

"Mer...?" She turned in the bed instinctively, pulling the sheet over her head to block out the sunlight.

"Cora." His voice deepened, commanding her like an army.

"Dude, I'm so tired—"

"Expect to always be tired from now on."

"Ugh."

"Now." His voice grew louder, the threat scary.

"Geez, okay." She threw the sheets back and rubbed the sleep from her closed eyes. "I'm awake. Just let me get breakfast started—"

"No breakfast. Get dressed and meet me downstairs."

"No breakfast—"

He was gone.

Freakin' psychopath.

Nothing.

Ashe?

Still nothing.

Wish I got to sleep in...

Callon struck down her branch. "Weak." He blocked her punch then threw her arm down, making her spin slightly. "Clumsy." He gave her a shove, sending her tripping backward across the grass until she regained her footing. "Have you forgotten everything I taught you?"

"No." She brushed off her pants and straightened. "I wasn't kidding when I said I was tired. Haven't slept in two days..."

"I've fought a battle for four days—and never slept."

"Well, I don't have a bazillion years of experience under my belt."

He tossed the branch aside, the instruction concluded. "I don't know how much time we have. But whether it's a lot or little, we can't afford to waste it."

She wiped her brow with the back of her wrist, getting rid of the sweat that had started to drip down her face. "I know. I'll be ready to go tomorrow."

"Why didn't you sleep for two days?"

"Traveling."

"You ran for two days straight?" he asked. "Were you chased by the Shamans?"

"No."

His eyes bored into her face, silently demanding an answer.

"We need to talk…" She headed to their packs by the waterfall.

He watched her walk away before he followed her. They sat together by the water, just as they had months ago.

Hungry, she opened her pack and took out the container Callon had packed for her.

The little red cardinal emerged, landing on the grass in front of her, giving out a few chirps. His mind suddenly felt strong against hers, like they were side by side, pressing against each other.

"Hey, honey. Nice to see you." She fed him a few berries then watched him fly away.

Ashe?

I'm here.

I need to tell him.

Be discreet.

Always. "I need to tell you something, but it absolutely has to stay between us."

Callon watched her with the same expression, and if that was the face she met on the battlefield, she would be thoroughly intimidated. "If anything you share poses a threat to Eden Star or my queen, I will report it."

"It doesn't. But if you share it with anyone…it could be a threat to someone else I love."

His eyes narrowed.

"Will you promise to keep my secret?"

"Yes, *Sor-lei*."

"You can't ask any questions either…just need to accept my information."

He gave a slight nod.

This is okay?

Yes.

"I have allies that have pledged to fight with Queen Delwyn—if she accepts."

His dark green eyes were different from her own. Deep. It was the only indication of age—because they were full of years of sorrow, of wisdom, of experience.

She lowered her voice to a whisper even though they were alone. "Free dragons."

As he'd agreed, he didn't ask any questions. His eyes shifted back and forth quickly, his only visible reaction.

"I've returned to convince her to accept the alliance."

He tore his gaze away, his eyes still frantic, absorbing the information with a display of emotions across his expression.

She let him have all the time he needed.

He didn't question you.

Because I was right—he can be trusted.

After a couple minutes of quiet reflection, Callon turned his attention back to her. "Your proposition will be unsuccessful."

"Why?"

"They are not our allies. I can speak on behalf of Queen Delwyn when I say we have no interest in helping the beings that caused all of this in the first place. The reason I've lost my wife...my son...my brother. The reason everyone has lost someone."

As I expected.

"Callon—"

"I will keep your secret. But you have no chance of convincing Queen Delwyn."

"I do...if you help me."

His head snapped in the other direction, dismissing the suggestion.

"You fear that King Lux will cross the desert and march on Eden Star. Can you think of a better ally than a fire-breathing dragon that wants to rescue their imprisoned kin?"

The dismissal continued.

"We have to put the past behind us if we ever hope to have a future."

Callon stared at the stream as if he didn't hear a word.

"I wish you knew how sorry—"

Cora.

The sigh released, slow and heavy.

He needs time. Give it to him.

I NEED TO EAT.

In the days that had passed, Cora and Callon trained in their hidden meadow, and once she had adequate sleep, her skills returned to her. She was still easily disarmed and had no chance against someone of his experience, but she redeemed herself from that first day.

But Callon barely spoke to her. If he did, it was about training, and that was it.

Cora failed to block the hit coming her way, striking her right in the ribs. She groaned and fell to her knees. "Geez, you got me good."

Callon threw down his stick. "I shouldn't be able to get you at all. Do better."

"I'm working on it."

"Work harder."

"What do you think I'm doing?" She cupped her ribs as she glared at him. "I'm out here every day, giving it my all—"

"Stop the excuses."

"They aren't excuses—"

"They are to me." He stepped away, his shirt showing his muscled mass through the thin fabric. When he was dressed in his armor, he was even thicker, far more ominous. But he was just as ominous in nothing but breeches and a tree branch.

Cora, I need to eat.

Yeah, heard you the first time.

Then obey.

Obey? Ooh, that was the wrong thing to say.

If you obeyed, I wouldn't be hungry right now.

Let's just remove that word from our vocabulary right now.

It offends you.

Yes.

But I'm Ashe, King of Dragons. I don't understand.

Would you ever tell Diamond to obey?

Silence.

Now you get it. She pushed herself to her feet, coated in slick sweat. **I'm not sure how to get you out of the forest...and then back in again.**

I need to eat every few days—so we need to figure this out.

Callon turned his gaze back on her, disappointment still there.

Yes, I know.

I could hunt here. They'd never know—

Yes, they would. That's not an option. Especially if we're asking for their aid. "Callon?"

Do not tell him.

We have no other choice. Unless you want to starve?

He gave a quiet snarl. *No.*

"Callon, I need you to help me with something."

"I'm in the middle of helping you with something else right now." He flashed her a look of annoyance, a growl with his eyes.

"Can you get me in and out of the forest without being seen?"

The annoyance faded like the sun setting over the horizon. It turned into razor-sharp focus. "Why?"

Do not tell him.

Ashe—

He's not ready. Trust me.

"I…I can't say."

His breathing changed, growing heavy, and his eyes sharpened.

"I need to come and go as I please…without being seen."

His jaw clenched next. "I grow tired of your secrets."

"Please. I promise that my intentions are innocent."

"Someone could follow you."

"I'm not meeting anyone."

His eyes kept their annoyance because no guarantee would be enough. "If the wrong person becomes aware of this passage, it could be catastrophic for all of us."

"I would never—"

"Promise me you will never meet anyone by route of this passage."

"Of course. I promise."

He stepped away. "After we eat, I'll show you the way."

She watched him walk away.

He loves you the way I love my hatchlings.

I know he does...

IT WAS A DEEP TREK INTO THE MOUNTAINS.

Callon led the way off the path, turning when he recognized a marker in the foliage.

I'm never going to remember this.

I will.

An hour of traveling led them to a mass of boulders between rocky mountainsides. When Callon halted, she knew they'd arrived. "Do you know the way back?"

"Yes."

He gave her a final look before he began the return journey.

"Thank you."

As if he didn't hear her, he kept walking.

Let's go. I'm starving.

She walked through the passageway, roots of trees crossing the gap and growing overhead. The path became narrower, just wide enough for her to pass through. Farther she went, reaching an opening on the other side. ***I'll wait here for you. Be discreet.***

Dragons aren't meant to be discreet.

She suddenly felt the world spin, felt her soul tear in half, her vision blur.

Her body was on the ground, and her eyes saw the wall of black appear.

Then a gray eye came into her vision, large and luminous. *Are you alright?*

"Yeah…just wasn't prepared for that."

I'll return shortly. He stepped away, each of his enormous feet making a distinct thud as he moved.

She pushed herself up and watched Ashe crouch down to become as small as possible as he slithered away, almost like a snake. Nauseated and weak, she felt as if her legs or arms had been torn off. Their connection had been brief, just a week, but once he was gone…there was a distinct void in her chest.

Like she would never be the same.

5

THE RIVERGLADE KING

Her training had completed for the day. She bathed at her tree house then sat at the table in front of the window with a bowl of greens and root vegetables in a lemon sauce.

That will not sustain a warrior.

"It sustains Callon just fine."

Then he must eat all the time.

"He doesn't."

Unnatural.

"We don't breathe fire and have jaws lined with ten rows of teeth. So, it is natural—for us."

Perhaps.

She stirred the contents without taking a bite.

You're sad.

"Just not very hungry."

I can feel it, Cora.

Her hand stilled on her fork, feeling his presence suddenly thicken, press up against her the way the red cardinal did—but on a much more intimate scale. Two souls in one body. Two hearts in a single chest.

When you were reunited with Callon, I could feel the way you loved him. Now I can feel this...

"I don't want to talk about it."

Ashe retreated from her mind, like he physically crossed the room to put space between them.

"Cora."

She turned at the sound of her name, seeing Callon in the doorway. "Hey."

With his arms rigid at his sides, he stood there, his eyes leaving her face and moving elsewhere.

"Everything alright?"

"I know I've been harsh. I'm sorry for that."

"You don't need to apologize—"

"I'd like to show you something." His face turned back to hers.

He wanted the awkwardness to pass, so she did too. "Sure." She abandoned her food at the table and joined him at the front door. "Where are we going?"

He led, taking the stairway of vines. "The Great Hall."

Fury

A FEW HOURS BEFORE SUNSET, THE LIFE IN THE FOREST WAS slowly becoming dormant. The sunlight hit the trees in a beautiful way, highlighting the canopy in a greenish glow from all the leaves. Elves walked the forest floor, mostly alone, but sometimes in pairs.

They took the path away from the tree houses and passed through the thick forest that obscured most of the sunlight. Moisture was heavy in the air, green moss on the north side of the trees.

Callon was beside her, quiet the entire way. "I understand you're no warrior, Cora. But I must try everything I can do to make you resemble one as much as possible. I will protect you with my life, but if my life is taken, I fear for yours."

"I know."

"I've lost enough." His eyes were rigidly fixed on the path ahead. "I can't endure any more. It was I who should have died, not my family. They should have outlived me. They should be the ones grieving me." He turned his head and met her gaze. "You must outlive me, Cora. You must."

Her hand went to his arm and gave a gentle squeeze. "I'm sorry."

"If you ever have children of your own someday, you will understand."

"I already do understand. I understand it every time I look into your eyes." Her hand slowly slid down his arm until it rested at her side.

He forced forward again, emerging from the trees and into the clearing where the large building sat in a field of orange poppies. Stalks broke under their boots as they approached, a quiet summer breeze passing through their hair.

They stepped inside, the hall answering their presence with silence.

"What did you want to show me?" She looked and listened for the sound of other elves in the building, but they seemed to be alone.

He took the lead down the hallway, made a couple turns, and then emerged into a large room that had benches and portraits on the walls. Enormous portraits, most of which were twelve feet tall.

He approached one in particular and stopped several feet back.

She examined the painting that captured his gaze.

Queen Delwyn stood there in a white gown, flowers in her hair, both of her hands placed in the palms of a man across from her. The couple faced each other—like it was a wedding ceremony.

Tall, muscular, with a hard jaw like Rush, she knew exactly who he was.

Tiberius Riverglade.

"This was painted on their Union."

"Queen Delwyn looks exactly the same."

"She's aged slightly—but it's hard to notice."

"I thought elves were immortal."

"They are. Doesn't mean we don't mature like humans and dwarves. We just do it very slowly."

She turned her attention on Callon and watched him examine the painting, his expression vacant.

She looked at the portrait again, looking at the man she'd never called Father. "I have his eyes…"

"You have other things too."

He was a man she'd never met, but somehow, her eyes began to tear. Memories had never been created. Moments never shared. His life came and went, on a timeline that never intersected hers. It wasn't the loss of the man. It was the loss of the opportunity. Blue eyes came into her mind along with a handsome smile, but she pushed it away to a place her mind couldn't follow.

"Whenever my brother was deep in thought, it was with a stern expression. You do the same thing." His hands moved behind his back, eyes straight ahead. "I doubt this is inherited, but…he was a bit of a smartass too."

Her eyes immediately flicked to him.

Callon shifted his gaze to hers, a slight smile moving to his lips.

She smiled back, her eyes still wet.

"At least, he was when it was just the two of us." His eyes moved forward again. "He was a good man and a great king. His infidelity was his only transgression, and I wouldn't have believed he was capable of such a thing if I didn't see your ring...and your resemblance to him. Don't think less of him for it. One mistake doesn't erase his lifetime of good deeds."

"I don't."

"He always wanted to have a child. Queen Delwyn didn't."

His strength was palpable through the painting, along with his love and affection for the queen he devoted himself to. How different would that painting look if she were there? "I wish I could have met him...even if it was just once."

His hand moved to her arm, and he gently pulled her away. "You can."

She regarded him as he guided her away.

"In the graveyard."

"Queen Delwyn forbade me from coming here." The trees were tightly scrunched together in the space, the evergreen leaves crowded together to create a ceiling that hid the sky from view. A single path was in the center, but the distance was obscured by mist.

"And she was wrong to do that." Callon took the lead, stepping onto the path between the trees and moving farther inside the forest. The mist was imminent, just like the mist that formed the barrier of Mist Isle, but the energy was different. Instead of thriving with the presence of mythical creatures, this was full of the absence of life.

The pathway opened, having clusters of graves with flowers growing around the headstones, even though sunlight didn't reach through the copse of trees. Trails led in other directions, to other groupings of fallen elves. Crickets and other creatures provided the background of a gentle hum of wildlife, but the mist amplified that noise to higher proportions. With the mist, the sound, the cool moisture against her skin, it felt like she was far away from Eden Star. "This is where you visit your family?"

He was about to take a path to the right when he turned to regard her. "Yes."

"Can I meet them too?"

His natural instinct was probably to say no, but instead, he considered the request and gave a nod. "They're your family too."

Fireflies lit up the darkness on their way, the shrouded mist refracting the light to make the circumference even larger. Cool moisture pressed against her cheeks as they moved, forming drops that sometimes slid down her face.

Callon stopped when he reached two graves, side by side. There was a third headstone, but it was unmarked. He stared down at the headstones, quiet and still.

She came to his side and read the first.

In Grace Lies
Weila Riverglade
Warrior. Wife. Mother.

She read the second.

In Grace Lies
Turnion Riverglade
Soldier. Son.

Her hand moved to Callon's shoulder, and her fingers dug into his shirt. Together, they stared at the graves, the flowers growing over both of the markers. Green ivy grew along their headstones, covered with white flowers. "I'm sorry."

Callon's expression was as hard as always, his dark eyes conveying nothing. He stepped away and lowered himself to the stone bench beside their graves, his hands coming together on his thighs. With straight shoulders and head slightly bowed, he looked at the earth beneath his boots.

She took a seat beside him.

Silence went on for a long time, the crickets echoing throughout the forest, the fireflies slowly floating from one point of the area to the next.

"Sometimes they come. Sometimes they don't."

"They come together?"

"Rarely. It's usually just one or the other." His eyes remained on the ground, and he gave a slow and deliberate breath.

They returned to their silence, waiting and hoping.

She stared at the forest, finding it both sad and beautiful. It was unlike any other place she experienced on this earth. Her focus would follow one firefly then shift to another. Drops of moisture would occasionally drip from the canopy, like raindrops that made their way down to the base of the tree.

Then she saw it.

A bluish haze.

It was a flicker that came and went. Translucent.

Callon closed his eyes. "She's here. I can feel her."

With a held breath, she watched the blue tint come back into focus, and this time, it was more distinct. It was the outline of a woman. Long hair in a braid, it flapped like there was a breeze wherever she was. Petite in size but strong in the shoulders and arms, she looked like the warrior Callon had described. There were no other features to identify because it was just an outline, an incomplete drawing.

Weila moved to her knees in front of him, her hand resting on top of his.

"Can you feel her?" he whispered.

Cora couldn't speak.

Weila bowed her head on top of their joined hands.

The moisture on her cheeks was no longer from the mist. Tears sprung to her eyes quicker than the snap of her fingers as she witnessed eternal love.

"Cora?" He must have heard the sniffles because he turned to regard her.

"She's on her knees in front of you…her hands in yours…"

His eyes narrowed.

"I know this because…I can see her."

6

BEST FRIENDS

You think they'll be there? Flare glided in the darkness, the lights of Karth in the distant background.

Yes.

And if they aren't?

Then we wait.

Flare drew closer, the darkness covering their arrival in Anastille. *How are you?*

Fine.

Rush—

I'm said I'm fine.

Flare maneuvered around the mountain and dived into the cove. His heavy body landed on the beach with a distinct thud, his talons digging deep into the grains of sand as they shifted under his weight. *I see lanterns.*

Good, they're here.

Rush emerged and approached the entrance of the cave. "Wake up. Daddy's home."

Bridge sat up inside his cot, his palm rubbing his eyes before he tried to focus on Rush's approach. "Finally." He pushed himself to his feet, his eyes still blinking to adjust to the world around him. "You have any idea how long we've been waiting around?"

"Yes, I made a full recovery. Thanks for asking."

Bridge rolled his eyes as he gave a sigh. "Shut up. I already knew you would."

Rush stopped in front of him and looked him over. "You look like shit, by the way."

Bridge gave a sly grin, a full beard on his chin, more awake now. "I've been living in a cave for months, so, no surprise there."

Zane left his cot next and embraced Rush with a handshake. "This guy's immortal—and not because he's fused."

"Just because I'm a lucky son of a bitch, I guess." He embraced him back. "You look good, man."

He rubbed his hand through his thick scruff. "I take care of the front lawn, you know." He cast a look at Bridge.

Bridge glared. "Not my fault I lost everything with the ship."

"What happened to the ship?" Rush asked.

Bridge brushed off the question. "It's a long story…"

Liam came next, walking up to him with his typical starstruck look. "How's your dragon?"

"He's good," Rush said, shaking his hand. "I'm good too...thanks."

He knows we're the same person, right?

He just likes me more. Understandable.

"So, what's been going on with you these past three months?" Bridge asked.

"Wait." Rush took a look around. "Where's Lilac?"

"Oh," Zane said. "She's with Captain Hurricane."

Rush turned to Bridge. "As in, she's gone for good?"

"No..." Bridge gave an uncomfortable look. "They're doing a long-distance thing, so she's with him for a few more days. Where's Cora?"

The instant she was mentioned, Rush gave a pause. "Eden Star."

"Is she joining us or...?" Bridge's eyes flicked back and forth.

"Not for a while." When he didn't hear from her, he assumed she made it safe and sound. She had Ashe, King of Dragons, to look after her, so he knew she was in good hands. "As for Flare and me, we've been at Mist Isle."

"With the dragons?" Liam immediately blurted, his eyes glazing over as he imagined it.

Rush dodged the question, always uncomfortable with the guy's obsession. "Long story short, we convinced some of them to fight with us."

Bridge's mouth gaped open in shock. "What?"

"So, they are there?" Zane asked. "I can't believe it…"

"How many?" Liam asked. "How glorious were they?"

He sounds like you.

A bit. I like it.

Rush exchanged a look with Bridge.

Bridge gave a slight shrug, telling him Liam was harmless.

Rush continued. "But their participation is contingent on the elves."

"That's why Cora is there," Bridge said, following his thoughts perfectly. "You think that'll work?"

"I'm still in shock that we got some of the dragons to agree in the first place." If it weren't for Cora, it never would have happened. He was still the number one enemy to the dragons, still considered General Rush. "I believe that she can do anything."

"Maybe," Bridge said. "I mean, that elf came with her to save you."

"Yeah…" A conversation had never taken place, but Rush could see the fury on Callon's face when their eyes met. They were enemies. If the circumstances had been different,

General Callon would have had his sword against his neck. "That was kinda a one-time thing."

"It still happened." Bridge nudged him in the side. "Pretty big deal."

Because of her.

"So, what's the plan?" Bridge asked. "Eden Star? When Captain Hurricane returns, we'll ask for a ride."

"No Eden Star," Rush said. "We've got to get more allies. Even if the elves agree, we still need more people."

"Really?" Bridge crossed his arms over his chest, his head tilted. "Even with an army of dragons?"

"We don't have an army." Rush gave a shake of his head. "We have twelve. King Lux has far more than that..."

Disappointment flickered across Bridge's gaze, but he covered it up. "Well...better than nothing. So, who do we ask?"

Rush gave him a blank stare. "So, you guys literally did nothing but grow beards while I was gone?"

Bridge glared. "How are we supposed to find an underground resistance group and wait for you at the same time?"

He has a point.

This is taking too long.

Why are you in such a hurry?

My father knows Cora and General Callon got me out of the prison.

Meaning?

I'm building alliances—powerful ones.

Flare considered what he said, his mind suddenly heavy. *Will he march on Eden Star?*

He might.

He never has before.

Well, when his son is rescued by the brother of the king he slew…things change. "The dwarves. Let's start there."

"Uh, do you have any idea where they are?" Bridge asked.

"You're the scholar, aren't you?" Rush said.

Bridge nudged him in the side, this time harder. "I know the location of their territory. But how to get inside? No idea. You're the only one who was alive last time they were seen, so you tell me."

Rush looked at the other guys. "Anyone have any ideas?"

Both shook their heads.

"We'd waste a lot of time going around knocking on rocks," Bridge said. "Time we don't have."

"I agree," Rush said. "So, we won't do that."

"Then what are we going to do?" Bridge said. "Use Flare to tear the rocks apart?"

"If you shut up, I'll tell you." Rush gave him a nudge back. "We're going to ask someone."

"Ask who?" He gave a slight wince where he'd been elbowed. "Who the hell would know how to contact the dwarves?"

Rush set his pack on the ground and rolled up his sleeves. "A witch."

Bridge's eyes narrowed. "Mathilda? You think she'd know?"

Rush gave an exaggerated shrug. "She knows how to get dragon tears. What else could she know?"

Days passed as they waited for Lilac to return.

Rush was the last one to finish eating. Before he was done, Zane and Liam retired to their bedrolls on the stone floor in the corner.

Bridge glanced at him. "Never seen you eat like that."

"Been a long time since I've had meat. Forgot how good it was."

"Why is that?"

Rush licked his fingers as he stared at the fire. "Cora doesn't eat meat, like the elves."

"What's that got to do with you?"

He gave a slight shake of his head. "Didn't want to make her uncomfortable."

"Does that mean what I think it means?"

"That I'm considerate of other people? Yeah, it was a shock to me too."

"Come on," he said with a laugh. "Did something happen with you guys? All alone on Mist Isle…dragons in the skies. Sounds pretty romantic."

His eyes remained on the flames. "No."

"No, it wasn't romantic?"

"No. Nothing happened."

"Really?" Bridge asked. "What about all that 'she's off-limits' crap?"

"She *is* off-limits."

"Because she's yours, right?"

"No, asshole," Rush said. "Because you aren't good enough for her."

Bridge chuckled. "You're totally right. She looked pretty badass breaking into that castle to save you."

Rush didn't recall much from that night, but he remembered the moment she threw a rock at the Steward's head to help Callon. It gave him a short-lived smile, quickly replaced by loss once more. "Badass…that's a good word for her."

"Did you at least go for it?"

None of your business.

Flare, it's fine.

Why does he pry?

He's not prying. It's just...guy talk.

I spoke to Ashe, King of Dragons, many times, and not once did I ask him about his personal life.

Well, he's a king—

Or any dragon, for that matter.

You aren't best friends with those dragons, so it would be inappropriate to ask.

Flare gave a quiet growl. *I thought I was your best friend?*

You are—

Best means singular. So, how can you have two best friends?

"Rush?" Bridge waved his hand in front of his face. "Yoo-hoo."

Rush pushed his palm away. **No need to get possessive—**

There is only one best friend—and it is I.

Oh my god, this conversation is so stupid...

"Are you and Flare having a go or something?"

Our minds, bodies, and souls are combined. I give you beauty, flight, and immortality. What has he done to earn the same status—

Alright, alright. You are my one and only. We good?

Yes.

Rush gave a sigh before he acknowledged Bridge once again. "Okay, I'm back."

"What were you guys talking about?"

Tell him. Make sure he knows where he stands.

Rush rolled his eyes because this was a side of Flare he didn't see often. Greedy, possessive, like Rush was a hoard of treasure that belonged to him alone. He acted that way toward Cora too sometimes. "You don't want to know…"

"So, did you make a move?"

Rush nodded. "She turned me down."

"Really?" Bridge asked in surprise. "She came all the way to Rock Island to save you…and she's not interested?"

"We're good friends." Images flashed in his mind. Their first kiss on the border of Eden Star. Her angry but playful eyes every time he grabbed her ass. Firelight casting a beautiful glow on her face inside the cave. Touches. Kisses. A sky full of stars. "If you and I had swapped places, she would have come for you too."

Bridge held his gaze, his unblinking stare cutting to the bone. "I'm sorry."

Rush gave a shrug. "It's fine. Other fish in the sea…" He turned away to look at the fire once more, even though the flames reminded him of a different fire in a different place…in a different time.

"I can tell it really bums you out."

"Come on," he said with a scoff. "I'm fine."

"It's fine not to be fine, Rush."

Rush refused to look at him now, eyes focused with all his strength, squeezing the emotions out of his heart like a wet sponge. "That elf that came with her...that's General Callon."

"I could tell he was someone important. He wields a sword like it's a stick."

"He's her uncle."

"What?" he asked in surprise. "I didn't get a good look at his face with the helmet to see the resemblance."

"And his brother is...the late Tiberius Riverglade."

Bridge caught on instantly. "Shit..."

"Yeah."

"Now I understand."

"Ironic, right? Meet a woman I actually like...but I killed her father." He released a sarcastic laugh even though it wasn't the least bit funny. Not at all. Not in the slightest. "I don't deserve her...she made the right call."

"Why did he come to your rescue?"

"He didn't have a choice. If Cora went alone, she would have been killed."

"Still..."

"I suspect he didn't know I was the one they were saving."

"What did he say to you afterward?"

"I was unconscious. Never spoke. But I can imagine what he might say..."

"Yeah." Bridge rubbed his palms together as he stared at the fire, the sounds of the small waves of the cove floating through the entrance and reaching their ears. The tide never rose above the sand, so they were never flooded with the sea. If there were a storm, that would be a different story. "What was it like with the dragons?"

He searched for the perfect word, but there was none. "I can't even describe it. It's been so long since I've seen free dragons that it was pretty indescribable." He dropped his head and looked at his own hands. "Made me feel like absolute shit."

Bridge gave his friend a look of pity, but he had no words to pull him from the sadness. "Guess that means Ashe didn't kill you when you came back."

"Thankfully."

"And he agreed to be your ally, so that's something."

Rush gave a shrug. "He *tolerates* me, but that's about it."

"Better than being dinner."

"Dinner?" Rush asked with a laugh. "Remember how big he is? I'd be a *snack*…"

"An appetizer." Bridge chuckled. "Good thing you shared that memory of your escape, when you freed those three dragons. Probably wouldn't have gotten out alive if you hadn't."

"I wish I had a better memory than that one."

Bridge watched him for a while. "I think it's a pretty good one. You saved those three dragons, saved Flare, took a stance against your father, and nearly sliced his hand off…"

"I didn't save those dragons. I *tried* to save them."

"You don't think they got away?"

Rush shook his head. "That's very unlikely. King Lux isn't going to let three dragons leave his treasury. I'm sure he sent the entire cavalry out, hunted them down one by one, and those that resisted...were probably killed. There's nowhere for three dragons to hide for long—at least, not in Anastille." He felt his heart break for the millionth time. The scar tissue made him wince deeper each and every time.

"Well, I like to think they got away."

Me too.

It was too hard to think about—especially when he remembered how terrified their eyes were. Their eyes probably looked the same before they were captured or burned alive. "There's something you need to know... I didn't want to share it with the others."

"When are you going to trust them?" Bridge asked with a sigh. "When we came to rescue you—"

"Which was stupid, by the way. What were you thinking?"

"I was thinking that I needed to save my friends and sister. Liam and Zane did too. They didn't hesitate, Rush."

"I don't know... Liam is a little odd."

"He's..." Bridge rubbed his jawline, his fingers going through his beard. "Okay, he's a little odd. But we don't need to question his loyalty. He just has a bit of an obsession with dragons.

Who doesn't? You think he's going to steal Flare from you or something?"

"Not possible."

"Then he's harmless."

"Your sister is an idiot, too, so it looks like you both inherited that gene."

Bridge dragged his hands down his cheeks as he sighed. "Yeah, I don't know what she was thinking."

I do.

Shut it.

His arms moved back to his knees. "What did you want to tell me?"

"When Cora returned to Eden Star, she didn't go alone."

Bridge's eyebrows immediately furrowed in a concentrated stare. "Okay...who went with her?"

"Ashe." Rush stared at his friend's face, anticipating the reaction.

"What?" he blurted. "She just walked into the forest with this ginormous dragon and assumed that would go just fine?"

"They didn't walk in together."

"Then how—" His eyes shifted away, his mouth wide open. Then his eyes came back, nearly twice the size they'd been before. "It can't be... There's no way... There's just... Ashe would never agree."

"Well, he did," Rush said. "Because he and Cora are fused."

7

POLOX

The galleon pulled into the cove, the cannons visible over the edges, the beams constructed with wood but also flecks of gold. It was an unsinkable ship, and Captain Hurricane wanted that to be known.

Bridge cupped his mouth and shouted to Lilac. "Took you long enough."

"Shut up." She gripped the rail then leaned over to shout back. "I can't control the weather." Her eyes shifted to Rush standing beside him. "Oh, you're back. Glad to see you're still in one piece."

"Thanks." Rush turned to Bridge and cast him a glare.

Bridge shouted back at her. "We need a ride."

Captain Hurricane appeared over the edge, in his dark-blue jacket and hat. "Do I look like a horse and buggy to you?"

"Kinda," Rush said. "Just replace the horse with some wind."

Captain Hurricane gripped the rail a little tighter, his eyes narrowed.

Bridge lowered his voice. "Why do you never know how to talk to people?"

"I'm a smartass," he said back, his voice low. "I can't help it, alright?" He projected his voice once more. "Come on, we're allies now. If we weren't, you wouldn't have come back for us."

"I returned for my fair maiden." He grabbed the top of his hat and gave a slight adjustment. "Not you. You didn't uphold your end of the bargain."

Rush took a step forward. "Say what now?"

Bridge grabbed his arm. "Rush, we need him. It'll take us forever to get to Polox—"

Rush threw his arm off. "A little hard to uphold my end of the deal when I was being tortured in a dungeon."

"Not my problem." His hands returned to the rail, his eyes cold on a warm day. "A failed deal doesn't constitute an alliance."

"Your ship is made of *gold*." Rush threw his arms up. "What do you need more money for?"

Now Captain Hurricane just stared.

Lilac came to the rescue and wrapped her arms around his shoulders. "Come on, Captain." She leaned into him, took off his hat, and placed it on her own head.

He turned to her on instinct, giving her a very different look than the rest of them.

Bridge exhaled a sigh of disgust.

Good thing you turned her down.

Would have turned her down, regardless.

"If I'm your fair maiden, then my allies are your allies, right?"

Until he finds out about the two of you.

Like he needs another reason to hate me.

Captain Hurricane gave a silent response—a simple nod.

She smiled and kissed him on the cheek before she turned to the guys down below. "So, boys...where we going?"

They sailed north for a few days.

They stayed away from the coastline, deep in the blue, completely alone.

Rush stood at the bow of the ship, taking in the sight of the blue water as it reflected the sunlight.

"What'd they do to you?" Lilac came to his side and leaned against the rail.

"Good ol'-fashioned torture."

"I'm sorry." Her back leaned against the sail, facing the opposite way of Rush. "For what it's worth, you can't tell."

"On my face..."

She crossed her arms over her chest, her eyes on the ship. "You shouldn't have saved me."

"You have an interesting way of expressing gratitude."

"I just feel so guilty that I'm the reason you were captured—"

"You should feel guilty." He turned his gaze on her. "It was a stupid idea. You shouldn't have come."

"I know. I just...thought you needed help—"

"I have a *dragon*. I don't need help."

Her head snapped in the other direction, severing the gaze like the edge of a sword. "I'm sorry...for everything."

He looked ahead again and sighed. "It's fine. I might have been captured anyway...no way to know."

"And I do appreciate you saving me, even if I wasn't worth saving."

"Of course you were worth saving." He turned back to her, his eyes narrowed.

Her eyes narrowed slightly, her arms a little tighter across her chest.

"We're friends. That's what friends do. I've always got your back—and I know you've got mine."

Like a bolt of lightning that struck the earth in darkness, the disappointment hit, coming and going instantly. She looked ahead again. The silence was broken by the waves as they crashed against the hull. After she cleared her throat, she pushed off the rail and straightened. "Your girlfriend is a fine piece of ass."

Rush gave a quick smile. "She's not..." He quickly swallowed the words and felt the smile disappear. "Yeah...she is."

"Pretty badass that she came to rescue you and all that."

"That's what she is—badass."

"Sounds like my kind of woman."

Alright, I like her a bit more now.

"I'm sure you two will hit it off whenever you meet."

"For sure—"

The pirate in the crow's nest shouted from the top. "Ahoy! Polox."

Captain Hurricane turned the ship, heading for land.

Rush left the bow of the ship and took the stairs to the wheel. "We can't dock in the harbor."

Captain Hurricane kept his eyes ahead as he continued to turn the wheel. "You want to jump out, then?"

Rush gave him a stare.

Captain Hurricane gave him a stare back—with a smug smirk on his face.

"Take us to a quiet beach."

He looked ahead again, turning the wheel the other way now. "That's not what you said before. Be more specific next time."

"You know the empire is searching for me high and low—"

"Couldn't care less."

"Well, you should care. Because if they find me, they find your fair maiden, alright?"

He righted the ship then gripped the top of the wheel with a single hand.

"Thanks." Rush walked away, knowing the captain was drilling holes into his back.

After a long and affectionate goodbye, Lilac got into the small boat, and one of the crew rowed them to the beach.

"How are you going to meet up again?" Rush asked.

Bridge gave a sigh, like he didn't want to hear about it.

"He said he'll come by the Hideaway and see if I'm there," Lilac answered.

"You don't have to come with us." Rush stared at Captain Hurricane at the side of the ship, his eyes on Lilac's back. "If you want to stay, we would totally understand."

"No." She didn't turn to look back. "This is more important. He knows that."

"You told him what we're doing?" Rush's eyes flicked back to hers.

"I told him we want to save the dragons. Didn't give any other details, and he didn't ask. And even if I didn't have more important obligations, I couldn't live full time on a ship anyway, and he'll never abandon his crew. It would never work—at least not long-term."

Bridge kept his eyes on land, doing his best to tune out the conversation.

They arrived on shore, gave a wave to the galleon, and then stepped into the brush.

"Maybe we should have thought about this before, but..." Bridge walked beside Rush, the other three behind them. "How are we going to get into Polox without being seen? Their security must be ramped up by now."

"You're going to sneak me in."

"Whoa, what?" His hand pressed into his chest. "Me?"

"Yep. You live here, remember? The guards might recognize your face."

"*Lived*. I haven't been home in a while." He kept up with Rush's quick stride, his hands gripping the straps of his pack. "And the guards might also recognize me from my little charade at Rock Island."

"Unless General Noose is at Polox, I doubt it. He's the only one who saw you. The guards will recognize me—because I look just like my father—but they won't recognize you."

"Guess that's true…"

"So, we'll steal a wagon. I'll hide inside, and you drive me in."

"May as well. You're already wanted for treason—no harm in committing another crime."

They approached the wooden gate of Polox, with the doors wide open, letting merchants and citizens come and go. From a distance, they squatted down, taking a look at the scene.

"Uh…guys." Lilac kneeled beside Bridge. "I don't think this is going to work."

"Why?" Bridge asked.

"Everything looks normal." Rush saw the citizens go in and out, wagons full of flour and corn rolling through the gates to sell in shops. Horses kicked up the dirt with their hooves. Quiet conversations drifted to their location. There were more guards than before, but that didn't matter.

"Do you not see those humongous posters on the wall?" Lilac pointed to the right of the gateway.

There were five sketches—showing each of their faces.

Rush let out a loud sigh of defeat. "Great…that's just great."

"Can you fly in?" Bridge asked.

Rush turned to give him a glare. "Sure. They won't notice a bright red dragon at all…"

Bridge elbowed him. "I'm trying to think of something, okay?"

Lilac opened her pack and pulled out a telescope. She extended it into position then placed it against her eye.

"Where'd you get that?" Bridge asked, eyeing his sister.

She turned the telescope and focused on the poster. "My hot pirate boyfriend."

"See anything?" Rush asked.

"Well, I have some good news." She rotated the dial, increasing the focus. "The drawings are terrible. I look like a hag in mine...and Bridge looks even worse. Rush, you're the only one with a spot-on drawing."

Not that they need it.

She contracted the telescope back into its smaller position and stowed it in her pack. "Since they've depicted me as a hag and I'm definitely *not* a hag, I have an idea."

"What?" Rush asked.

"Let me see that." Bridge grabbed the top of the telescope visible at the edge of her pack and placed it against his eye. He made the adjustments until he got the posters in view. "You're right, that looks nothing like me. Yours is dead-on, though."

She slugged him in the side.

Bridge gave a jerk, slamming the telescope into his eye as he fell forward. "Ouch, that hurt."

Rush ignored him. "What's your idea?"

Bridge stayed down on all fours, rubbing his face. "Great, now I have a black eye."

"I distract them," she said. "I'll walk up to the gate. Do a bit of flirting. You slip right in."

"What about on the way out?" Rush said. "I don't know how long I'll be, and you can't keep that going for too long."

"Look." She nodded toward the gate. "They're only checking people entering—not leaving."

Rush watched the guards check every person who came to the gate, ordering them to take down their hoods so they could have a thorough look at each person as they entered Polox. Everyone who departed the city was ignored. "You're right."

Lilac took the telescope from her brother and stowed it away. "Let's do this."

"What are you going to say?" Rush said.

"I don't know," she said as she got to her feet. "It's not like men listen anyway…"

The second Lilac strolled up, she captured their complete and undivided attention.

Rush didn't catch anything she said as he slipped past the guards and entered Polox, his hood still up to hide his face from everyone in the street. It was past midday, so there were only a couple hours left before sundown. Once that happened, the gates would close, so if he didn't want to be stuck on the street all night, he had to get to work.

He made it to the potions shop and slid inside, the bell ringing over the door.

There was already a customer inside, so Rush immediately walked to the rear of the shop, eyeing the strange things that no one ever bought. How did he know that? Because there was dust everywhere.

He moved toward the window, spotting another flask of dragon tears.

Interesting.

How does she always have tears on hand?

Good question.

The customer paid at the counter then departed the store. The bell rang again.

"What can I do for you, Rush?" Mathilda's deep voice came from the front of the store.

Rush pushed his hood back as he approached the counter. "How'd you know?"

"The way you move." Her long hair was in thick curls, and she was dressed in purple. The counter separated them, and there was a doorway behind her that led to a private storeroom. "Entitled men always move in the same way—like they own the place."

He took the insult with a shrug. "Someone said I was arrogant once...maybe a couple times."

"Whoever told you that is a good friend—because a good friend will lie about your flaws behind your back but speak them to your face." She gave him a long and hard stare, one hand on the counter. "Looks like those dragon tears did you some good."

He met her look, not the least bit surprised by her assumption. "How'd you know?"

"The empire told me—with their posters on every wall."

He gave a subtle nod before he planted his hands on the counter between them. "I've always been a popular guy." He stared at her, people passing by the windows, having no idea that the person the empire wanted most was right inside. "Why'd you do it?"

"I do a lot of things."

"You gave it to her at no cost. Why?"

"It was at a cost—which she'll pay later."

"I was the one who needed them, so I should be the one in debt."

"But you aren't a half-elf who would risk her life to save a man and a dragon, are you?" She gave a smile, but her eyes remained shrewd. "What can the empire's number one fugitive offer me?"

"Touché." His eyes narrowed, looking at Mathilda in a whole new way. "What do you want?"

"That's between her and me."

Why did you think this was a good idea?

Never said it was. "Where do you get the dragon tears?"

A slow smile moved on to her lips, more like a taunt. "From a dragon, obviously."

"But *which* dragon?"

Her hands planted on the counter and she leaned forward, her head tilted up to regard him at his greater height.

She must get them from the empire.

You're right. "Why haven't you ratted me out to the guards?"

"It's not my place to interfere with another's journey. No one interferes with mine."

Rush withdrew his hands from the counter and straightened.

"You came here for something, Rush Hawkehelm. Not to buy, because your hands are empty, but something, nonetheless."

"I need an introduction to the dwarves."

"That, I can't give you."

"Do you know them?"

"Once upon a time."

"Then tell me the way. I'll introduce myself."

She withdrew from the counter, her eyes hazing over with a foggy memory. "You waste your time going there."

"What happened to not interfering with another's journey?" An audience with the dwarves was happening—and a witch wouldn't stand in his way.

She stared hard and deep for a very long time, her eyes still and focused. "As you wish. But this information comes at a price."

"Of course it does…"

"The shelf life of the Galeco Frogs is short. I need another batch, but last time I ventured west, there were no frogs to be seen."

She knows.

"How do you know about the venom?"

"Honey, *everyone* knows."

"But…how?"

She gave a shrug. "When a weapon is discovered, word travels fast. Bring it to me—and I will give you what you seek."

This will be easy.

But take weeks of our time.

It'll take even longer climbing up and down the mountains like goats looking for a way in.

I see your point.

Rush left the counter and headed to the door, knowing he had to get out of the city before sundown. "I'll be back in a couple weeks."

"Or perhaps not at all."

He gave her a glance over his shoulder. "Way to stay positive…"

8

THE ARMY MARCHES

THEY TREKKED THROUGH THE WILDERNESS, staying clear of popular roads and trails taken by merchants. It was hot and miserable, and they only made a fire long enough to cook dinner before it was stamped out again. Enemies were in the skies. And Rush had no doubt they were on the ground too.

"I can't believe this." Bridge kept up with him while the others trailed behind. They crested a hill then moved back to the flatlands, cutting through condensed trees and brush, heading west. "I hate those big-ass frogs. I literally have nightmares about those guys."

"They aren't my favorite either."

"I'd rather deal with an orc than one of those guys."

"Really?" Rush asked. "Why?"

"Uh, because orcs don't jump ten feet in the air while they chase you—and *roar* while doing it."

Rush chuckled. "Orcs are seven feet tall, have skin thick as armor, and wield swords like decent fighters. That doesn't scare you?"

Bridge shrugged. "They don't jump on you."

Rush rolled his eyes.

"And they aren't as angry. Frogs are pissed, man. Their eyes literally pop out a bit and they do that stupid thing with their mouth—"

Hide!

Rush grabbed Bridge by the arm and yanked him so hard his shoulder nearly popped out of the socket.

"What the—"

Rush cupped his mouth and forced him down behind a boulder.

The others copied their movements, all giving Rush looks that demanded answers.

He pressed his finger against his lips.

The thud of footfalls was suddenly distinct.

Thud. Thud. Thud.

It grew louder until it was right on the other side of the boulder.

Bridge mouthed to him. "Orcs?"

Rush shook his head.

The thudding didn't stop. It just kept going—for a solid twenty minutes.

Rush felt the blood drain from his face because he knew what it was.

When the thud turned faint, he popped his head over the edge of the rock to see what he'd already imagined in his head.

General Noose rode his steed in the lead—followed by an army of two thousand men behind him.

Bridge and the others did the same, popping their heads to get a look.

They're searching for us.

THEY STAYED LOW FOR A FEW DAYS BEFORE THEY CONTINUED toward the desert.

"The frogs don't seem so scary...after seeing that." Rush moved faster now, wanting to get to their destination as quickly as possible to decrease their odds of running into General Noose...and whoever else was looking for him.

"Dad must really miss me."

Bridge gave a slight snort that came out as a pained laugh. "What will happen if he catches us?"

Torture us. Kill the rest.

"They aren't going to catch us, so don't worry about it."

"What if he sent out another army—"

"An army isn't going to sneak up on us. My dad is an idiot if he thinks Flare and I aren't going to notice two thousand soldiers."

"I don't know. We didn't notice them that quickly."

"It'll be fine, Bridge."

What if they weren't looking for us?

What do you mean?

What if they're preparing to march on Eden Star?

Rush halted next to a tree.

Bridge kept walking and took several seconds to notice that Rush had fallen behind. He looked over his shoulder. "You okay, man?"

Why do you say that?

I didn't see crossbows.

They were pretty far away by the time we looked.

I see much better than you do.

Rush replayed the march in his head, mapping out their direction. **They weren't going in that direction.**

I guess you're right. Still worries me.

Yeah, it worries me too.

"What are we looking for here?" Lilac kicked a pinecone as she walked forward, glancing at the grassy area next to the stream.

"Galeco Frogs," Liam said. "In various pastel colors, their skins are slick with venom along with their saliva. They're six feet tall and can propel themselves to great heights, sometimes launching themselves to a height of twenty feet for the most mature individuals."

Lilac spun around in a circle. "Well, I don't see any monster toads. And they sound like they'd be easy to spot."

"If you don't see them, you'll hear them," Liam said. "Because they roar."

"Whoa, what?" Lilac turned to regard Liam. "Roar? Like a dragon?"

How dare you.

She doesn't mean it like that.

I'm a beast. Not a pink frog that hops around like a rabbit.

Just let it go, Flare.

I dislike her again.

Rush moved forward, crossing the shallow stream and moving deeper into the tree line. "This is where they should be—near the river."

"How many are there usually?" Zane asked.

Rush gave a shrug. "I don't know...dozens in each group."

"Maybe they moved upstream?" Lilac asked. "Downstream?"

Rush took the lead. "Let's try upstream. The water will be fresher closer to the waterfall."

They hiked for a full day—and didn't see anything.

"Where the hell are these guys?" Bridge asked. "Do they migrate?"

"Not that I know of," Rush said. "This is their territory. Anytime I've come this way, they're here."

"Maybe soldiers are coming through this area, so they moved."

"Yeah, they aren't really the turn and run kinda creatures."

That's the only thing we have in common.

You're still on that?

She compared me to a FROG.

"Rush, over here." Lilac gave a loud whistle.

Rush turned to see her across the river near the base of one of the rock walls embedded with soil. It was a mossy area, evergreen bushes everywhere, moss growing over the soil. "What is it?"

She rounded the corner before he could catch up.

He jogged, the rest of the guys along with him.

When he turned the corner, the sight brought him to a halt. "No..."

An old bonfire sat there, desiccated bodies and bones of the Galeco clan on top. Most of it was dust. Individuals couldn't be discerned. It was an ashy graveyard.

This is wrong.

"Who would do this?" Liam kneeled down and looked at the pile, his face tight in agony. "They wiped out an entire species..."

Rush closed his eyes and released a pained sigh. "The Shamans or the empire. But nowadays, they're one and the same."

Bridge kicked a bone into the pile. The fire was old because there was no hint of smoke in the air. The graveyard had been there for months, probably. "Smart. Now they can't be killed...again."

Rush stood with his hands on his hips, looking at the dead creatures that were all now a single color—black. Their pastel luminosity was gone. Their roars would never echo in this forest. King Lux wiped out the race of free dragons, so of course, he wouldn't hesitate to do it to something else. Rush had no particular fondness for the frogs that had chased him down more times than he could count, but this...was despicable.

What are we going to do?

Don't ask me.

Who else can I ask?

I'm not in the mood, Flare. This was my one way to get to the dwarves, and now—

Ribbit. Ribbit.

The group shared a look before they turned toward the sound.

"Somewhere over here." Bridge took the lead.

Ribbit. Ribbit.

"Break into groups." Rush went his own direction. "We gotta find these guys."

"Shouldn't we be able to see them?" Lilac asked. "Or hear them roar or whatever?"

Ribbit. Ribbit.

Go right.

Rush felt Flare's mind press up against his, a knock on the door, and then they became one. The energy donated by his dragon heightened his senses, and the sounds of the Galeco Frogs were amplified.

Ribbit. Ribbit.

It's louder.

Keep going.

Rush kneeled near the copse of ferns.

Careful.

Are they underground?

Maybe it's a regular frog that we're chasing.

Rush gently pulled back the ferns and revealed a hole in the ground.

Several pairs of eyes darted to his face, swelling in anger and fear, and then their lips started to snarl. There were a dozen, all with the pastel skin that made them so easy to spot, all the size of his palm. They didn't jump. They didn't attack. They just stared with their snarls. "Guys, over here."

Bridge got there first. "Are those...?"

The frogs shifted their hostile stare to him.

"They're actually pretty cute...when they're small." He looked at Rush. "I guess they must have hidden them when they were attacked."

"Yeah," Rush said, imagining a mother frog burying her young before she could be slain.

Liam kneeled. "The last survivors..."

They all sat there and stared, looking at the frogs as they looked at them.

"She didn't specify how much venom she needed," Bridge said. "So maybe we can just take one or two—"

"No." Rush dropped his pack and dug inside until he found an extra bag with a drawstring on top. "We aren't doing that."

"Then what are we going to bring to Mathilda?" Lilac asked. "We don't have to kill them all—"

"We aren't killing any of them." He set the bag sideways close to the edge of the hole. "Come on." He shook the bag, trying to entice them to hop inside.

"Then what's the plan?" Bridge asked. "Why are you taking them?"

"Because they can't stay here." He waved his hand toward the bag. "Come on, guys. I'm not going to hurt you. Ugh, how the hell am I going to do this?" He shook the bag again and pointed inside the flap. "If they stay here, they'll get bigger, and when they do, they'll be killed too."

"Then…where are they going to go?" Bridge asked. "They're just as vulnerable anywhere."

Rush gave an angry sigh as he looked at one of the frogs. "Get in this bag, or I swear—"

Ribbit.

"Get." He pointed at the bag. "In."

Ribbit.

"Don't be a dick—"

The frog hopped inside.

Rush's eyebrows both shot to the top of his face.

Then the next one joined him.

One by one, they went, hopping into the bag until the hole was empty.

Rush righted the bag and cinched the drawstring before he got to his feet. **Never imagined I'd be holding a bag of baby frogs.**

That makes two of us.

He put his pack back on his back and held the bag at his side, like it was a bag of flour or something. "Next, we cross the desert."

"Uh, Rush," Bridge said. "Those guys won't survive out there…"

"I'm not an idiot," Rush said. "I'm taking them to the one place where they're safe—Eden Star." He took the lead, heading in the direction of the desert, which would have to be crossed under darkness.

"Rush?" Bridge was close behind. "What are we going to do about Mathilda? We're supposed to earn the dwarves as allies, not go on a conservation escapade. It would be a lot easier if we just harvested the venom—"

"I can't do it, alright?" Rush said as he kept walking. "I just can't…"

Bridge let it go.

They headed west—right for the unbearable sands.

I'm proud of you.

Shut up.

I am.

I'm only doing it for her.

No, you aren't. You're doing it because of her.

9

WOR-LEI

Mist filled the air around them, fireflies illuminating the area where the sunlight couldn't reach. Callon locked his eyes on hers with the greatest endurance he'd ever shown, not needing to blink, not even when minutes passed.

Cora's fingertips touched her face, wiping the last of the tears that had streaked down her cheeks. The blue outline of Weila was still there, holding on to her husband like their separation was as hard for her as it was for him. "I can't see the details of her face. It's just an outline, a hazy one..."

His hands tightened on Weila's—as if he hoped he could feel her.

Cora watched his fingers move through hers without touching. "I know I must sound crazy, but—"

"I believe you." He turned to his wife, seeing nothing but the ground in front of him. He gave a sigh in disappointment, closed his eyes in pain, as if he'd give anything to see what she could see.

Cora watched Weila bring her head back to look into her husband's face. "She's looking at you…"

Callon opened his eyes and met the look he couldn't see.

"*Wor-lei*…"

Cora sucked in a deep breath when she heard it, the quiet voice of the woman on her knees. "I can hear her too."

Callon turned back to her, his breaths now labored.

"She said…*Wor-lei*."

He sucked a deep breath instantly. He closed his eyes briefly, and once they reopened, they began to water.

"What…what does that mean?"

He looked at Cora again, squeezing the hands he couldn't feel. "Husband."

Weila turned her head in Cora's direction.

"I think…she can hear me too."

"Then speak to her." Callon's voice gripped her body the way he tried to grip the hands of his wife. "Tell her…tell her that my love has not abated in the years we've been apart. Tell her…I'm lost without her."

Her eyes watered again, her heart wrenching at the pain her uncle shared so vividly. His words matched the sorrow in his eyes, the sorrow she saw on a daily basis. "Weila, Callon wants you to know that his love for you still lives on…and he misses you so much."

Callon stared at her invisible face, eyes wet, his grief taking over. "What did she say?"

"Nothing yet."

A full minute of silence passed. Weila looked at her husband once more. "*Wor-lei*..." Her voice came from every direction, not from the invisible mouth that Cora couldn't perceive. The sadness was heavy. The sorrow worse than her husband's. "Grief is the perseverance of love. An unbearable burden, but one that keeps us together, across the veil, forever."

Cora repeated it word for word.

Callon closed his eyes to restrain the tears.

"Our spirits will touch once more, not as they did in life, but in death. Reunited once more, we will float on the wind, between the leaves, through the trees. We will be the flowers we once admired. The birds that sang to us in the morning. The river that brought our forest life. We will wait until your time has come—and go together."

Callon sucked in a breath, the tears escaping his eyes.

Too difficult for her to watch, Cora looked away. She became the vessel of communication between them, but nothing more.

He spoke through his tears. "I wish to join you now..."

"Now is not your time, *Wor-lei*."

He shook his head, his eyes closed.

"We will wait," she said. "We will wait until that time has come."

"I...I can't wait..."

"I am here for you—always. We both are. But I must go now..."

"No." His eyes opened, his fingers tightening into fists. "Please...don't go..."

"*Wor-lei, Hei Nu Sen.*"

He sucked in a breath, his eyes closed. "*Hei Nu Sen, Sun-lei...*"

The blue outline disappeared.

Callon's hands suddenly dropped.

Cora looked away, to cover her own tears as well as avoid his.

He leaned forward with his head in his hands, breathing through the pain, like Cora wasn't even there.

Her hand reached out until her fingertips felt his shoulder. Gently, she slid it across his back, resting her palm against him, the only comfort she could provide...and she wasn't even sure if he wanted it.

There was no reaction to her touch. His breaths still came and went, a quiet breakdown that he couldn't control.

"I'm sorry, *Tor-lei*..." She spoke through her tears, broken apart by the raw grief he carried every single day.

He pulled her arm from his back.

She immediately withdrew, remorseful for invading his space. Her eyes went down to her hands in her lap, wishing she could disappear entirely.

His arm circled her shoulders, and he drew her close, resting his head on hers.

She closed her eyes, enveloped by the kind of affection she'd never felt in her life.

"Thank you, *Sor-lei*."

CALLON KEPT TO HIMSELF FOR A FEW DAYS.

Her daily training had ceased, so she spent her time in the tree house, meditating in the fields, going to the market despite being ignored by everyone there.

I feel your sadness.

She looked out the window with the cup of tea between her fingertips. Steam rose to the ceiling, the rosebuds floating on the surface of the hot liquid. She looked down into the dark tea and gave it a couple stirs with her spoon. **Not sadness...more like heartbreak.**

For your uncle?

Yes.

If I lost my Zuhurk...I'd feel the same way.

Yeah...

But he still has you.

I'm not enough to replace what he lost.

It still gives him reason to go on.

She stirred her tea, her eyes down.

Is there more?

After a deep breath, she gave her answer. *No.*

A knock sounded on the open doorway.

She flinched because she hadn't heard him approach. His elven footsteps were impossible to detect. Unless she happened to stare straight at the door at his arrival, she'd never know he was there. "Hey...how are you?"

He crossed the room with his silent authority, his powerful arms still by his sides, the muscles and tendons visible because he wore a short-sleeved shirt that day. His large frame sank into the chair across from her.

They stared, back and forth.

She held her breath, waiting to hear what he had to say.

But he never answered her question.

"Want some tea?"

He gave a slight nod.

She poured him a cup before she returned to her seat.

He stared at the rising steam for a moment before he regarded her once more. "Needed some time."

"I completely understand..."

His elbows rested on the table, one hand cupping his chin, a heavy shadow there because he'd skipped the shave for several days. His fingers rubbed the coarse hair, his eyes down. "I was too overcome with the moment to think about its implications. But I've thought about them now."

"So, you know why I can see her?"

He shook his head.

"Do you know why I can talk to her?"

"I don't know that either."

Is it because I'm fused with you?

No. Dragons don't possess those kinds of powers. We also have no concept of the afterlife.

You don't?

Why would we when we're immortal? We lived in peace. There's been no reason to question our mortality and speculate on the afterlife when we've never needed one. That all changed when King Lux arrived...

"Has there ever been another elf who can—"

"No." He dropped his hand to the table. "You can push your mind in a way I've never seen before. Maybe there's an elf in our history that could, but I'm not aware of it. Perhaps that is the reason."

No.

No, what?

That's not the reason.

Okay...then what do you think is the reason?

Death Magic. Ask him.

I know it's not Death Magic because I didn't do anything. Didn't perform a spell. It just...happened.

You can perform the Skull Crusher without a spell. Death Magic is not what you can do—but what you are. Now ask.

"Uh...what about Death Magic?"

That's not how you ask such a question.

Hey, you gave me zero advice.

Callon stiffened at the question. His eyebrows drew close together an instant later.

"What about Death Magic?"

"Is that...what I'm doing?"

"Are you dead?"

"No."

"Then no."

"Wait...so you have to be dead to use Death Magic?"

He must have assumed it was rhetorical because he stared.

"Because I can do the Skull Crusher, and now I can talk to dead people."

"Not dead people," he said quickly. "Spirits of the living."

Careful. Do not offend him.

"I just...don't understand. How can I do these things?"

His eyes dropped in quiet contemplation.

"So, is there a difference between dead people and spirits of the living?"

"Night and day difference."

"How are they different?"

"Shamans are dead. My family has passed on and become spirits."

She'd been close to a Shaman but had never seen inside that hood. Her knife sank into something soft, like a pillow, like they were physical, but barely. "That's why they can't be killed...because they're already dead."

"Yes."

"But, like, what the hell are they?"

He lifted his chin, his eyebrows high.

"Where do they come from? Where do they live? How can something be dead but go around and kill people? Have powers like that?"

He's hiding something.

No, he's thinking.

Callon looked out the window for a moment, his lips pressed tightly together. "It's forbidden."

"What's forbidden?"

"To speak of such things."

Told you.

"To talk about the Shamans?"

He nodded.

"Why?"

"It's…" He pressed his lips tightly together again. "It's a part of our history that we want to erase. It's been removed from our textbooks in the library. It doesn't exist in our conversations in the market. It just doesn't exist anymore."

"Why? I don't understand."

He kept his eyes out the window, his chest rising with every breath he took. "Because we're ashamed."

Ashe's voice deepened, turning hostile the way it did on Mist Isle every time he interacted with Rush. *Make. Him. Answer.*

"Callon…you need to tell me."

"It's not lore that should be passed down—"

"You watched me get rid of those Shamans on the way to Rock Island. Now you've seen me speak with the dead. I need to know this information."

His eyes shifted back to hers. "You aren't a Shaman, Cora—"

"How do we know for sure?"

"Because I'm looking at you right now. Your eyes illuminate like the fireflies in the forest, and your heart beats with the soul of the trees. I feel your presence, and it's vibrant, honest, and beautiful."

She released a slow sigh. "Please tell me."

"You have a powerful mind. That's all."

"*Why* do I have a powerful mind, Callon?"

"Because you're the daughter of the greatest king who ever lived."

"Are you seriously not going to tell me?"

He looked away again, his features tightening into a grimace. "You have your secrets, Cora. I've respected your privacy, have betrayed my own queen to protect your interests. It's your turn to give me the same kindness."

No.

She closed her eyes in defeat. *Ashe, he's right—*

We need this information.

There's nothing I can do.

Grrrrrrrrrrrrrr.

I'll try again later, but I have to let this go for now.

A louder growl, like the stove trying to light the gas. *Grrrrrrrrrrrrrrrrr.*

She did her best to ignore the growl in her head. "Okay, I understand."

Callon instantly grabbed the cup of tea and brought it to his lips for a drink. "The last thing I'll say about this topic... You are not a Shaman. Yes, your powers are similar, but there's another explanation for it. Now we're finished."

If that were the truth, he would have no problem giving you this information.

Not necessarily. He can prove that I'm not what I fear, but in doing so, he'll reveal something he doesn't want me to know.

Now I don't like him.

Ashe, I've brought a dragon into their borders without their knowledge or permission. I have access to a private passage that takes me in and out of their lands undetected. He saved Flare from the empire. He's earned your respect a million times over.

Ashe turned quiet, simmering in silence.

Callon drank his tea, his eyes on the window most of the time, the sounds of the birds all around the tree house.

Rejection stabbed her deep, and the disappointment was difficult to overcome. It drew her out of the conversation.

"I've wanted to return to *Sun-lei* ever since we left. I can't see her. I can't touch her. But I can feel her, so it's like she's there. You speak her words, but I hear them in her voice. The details of her face have never left my mind, so I see them when you speak. We're together again. It brings me joy...albeit short-lived."

"We can see her whenever you want, Callon. I'm happy to do that for you."

"I know, *Sor-lei*." His eyes glazed over as he looked out the window, filling with the pain she'd witnessed countless times since they'd met. "But I wonder...if she's the only one? Can you see others?" His eyes shifted back to hers.

I have the same wonder.

"I...I don't know. I didn't see anyone else while I was there."

Perhaps you can see more than your father's grave.

She instantly sucked in a breath. ***I...I didn't even think of that.***

Nor did I.

"My *Vin-lei* doesn't come to me as often as my *Sun-lei*. I don't know why—and I wish I did."

The potential meeting with her father had taken her focus, but the sorrow in Callon's voice pulled her out of it again. "Let's ask him."

Callon inhaled a slow breath, the surface of his eyes forming a nearly invisible film. "I'm afraid." He'd stormed the castle and had taken out the guards as his elvish blade reflected the torches mounted on the wall. With dark and focused eyes, he'd slain men and left their bodies in his wake. He moved with a swiftness that defied his size, a calmness that rivaled a stream. General. Soldier. Hero. But this was a different version of him entirely. Grieving father. Broken widower.

"Afraid of what?"

"What his answer will be."

10

DEATH WILL HAVE TO DO

On the same bench as before, they sat together.

Whether it was morning or evening, the graveyard looked the same, the mist heavy in the trees, the coolness sticking to their clothes. Both times she'd visited the Cemetery of Spirits, no other elves were present.

Maybe because there were far more living elves than dead ones.

With his hands together on his lap and a straight back, he sat there, watching a firefly float past his face then leave his vision. Sometimes, his head would bow and he would close his eyes. He seemed to have forgotten her presence because there was no conversation or eye contact.

Hours passed—and there was no sign.

Callon showed his unease in his breathing, which had grown more labored over the past hour.

"He'll come, Callon. Maybe not today. Maybe not tomorrow. But he will."

Callon released a heavy breath, giving a slight nod at the same time.

Her hand went to his back, her palm running over the large muscles that flanked either side of his spine. "But we can stay as long as you want."

He dismissed the suggestion by rising to his feet. "His spirit is elsewhere."

She got to her feet too, but her eyes pierced the mist to see the headstone that was barely visible in the haze.

When Callon realized she wasn't behind him, he turned back.

"I think I'm going to stay."

His eyes immediately flicked past her, looking at the same headstone. It was a confirmation—that was Tiberius Riverglade's final resting place. His eyes drifted back to hers a second later. "I apologize for my self-absorption."

"Please don't apologize. I understand."

"Would you like me to stay?"

"No, I'll be okay."

He gave a final nod before he departed, disappearing into the mist.

Once his presence was gone, she felt the solitude all the way to her bones. It was still the afternoon, but the crickets chirped their song into the glade like it was twilight. Fireflies floated across the clearing, giving off a beautiful glow.

She left their graves and traveled to the one that stood alone.

It was a distinguished area compared to the rest, a private niche with several trees. A large statue carved in white was next to the grave. Over six feet tall, Tiberius Riverglade stood in his battle uniform, medals made of flowers pinned to his chest. His thick vambraces were scarred with sword marks, and his gloves were weathered at the knuckles. He was depicted in reality—a battle-worn king.

Her eyes shifted to the headstone.

In Grace Lies
King Tiberius Riverglade
Lord. Protector. Husband.

IVY GREW OVER THE CORNER OF HIS HEADSTONE, WHITE FLOWERS in full bloom like the summer sun shone in a cloudless sky. Drops sprinkled the petals and the vines, reflecting the lights of the fireflies as they floated across the glade.

Lord. Protector. Husband.

Something was missing.

Father.

Her lungs took an involuntary breath, a jerk of her chest that she didn't see coming. The loss fell across her shoulders like a warm blanket in winter, except the weight wasn't cozy. It was a burden. A heavy one.

There was no reason to grieve a man she'd never known, but if he shared her uncle's likeness, it was a real loss. Strong. Intelligent. Powerful. He would have been the grace she aspired to be. A role model. An inspiration. But he would have been more too... Loving, affectionate, fatherly.

She'd never had the opportunity to feel it herself. And now she never would.

She lowered herself to the blue bench at his side. Automatically, her fingers went to the ring on her forefinger, feeling the green gem against her skin. It was cold from the mist.

She saw the blue eyes. The sly grin.

She felt the warmth of his touch like his hand was on hers.

Firelight. Starlight. Joy.

She swallowed it back with a painful sigh.

Then she felt it.

A presence so thick it was solid, it drew close, real enough to cast a shadow. Invisible footprints marked the soil. Fireflies drew closer, attracted to the energy that entered the clearing. A majestic soul. An authority that was kingly but intimidating. The command of his reign continued—even from death.

Her eyes lifted from the soil—seeing the blue outline of King Tiberius.

Still, with his arms by his sides, he remained there, watching her without a sense of familiarity.

Her heart had never raced so quickly. War drums sounded in her ears. As if she awaited an execution rather than a meeting, her body went into duress. When she'd occupied the bench, she hadn't expected him to come.

Let alone so quickly.

There was no face. Just the outline of his head.

His body pivoted away—and then he began to fade.

"Wait." Her hand flung out, swooshing through the blue outline without contact.

He stilled.

She drew her hand close again, her fingers closing into a fist like she'd been burned by a fire.

He turned back and drew close.

"Cora... I'm Cora."

A deep and powerful voice broke the silence, having the same regal strength as his presence. "Your face is not in my memories."

"Because we've never met..."

He stilled again, this time taking a step backward. His head turned to one side. Then the other. He drew close again. "You stare like you see. You speak like you reply."

"Because I see you...and I hear you...King Tiberius."

His invisible eyes stared. "Who are you?"

"Cora—"

"That was not the question. *Who* are you?"

Her fingers removed the ring from her hand then held it in her open palm. "Your daughter."

His blue outline was on the bench beside her, several feet away even though they couldn't touch. "As much as I wanted children, I sired none."

"It was twenty-one years ago…shortly before your death."

The outline of his head was turned her way, his invisible stare focused on her.

"You…had an affair."

His head faced forward, the silence so long that it seemed like the conversation was over. When his words emerged, they were filled with a hint of anger…and a storm of regret. "It was no affair."

"I was left at the gates of a village—with just a note and this ring." The ring had been removed from her finger and placed in her palm, on display for him to see. "I've never seen the note, so I don't know what it says."

He gave a slight turn of his head toward the ring.

Her fingers tightened around it again before she slipped it back on. "When I showed it to Callon, he knew who I was."

"Because that ring belongs to me."

She looked at the ring again, this time in new appreciation. "Tell me who my mother is." That secret had been taken to the grave, but she could go to the grave too. Her eyes left the ring and moved to where his face would be. The green eyes were invisible to her, along with the strong jaw, the tightened brow.

"I remember life with the same vividness in death, but I cannot give you what you seek—because I don't know the answer. As I said, it was not an affair. We made camp on our journey, and in the middle of the night, when the campfire burned the lowest, I was pulled out of my tent by an unseen grip. She slipped past my guards with the quietness of a butterfly and locked her eyes on mine." He looked forward once more, his head slightly bowed. "Like a humid storm, my mind was muffled with heavy clouds. All I knew was she was the most beautiful woman I'd ever seen. The flap of the tent closed. That's the last I recall."

This pill of disappointment was too heavy to swallow, so she let it sit on the back of her tongue.

"Perhaps she snuck something into my food or drink the night before, creeping past the guards just as she did then. All I know is, I wasn't myself, and I can't remember my misdeed. But you are here—so it must be true."

"Does that mean she was a witch?"

"That's an answer we'll never know. But I recall her deep, dark hair, her petiteness, the way she moved like a wild cat stalking its prey." His head slowly turned back to her. "I'm sorry I couldn't be of more help."

Her eyes returned to the ring.

The glade turned quiet, even the crickets lowering the volume of their song.

"Now I understand why she hasn't come to me."

Cora spun the ring on her finger, wondering how it'd been changed from fitting a king's hand to hers. "Queen Delwyn?"

"Shortly after we married, she confessed she did not want to mother a child. The Tiberius line needed to continue. I needed an heir if we ever grew weary of the burden of rulership. But we were young, newly married, and I knew she would change her mind later." It wasn't the volume of his voice that hushed everything else around them, but the depth of his command. Even in death, he ruled over the forest. "On the eve of my departure, I propositioned her once more. It wasn't just the fear of my own mortality that rekindled my desire for a legacy, but I wanted to share the forest with someone I would love more than anyone else I'd ever known, if I returned. Envy is not something I feel often, but I felt it when I stepped onto the training ground. Watching General Callon impart his wisdom to his *Vin-lei* made me realize how much I wanted that myself."

The emptiness of his face had filled with the detailed features of his identity. The scruff on his jaw. The tightness of his jawline that shared the sharpness of her blade. His figure was distinct too. In the attire of his sculpture, it seemed like he was right there—in the flesh.

"Her stance hadn't changed. She didn't want children—nor did she ever."

"That doesn't surprise me..."

He didn't seem to hear her because he continued. "The conversation escalated, an exchange of unforgivable insults, and then I left without a goodbye. She probably assumes I broke my vow in anger, but that's not the case. I wish she knew."

"I could tell her."

His face turned back to hers. "You would do that for me?"

"Of course."

"Thank you, Cora."

A distinct chill moved down her spine, savoring the sound of her name on his tongue. "Callon speaks highly of you."

"Really?" He gave a slight laugh. "I gave him many reasons *not* to speak highly of me."

She smiled.

"I imagine my brother has filled my shoes in my absence."

"Yes, he has."

"He comes to me often, but sometimes I wish he wouldn't."

"Why?"

"His sadness... Sometimes, it's too much."

Green eyes full of sorrow were the most distinguished feature of his handsome face. "He's looked after me ever since I've arrived. He's trained me in the sword. He's protected me against Queen Delwyn's wrath. He even forfeited his title to keep me safe as I rescued my friends…"

"General Callon is no more?"

She gave a shake of her head. "Because of me."

"I assure you that it doesn't bother him in the least."

"Why?"

"Because I would do the same for Turnion—with no regrets."

She fidgeted with her ring once again.

"Cora, I'm very happy to meet you."

Her chest suddenly felt tight. Everything else did too.

"This isn't how I imagined I'd have a daughter—but I'm grateful for the opportunity."

"I wish…I wish I could have met you in life." A tear splashed onto her ring, right onto the green gem inside the wooden material.

"Me too, Cora. But death will have to do."

11

INVINCIBILITY

You failed to ask him.

It wasn't the right time.

It was the perfect time. You're crossing the veil from the living to the dead. I'm surprised he didn't question you himself.

Because he cared more about the fact that I'm his daughter. As should you. She walked up the vines to her tree house, ascending to her home with such grace that she looked like an elf born and raised in Eden Star.

I apologize, Cora.

When she stepped into her tree house, it was sunset, and she wasn't alone.

Callon sat at the dining table, looking out the window. When he heard her entrance, he rose from his chair and faced her, his eyes quickly examining her face for an indication of what had transpired in the Cemetery of Spirits. "I have no desire to intrude. If you wish to be alone, I will excuse myself."

"You're always welcome wherever I am, Callon."

His eyes tightened slightly, as did his jaw.

"I'll make some dinner." She whipped up something in the kitchen before she set the bowls on the table. They sat together and ate. Callon wore an anxious look but never asked a question.

"He came to me."

Callon swallowed his bite and didn't take another.

"He's exactly like his portrait…strong but kind."

His eyes shifted back and forth between hers, his hands on the table.

"He said he always wanted to have children, but Queen Delwyn didn't."

There was no reaction.

"He said this isn't the way he wanted to have a daughter, but he's grateful that it happened."

"That doesn't surprise me."

"I told him everything you've done for me, and he said he wasn't surprised either."

He drew breath, his eyes briefly dropping to the table before raising back up.

"He said he would do the exact same thing for Turnion without regret."

He dropped his eyes again.

She knew this was as emotional for him as it was for her, so she gave him a minute to process all of that before she continued. "I asked him about my mother..."

Callon was back at attention, eager for this information.

"He doesn't know. He said he was poisoned or bewitched...has no memory of it."

Callon shifted his eyes out the window, lost in thought.

"He said she had brown hair...that was about it."

"I wonder if it was a witch from the empire."

"Maybe, but why?"

"So, they could use the child for leverage. If they threatened to kill his only heir, Tiberius would comply with any and all demands."

Perhaps.

"That doesn't explain why I was left at my village. But I guess we'll never know."

"Probably not. Did he say anything else?"

"That he wishes Queen Delwyn didn't believe he broke his vows. She hasn't visited him once, and he suspects that's the reason."

Callon's eyes instantly narrowed.

"I offered to tell her the truth on his behalf. It's obvious that clearing his name is important to him."

Callon kept up the same perplexed stare.

"What?"

"Queen Delwyn was unaware of your existence until a few months ago."

He's right.

Callon continued. "It fails to explain why she hasn't visited his grave these past decades."

"Then, why hasn't she gone to see him?"

"I don't have an answer for that."

"He said they had a fight before he left. He wanted children, and she said no."

"Still doesn't explain why."

"Maybe it's just too hard for her—"

"No amount of emotional difficulty will prevent you from feeling the spirit of someone you love. That connection is addictive, regardless of the pain, and you return time and time again just to feel it."

"Then…I don't know."

"Nor do I." His eyes flicked away out the window.

The queen is corrupt in more ways than one.

Just because they had marital problems doesn't mean—

Then it means she's heartless—not a quality you want in a ruler.

Callon shifted his gaze back to her. "It would be unwise to go to Queen Delwyn and relay that message."

"But I told him I would—"

"She's desperate for a reason to eject you from Eden Star. Don't give her one."

"Wouldn't she want to know that I can speak to her husband beyond the grave?"

"She'll be more concerned that you can speak to *anyone* beyond the grave. Your lineage is a threat to her power, and these abilities will make you an even bigger threat than before. The moment you confide this information to her, as well as the acknowledgment that you're aware of your relationship to King Tiberius, she'll do more than expel you. She'll execute you. There's only so much I can do to protect you—and taking on all the elves of Eden Star is beyond my abilities."

"But...I have to do this for him."

"The last thing he wants is for anything to happen to you, *Sorlei*."

"Then what do I do?" Sunset had deepened into twilight, the shadows shifting across the tree house. "I'm afraid if I tell him how I feel about Queen Delwyn, he'll refuse to talk to me. How can I sit there and say terrible things about the person he loves most?"

"She's not the person he loves most—you are."

"He just met me—"

"Doesn't matter. It's hard to understand until you're a parent yourself, but when you are...that love is instant and unconditional. Trust me on that."

She dropped her gaze when she felt the burn of his stare. "Actually, I think I do understand…"

He looked out the window again, a minute of silence heavy in the air. "If you still intend to do this, there's only one way. The queen rules us, but it's the elves who rule Eden Star. Gain the favor of the elves—and she can't touch you."

"Come on, that's never going to happen. You've seen the way they look at me."

"Because you've never integrated into society."

"And how am I supposed to do that?" she said. "Trade my smartass comments for fruit?"

His eyes showed his laughter, but he didn't let it escape his lips. "You're forgetting your greatest ability, *Sor-lei*. When you lose someone you love, you spend your life feeling their absence, pining for one more conversation, wondering how they are…wherever they are. You can answer all those questions."

She dropped her gaze.

"Give the elves the one thing they want above all else—and you're invincible."

HE TESTED THE SWORD IN HIS HAND, SPINNING IT AROUND, making it whirl in a flash of bright red color. "This is a powerful sword." He held it up to the light, taking a closer look at the scales fused together. "It can slice a stalk of grass and break through a shield—if you know how to use it."

"Well, we both know I don't."

"I've fought against a blade such as this in battle many times. To say I was unintimidated would be a lie." He spun it around his wrist again before he lowered it to his side. "But a blade is only as powerful as the one who carries it. It takes time—a lot of time. But we don't have the luxury." He turned the blade, holding the hilt out for her to take.

The blade suddenly felt heavier once it was in her grasp. It had hung on her hip over the last few months, but she never removed it from the scabbard. "Damn, this is a lot heavier than the branch."

"Which is why we're in armor." He was in the same attire as the first time they'd met at the border—except his flower medals had been removed from his chest. His chest plate was black with a flower in the center, but instead of it being metallic and shiny like the guards of Anastille, it had the ability to bend but not snap. The armor on his shoulders was dark green and sleek, so a blade would slide away from his arm. His black vambraces were jagged and sliced irregularly, so he could catch a blade and fling it from the hands of his opponent.

She wore the same attire, and it wasn't as heavy as she imagined it would be. It was still uncomfortable, but she wouldn't complain. She wanted to wield her weapon like she knew how to use it—and that was finally happening. "Where did you get this armor?"

"A favor from a friend."

"They made it even though they knew it was for me?"

He gave a nod. "Their loyalty to me is stronger than their contempt for you."

"Contempt...ouch."

"Let's begin." He stepped back and unsheathed his green sword. "I apologize in advance for hurting you—but there is no other way to train you. You've been taught maneuverability, defense, and balance. Remember those skills because you will need them. You can't beat me, or any other opponent, with strength. But you can be quicker, smarter, swifter."

She held up her blade and took her stance. "I'll do my best, so you do yours."

He spun the green blade in his hand and took his first steps, moving sideways, immediately circling her like prey.

She pivoted as he turned, waiting for his attack.

He continued to spin the blade around his wrist, his dark eyes staring her down like a real opponent.

This isn't terrifying at all...

Focus.

Callon made his move, launching several feet forward, his blade striking down.

She blocked it just in time, stumbling backward from the immense force he exerted.

He moved again, his blade clashing hard against hers. He pushed her back, controlled the fight, and then he gave a flurry of hits that happened with lightning speed.

She caught each one—but barely.

Callon stepped back, spun the sword around his wrist, and then stared her down.

I swear, he never blinks.

Focus.

He leaped forward again, this time moving so fast that she couldn't keep up.

Her knees were kicked from underneath her, and then the blade ended up at her neckline.

She breathed, the blade just an inch from her neck.

He released her and stepped away. "You exceeded my expectations. But we have a lot of work to do."

At least I got a compliment in there...

Enough with the jokes, Cora.

What else am I supposed to do? Just sit and cry?

FOCUS.

Callon rushed her again, sword clashing against hers, her body forced back as he took over the fight.

She barely met his hits, her forehead already coated in sweat.

He was at physical ease, his endurance and strength giving him an advantage she couldn't match. There was no sweat. No exertion. No breaths. "You can't win a fight with defense. You can only hold it. Make your move."

"You're too fast—"

"Then be faster."

Pretty.

Her fingers lost their grip on the hilt, and the blade tumbled to the grass.

Callon didn't bother with the killing blow. Her defeat was obvious enough. "Pick up your blade."

She moved to her knees but didn't reach for her sword. ***Flare?***

Yes.

The smile took hold of her face as she pictured the beautiful red scales and yellow eyes. ***How are you?***

"Cora. Up."

Exhausted.

Why?

Because I crossed the desert with four people on my back.

What...? Are you...are you here?

If here is Eden Star, then yes.

"Cora?" Callon kneeled and grabbed her shoulder, his face taking up her entire view. "Are you alright?"

"Yeah, I just need a second..."

He took her hand and helped her to her feet.

Come to us. We have something for you.

I'll be right there!

"You're speaking to someone." Callon's face came back into view.

"Yes. It's Flare."

Now he looked even more intimidating than he did in battle. "We're training right now. Your time is mine. Whatever he has to say is not more important than the instruction I'm desperately trying to give you."

Flare? Ashe asked.

I'll tell you about it later. She reached out to Flare once more. **I need a couple hours. Callon is training me.**

We'll wait, Pretty.

Thanks. I'm sorry I can't come sooner.

You're worth the wait.

THE MOMENT THE INSTRUCTION WAS FINISHED, SHE THOUGHT about her friends waiting for her. "Callon, I need your help."

"What is it?" He sheathed his sword and drank from his canteen.

"Flare is outside Eden Star. Wants me to meet him."

He lowered his water, as livid as she anticipated.

"I can't take the passage because I'm meeting someone. So... can you get me in and out?"

"Why?"

"He says he has something for me—"

"*They* have something for you. General Rush, the murderer, and his mindless dragon."

Grrrrrrrrrrrr.

"Callon, please."

"He's not welcome here."

"They aren't coming into Eden Star—"

"But they are close enough." He whipped away, marching to his pack by the waterfall.

"Callon—"

"Haven't you asked me for enough?" He spun back around, his eyes snarling.

She faced his rage with a slow and steady breath. "I know this is hard for you—"

"You've met your father, the greatest king that ever ruled Eden Star, and this is not hard for you? I hoped a single conversation with him would be enough for you to hate Rush as much as you should. But I was wrong."

"Callon..." She was choked up with wet eyes, and her following words emerged with a long pause. "You have no idea how hard it is for me..."

He turned his head away, closing off entirely.

"But if King Lux and his army marched on these lands, he'd be the first to come to our defense. As much as you don't like it, he's our ally, and he's the most powerful ally we can have."

His stare remained on the waterfall.

"He's not that person anymore—"

"No amount of contrition will bring my king, my brother, my best friend back from the dead." He stepped away and grabbed his pack from the ground.

She stared at his backside, watching him sort through his rage.

He won't help you—not this time.

He will.

Cora—

He just needs a minute.

We must use the passage.

Cora watched her uncle.

Cora?

Callon turned back around to face her, releasing a deep sigh. "Return your weapon and armor. Then I will take you."

Callon escorted her out of Eden Star.

General Aldon was at the perimeter, decorated in the medals of his status. With his guards, he intercepted Callon and Cora. His stare lingered before it shifted to Cora. Then it went back to Callon again.

"I'm escorting Cora on a tour of the wildlands."

General Aldon stared.

"We'll return in a few hours."

"She doesn't have the clearance to come and go—"

"But I do. I take full responsibility for her actions while she's in my care."

Just as before, General Aldon didn't impede. He gave a nod to the guards and stepped aside.

Callon moved forward, Cora close beside him.

They moved deeper into the forest, far away from the sights of the guards.

"Callon?"

He took the lead, moving through the stalks of grass with little disturbance to the ecosystem around him. "Yes?"

"Have you ever…thought about being king?"

He halted in his tracks and, after a long bout of silence, turned around to face her. "Why would I?"

"Because people treat you like you are."

"You confuse respect with obedience."

"When it comes to you, they do both."

He faced forward again and continued on his walk.

"Aren't you as entitled to the throne as she is?"

"No."

"Why not—"

Callon spun back to her. "Queen Delwyn is our rightful queen. I don't have to agree with her decisions to respect her as my ruler. I serve the crown—regardless who wears it."

"Even though she's lying to her people about my existence? Even though she removed your rank because you needed to save your niece? The *king's* daughter?"

"Cora." He lowered his voice, his eyes angry. "Tread carefully. You speak of treason."

"To question King Lux's rule is treason because he's a tyrant. Is Queen Delwyn a tyrant?"

His eyes narrowed. "We will speak no more of this."

"She doesn't seem like the best person for the throne...at least not from where I stand—"

"Because you're a child."

She shook her head. "I'm old enough to know corruption when I see it."

He knows it too. Just doesn't want to see it.

Angry eyes bored into hers, but nothing more was said. He turned around and continued his trek into the wildlands. "Where are they?"

"I'll ask." *We're southwest of Eden Star. Where are you?*

Flare's voice emerged. *Pretty, you're close.* He sent an image of the rocks at the edge of the forest. *Come quickly. I've missed you.*

CORA STEPPED OUT OF THE TREES AND SAW THEM GATHERED together near the rocks. They sat around a cold campfire. Cora recognized three of them from the prison cell, along with Bridge. But there was only one person she stared at.

He sat on a rock near the pile of cold wood, arms on his knees, head slightly down as he listened to Bridge across from him. Scruff was on his jaw, his hair was a little longer, and his long-sleeved shirt fit the muscles of his arms a little tighter.

"She's here." The woman with dark hair stood up first and dusted off her pants with her palms.

The rest turned their heads.

Blue eyes locked on hers.

Hers locked on his.

Shit...I forgot how hot he is.

Hot? Is someone on fire?

No, it's an expression... Never mind.

Fire safety is no joke, Cora.

Bridge and the others rose to their feet.

Rush remained seated.

Bridge took the lead with the others behind him. "We meet again." A smile was plastered on his face, and he embraced her once they were close enough. "It's been so long. We saw each other at Rock Island, but...didn't really count."

"Wish that were under better circumstances too." She pulled away and reflected his smile with her own.

Bridge gestured to the woman beside him. "This is Lilac—my sister."

Lilac sized her up and down before giving a nod. "Hey."

Cora gave her an awkward wave. "Hey."

"And this is Zane." Bridge patted him on the back. "And then Liam. He's a scholar too."

"It's nice to meet you all," she said, her eyes shifting between them, heart racing in her chest. A distinct thump sounded in her ears, just the way it did when she got a shot of adrenaline before all hell broke loose.

Bridge glanced behind himself then stepped out of the way.

Rush came into view, a sack held at his side. Their eyes made contact and stayed there.

Bridge nudged the others to head back to the camp.

Anguished blue eyes looked into hers, still and steady, absorbing her appearance as if it was the first time they'd met.

Like a flower facing the sun, she took in the heat of his stare like a summer afternoon.

He gave a breath. A drop of his shoulders. And then he gave a smile. Not the kind that reached his eyes. "Let me guess. Still haven't made any friends."

Her eyes dropped momentarily. "You know me so well."

His smile faded and the stare continued.

Silence.

Stares.

More silence.

Cora cleared her throat. "I can see dead people…"

The intensity of his stare vanished as his eyebrows hopped to the top of his face. "Whoa…what now?"

"At the Cemetery of Spirits. I went there with Callon to visit his wife and son…and I saw his wife."

"What do you mean, you *saw* her?"

"She was this bluish outline. I watched her kneel on the ground and take his hands."

His fingers ran through his hair before he gave a shake of his head. "Did you tell Callon this?"

"Yes. And I could talk to her too."

Rush took a long pause, processing that information with a gaping mouth. "So, when you go to the graveyard, you just see and hear a bunch of dead elves?"

"No, it's not like that—"

"Because that sounds like the scariest shit I've ever heard."

"It's not scary. It's...peaceful... And sad," she said. "When I visit their graves, sometimes they come, and when they do...I can talk to them."

"So, it's not just Callon's wife?"

"No."

"Who else?"

Her eyes shifted away. "Other elves at different gravestones..." When she turned back to him, his eyes were fixated on hers. She ignored the question in his eyes. "When I asked Callon about it, he said no other elf has ever had this ability. He attributes it to the size of my mind, but I think it has something to do with the Shamans."

"You aren't a Shaman, Cora."

"I know, but...it's gotta be related, right?"

He gave a shrug. "I really don't know."

"But listen to this..." She lowered her voice even though Callon was out of earshot. "When I asked Callon about the Shamans and Death Magic...he wouldn't talk about it."

His eyes immediately flicked past her to look at Callon.

"Don't stare."

"Well, he's staring at me, and he still doesn't like me very much." He looked at her once more. "So, he knows something."

"He said it's forgotten lore among the elves."

"Forgotten or forbidden?"

"The second one."

His eyes flicked back to Callon. "He's done everything for you up until this point. So, the only reason why he's not helping you now is because…it compromises the elves."

Her eyes dropped.

"You need to get this information from him."

I agree with General Rush.

Stop calling him that.

I will call him—

Stop. Calling. Him. That.

Ashe retreated from her mind.

When Cora focused once more, she felt Rush's stare.

"I know how that is, carrying on two conversations at once."

"I'm still not very good at it."

A smile moved on to his face, this time reaching his eyes. "You'll get better at it."

"So...what are you guys up to?"

"Oh, it's a long story, but we're basically going to the dwarves after this."

"Never even seen a picture of a dwarf. Wish I could come with you."

"No, you don't," he said. "Come on, you can talk to dead people. That sounds way more interesting than trying to forge an alliance with rats that live underground."

She gave a slight chuckle. "If you call them rats, you won't make any friends."

"Maybe I'll let Bridge do all the talking, then."

"That'd be wise."

His eyes shifted past her to Callon. "His eyes have been trained on me like an arrow this entire time."

Cora glanced over her shoulder.

Callon stood in his armor, dark eyes driving into Rush with menace. Just like the poisonous frogs, that hatred was etched into the features of his face, and he looked like he might snarl just like them too.

Cora gave a sigh as she turned back to him. "Just ignore him."

"I'd like to thank him for what he did...if that's okay." Rush turned back to her.

"I...I don't think he wants to hear it."

"I owe him my life. He deserves my gratitude." He stepped forward to cross the field and approach Callon.

The slide of metal against his scabbard was loud in the trees, echoing in the canopy up above. Birds immediately vacated their nests and cawed as they flew away. His sword was at the ready, his defensive stance identical to the one he used when he trained Cora. The weapon in his hand wasn't the only one he possessed. His eyes were sharp blades themselves.

Rush halted.

Cora placed her hand against his chest, her fingers digging deep through the fabric as she felt his hardness. The touch prompted a series of images across her mind in a split second. She sucked in a breath as she guided him back. "I'll tell him for you."

Rush dragged his look away from Callon until it was on Cora again.

She pulled her hand away, her fingers curling into her palm.

"Have you told him about Ashe?"

"No."

"Are you going to?"

"Yes."

"I know Ashe would never eat rabbit food, so what's he eating?"

"Callon showed me a secret passage in and out of Eden Star…"

He gave a slight nod. "His secret must be pretty big...if he has no problem sharing that secret."

"I'll get it out of him eventually. Or...I'll ask someone else."

Rush stared for a while, his eyes reading hers like words.

She cleared her throat. "Flare said you had something for me?"

"Yeah." He held up the sack. "Bad news. I made a deal with Mathilda. Venom for access to the dwarves. But when I got there, they'd all been wiped out."

"What?" She took a step back. "No...that can't be."

His eyes dropped, and he lowered the bag. "Makes sense. Once the empire realized we had a way to kill them, they made sure we couldn't do it anymore. I'm sorry, Cora. I should have foreseen this. I could have stopped it."

She lowered her gaze to the sack in his hands. "They wiped out an entire species..."

"Not the *entire* species." He uncinched the drawstring and opened the bag. "I found these guys hidden away."

She peered inside, seeing the snarling frogs staring at her, various bright colors. The breath she sucked in was automatic, along with the film that layered over her eyes.

"I knew they'd be safe in Eden Star, so..." He cinched the bag once more before he set it on the ground. "The Galeco Clan can raise them. Maybe when this is over, we can introduce them to the area again and help them repopulate."

She stared through the small opening at the top, seeing shadows move as the frogs crawled over one another to get comfortable. "What are you going to do about Mathilda? Did you...get some venom?"

With his eyes on the bag, he gave a subtle shake of his head. "No." His eyes flicked back to hers. "I'll find another way... Always do."

With soft eyes, she stared at him, the bag between her feet. "Why?"

Rush gave a stare he had many times before, on an island, far away from this place. "You know why."

Her chin immediately dropped to the bag between them, and she kneeled to grab it. The bag was light, and as soon as she picked it up, she felt the frogs shift and rock the sack.

"You're the one who thinks they're cute, so...they're your problem now."

She pulled the strap over her shoulder and let it hang at her side, feeling the bag shift and move slightly as they got comfortable once again. "Thank you."

Without looking at her, he gave a nod. "When we get to the dwarves, I'm not sure if you'll be able to reach me. We'll be deep underground, so I'm not sure if we'll remain in contact. Just want you to know so you don't assume the worst."

"Thanks for letting me know. Good luck."

"I'm sure we'll need a *whole* lot of it." He gestured behind him. "Especially with those idiots."

"You're an idiot too."

He chuckled. "Am I now?"

"Always have been."

He gave a shrug. "Yeah, you're probably right."

There was nothing left to say, but Cora couldn't say goodbye. She looked at his chest for a moment before meeting his gaze once again.

"Don't be a stranger. Gonna need some company being stuck with these circus freaks for who knows how long..."

She felt the smile move on to her face, but just like his, it didn't reach her eyes. "Alright."

"One thing before I go..." He chewed the inside of his cheek and shifted his gaze in the other direction. "General Noose crossed our path with an army two-thousand strong. He didn't head in the direction of Eden Star, but I'm still wary he might. The empire knows I have an existing relationship with General Callon, and therefore, Eden Star. He might try to eliminate you—just the way he did with the frogs."

"Callon shares your fear."

"Then your queen is aware?"

She nodded.

"Then prepare for war—because it might show up on your doorstep."

She nodded again.

"If that happens, I will come to your aid as quickly as I can—hopefully with an army of dwarves."

"I know you will."

"If it happens, it's because of me. And I'm sorry for that."

She gave a shake of her head. "It would have happened eventually."

His stare lingered, his eyes hard on her face.

She stared back, picturing the cool mist that fell from the clouds, remembering the sounds of the waves as they crashed against the cliffs below. Eden Star was a place of serenity, but because of magic. Mist Isle was a place of innate peace. Moments like this made her wish to return.

He gave her a final nod before he turned away and retreated to Bridge and the others.

She watched him go, and it felt exactly the same as the last time he left.

Like she was alone on an island—watching a fire-red dragon fly across the ocean.

12

SUICIDE MISSION

You handled that well.

Really? Didn't feel like it. Never had to do that before.

What?

Going from being that...to being friends.

You did it with Lilac.

Yeah, that's not the same thing.

It is the same.

What I had with Lilac is *not* what I had with Cora.

Flare let seconds of silence trickle past. *Wish I could have seen her in the flesh. Watched her admire my beauty with appreciation.*

Rush rolled his eyes. **You just want compliments.**

Yes. She gives plenty. But she's also my friend, and I enjoy her company.

Rush remained in the lead as they trekked through the wilderness. The dry and blistering desert was behind them, and they were back in the evergreen trees near the stream. He set the pace, and everyone groaned in protest behind him. **Yeah…I enjoy her company too.**

Hope she contacts us.

She will.

Do you think she's spoken to her father?

Rush stopped at the top of the crest and looked at the path below. It was a quiet afternoon, no travelers or armies in their vicinity. Their only company was the birds. The poisonous frogs would have been there…if they hadn't been annihilated in a gruesome death. **Yes.**

I think so too. Just wanted to spare your feelings.

I didn't have much of a chance before…but now I have none.

Not necessarily.

Yes. That's the exact reason why she didn't mention it. He's her family—and I'm just some mistake.

You know that's not how she feels about you.

If not now, she will soon.

Rush headed down the hill, past a couple boulders, and then came to a stop when Bridge's voice came from the rear.

"Do you *ever* stop?" He paused at the top of the hill, hands on his back, head tilted to the ground. "You've got some good shit in your pack or what?"

"Got some beef jerky you aren't sharing with the rest of us?" Lilac stopped next to her brother, her forehead shiny with sweat. "Or maybe some cookies? Did your girlfriend hook you up with some cookies?"

It's time to rest, Rush.

We have a lot of ground to cover.

You can cross all of Anastille, and you'll still never outrun your thoughts.

"Fine. We'll rest here for the day." Rush dropped his pack in a grassy area between the trees and readied his bow. "I'll grab dinner. You guys make a fire."

BRIDGE WAS THE LAST ONE AWAKE, AND HE CONTINUED TO CAST glances at Rush. "I'll take the first shift."

"It's fine. Not tired."

"How?" he asked incredulously. "Now I'm thinking she gave you more than cookies..."

"I just don't want to be out in the open longer than necessary."

"Because of General Noose?"

"Because King Lux stepped up his game. His dictatorship has been peaceful for a very long time...until now. I know my father. He's unnerved. And he's especially unnerved that I'm the one who's challenging him."

Bridge shifted his gaze to the fire.

"War is brewing."

"You think he'll go after Eden Star?"

Rush gave a nod. "Unfortunately."

"What about the dwarves?"

"His focus is on the half-elf that's immune to the Skull Crusher and the general of the elven army that dropped ancient hostilities to rescue their enemy. Nothing else is his concern right now. We have to keep Ashe a secret as long as possible. Because once that's out...he'll give everything he has. At least right now, he'll continue to underestimate us. That's our only advantage."

Bridge nodded. "You think it makes sense to go into the mountains without any idea where we're going? That's like searching for a broken fingernail on the rug."

"You got a better idea?"

"Can you offer Mathilda anything else?"

"Other than the shirt off my back, no."

"She gave Cora the tears for an IOU. Maybe she can do the same for you?"

"Doesn't think I have anything to offer...and she's not wrong about that."

Bridge rubbed his palms together and held them out to the fire. "If she's not ratting you out to the empire, then she can't be a supporter of King Lux. So, it's in her best interest to help you. Maybe you should tell her what we're trying to accomplish."

"Too risky."

"Well, combing mountains we're unfamiliar with is more risky, if you ask me."

"It's going to take us twice as long to go all the way back, and she may not even cooperate."

"All I know is, I'm not familiar with anything north of Anastille. There's no passage through the mountains by foot, so the only way to get there is by flight. So...who knows what's out there."

"Sounds like you're scared, Bridge."

"Uh, you aren't?"

He shrugged. "I've seen it all. Nothing scares me anymore." His eyes went back to the fire.

"Whatever. This is your mission, so I'm down for anything. But if time is of the essence, we've got to spend it well."

I agree with him.

Didn't ask for your opinion.

Rush.

How am I going to convince a witch to help me?

I don't know. But it's a better use of our time than hiking up a mountain in the dark. We don't know where we'll find water. How will we hunt?

Rush gave a sigh. "Fine...we'll go see Mathilda first."

"Tell Flare I said thanks."

Tell him I like him.

I'm not saying that.

Bridge looked at the fire for a while, rubbing his palms together again. "Things seemed tense with you guys..."

This is exactly why I didn't want to stop.

You don't need to be ashamed of your feelings.

Not ashamed. Just don't want to talk about it. "It's a bit awkward when a woman says she just wants to be friends."

Bridge gave a nod. "Sorry, man."

"That was the first time we'd spoken since she shot me down. It'll get easier from now on."

"I'm sure it will."

Despite their hustle, it was a two-week trek back to Polox.

They made fires during the day to cook their meals and immediately snuffed them out with a fire blanket instead of water. Otherwise, it would create a cloud of smoke that could be seen by unwanted eyes.

They didn't cross paths with General Noose and his army.

But they came across something worse.

"Just saw it..." Bridge lay beside him in his bedroll in the dark. "And there's another one." If he pointed at the nighttime sky, Rush couldn't see it because it was pitch black without a campfire.

I've counted twelve.

That's not good news.

They're searching for us—everywhere.

"Flare counted twelve."

"Twelve?" Bridge asked in surprise. "I didn't even know there were that many."

"Neither did I."

They were either really lucky, or the Shamans only searched by night because they hadn't seen the cloaked Shamans and their steeds in the blue sky. If they thought Rush would light a fire in the dark to keep warm or cook a meal, they were idiots.

They continued on their journey, just a few days from Polox.

It's Cora.

His heart already raced from pushing himself physically, but his pulse gave a sudden spike. **Put her through.**

Her beautiful voice came into his mind, loud like she was right beside him. ***Where are you guys now?***

Almost to Polox.

I thought you were going to the dwarves.

We were. But Flare and Bridge decided that it would be more worthwhile to get directions from Mathilda…even though we're gonna be empty-handed.

It sounds like she already knew about the frogs…so she won't be surprised.

True.

Hello, Pretty.

Hey, Flare. How's it going?

Tired, hungry…hide!

What?

"Down." Rush grabbed Liam because he was the closest person to him and yanked him to the base of a tree.

Bridge did the same with Lilac, pulling her under the canopy as they searched around for enemies.

Zane was at the tree beside him, turning his head frantically back and forth.

Is everything okay?

Before Rush could answer, he saw the enormous outline above the trees.

The outline of a dragon.

Who is it? Flare?

Flare was silent.

What's going on?

Rush felt Flare disappear from his mind completely.

Everyone else saw the big outline above the trees and pressed their backs even deeper into the trunks.

Liam looked completely awestruck, his mouth agape, his eyes wide.

Rush watched the dragon soar overhead and continue across the sky. **We just spotted a dragon.**

Do you know who it is?

Rush moved between the trees, getting to the edge so he could see over the horizon.

He recognized the blue scales immediately.

Obsidian.

It was several hours before Flare returned to his mind.

I'm here.

Why'd you leave?

I feared he would feel my mind.

Didn't even consider that... Good thinking.

They were close to Polox but didn't move from their hidden location. The skies were clear of dragons, but the fear had just reached a crescendo. **He's looking for me—personally.**

And he wants you to know that he's looking for you.

This is bad.

Yes.

"What's our plan?" Bridge asked.

"Should have headed straight to the mountains…"

"He could be looking there too."

"Unlikely."

"What if he thinks you're going to the dwarves?"

Rush gave a slight shake of his head. "No one knows anything about the dwarves, so I doubt he would assume that."

Rush, we have a problem.

What?

What happens when he doesn't find you?

I'm not following.

If he can't find you anywhere *in Anastille, where's the last place he can't check?*

Rush released a sigh. **Fuck.**

Eden Star.

They were stationed outside of Polox and ready to slip inside.

"I have a plan...and you aren't going to like it." Rush approached their group, leaning against a big log as they rested after their long trip.

Bridge finished drinking his water before he secured the cap back in place. "We already have a plan. Lilac will get you in just like last time."

"Yeah...a plan after that plan." His hands rested on his hips, his pack at his feet.

Lilac folded her arms over her chest. "What are you up to, Rush?"

"You aren't going to like it," he said. "Spoiler alert."

"What is it?" Bridge asked, sitting beside Zane.

"Dragons, Shamans, armies...they aren't going to stop until they find me." He crossed his arms over his chest and shifted his weight to one leg. "And when they comb every inch of this land and I turn up nowhere...he'll assume I'm in Eden Star."

Bridge set his canteen down slowly then rested his palm on the lid. "I already see where this is going."

"I don't," Lilac said, glancing at her brother. "We skip the dwarves and head to Eden Star?"

"No." Bridge shook his head. "That doesn't fix the problem."

"Then what does fix the problem?" Zane asked.

Bridge gestured to Rush with his hand. "Suicide mission...but whatever."

They all looked at him and waited for an answer.

"You get me into Polox. I talk to Mathilda," Rush said. "Then I lie low for a couple days so you guys can get clear of this place. We'll agree on a meeting spot. I'll meet you there when I can."

"Whoa…what?" Zane asked. "Meet us after what?"

"If my father doesn't find me in Anastille, he'll hit Eden Star," Rush explained. "So, I basically have to tell him where I am."

"Rush." Bridge closed his eyes and shook his head. "You literally have no chance of getting away."

"Seriously," Lilac said. "And you have no idea if King Lux will actually attack Eden Star—"

"He will," Rush said with a sigh. "Eventually. And I can't let that happen. Eden Star won't stand a chance against dragons, armies, Shamans… It's a forest. Their magic will protect it for a short while, but then my father will obliterate the place."

"Then why hasn't he done it before?" Bridge asked.

"Too far away," Rush said. "But it's not going to feel too far away very soon."

Bridge pushed himself to his feet and dusted off his trousers. "You do realize that if you're recaptured, all hope is lost? You're literally the one person we can't afford to lose."

"Not true," Rush said. "Cora is the one person we can't afford to lose. She's the one person who can unite the dragons and the elves. My life is inconsequential compared to hers. Eden Star must be protected at all costs."

We must keep Pretty safe.

"The reason this is happening in the first place is because General Callon came to my rescue. If he hadn't done that, King Lux wouldn't even be thinking about Eden Star. Doing nothing is a really shitty way of repaying that sacrifice. I have to do this. There's no other way."

Bridge dropped his arms to his sides, his shoulders falling too. "What would Cora think if she knew?"

Tell us no.

"She doesn't need to know. And hopefully...there'll never be a reason for her to know."

13

THE ASSASSIN

Rush instructed the others to go to the Hideaway if he didn't escape. Hitch a ride with Captain Hurricane and figure out their next plan.

Lilac's plan worked once again, and he slipped inside Polox just before dark. He returned to the shop, rang the bell overhead when he opened the door, and stepped inside the store that held an arrangement of odd objects.

"You're back."

He sauntered through the aisles and stopped near the window when he saw the dragon tears. "Business been slow?"

"Not a lot of people in the market for dragon tears. Most people don't need it once—let alone twice."

He moved to the front counter where she stood. The walls behind her were covered in colorful tapestries, feathered necklaces, and various jewels. On the counter, there was a bowl of transparent crystals. "Does any of this stuff work?"

One hand moved to her hip, cinching her purple cloak into her side. "Did the dragon tears save your life?"

He gave a slight nod. "You got me."

She glanced down at his hands, as if expecting to see the jar of venom she requested. "Didn't go well?"

"You were right. Frogs were massacred."

"The empire made the right decision."

"They killed off an entire species—"

"And now the Shamans are invincible. Smart play."

He pulled his hood back and revealed his face, a full beard on his jawline because there'd been no time for anything on their travels except hauling ass. "I know I didn't fulfill my end of the deal, but you still need to tell me what I want to know."

"I don't need to do anything, General Rush."

"You were interested in that venom for a reason. It means you're an enemy of the empire. I'm an enemy as well—which means we're allies."

"Or it just means I want something good to sell in my shop."

"Would you really sell that?" Skepticism shot out of his mouth like an arrow released from the string. "You don't think the empire would come knocking?"

"I sell dragon tears, and they still haven't come knockin'."

"Maybe not yet…but they will."

She gave a shrug. "I'll take my chances."

"Look." He pressed a hand to his chest. "I'm an enemy of the empire. So, you should *want* to help me."

"I see starving children on the street, and I *want* to help them. Doesn't mean I do."

"Okay...anyone who doesn't help a starving kid is an asshole. But that's not the point right now. Just tell me how to reach the dwarves, and I'll be on my way."

"What do I get in return?"

"The hope that I'll be able to overthrow King Lux because of your help."

She popped out one hip and came closer to the counter, her other hand on the surface. "You shouldn't make such assumptions. Maybe I'm a friend to the empire. Maybe I'm a foe."

"If your allegiance is to the crown, you're doing a terrible job showing it by letting me come and go from your shop without repercussion."

Her eyes narrowed. "As I've said before, I don't interfere with a person's travels."

"Then don't impede me now. Tell me how to get to the dwarves."

Her fingers started to drum on the counter, her long nails creating a loud clicking sound. "You would waste your time there."

"That's for me to decide."

Her fingers continued to drum against the counter.

"Mathilda, come on. Don't make me crawl all over those mountains like a damn goat trying to get inside."

"You expect me to help you when I'll receive nothing in return."

"That's called being a good person. Try it sometime."

Her nails went silent. "Didn't realize you were so virtuous, *General Rush*."

It was a fist to the stomach. "I'm no longer that man."

"Being a good man serves me no purpose."

"Then what do you want? If it's in my power, I will grant it."

Her nails started to drum once more. A stare deeper than the ocean penetrated his face, hot like the summer sun. "A sword of dragon scales."

Grrrrrrrr.

"To sell in your store?"

"What I do with it is none of your concern."

"That's not going to happen. I'm not a blacksmith—"

"I can find one. Just need the scales."

What do I do?

She doesn't deserve my scales.

I can't think of a substitution.

"What's it going to be?" Her nails continued to drum on the surface. "I have warned you that this trek into the mountains is pointless. To sacrifice your scales would be a mistake on your part. As a *good person*, I've given you fair warning. But if you want to go anyway, it'll cost you."

We need the dwarves.

I know.

But I won't do anything you don't want to do. I'll hike up those mountains day and night until we find them.

We don't have the time.

Then it's your call.

After a long pause, Flare agreed. *Okay.*

"Why do you say it's pointless? And fatal?"

"Because it is."

"Mathilda—"

"You asked for directions. I will grant them. But I'm not obligated to tell you anything else. Do you accept?"

"Fine...I accept."

"Alright." She pulled her hand off the counter. "Once I have the scales, I'll provide a map."

"Okay, that's going to be a problem," Rush said. "You do realize everyone and their mom is looking for me right now?"

"And?"

"I can't just transform into a dragon in your shop or in the street."

"Then let's go somewhere you can."

I have an idea.

What?

You need the empire to see us. Perhaps she can help us.

That wasn't part of the deal.

Then make it part of the deal.

"You also need to help me escape."

"The sword in exchange for the map."

"We both know the value of my scales. I can ask for anything I want—and this is what I want."

She chewed on the inside of her cheek before she gave a raw look of annoyance. "Fine."

"We'll sneak out and harvest my scales. And then I need to be seen by the guards before we return to your shop so I can hide for a few days."

"Cat's piss, are you kidding me?"

"Wish I were."

"Why do the guards need to see you?"

Rush kept quiet.

She tells us nothing. We tell her nothing.

"Do you have a secret way out of the city?"

"You think I use the front gate every time I come and go?"

At least we'll have a secret way into Polox from now on.

That would have been helpful a long-ass time ago.

THE STREETS WERE DESERTED.

Shops were closed. Inns were no longer serving pints of beer. The occasional window was lit up with a candle from a sleepless resident. The dark sky was dotted with little stars that were bright enough to cast a subtle glow on the cobblestone pathway.

Mathilda led the way, her dark purple cloak masking her quite well.

She maneuvered between buildings then reached an alleyway where a group of rats munched on moldy bread. Right up against the thick fence that defended the city from outside invaders, her palm slid across the wood until she found the dial. She turned it, an audible click sounding.

Then two planks spun on an invisible dial.

She lifted the plank above her head then stepped through the opening.

"Did you make this?" Rush followed her, keeping the wood above his head as he stepped onto the grass beside her.

"Shh!" She let the plank slide back into place before she clicked the dial on the other side of the wall.

"Let's go." She led the way along the fence, invisible to the guards that manned the wall up above. Silently, they moved, reaching the rear of the city that received little to no attention from the guards watching the perimeter.

They used the darkness as cover and snuck into the trees, getting far enough away from Polox to have a conversation at normal volume.

"Did you build that thing?"

She pulled out a knife. "I didn't come here to gossip."

"Asking how you made that passageway is not gossip—"

"We don't have time for this."

Sure you're okay with this?

I gave my scales to Pretty as a gift. But she's harvesting them as a butcher.

Still time to say no.

No. We need that map. And we need to keep King Lux away from Eden Star.

Alright. Rush transferred into the fiery red dragon.

Mathilda paused to absorb the sight, her eyes glossing over with a dreamy haze. She took him in from head to toe, pressed her palm against his flank, even came close to his snout and reached for a tooth. "Magnificent."

Thank you.

She extended the blade and got to work.

"I will wait for you at the dial." Mathilda disappeared into the darkness, her cloak hiding her form from view within a few seconds.

Flare looked at the stars in the sky, his flank dripping with blood from the scales that had been harvested.

You okay?

It didn't hurt.

Well, it's going to hurt me like a bitch when we get back to the shop.

Flare's head turned when he saw the glimmer in the sky, when the stars were blocked out for just an instant. *They're here.*

Of course they are…

This is going to be difficult.

When do we ever do anything that's not difficult?

Here we go. Flare opened his wings and pushed off the ground. *Roooooooaaaaaaaarrrrrr!*

The scream pierced the night, shook the mountains in the distance, made the guards falter along the fence line.

That was quite the entrance.

Flare got to altitude immediately and soared right over Polox, breathing a stream of fire without actually burning anything.

Don't set anything on fire.

I'm not.

Flare flew low enough to be visible to all the guards, his bright-red scales unmistakable.

Okay, enough. We gotta get outta here. Shamans are probably already here.

Flare glided around the city then circled back, returning to the darkness away from Polox. He extinguished his breath of fire before he landed with a thud on the earth.

Let's go. Rush came into being, tripping over himself and landing back on the ground. **Damn, this hurts.**

Move.

Rush gritted his teeth then pushed himself upright. He forced himself into a quick jog, heading back to Polox to reach the secret passage.

Whoosh. A gust of wind passed him, making his hair blow back.

Run.

He silenced his grimace and forced himself forward, beelining straight for the fence line.

I said run!

Bitch, I'm going.

A loud cackle filled the night, an eerie sound that Rush had heard more times than he could count.

They're following you.

His palm slid across the wood, searching for the dial. **Where is it?**

Rush!

I can't find it!

The cackle grew louder.

Now!

The wood plank lifted, and a hand shot out to yank him inside.

That was close.

Too close.

Mathilda dragged him down the alleyway and they ran together, crowds in the streets as they came out of their homes to see the dragon they just heard. Guards pushed past them as they rushed to other parts of the city.

She moved to a walk, and Rush mimicked her movements.

I feel like shit.

Hold on.

The adrenaline wasn't enough to numb the pain. **Why do I feel like I'm always in pain?**

We're here.

Mathilda pulled him inside and locked the door behind her.

Rush immediately leaned on the counter, breathing hard as the gapes in his flesh bled into his clothes. "You got a bandage or something?" Too weak to stand, he dropped into a chair behind the counter, breathing through the pain.

Mathilda walked off.

I would change back if I could fit.

I know. I'll be fine. Just hurts more than last time...

Probably because of all the scar tissue from Rock Island.

Yeah...maybe.

Mathilda extinguished all the lights in her shop, plunging them into darkness.

"I need something to stop the bleeding. Got gauze or anything?"

"Lift up your shirt."

He turned in his chair then yanked the shirt over his head and to his shoulders.

Instead of feeling tight fabric wrap around his body, he felt drops.

Water poured down his back, and instead of burning like a disinfectant, it felt good. Really good. Immediately, he felt better, like he was brand-new. "What is that?" He turned back in his chair.

She corked the lid. "You owe me. This wasn't part of the deal." The bottle was returned to the locked cage in the shop for someone else to buy.

He pulled his shirt back on, no longer soaking blood into his clothes. "Thanks."

She ignored his gratitude and stationed herself by the windows, seeing the silhouettes pass by the curtains as people frantically moved up and down the street. "You wanted to be seen. Mission accomplished."

Hours passed.

They sat in the dark at opposite ends of the shop, waiting for the crowds in the street to vanish. The shadows in the window slowly lessened as people gave up on their curiosity and returned to their now-cold beds.

Just when Rush thought they'd gotten away with it, a knock sounded on the door.

Mathilda stiffened in her chair, and the look she gave Rush was murderous.

Oh no...

The knock sounded again. "By order of the king, we are to search your premises."

Jump out a back window.

Rush crossed the room but stilled when he saw the outline of soldiers on the other side.

"Psst."

His head snapped in Mathilda's direction.

She waved him over frantically then gestured to one of the shelves.

Witches always have tricks up their sleeves...

They lifted it together, revealing a hatch in the floor.

She opened it. "Go, go."

He grabbed the ladder and slid down to the floor.

The shelf dragged over the floor as she moved it back herself, doing one side and then the other.

Rush kept his eyes on the ceiling, his ears straining to listen.

The door opened.

Footsteps entered. Heavy footsteps. Bootsteps.

Then clicks.

Shamans are here.

"Step aside." The footfalls fanned out to different parts of the room.

Mathilda shrieked with annoyance. "Just don't take anything!"

Uh, Rush?

His eyes remained on the ceiling, seeing little flecks of dust fall from the floorboards. One of the guards was right on top of him now.

Rush?

Rush stepped back, watching the dust and listening to the sounds as the guards maneuvered around the shop. The

Shaman was impossible to detect because the footsteps were too light. There were no clicks.

What?!

There's someone here.

Yes, I'm aware. It doesn't seem like they have a clue there's a basement, so we should be good.

No. There's someone in here—with us.

His body turned as rigid as ice, frozen over in a chill. Suddenly, the search party up above didn't seem that important anymore because his head slowly turned to the man standing there, against the other wall, eyes on the ceiling.

Dressed in black street clothes, he was unremarkable, but that changed once he met Rush's gaze.

His eyes weren't ordinary.

Intelligent. Confident. Powerful.

He held Rush's look with a ruthless calmness.

The steps overhead left as they ventured farther into the shop. "We need to go upstairs."

"To my bedroom?" Mathilda shrieked. "What on earth do you hope to find there?"

He's somebody.

I agree. Nobody wouldn't be hiding under Mathilda's shop.

And he's looking at me like he doesn't like me very much.

You did just compromise his hiding place.

It's more than that. I can tell.

Do you recognize him?

No.

The man continued to hold his gaze, refusing to look away first.

Rush did the same.

Minutes later, the footsteps returned, followed by Mathilda's attitude.

"Are you done waking me up in the middle of the night to ransack my home?" Her quick footsteps followed them. "And if you've taken anything, I'll hunt you down and gut you like a fish."

The guards filed out. The door shut.

Both men looked up at the ceiling.

Silence.

Rush waited for Mathilda to push the shelf away and open the hatch.

She didn't.

She probably wants to make sure they don't come back.

Yeah. Rush turned his stare back to the man. "Who are you?"

Brown hair. Brown eyes. High cheekbones. His eyes stared coldly before a quick smile appeared on his lips. "Not surprised."

"Not surprised what?"

He moved to the chair against the wall and lowered himself, his knees planted firmly apart, his arms on his knees. "That you don't recognize me, General Rush."

Rush sat in the other chair on the other side of the room, but the hostility crossed the space, radiating from the man's eyes and landing on his skin. It was hot like a sunburn, slowly growing more uncomfortable as the skin bubbled then peeled.

You know everyone—but everyone hates you.

But I remember everyone who hates me. I have no recollection of this guy—or what I did.

Ask.

He doesn't seem like a talker.

Know your enemies, Rush.

"Care to enlighten me?"

The basement was a storage room. Shelves along the walls carried canned goods and dried nuts. There were also extra supplies that would replenish the stock on the shelves once they were purchased. It was a cold and dark place, the only illumination the white candles sprinkled around the room. The man looked at the shelf as he sat with a relaxed posture, but the way he carried his shoulders suggested he was a fighter. His arms stretched the fabric of his sleeves, indicating he knew how to wield both sword and shield. "Just like you, I served King Lux."

Past tense. That's good.

"There are a lot of soldiers at High Castle."

"Wasn't a soldier."

"Then what were you?"

His eyes shifted to Rush's, cold. "An assassin."

It suits him.

"I spied on his enemies—then I killed them."

"King Lux doesn't have a lot of enemies—"

"Because he kills them before they become a threat."

That's why there's never been a coup—because of him.

Rush searched his memory, coming across a name he'd heard his father mention. "Maverick."

He cocked his head slightly. "You remember me, after all. In part."

What happened to him?

"King Lux assumed you were dead." **He left for a mission and never returned. My father sent out scouts to find him and**

recover his body. When that didn't happen, he just assumed he'd been killed. That was years before I left.

"Well, he assumed wrong." His eyes narrowed. "But I'm grateful for the assumption."

We have an ally—a good one.

"Why did you leave?"

His eyes flicked away.

Alright, I'll go first. "I told my father things needed to change. He refused. So, I left. My intention is to remove him from power."

"So you can take the throne."

"Because he's a tyrant. Because he's enslaved an innocent race of beings and rules over Anastille with cruelty and fear."

He continued to look away.

He doesn't trust you.

Picked up on that. "Why are you down here?"

"When did I give any indication that we're friends?" He turned back to Rush, his confident eyes covered with ice.

"I've publicly marked my father as my enemy. I say that makes us allies."

Maverick gave a subtle shake of his head. "You're an arrogant, entitled brat. That's all."

Rush's eyes narrowed.

Rush. Don't.

He took a slow breath and let it release just as slowly. "You left King Lux's service. You're under Mathilda's shop. We're the same—whether you like it or not."

Maverick gave a subtle clench of his jaw.

"We both did vile things in service to a dictator. Judge me? Then you better judge yourself too."

He looked away.

"Let's work together here."

He ignored him.

"Maverick."

The shelf started to slide across the floor as Mathilda pushed it.

Rush kept his stare on the former assassin. "Come on. You and Mathilda are working against the empire. I know it."

I know it too.

The hatch opened. "All clear."

Maverick turned to her.

"You should go now while they're still searching for Rush," Mathilda said. "No one will give you a second look."

He got to his feet and readied his weapons. A sword at his side, a shield and bow across his back, and his pack over one shoulder.

Rush, we need allies—and they're right here.

Rush jumped to his feet. "Why won't you let me help you?"

Maverick's reaction was so fast, his body turning to face Rush with his hand already on the pommel of his sword.

Rush glanced down at his hand, immediately taken back to the outside of Eden Star when Callon had reacted the same way. It was an insult—each and every time. "Tell me."

His fingers released their grip, but his eyes increased their might. "Loyalties can be severed with a butter knife. But family...there's nothing that can break that bond. The empire hunts you day and night. You will be recaptured, and when that happens, your loyalties will turn once more."

14

SEE THE TRUTH

Mathilda never answered his questions.

The only answer he got was stony silence.

The map was in his possession, and once the guards assumed he was long gone, he left the city through the secret entrance and trekked through the wilderness toward the location where they'd agreed to meet.

You're angry.

You think?

Why?

I don't know...maybe because I can't get anything done because literally no one trusts me?

It takes time—

I don't have time, Flare.

I understand their position. King Lux is utilizing every resource to find you. Any information they give to you could be shared once you're captured.

I would never do that.

But they don't know that. Would you do anything differently?

He kept his eyes forward, his gaze targeting the tree line so he could hide from the hot sun.

Mathilda has helped us many times—so at least she doesn't see us as a threat.

I guess.

If we secure the dwarves, we can return to Mathilda with something to offer.

I don't know… I've gotta survive all that death she mentioned.

If the dwarves get in our way, I'll just eat them. They're bite-size.

He cracked a smile as he imagined it. **Not the best way to proposition allies.**

A little fear never hurt anyone.

When there wasn't enough light to see several feet in front of him, he stopped for the night. No campfire. Just his bedroll in the grass. **We should be there by early afternoon. Hope the others are alright.**

I'm sure they went unnoticed with all the commotion.

His hands folded underneath his head, and he stared at the stars. Despite the long day, he was still wired. His eyes focused on the heavens, expecting the stars to dim momentarily as a Shaman passed. Thankfully, that never happened.

Should I contact Pretty?

No. It's okay. I'm sure she's busy...

A moment later, Cora's voice appeared. *Rush?*

He rolled his eyes in annoyance. "Flare..." **I'm here.**

What's going on with you guys?

Chaos. Like always.

You're okay?

Yeah...we're all good. What about you?

Callon has been teaching me with an actual sword.

How's that going?

I can barely move. I'll leave it at that.

He gave a slight chuckle under his breath. **You'll get better.**

I'm a lot better than I used to be, but I could never imagine holding my own against Callon in a real fight...

You probably never will.

You just said I'll get better.

And you will. But General Callon is one of the best living swordsmen. You would need a good thousand years to get on his level.

Her words didn't emerge for a while. *Actually, it's just Callon now...*

Rush closed his eyes, guilt pulling him under. **No wonder he drew his sword.**

That wasn't why. He said he would do it again.

Because of you.

She turned quiet.

He did too.

Conversations by the firelight had been effortless once upon a time. Laughter and jokes, smiles and long stares. Those times were long gone. They were just memories now. **How's talking to dead people?**

She released a chuckle. *I should have phrased it better.*

No. A lot funnier this way.

I haven't been back yet. Callon and I have been training pretty hard.

Good. Have you asked him about the Shaman thing?

No. He's been...in kinda a bad mood lately.

And I know why...

I'm not sure if he'd ever tell me anyway.

Ask your father. He forced it out into the open, pushed through the awkwardness, ripped off the bandage.

For a while, it was just her silence.

It's okay, Cora. You can tell me anything.

The silence continued. *I've only spoken to him once. Next time I see him...I'll ask.*

Rush closed his eyes again, another tide of despair filling his lungs. **How was that?**

I don't know...a bit indescribable.

Did you tell him who you were?

Yes...

I'm sure he was thrilled.

Yeah, he was.

He wanted to force the conversation, but he just couldn't, imagining their reunion on two sides of the veil.

I found out what happened with my mother.

Yeah? Who is she?

He doesn't know. Said he was bewitched or poisoned. Doesn't remember anything except seeing her outside his tent. The rest...is lost.

She might be a witch...but I guess anyone could have bought a potion. But what is the purpose of seducing a king and siring a child?

Ashe thinks it was the empire. If they had a child of King Tiberius, they could use that as leverage to get the cooperation of the elves. They could get past the magic of Eden Star and invade.

Possibly...but I was never aware of this plan. But then again, I served King Lux like everyone else. Wasn't necessarily privy to a lot of things.

So maybe that's what happened.

Unlikely. I can't see any king sacrificing all of his people for one person—even if it was his daughter. Sacrificing himself? Yes. But not everyone.

True. I can't see him doing that either...

We'll uncover this secret—eventually.

Her voice turned quiet, withdrawn. *Hope so.*

As if she was right beside him next to the campfire, he turned quiet because it was always comfortable—even when it wasn't comfortable.

Did Mathilda end up helping you?

She did.

Without the venom?

I gave her scales again.

Oh...are you okay?

Totally fine. She gave me some dragon tears.

That was generous. And out of character.

I don't know...she gave it to me with nothing in return.

So, you know how to get to the dwarves now?

Got a map.

That's great!

But she did warn me about going...said there was lots of death and stuff.

There's death anywhere you go—except Eden Star.

I'm not worried about it. It's gotta get done anyway.

True.

I'm pretty sure Mathilda is actively working against the empire.

Why? Though, I guess that would explain why she helped us.

She had a former assassin for King Lux hidden in her basement.

Why were you in the basement?

Long story. Doesn't matter. I didn't remember him right away, but it eventually clicked. His name is Maverick, and when he didn't return from a mission, King Lux assumed he was dead. But it looks like he changed his loyalties instead.

Wait. Then that must mean...

That they're working together—so there must be others too.

That's great news! Maybe this is part of the underground group that you mentioned before.

Maybe. But they want nothing to do with me.

They said that?

Yep. Because the same blood that runs in his veins runs in mine...

She clearly didn't know what to say.

You're the only person who sees me for who I really am. The only person who looked at him with joy rather than disdain. The only person who saw a future behind his past. The only person who thought he was worth another chance.

That's not true, Rush.

It is.

It's not just me. It's Flare. It's Bridge. Even Ashe.

He despises me more than anyone.

No, he doesn't.

Sorry...forgot about Callon.

If Ashe didn't believe in us both, he wouldn't be here right now.

You're the one he believes in, Cora.

And I believe in you.

He closed his eyes, the mist against his skin, the crackle of the fire in his ears, her fingers wrapped around his.

It'll happen, Rush.

He let the silence trickle past, holding on to that connection until it slipped away. When he opened his eyes, it was just dark. Solitude. Emptiness. **If we can get the dwarves on board, maybe they'll reconsider.**

That's a good plan. I like it.

He stared at the stars, wondering if she stared at the same thing through her window.

Tell the others I said hello.

He sighed as his hands squeezed on an invisible hand, keeping her close even though she was already gone. **I will.**

Goodnight, Rush.

Goodnight...Cora.

"How are you still alive?" Bridge was the first to run up to him. "It was pandemonium, man. Even from here, we could hear everything."

"Flare can be loud sometimes."

"I'll say..." He gave Rush a quick pat on the arm. "I can't believe you pulled that off."

"When do I not pull off anything I do?"

Bridge rolled his eyes.

The others got up to greet him.

"You aren't bloody or bruised..." Lilac looked him over. "Lucky son of a bitch."

"If you're referring to my father, then yes, that's very accurate."

She cracked a smile.

"You got the map?" Liam asked.

Rush pulled it out of his pack. "Yep."

Liam unfolded it and took a look. "This is going to take a while..."

"I'd be suspicious if it didn't." Rush turned back to the others. "So, you want the details or what?"

"Not really," Bridge said. "Just assumed there was a lot of action, stupidity, and maybe a pretty girl in there somewhere."

"I guess Mathilda can be the pretty girl because she saved my ass," Rush said.

"So, what happened?" Bridge said.

"Well, I did meet someone..."

Bridge's eyebrows furrowed. "You somehow managed to score a date during all that chaos?"

"No," Rush said quickly. "It was a guy."

"You're into guys too?" Lilac asked.

"No, no, no." Rush waved his arms. "Okay, maybe I should have phrased that better."

I think it's hilarious.

Rush told them about Maverick in the basement and all that transpired.

"You think they're involved with the people who changed the maps?" Bridge asked. "Because this could be huge."

"I have no idea." Rush shook his head. "They wouldn't share anything with me. For all I know, it could just be the two of them...no idea."

"An assassin from the empire and a witch who has dragon tears..." Bridge folded his arms. "It's got to be more than just them."

"I think so too," Lilac said.

"Unfortunately, they hate me, so unless I bring them a dwarf on toast, they're never going to share a drop of information with me." Rush took the map from Liam and stowed it back in his pack.

"Then let's get the dwarves." Bridge gave a rise and drop of his shoulders. "I mean, we found the dragons at Mist Isle. We got Cora into Eden Star. General Callon bailed you out of Rock Island...and we got an infamous pirate to chauffeur us around the deadly seas. I'm pretty optimistic."

15

TRUST

It was a flurry of hits, the green blade striking hers then whipping around to strike her again, over and over, sparks igniting off the steels and scales. With all the expertise of a lifetime of battles and experience, Callon wielded his blade as if she were a foe on the battlefield, menace in his eyes, driving her back farther and farther.

Cora blocked the hits with slippery hands, and when she finally got an opening to strike back, she was quickly shot down.

"Come on, Cora." Furious. His look was furious.

His disappointment gave her a surge of energy, and she kept up the volley, blocking his hits and swinging his sword aside to strike at his armor, only to miss after his graceful side step. Sweat poured from her head, dampened her hair, made her hands slip on the handle.

Callon gave a final flurry of strikes, his sword glinting in the sunlight, and then made a maneuver to steal the sword directly out of her hand before he stabbed it deep into the grass between them.

His sword was sheathed, and he stepped away, his muscular back to her, rising and falling with deep breaths.

Better. But still not good enough.

Don't need the commentary.

She grabbed her sword and yanked it out of the ground, but it wouldn't budge. It required two hands to get it out of the inches of soil. "I'm ready. Let's go again."

Callon looked into the trees.

She wiped the sweat from her forehead with the inside of her wrist before she dragged her hands down her pants, getting the sweat to wick off her skin. "Come on."

Callon slowly pivoted back to her. His dark eyes were narrowed with coldness, like the battle still raged.

He's still angry.

No kidding... "Callon, it's been a week."

"A week for you is a second for me. Elves experience time—"

"Differently. Yes, I know." She sheathed her sword as she approached him. "But you need to let this go."

Ooh...not the right thing to say, Cora.

His eyes managed to narrow even further—with a spark of fire.

It was the right thing to say.

Callon came closer, each step slow and purposeful, like she truly was an opponent on the battlefield. "To stand idle as my brother's murderer breathes..." He shook his head. "The restraint, the sacrifice...your childish mind has no idea."

"Callon—"

"A betrayal to my king. A betrayal to my people. He was outside Eden Star—and I didn't strike him down."

"He's our ally that we can't afford to lose."

"If he didn't vow to claim his life once this is over, my sword wouldn't stay in my scabbard. It would swipe his head clean from his shoulders until it rolled down the hill and splashed into the river, to be feasted on by crows—"

"*Stop it.*" Her hand had risen of its own accord.

His jaw clenched before his eyes flicked away.

"I understand this is difficult for you—"

"And I see very clearly why this is not difficult enough for you." He turned back to her, his eyes piercing.

She held his look with uneven breaths, the paralysis taking over her entire body. Confronted head on by a raging bull, she had nowhere to run, nowhere to escape.

When he couldn't look at her anymore, he stepped away.

HER PALMS WERE COATED WITH BLISTERS, EVEN WITH THE gloves she wore, so she applied the cool gel that Callon had given her weeks ago. It burned at contact, but then it was soothing, lubricating the wound and helping it heal.

I feel what he sees.

She stared at the inside of her thumb, where the worst damage had been done.

I didn't understand the origin of your sadness—until then.

She gave neither an agreement nor a denial. Nothing at all.

He doesn't deserve it, Cora.

Well, I can't help it, alright? It's not something I can just control…

You shouldn't have allowed it to happen in the first place.

Couldn't control that either.

Ashe turned silent, floating in her mind like an apple that had dropped into a lake. He was physical, with a heftiness that increased the load on her shoulders.

I don't want to talk about this anymore.

Nor do I.

She wrapped her hands in the leaves, securing them in place with a wooden pin.

I pity your heartbreak. But I don't pity the one who gave it to you.

This conversation is over, Ashe.

His mind retreated slightly, as if her hand had pushed him away. *It's time we speak to the queen. We've been here too long as it is. Our fusion has become easier, but it still feels like a mountain sits on top of my chest.*

I'm sorry.

It's not you. Just the circumstance.

Would it help if we ventured outside Eden Star every day so you can stretch your legs?

We don't have time for that. Have far more pressing obligations.

Then I don't know what the solution is.

I do. Go to the queen.

She closed the jar of goo then sat at the kitchen table. **She's corrupt, remember?**

But she's still the queen. She's the one I need to address.

I agree. But I don't trust her. And the second I reveal you…I fear for my own safety.

Then what is the plan?

I don't have one.

Then this mission is over. I must return.

I said I don't have a plan right this second, not that I give up. She slumped at the table, her chin on her folded knuckles. **Never thought that convincing a dragon would be easier than convincing an elf.**

Queen Delwyn isn't a good representation of her people.

No, she's not.

If Callon were your ruler, this would have been a simple acquisition.

I agree.

I say Callon takes the throne.

She shook her head. **You heard him. He's too loyal.**

He wouldn't be so loyal if her corruption was exposed. Neither would the elves.

What are you saying, Ashe?

As Callon said, gain the favor of the elves. Then reveal who you are. Her reputation will be destroyed and irreparable.

I promised Callon I wouldn't tell anyone.

Then ask his permission to break that promise.

He said he would keep this secret as a way to keep me in Eden Star.

But that's an agreement he never should have had to make. The Princess of Eden Star should not be shunned or ostracized from her home, let alone her identity. After what King Tiberius shared, I believe her corruption goes far deeper than the surface. We expose that—and she's done.

It was a treasonous coup, but was it treasonous if Cora was exposing the queen's treason?

We continue our conversations with King Tiberius, integrate with elven society, and continue our training. That's the plan.

Okay.

And we need to reveal my presence to Callon.

I don't know...you saw how he was today.

He needs to know.

Why?

Because he isn't the only one that needs to train you.

He's going to be so overwhelmed with this. I'm not sure how he'll handle it.

He'll be fine.

This is different. He'd be harboring an enemy inside his lands. It's one thing to sneak me out of Eden Star, another to protect me at Rock Island, but this...this is knowing that the King of Dragons is behind enemy lines.

It does not concern me.

How? How does it not?

Because I trust him.

Cora landed on the ground, her sword at her side.

"Get up."

She closed her eyes as her cheek rested against the grass.

"I said up!"

She gave a groan as she reached for her sword, the blisters of her hand immediately stinging. She dug the tip of the sword into the ground and used it to raise her body upright, her entire body protesting with soreness. "I know I'm not meeting your expectations, but don't you think my progress is remarkable?"

He held his sword at the ready.

"You've had thousands of years to be this good, and I've had what? A couple months—"

"Are you dead?" There was a bite to his words.

"What?"

"Are. You. Dead?" He made a gesture with his sword.

"Yes..."

"Then it's not good enough." He switched the sword to the other hand because he could use either one with the same strength, apparently. "Don't give yourself a pat on the back—because you haven't earned it."

I like him.

Really? I think he's being an ass right now.

I would never lower my expectations of my hatchlings to meet their potential. I would demand their potential meet my expectations.

She caught her breath as she readied the sword.

But I think I have something to add to his training.

Now isn't the time to tell him, Ashe. You see how pissed off he is?

Ashe pressed his mind against hers, but this time, it was the hardest push she'd ever felt, like when Flare blasted through the parameters of her mind. Everything shattered, and the thin veil that was once between them was gone.

What are you doing?

Her hand suddenly felt empty because the sword weighed nothing. The aches in her muscles and the pains in her joints suddenly vanished, like a wave of pain medication took away all her suffering. There were no blisters. No fatigue.

We are one.

Callon spun his sword around his wrist as he began to circle her.

You will learn battle quicker this way.

What way?

When you can actually finish it.

Callon lunged, swiping his sword at her shoulder.

Her reaction time was instant, meeting his fast blade with the block of her sword.

He hesitated, as if expecting her to miss. He swung his sword again, giving her a flurry of blows with a rush of speed.

Her sword met his every time without taking a step back.

She saw the opening and took it, slicing the sword across the armor of his stomach.

He faltered back, his eyes wide.

Okay...this is pretty cool.

Focus.

He spun the sword as he circled her. Then he moved again, attacking her harder than he ever had in their training.

Cora felt weightless, moving her arms without consequence, without the scream of her muscles. She possessed the strength of ten strong men, had more energy than her body could store, and she used it all to meet his blows.

Callon stepped back—again.

His furious expression was gone—replaced by a shine of pride. "Yes, *Sor-lei*."

For the first time, she attacked him. She swung her sword and met his block, but she kept going, slashing and fighting, matching his energy and strength with her own. Swords collided then broke apart. Grunts came from both of them. They circled each other and moved, each one giving their all.

She went for the killing blow.

He stopped her blade then tripped her feet from underneath her.

She fell to the earth, her face pressed against the grass once more.

Ashe pulled his mind away, ending the connection.

The second he was gone, she felt the consequences of her actions. Her muscles screamed. She gasped for breath. Her fingers stung like salt had been poured into the cracks. *No... come back.*

That's how battle should be. Recreate it.

Yeah, I'm never going to be able to do that.

You will.

I don't have the strength or energy to do that on my own.

My expectations won't change for your potential. Your potential will change for my expectations.

Callon kneeled beside her, his arms resting on his propped knee. The anger in his eyes had changed. Now they were calm like the stream. Bright like the sunrise. Gentle like the raindrops that dripped from the leaves to her cheek. "You did well, *Sor-lei*."

I have to tell him the truth.

You don't have to tell him anything—if you do better.

16

BROTHERS RIVERGLADE

"Can I ask you a favor?" Callon walked beside her on the path between the trees, his shoulders square, his muscular arms hardly swinging at his sides. His sword was across his back, his black armor giving his strong body another layer of protection.

She already knew what that favor would be. "Always."

They approached the base of her tree house. "I'd like to speak to my brother."

"Of course."

A day of training never slighted him. His body didn't droop because of the fatigue, and he carried himself like a general even though the title was no longer his. There was an integrity to every step he took. Honor in his countenance. "I'll meet you there."

"Okay." She turned to the vine stairway so she could drop her armor in the tree house and have a quick bath.

His hand moved to her arm.

She stilled at the touch.

"You are your father's daughter."

Everything in her body tightened.

His hand moved to her back next, where he gave her a pat. "And you are your uncle's niece, too."

They sat together on the bench in the mist, the rest of the cemetery obscured from the fog that provided privacy to anyone else there visiting a lost loved one. The statue stood tall, perfectly capturing his regal bearing in life. More flowers had grown over his tombstone.

Cora felt the droplets stick to her skin. Once they became big enough, they slid down her arms and plopped into the soil. Every time she drew breath, she felt the cold droplets enter her lungs, cleanse her soul.

Then she felt it.

Callon felt it too—because he raised his chin.

Cora saw the blue outline of her father's figure, just a blur of color before it solidified into his strong frame. His head was tilted down, his eyes on his brother.

Callon straightened his back and sat with an upright posture, his hands moving to his thighs. His eyes were straight ahead, unaware of his brother's proximity.

King Tiberius turned his gaze on her next. "Hello, Cora."

"Hello…Tiberius."

"I'm very happy to see your face once more."

"Me too."

Callon turned to regard her, listening to her speak to someone who wasn't there.

She shifted her gaze to his. "I'm here for Callon. He wishes to speak with you."

King Tiberius moved to the bench on the other side of Callon, sitting with the exact same posture.

"He's beside you," she whispered. "Looking ahead the way you are."

Callon turned his head slightly, as if he hoped to see him in the flesh. "My King…"

Cora acted as the translator through the veil, connecting their conversation.

"You never called me that in private. Please don't start now."

Callon cracked a smile, giving a slight chuckle. "Brother, it is…"

"I will not ask about your well-being because I see it in your eyes every time you visit my resting place. You carry a weight that doesn't belong to you. You carry more sorrow than any man ever should."

Callon faced forward again, hiding his face from a ghost.

"Release it."

"I can't. Grief is permanent. The only change is the way I handle it—which is different every day."

The outline of Tiberius shifted, his gaze moving to his brother's face. "Do not grieve me."

"How can I not?" He stared at his hands as they came together, sucking in a deep breath to stifle his emotion.

"Honor me. But do not grieve for me. The same for Weila and Turnion—who are waiting for you."

He sucked in another deep breath.

"We will be together again—when the time is right."

Callon kept his head bowed, his hands clenched.

"For now…it looks like you have someone else to live for."

Callon gave a nod, his eyes still down.

"Thank you for looking after her in my stead, Callon."

He stared at his hands, rubbing them together as he gave a subtle shake of his head. "It has been my joy."

"I know it has, brother."

They sat together in a long pause of silence, each man overcome by the presence of the other.

Callon turned his head slightly, regarding the position his brother would have if he were alive. "Have you found peace?"

"That's all there is on this side of the veil—peace. There are times when I miss my queen, there are times when I miss you, but that pain can never truly manifest. It's always quieted, in some inexplicable way. When you wake up first thing in the morning, you're aware of your world, of the sunshine, of the birds, but you don't open your eyes because you're still in that state of slumber. That's how it feels…all the time."

Callon gave a subtle nod in understanding.

"How is my queen?"

"Her reign has been peaceful—until now."

"Cora told me that she stripped away your title. I'm sorry for your loss, but I also understand why she did it."

"As do I."

"She must keep everyone accountable—even Eden Star's longest-serving general."

"I understand that. But…"

Tiberius stared.

"I don't trust her. Not anymore, at least."

"I don't condone her treatment of Cora, but I understand it."

"That's not the only reason," Callon stared. "If she had it her way, no one would ever know who Cora is."

"Give her time."

"I don't think time will change anything, Tiberius."

Tiberius turned quiet.

"I don't mean to speak ill of your *Sun-lei* or my queen...but I'm concerned. She hasn't come to see you since you've passed, but she didn't know of Cora's existence until a few months ago. That doesn't explain her over twenty-year absence."

"I suppose it doesn't."

The silence fell again, this time longer.

Callon spoke some time later. "War is coming."

"It can't come when it's already here, Callon. We've been at war with the empire for thousands of years."

"But the end is nigh."

"Speak your mind, brother."

"Cora has gained an alliance with the remaining free dragons, along with some high-ranking officials in the empire..." He faced forward again, his hands clasped together. "Her purpose in Eden Star is to forge an alliance between the elves and the dragons. It makes me sick to even consider it...after what they've done. I've lost everyone...because of them."

Cora watched their interaction, feeling like an observer rather than a participant, watching two members of her family interact like the veil wasn't enough to keep them apart.

Tiberius held his silence.

Callon turned back to him slightly, expecting a response.

"Those kinds of resentments run deep. So deep, they become who we are."

"So, this errand is foolish?"

"No." Every word in the king's speech had purpose, never rushed, matching the flow of a gentle river. "It is foolish to think this world will become better if we continue to do nothing. It's our right to hold on to the past, to store resentments in our hearts, to continue our prejudice. But what will that accomplish? Cora is the youngest elf in Eden Star, born in a different time, experiencing the world through a lens we can't comprehend. That gives us a perspective we wouldn't have otherwise. You can call her optimism foolish and insensitive. Or you can call it a gift. I choose the latter."

"So, if you still reigned…you would consider an alliance?"

Tiberius turned his head away, regarding the statue that captured his essence in life. "You can do your best to prepare for a battle you might win—or you can ignore it and wait for it to slaughter you and everyone you love."

"You didn't answer my question."

"Ashe made a decision to the detriment of us all. But let's not forget—we are not innocent ourselves."

Cora's eyes narrowed.

Callon looked forward again.

"Yes," Tiberius said. "I would do everything necessary to defeat King Lux once and for all. I would forge an alliance with anyone who would have me. I would sacrifice my life and the lives of those I love for a chance for peace. It's them or us —and it'll be us unless we do something."

Callon said goodbye and dismissed himself. He disappeared through the haze, but Cora suspected he stopped at Weila's grave to visit. Even if he couldn't speak to her, her presence was both depressing and addictive.

Once his brother was gone, Tiberius turned his attention on Cora. "Have you spoken to Queen Delwyn?"

"No. I'm sorry."

"I'm sure she's occupied with regal obligations." He looked forward again, but his disappointment couldn't be sheathed in his voice.

"Actually…I thought it was best if I wait."

"Why is that?"

"She won't be happy when she knows I can do this."

He dropped his chin slightly, his eyes on his own grave.

"But I will. I promise."

"When it's meant to happen, it'll happen."

"Can you keep a secret?"

His head turned her way, slow and purposeful. "The dead are the greatest secret-keepers. But even if I were living, your secrets would die with me."

King Tiberius is an honorable man.

I know he is.

Just like his brother.

I'm proud to be a Riverglade.

Yes.

I'm going to tell him about you...if that's okay.

The response was immediate. *Yes.*

"Speak your truth, Cora Riverglade."

"I've...I've never heard my full name before."

"Beautiful, isn't it?"

She nodded. "When King Lux overtook Anastille, some dragons escaped. Ashe flew them to safety on Mist Isle, an island far away from here. Another sacrificed himself so others could live...Obsidian."

He had no expression, so if he showed surprise, it was invisible. "How do you know this?"

"Because I found the island."

He remained still. "That's quite the feat, Cora."

"Well, it wasn't me, exactly. More like we...me and my friends."

"They must be pretty powerful friends."

Will you tell him?

No...I don't think I can do it.

"And what did you discover?" Tiberius asked.

"Ashe, King of Dragons, continues his reign. I asked him for his aid, and after several months of discussion, he agreed. But it's conditional."

"On the participation of the elves."

"Yes."

He gave a nod. "Cora…I have no words. You accomplished something that would have been impossible for anyone else. The dragons would be wise to remain on their hidden island rather than risk what they have left when the odds are stacked against them. How did you convince them otherwise?"

"Honestly, I don't know…"

"Remarkable."

"But I think convincing Ashe is going to be much easier than Queen Delwyn and the elves."

"You're right, unfortunately."

"Even Callon…he thinks the dragons deserve their eternal suffering."

"He doesn't mean that. He's just bitter."

"And the rest of the elves?"

"Also bitter and angry. My death must have been the end of their resistance. It's easier to hide in the serenity of the forest and forget what lies across the desert. I understand the temptation."

"I have to change that...or we'll all die."

"You and I are in agreement, Cora."

This would be so much easier if he were still here.

Yes.

"How many dragons have pledged their fight?"

"Twelve, but I hope we can get more."

"Dragons are the most powerful beings in existence. Just one is enough to tip the scales of war."

"But they have more dragons than us."

"You will find a way, Cora."

She stared at his outline, wishing she could see the eyes identical to her own. "Why do you say that?"

"You've made it this far—farther than anyone else."

Her eyes dropped, her stomach warm. "I could always use the wisdom of a king. Will you help me?"

"Always."

"I wish the others felt the same way. You're the only person I've met who didn't need to be persuaded."

"Because I want the elves to persevere. And that can't happen while evil invades this land. We can't turn away. We can't ignore it. If we don't knock on their front door, they'll knock on ours. Elves view time differently, experience it so slowly, so as long as nothing has challenged the border of their forest, they will continue to hide behind it—and leave the others to be damned."

She gave a nod.

"Not that I don't have great empathy for my people. They've lost so much. There are others just like Callon—lost without their loved ones."

"Yeah…"

"But if we don't fight now, we'll be slaughtered later."

"There's something I need to tell Callon, but I fear his reaction."

"In what way?"

"He's done so much for me up until this point. But since this is treasonous…I'm afraid it'll be too much."

"You do not have ill will toward our people—so it is not treasonous. Trust him with your secrets as you trust me." With his head turned her way, he regarded her. "What is it, Cora?"

"Ashe, King of Dragons, is here in Eden Star…"

Silence. Stillness.

"Because we're fused."

A long stretch of time passed, full of silent intensity, a long moment of reflection.

She waited for something to be said.

"Ashe must trust you deeply to agree to that arrangement."

"It's not permanent. It's just until we can speak to Queen Delwyn. Once our mission is complete, our separation will be permanent."

"Their race has been enslaved by cruel men who have turned them into flying horses. Ashe has had to watch every one of his subjects become an object to somebody else. Immortality. Power. Fire. They're all gifts that are too valuable to part with. You could do the same to him—but he believes you won't."

"Because I would never..." Just the thought made her eyes tear.

"If I were in his place, I wouldn't have taken the risk."

"He knows I would never do that. That goes against everything I'm fighting for. Plus...I simply have no interest."

He turned quiet again. "No interest? You're bonded with someone in a way that you'll never be bonded with anyone else. Even if you have children, that bond will never compare. A passionate relationship with your spouse will not either. You share your entire soul with this other being, every thought, even feelings you wish to hide. There is nothing like it...and you could just let that go without reservation?"

He speaks like he understands.

You're right. "It's a special relationship. It's been short-lived, but so potent. To feel this connected to another person...is indescribable. Yes, I will miss that once it's gone, but...we will still have this closeness even when we separate."

"You'll never be able to communicate with him again, Cora."

"Actually, I can."

The air grew heavy. The mist cold. The energy changed between them. "How?"

"I...I don't know."

He continued to stare, his invisible eyes piercing her face.

"I have a feeling I'll never know."

17

KING OF DRAGONS

CALLON DISARMED her with an effortless flick of his wrist. "Come on, *Sor-lei*."

She stepped back, her arm falling to her side because all of her muscles screamed from holding the weight of the sword.

Callon continued to circle her, his green sword in his grasp. "Show me that fire."

I have to tell him the truth.

You would deny him that pride?

Ugh.

I've shown you the flow of battle. You know the way.

I just don't have the strength—

But you have the speed. Do it, Cora.

"I just need a second…"

Callon remained light on his toes, his eyes eager for the swing of her sword.

She took a drink, caught her breath, and rubbed the kink in her neck.

He spun his sword around his wrist again and approached.

"Alright." She gripped her sword with both hands, held it at the ready, and did her best to disconnect her mind from her body, to ignore the fatigue, the aches and pains.

Focus.

She drew breath then moved.

Their swords came together in a loud clank, steel sliding across scales, sparks flying. The air was sliced with a whoosh as Callon's sword made a swoop toward her torso. When her performance improved, so did his.

She ducked before the blade hit her armor, her hair flying past from the speed of the wind. She stood upright again, taking advantage of the opening to slam her blade down on his arm.

He caught it in his vambraces and pushed it back.

The blade toppled from her hand to the grass.

Don't stop.

Cora continued the flow by pushing down his sword arm and punching him square in the mouth.

Yes.

She rolled away and grabbed her sword from the ground and jumped to her feet, knowing he was right on her with his sword aimed for her neck.

But he was where she'd left him, his mouth bloody. He sucked the liquid into his mouth before he spat on the ground, a noticeable pool of blood staining the grass. His teeth glimmered with the red liquid.

Oh man...I feel so bad.

Don't.

Why?

Callon looked at her, raised his sword, and grinned.

That's why.

"Very good, *Sor-lei*."

You did that on your own. I did not help you.

That was a very small victory...

With perseverance, small victories can become big victories.

Their empty bowls sat beside them on the grass as they faced the passing stream. The red cardinal joined them, enjoying the extra berries she brought just for him. When the sun was the brightest overhead, the outline of fish were visible, swimming in the water.

Callon was as still as the statue next to her.

"I'm ready whenever you are."

"We'll meditate first."

"I don't think meditation is going to win battles."

"Not for me. But it might for you." His eyes remained on the stream, speaking slow and easy, relaxed despite the soreness he felt in his mouth. "Let's not forget that your mind is your most powerful asset. Use it to your advantage."

I agree.

His hands rested on his thighs, and he closed his eyes. "Besides…it's good for your soul."

It took her a while to settle down because she was eager to train, eager to get better, to feel worthy of the pride her uncle had shown her. But eventually, she did, and she pushed her mind out, feeling the heart of the forest at the center and the veins that stretched to the border.

She could feel the presence of the life in the trees, the elves throughout the forest, the magic that couldn't be touched or conjured, only felt. Every time she felt it, it brought her peace in a way nothing else ever had. It was the same relaxation of sleep, but in a conscious experience.

She pushed her mind further out, exceeding the border into the wildlands.

"Your presence is…immense."

Her mind floated in space, her breathing so deep and slow.

"I have never felt it at this magnitude."

The trance ended, and her eyes opened.

Callon stared at her.

She met his look.

He may sense me.

Can elves do that?

They can feel—but not discern.

Callon watched her. "You continue to grow in many ways, *Sorlei*."

When will you tell him?

I don't know. Maybe tomorrow. Cora walked behind Callon on the trail, taking the long trek from their secret training grounds and back into the heart of the forest.

You're worried.

Can you blame me? You should have seen the way he looked at Flare...

I'm much bigger than Flare.

Exactly. He's going to lose his mind.

When your mind is attached to your body, you can't lose it.

You know what I mean.

Your father is right, so there's nothing to fear.

He may keep our secret, but that doesn't mean he's going to like it. Her eyes took in the scenery around them, the wildness of the lands. There was always a bird in a nearby branch, always a rabbit hopping across their path, completely unafraid. Wild flowers were in abundance, something she'd never seen in her travels across Anastille.

Black as the darkest night, it contrasted against the evergreen, the colors of the flowers.

She stopped in her tracks.

What is it?

She'd never seen something so out of place in her life.

Sunlight reflected off the black petals. Metallic in sheen, the surface was covered in a substance that caused a glint so bright, it was like a glare in the steel of a sword. With vines made of thorns as thick as the width of a blade, it was untouchable.

She left the path and stepped onto the grass, approaching the black flower that hardly protruded from the grass. If it were any other color, she would have walked right by without a second glance.

She kneeled, bringing herself closer.

Birds sang their song in the trees, the breeze moved through her hair, life bustled around her.

But she felt nothing from this little flower.

Then there was a faint whisper.

A whisper she couldn't decipher.

Her hand instinctively reached out to swipe her finger across the petal, as if she hoped to catch a streak of dust from a forgotten heirloom.

Cora. No.

She reached for it anyway.

A hand grasped her by the arm and yanked her away.

Her fingers missed contact by just a stalk of grass.

She fell on top of her backpack, uncomfortable like a turtle flipped onto his shell.

Callon swiped his sword through the stem, right where the stalk met the earth, and it tipped over. When the breeze caught it, it began to roll away, slowly migrating deeper in the brush of the forest.

He sheathed his sword then stood over her—looking more pissed off than ever before.

She rolled over and got to her feet. "What was that?"

"Don't touch it. Ever."

"Okay…but what is it?"

"You see one again, kill it."

He marched away, the conversation dismissed.

She turned to look at the flower once more, but it was gone. "Callon?" She returned to the path, catching up to his heels. "Are you not going to tell me what that was?"

He looked straight ahead—like she wasn't even there.

"I've never seen a flower like that." She came to his side, holding his stride even when he moved faster. "Why does it grow here? When I came close to it...I heard a whisper."

He halted.

She did too—a second later.

His nostrils flared with the deep breaths he took, and he was maniacal. "It's death, Cora."

Her eyes shifted back and forth as she looked into his.

"Death."

Flare? You there? She pushed her mind out, finding his front door easily because he was much closer than he'd been at Mist Isle. *Hello?*

His majestic voice spoke. *I'm here, Pretty.*

How are things?

Not so good.

Everything okay?

Everyone is fine. But we were attacked by goats yesterday.

Goats?

Mountain goats.

Oh...that sounds a bit hilarious.

It is. It's especially hilarious because it wouldn't have happened if Rush had listened to me.

Typical Rush.

You get it, Pretty.

She smiled, picturing all of his sharp teeth as he showed his form of a grin. **You made it to the mountains, then?**

Yes. But we're lost.

I thought you had a map?

Even with the map, we're lost.

Oh no.

We'll figure it out. Always do. What about you?

Just exhausted.

General Callon is training you well?

He's trying.

You'll get there, Pretty. I have no doubt.

I've gotten a lot better. Pushed my body in ways I didn't think were possible.

And you'll continue to do so. How's Ashe, King of Dragons?

He's helping me out a lot too.

Kingly.

Can Rush join us? I have news.

Was hoping to keep you to myself... One moment.

Rush's deep voice came a moment later. **He told you about the goats, didn't he?**

She chuckled out loud as well as in her head. *Yeah...he mentioned it.*

They're like the frogs—but with horns.

At least they aren't venomous.

Their looks sure are. And they've got horns...big horns.

Just be nice to them, and they won't attack you.

You think we haven't tried that? Gave them the last of my bread...and they still mauled me down.

She chuckled again. *Then I guess they just don't like you.*

You think?

Most people don't, so it's not surprising.

Enough outta you...

Glad you guys are doing well...goats aside.

What about you?

Where do I start...? She told them about the conversation with her father, the training with Callon, and the black flower she discovered.

Wow.

That's a lot of information to get in fifteen seconds.

Sorry.

So, Ashe lent you his strength. Nothing like it, huh?

Yeah...I felt invincible. Do you do that with Flare?

In battle. It gives you an edge.

Even with the strength of a dragon, he could still defeat me.

Well, Callon is the greatest swordsman ever. Like, literally. General Noose is good too, but I would have beaten him if he hadn't cheated. Your dragon doesn't just give you his strength and energy, but his focus and sight. He allows you to navigate your terrain without effort, so you can focus on the battle with even greater detail. Keep practicing because it's overwhelming at first.

Ashe only did it so I could really experience battle. Before that, it was just Callon destroying me immediately over and over. It's helped a lot. I'm a better fighter for it.

That's good. But you should still practice anyway.

We won't be fused after we speak to the queen—so there's no point.

Rush turned quiet for a while. So, it sounds like Tiberius is an ally.

As much as he can be.

If only Queen Delwyn were as open-minded.

I think he's the only one who is.

Maybe he can help you change that.

Yeah, hopefully.

He say anything else?

Well... His words echoed back to her, the way he described a fused relationship. *I told him about Ashe...and he understood perfectly how that union feels.*

He wasn't upset? Having a secret dragon in Eden Star is kind of a big deal...

He didn't care at all.

Huh.

Is it possible...that he's fused with a dragon?

Since he's cool with Ashe, I assume he would be forthcoming about it if that were the case.

True. But I mean...do elves ever fuse with dragons?

A long time ago and only for the purpose of communication. That was before he was king, so I highly doubt it.

Cora looked out the window as she sat at her dining table, her finished dinner in front of her. Starlight was visible in the opening of the trees at the canopy.

So, you saw an ugly flower?

I didn't say it was ugly. Said it was black and metallic...

That sounds pretty ugly for a flower.

She chuckled. *Yeah, it definitely felt out of place for Eden Star. That's why I could see it so well. It just stood out. Before I could touch it, Callon yanked me away and sliced it from the stem. He told me it was death.*

Did he say anything else?

No. And I don't think he's going to. Do you know what it is?

Not a clue. I've never seen anything like that before.

The image of the flower was seared in her brain, the way it contrasted against the stalks of grass, the color of the nearby flowers. Eden Star was a vibrant place of life...so how could death grow there? *I also heard a whisper when I came close to it.*

A whisper?

Rush paused for a bit. **What did it say?**

I couldn't make it out...like it was in another language.

That's not creepy at all...

You must ask your father.

I think I will...since I have no one else to ask. Wait... An image suddenly flashed into her mind, seeing the flower alive on a shelf, growing out of a small pot near the windows. *I've seen it before.*

Where?

Mathilda's shop...last time I was there.

Rush gave a loud sigh. **Ugh, witches are the worst.**

Why?

Because you can't get a straight answer out of them. If you wanted to ask her about it, it would come with a price—a big price.

A price she hadn't paid yet.

I don't have a clue what it is or what it means, but it's bad. If Callon doesn't tell you, then ask Tiberius.

I think I will.

And if you see it again…don't touch it.

Callon was in the lead, hiking to their training ground as the sun rose over the horizon. His backpack was over his shoulders, his sword on his hip.

"Callon?"

"Yes?"

"Can we go somewhere farther away from Eden Star? Like, really far away…with lots of space?"

You make it obvious he's about to meet the most ferocious dragon that ever lived.

He needs to know the requirements. Last thing we need is for you to be seen.

Callon halted and slowly turned around. His eyes narrowed, and he asked the question. "Why?"

"I need to show you something…in private."

His shoulders slumped as the annoyance deepened in his features. "It never ends with you, does it?"

She didn't know what else to do, so she shook her head.

He sighed and continued forward again. "We'll stop at the stream halfway to replenish our canteens. We've got a long day ahead of us."

This is happening.

Nervous?

I'm never nervous.

Well, I am.

I have no concerns. He's shown his loyalty to you.

Doesn't mean he's not gonna be pissed off. Really pissed off.

They stopped at the stream and refilled their empty bottles and then continued ahead. They were far away from the path, but Callon seemed to know exactly where he was going because he moved with purpose.

"Callon?"

His response took a little longer this time. "Yes?"

"If that flower is death...why does it grow here?"

The sigh he gave trailed behind him and entered her ears.

"So, all you have to do is touch it, and you just collapse?"

He ducked under a low-hanging branch.

"Why won't you answer me?"

He spun back around. "Because I told you everything you need to know."

"If that were true, I wouldn't have questions."

His eyebrows furrowed together, flashing his signature look of annoyance. "I suspect today is going to be enough as it is. Give it a rest."

He's hiding something.

I think so too.

We shall ask King Tiberius.

Callon faced forward once again and powered through the forest, his armor, weapons, and backpack having no impact on his speed.

They continued that way for hours, getting farther away from the center of Eden Star than she'd ever been. It was midday when they arrived in a large clearing of trees, in a valley somewhere deep in the forest.

This will work.

It was much bigger than the glade near the stream, but it came at a heavy price. She dropped her backpack and took a seat, needing water and a small snack.

Callon glanced around the area before he did the same.

"How do you know the forest so well? I mean, it's so big."

"I've lived a very long life."

"And that life was spent out here?"

"As the General of Eden Star, it was my job to protect the entire forest, not just Eden Star proper. I know this forest better than anyone."

"Do any elves live away from Eden Star?"

"Some."

"Like, alone?"

"Yes."

"Why would they want to do that?"

He drank his water then turned the cap back into place. "Because as you say, they're 'old and grouchy.'"

"Even on my worst day, I'd rather be with people than be alone."

"Company is for the young. Solitude is for the old." He stored his things back in his pack then got to his feet. "What is it, Cora?"

Here we go.

He's going to be in shock.

And mesmerized by my brute strength and glorious beauty.

Okay...so Flare's not the only one that does it.

Does what?

Nevermind.

She got to her feet and brushed off her trousers before she faced him. "Alright, well...yeah."

His eyes narrowed.

"You're going to be upset—"

"What is it, Cora?"

"I just need you to be calm—"

"I'm always calm."

"Well, you don't look calm right now."

He stepped closer to her, his dark eyes vicious. "You're my *Sorlei*, so you've never seen me as anything else but calm."

She took a slow breath, unsure if she should start at the beginning or just cut right to the chase. "When I found the dragons, I met their king. Ashe, King of Dragons."

His expression remained hard like the blunt end of an ax. The hatred for their race was so deep in his blood that he couldn't feel an ounce of awe. He was a still lake, never changing, raindrops only disturbing the surface but not affecting anything underneath.

"He, along with others, wish to free their kin. But they can't do it alone. They need allies—they need the elves."

His arms remained at his sides, the only movement of his body his slightly shifting eyes.

"I knew there was no way I could convince Queen Delwyn to agree by myself. I thought it would be best if she spoke to him herself. King to queen. Ruler to ruler."

His eyes narrowed, just slightly.

"So…I brought him with me."

The reaction was so slight, but it was there. A subtle tightening of his jaw. A slight turn of his head. The tightening of the cords in his neck. And the eyes...glazed over like a fog of mist rolled in.

Cora took several steps back, putting twenty feet between them.

Callon wore the same expression.

Cora felt Ashe take over, felt her body become devoured by his. She was suddenly high in the air, looking down at Callon below. Her claws punctured the earth. Her belly felt hot with the eternal fire that filled her lungs with every breath. No longer small and insignificant, she was the most fearsome dragon that ever flew across these skies.

Cora was herself once again, the enormous black dragon somehow deep inside her.

Callon still hadn't spoken.

She gave him plenty of time to speak first, but no words were forthcoming. *I think he's in shock.*

I don't know what he is.

"Callon?"

His clipped response was immediate. "What do you expect of me? A sworn enemy has been hiding among us, unknown to Queen Delwyn and General Aldon, and is now intimately acquainted with Eden Star. Now I must carry the burden of this treasonous secret."

"He's not your enemy—"

"But he's ours." The anger started to burn, his eyes on fire, his jaw so tight his teeth were about to crack. "My wife...my son... dead because of *him*. Countless other elves who should have lived so long, they ended their lives themselves...gone. *Because of him*. Because of his stupidity. You shouldn't have brought him here. You bring Riverglade Clan shame. You've brought us nothing but shame since you got here."

This...this was a bad idea.

He speaks in anger. Not truth.

Callon marched off, snatched his pack, and departed the clearing.

"Cal-lon?" Her voice broke before she could finish saying his name.

He didn't look back.

Cora, it'll be okay.

He just left me here...

I know the way.

But...he doesn't know that.

18

THE BLACK CURSE

She lay in the middle of the clearing with her pack as a pillow. It was a warm night, so her skin didn't erupt with bumps without a blanket. There was enough food in her pack to last until morning, and there was a nearby stream that Ashe had picked up on with his remarkable hearing.

We all say things in anger, Cora.

He's never said anything like that before.

He's a hot coal. Even when the fire is gone, it'll still glow red-hot. But give it time...and you'll be able to touch it again.

He was just proud of me a couple days ago.

And still is.

What if he tells Queen Delwyn?

He won't.

But what if he does—

He. Won't.

I thought you would be upset...because of all the things he said.

I can't be upset when it's the truth. I can't be upset when I've seen firsthand how my mistake has impacted others. To watch this honorable man grieve for what he's lost...it breaks me. He's entitled to his anger. He's entitled to his sorrow. Ashe drifted away, curling up in her mind, like he wished to speak no more.

Her eyes remained on the stars, feeling more alone than she had before.

She reached out her mind and felt the door. She pressed into it, her hand knocking on the surface.

His answer was instant. *Pretty.*

Hey...is Rush around?

There was a long pause before he spoke, like he could hear all her pain in just the tone of her voice. *I'll get him.*

He arrived an instant later. **I'm here.** No jokes. No taunts. Just himself. **Talk to me.**

With her eyes on the stars and the grass cushioning her back, it was easy to pretend he was right beside her, admiring the same sky at the same time. Whenever the breeze brushed over her face, it took her to a different time, a time when everything felt right, even if it was short-lived. *I told Callon about Ashe.*

A long, heavy sigh. **He'll come around. If he can let me live, then he'll accept this too.**

I hope so.

He will. I know he will.

The tears bubbled from her eyes and streaked down her cheeks. As much as she tried to restrain them from entering her voice, they broke through. *He said I've brought him shame... that I've brought him nothing but shame since I got here.*

Treasure, please don't cry...

He was proud of me a few days ago. And now...I feel like I've lost him.

You didn't. He's like everyone else—says things he doesn't mean when he's upset.

I don't know... I've never seen him like this.

It was a lot to take in. Just remember that.

I just don't want to lose what we have.

Impossible. I see the way he loves you—unconditionally.

She continued to cry.

I know you're scared, Cora. But he's not going to abandon you. He's not going to leave you outside a gate and walk away.

Her arms folded over her chest, and she gave a nod.

I promise.

Cora.

What?

She sat under the shade of a tree with her empty bowl beside her, the last of her rations. When she lifted her chin, she saw him across the clearing.

His shiny forehead glinted in the morning sun. His wide chest rose and fell in quick intervals—like he'd run the whole way there. Frantic eyes swept across the clearing, unable to see her in the shady spot under the tree.

She got to her feet and stepped into the sun.

His eyes immediately spotted her, and a long, deep breath followed. His eyes closed briefly, all the tightness of his face disappearing. He let his pack drop behind him before he ran to her.

Her eyes watered when she saw the look on his face.

She thought she'd never see it again.

His arm circled her waist, his other hand cupping the back of her head as he drew her close. His chin rested on her head as he gave her a tight squeeze, his breaths still labored and strained. "*Sor-lei.* You're okay."

"I'm fine."

He held on for another moment before he pulled away, his palm still cupping the back of her head. He gave her a once-over before he pressed a kiss to her forehead and released her entirely. "I went to your home this morning…and my heart dropped into my stomach."

"I'm totally fine—"

"I'm sorry—for everything."

"It's okay..."

He dropped his head and averted his gaze. "I just—"

"You don't have to explain, *Tor-lei*. I understand..."

His eyes remained down for a moment before they rose once more. "Doesn't excuse my behavior. Or the things I said."

"Did you...mean what you said?"

He winced, like a blade pierced his stomach. "No, *Sor-lei*. I'm the one who's brought our family shame."

"Not true."

"What would your father think if he knew I abandoned you out here...alone?"

"I wasn't alone."

His eyes remained soft.

"And I'm very capable, Callon. All I had to do was feel the heart of Eden Star—and follow it home."

After a breath, he gave a slight nod. "You're right."

"Let's just forget about it, okay?" Her hand reached for his arm and gave it a squeeze.

His hand pressed over hers, gave it a squeeze in return, and then he stepped away. "Thank you, *Sor-lei*."

I wish to speak with him.

Is now the best time?

Yes.

"Um...Ashe would like to speak with you."

The softness in his features instantly disappeared. His eyes were guarded. He was cold. But he wasn't livid like he was before.

"I'll speak his words for him."

Not a day goes by that I don't carry these regrets. If I could go back in time, I would ban them from our lands—and annihilate them if they refused. Our time of peace and prosperity was destroyed by my naïveté. This doesn't mean much, doesn't erase what you've lost, but you have my remorse.

Callon's face was a solid wall—with the exception of an occasional blink.

I understand if you don't accept my apology.

"I don't."

We're all on borrowed time—all the free folk that remain. The elves are the biggest threat to King Lux—so you'll be the first to go. It took a very long time for Cora to convince me that this alliance is necessary, that this war is worth risking what we have left. I hope we can put the past aside temporarily to join our forces and do what must be done. Because without each other, we have no chance to prevail.

"You speak to me as if I have any authority in this matter."

You do.

"That power belongs to Queen Delwyn."

It belongs to the elves of Eden Star—and you lead the elves.

"You're mistaken."

I am not. I know a king when I see one—as do your people. They follow your orders—not hers. That tells me what I need to know.

Callon stepped away. "I've served as General Callon for thousands of years. They respect my dedication and sacrifice to our people. That's all."

They respect the general more than the ruler he serves—that's telling.

"If your suggestion is to overthrow Queen Delwyn and take her crown, that's barbaric. We're not power-hungry and bloodthirsty like the very enemy we oppose."

She's corrupt—and you know it.

Callon looked away.

You may not be the general in name, but you are in heart. It is your duty to protect your people from this tyrant.

"Tyrant...that's a strong word."

We don't trust her. Neither do you.

His eyes remained elsewhere. "I served King Tiberius, and I will serve his queen just as loyally."

Your loyalty is unflinching. A great quality in a servant to the throne. But she does not have the same loyalty to her own people—otherwise, she wouldn't hide Cora's identity. I understand the struggle to reconcile the two parts of your identity. You want to serve—but you're meant to lead.

"I have no interest in the throne."

That's exactly why it should be yours. A true leader understands the sacrifice the job entails—so takes it with reluctance rather than ambition.

Callon kept his eyes focused on the tree line, peering into the shadows.

The armies of the empire will march on Eden Star. And Queen Delwyn is unsuited to defend it.

He turned back. "Our armies are always prepared to protect our borders."

It's not the soldiers that concern me, but the one who gives the orders.

"She would do whatever was necessary to protect her people."

She denies her people the daughter of Tiberius Riverglade, so I'm skeptical.

"Not the same thing…"

Cora is a threat to her power. Seems to me that she will do everything she can to protect that power—whatever the cost may be. Retaining her power comes first. Everything else is second.

Callon looked away again.

This time in Eden Star has given me a glimpse of your remarkable character. You care for your Sor-lei *like a hatchling. The love you have for your family continues beyond the grave. You tolerate Queen Delwyn out of respect for your late brother. I've never known a man with greater loyalty.*

"Let me make this clear." Callon pivoted his body, his eyes on the ground. "I will not challenge my queen for her seat. I will not plot to overthrow her. I will serve her as I always have. This conversation is over."

Then will you help us convince her to do what is necessary?

His eyes remained on the ground.

Because she will listen to you, Callon.

"I betrayed her, and she stripped me of my title."

Because she had to—not because she wanted to.

"I blackmailed her."

You shouldn't have had to in the first place.

"I'm not entirely convinced I want this to happen anyway." He lifted his gaze, a glimpse of anger on the surface. "You may admire my character, but I don't admire yours. It's ironic to listen to you question Queen Delwyn when you destroyed us all with your rulership."

Ashe remained quiet, his mind withdrawing as if the words had physically marked him.

Cora spoke. "This is me now. There are a million reasons not to do this. But we need each other if we want to survive."

"We've survived this long."

"But not much longer. And is surviving the same as living?"

Callon clenched his jaw.

"I told my father about Ashe."

His eyes immediately shifted, focusing on her face with deeper penetration.

"He's lost as much as you have, but he knows we need to put our animosity aside. The preservation of Eden Star is all that matters in the end. Whatever that requires is insignificant."

"He said that?" His anger dulled like an old blade.

"Yes."

His eyes flicked away once more, deep in reflection.

"He is still your king, is he not?"

"Always."

"Then this is what your king commands."

After a deep breath, he looked at her once more. "Tiberius is like a flower. He can be plucked off the stem, but he'll just grow another blossom and forget why he needed to grow it in the first place. His memory is short, his grudges even shorter. Me…I've never been that way."

"I've noticed."

His eyes narrowed.

"Sorry."

"I will speak to her on your behalf. But I can't promise it'll work."

"Even if she doesn't listen to you, the elves do. And that can make all the difference."

"They won't listen to me if they dislike you, Cora. So, that's something you need to work on."

"I know." She gave a nod, hearing Rush's voice in her head. "Gotta make some friends..."

Ashe sat near the tree line, a dark contrast against the green canopy of the trees. With his shoulders back, his chest puffed up, he watched with ancient eyes.

With his sword in hand, Callon glanced at the dragon—time and time again.

Ashe met his look with gray eyes.

"Is this okay?" Cora asked. "He's been cooped up for so long."

Callon focused on Cora and gave a nod. "It'll take some time to get used to." He prepared his sword and took his stance.

Cora.

She held her sword at the ready, eyes on Callon. ***I need to focus, Ashe.***

You need to use your other skills.

What other skills?

The power of your mind.

But...that's cheating.

Is my fire cheating?

Well, no.

Then this is not cheating. This is a skill you have—and you need to use it to your advantage. You're a hatchling, so you've never seen battle. It's barbaric, brutal, and bloody. All that matters is the one who survives. Be the one who survives.

Callon circled her, spinning his sword with his wrist.

Do it, Cora.

Callon launched himself, swiping his sword down on her.

She blocked the hit then pushed her mind out.

Callon felt the effects and immediately backed away.

She moved forward, slamming her sword down to defeat him.

He blocked the hit with a weak hand, his eyes wincing from the assault to his mind. He recovered and responded with even more aggression, swiping left and right, murder in his eyes.

She blocked his hits then pushed again, assaulting his mind with invisible daggers.

Fuming, he gave a growl and pushed on harder.

Great. Now he's just pissed off.

And unfocused.

His sword drove her back, his momentum forcing her backward across the grass. With gritted teeth and rage in his blood-red face, he was determined to strike her down. With speed and agility he'd never executed before, he came for her like she was King Lux in the flesh.

She instinctively pushed her mind out again, this time just to survive.

He gave a snarl as he grimaced, but he kept going.

She blocked hit after hit, but all her energy was focused on staying afloat, not striking back.

Come on, Cora.

I won't do it more than that.

You must.

It might kill him.

You underestimate General Callon's abilities.

She pushed again.

He faltered for just an instant.

And that was enough for her to slam her knuckles into his face, kick him back, and yank the sword out of his hand.

The pride was in Ashe's voice. *Very good, Cora.*

Callon was on his back for just a second. He recovered quickly, getting to his feet as if nothing happened. He yanked the sword out of the ground and drew it close to his side.

"I'm sorry. Ashe told me to do it..."

"Don't be sorry."

"Really?"

"You'll never have the time to train the way I did. The way Weila did. Turnion. Any powerful warrior. This is the only way you're going to compete against fighters like me, soldiers, other generals. Use it to your advantage, Cora."

"Do you still want me to use it while we train?"

"Yes."

"That seems a bit unfair to you..."

"How? I'm training you—and you're training me."

"What do you mean?"

"If I face someone with your powers, I'll be prepared. It's been a while since I've been challenged. I welcome it." He took his stance with his sword at the ready. "Let's go again."

SHE ENTERED THE CEMETERY OF SPIRITS AND PASSED THROUGH the mist.

General Callon is more exceptional than I realized.

Why do you say that?

A man who relishes new challenges is unafraid of failure. If you're unafraid of failure, it means you're confident in your abilities, that there's success at the end of the road.

Yeah, he's pretty great.

You're very lucky to have him, Cora.

I know I am. She passed through the cemetery, the mist immediately cool against her warm skin. She passed gravestones until she reached her father's final resting place. She sat on the bench and stared at the fireflies as she waited.

It took some time—but he came.

His power and majesty filled the space the instant he came into being, sending invisible ripples through the air around him. His bluish outline was visible, a subtle definition of his height and musculature. He joined her on the bench. "Hello, Cora."

"Hello, Tiberius."

"Give Ashe, King of Dragons, my regards as well."

She smiled. "I will."

I appreciate and reciprocate his hospitality.

"He gives you his regards as well."

"His scales are midnight black, are they not?"

"Yes."

"Gray eyes?"

"Yes."

Tiberius gave a nod. "Wish I could see him for myself."

"Callon has."

A light chuckle escaped his lips. "I already suspect his reaction."

"He wasn't happy…"

"But I'm sure you made him come around."

"He stormed off, actually."

"Callon…he was always uptight."

She chuckled. "I don't know if I would describe him as that."

"Ever since we were children, Callon has always been a devout rule-follower. I was the opposite…as you probably guessed."

"I've never cared for the rules either."

"Then you got something from me, after all."

"Guess so."

Tiberius turned quiet. "He came around?"

"A day later. I was actually afraid that would be the end of it…"

"Callon has his tantrums, but he always comes back around."

She stared at her hands in her lap. "I don't mean this in a disrespectful way…but I'm surprised you were the one who became king."

"I'm difficult to offend, so you don't need to worry about that." He looked ahead at the statue of his likeness. "I believe an important quality of a ruler is the ability to adapt to change, to shift your perspective, to question practices rather than blindly following them. That's exactly what I did as I led the elves. I challenged social norms when it was impossible for others. Perhaps that's what got me killed…but I wouldn't change it for anything. Callon is the longest-serving general

Eden Star has had because his upstanding qualities make him suitable for the job. He's selfless and dedicated. He wants to serve. He wants to sacrifice his life for something greater than himself. I think we both ended up exactly where we were meant to be."

"That makes sense. Was it weird having your younger brother as your general?"

"I got to boss him around all day. It was wonderful."

She chuckled.

He turned serious again. "It wasn't weird at all. We were a perfect team, he and I. A king is only as good as the general who serves him."

"What do you think about him being king?"

His eyes turned to regard her. "Is Queen Delwyn unwell?"

"No. I just...I'm not sure if she's the best for the position."

"I know you both have questioned her integrity. But until we know more, she deserves the benefit of the doubt. Ask her why she hasn't come to me for these past twenty years. Ask her to join with the dragons and prepare for war. Her answers will tell us what we need to know."

She gave a nod. "I think I already know how this will go...but I'll try."

He looked at the statue again, which was covered in a vine that wrapped around toward his arm. "Has Callon pledged his support?"

"Yes."

"Good."

"But only because of you."

He turned back to her.

"You're still his king."

"I wholeheartedly believe he would have come around on his own. Because your influence is much more potent than my own."

She looked at her hands once more.

"Is he still teaching you the sword?"

"Yes."

"How have you progressed?"

"I'm much better than I was, but Callon agrees I'll never meet his standards."

"That's an unfair thing to say. You're a child, not a woman with the same years of experience."

"When it comes to war, it doesn't matter. I'm not good enough. I'll never be good enough for what we're about to face."

He bowed his head.

"But I started using my…powers. I'm not sure what else to call them. That gave me an upper hand."

"Powers?"

"It's hard to explain, but...I can basically disarm someone's mind with my own."

Silence.

"It's basically the Skull Crusher, but at a nonlethal level."

More silence.

She regarded her father. "What is it?"

"That's Death Magic."

"I know..."

He remained quiet.

Ask him. Now's your chance.

"I asked Callon this...but he refused to tell me."

Tiberius straightened his body.

"Said it's forbidden."

"Because it is forbidden."

"I need to know anyway. Because Death Magic is as intuitive to me as breathing."

Silence.

"Please tell me, Tiberius. I'm entitled to this information. It could make all the difference in the world."

He seemed to draw breath because his chest slowly rose before it fell once more. A moment was spent looking straight ahead, but then he eventually turned to regard her. "I can tell you what I know—but that doesn't mean it'll answer your questions."

"Okay."

Yes.

"But I will only share this with you—and not your other half."

No.

"Why?"

"Because he's not an elf."

"We are one." The comeback was harsh, flying out of her mouth like spit. "I have no secrets from him."

"That's my condition."

It's okay, Cora. You can tell me when the conversation has concluded. He drifted away, further and further until he was gone from her mind, like he was asleep. He had no conscious presence.

"Okay, he's gone. But I'll tell him everything you share with me."

"I don't think you will."

"Why?"

He looked ahead again. "Because you won't want to. That is the real reason I requested privacy."

Her heart fell into her stomach, followed by an avalanche of discomfort. Her core temperature spiked, and the mist no longer had a cooling effect on her skin. Her fingers immediately curled in and formed fists as she drew them closer to her body.

"Are you ready, Cora?"

She gave a nod, a hesitant one.

"Shamans aren't any different from you or me—because they're elves."

Seconds turned into minutes.

Cora absorbed his confession like a dried-out sponge, soaking in every drop without saturation. Her steady breathing spiked into deep inhales and exhales. Overwhelmed, she didn't know what to say. "I don't understand…"

"A cursed elf becomes a dark elf. Then, in time, they become a Shaman. When men die, they go to heaven or hell. It's our version of eternal suffering."

She stared. "How does an elf become cursed?"

"By being cursed by another elf."

"What…?"

"It's a practice that has been outlawed for a very long time. The elves who commit atrocious crimes against their people have to be punished in some way, and the punishment must reflect the degree of their betrayal. The elves who can't be forgiven…are cursed. They are dead, but they never pass on to our spirit world. It's eternal damnation."

She inhaled a slow and deep breath. "I think I'm in shock right now…"

"It never should have been done. It's a shameful part of our history that we wish to forget."

"So…where do they go?"

"No one knows."

"So, all those Shamans I've seen…"

"Are elves cursed long ago."

She remembered the black flower on the hike, the petals that whispered to her. "I saw this black flower outside Eden Star… Callon pulled me away and sliced it from the stem. He said it was death."

"The Black Curse. That's what we call it."

"Is that…how you cursed them?"

He nodded. "We removed it from Eden Star…but sometimes it grows back."

She turned away, her eyes back on her hands. "I understand why Callon didn't want me to know."

"It was a barbaric practice. Regardless of the crime the elves committed, they didn't deserve that cruelty. It's a dark time in our society that we wish to forget. If you question any elf about it, they will disregard your words. The only reason I share this with you is because you're right—you need to know."

"Why would I not share this information with Ashe?"

He turned to regard her.

She could feel his stare even if she couldn't see it.

He remained quiet.

She raised her chin and faced him, looking into the blue outline of his face.

"Please don't make me say it, Cora."

The truth fell onto her shoulders with the weight of the world. "Because King Lux used the Shamans to enslave the dragons..."

19

PEONY

The mist parted and revealed her sitting there.

Long blond hair with flowers pinned into her braid. Dark green trousers and a matching tunic. She sat on the bench beside a grave, her hands together in her lap, her eyes on the tombstone that marked the final resting place of her loved one.

She had no idea that the outline of a woman was right beside her.

Cora stared, enticed to walk away and push this attempt to another day.

The blonde turned her head slightly and locked her eyes on Cora. They were blue and clear, but they instantly turned hostile once she narrowed her eyes. Her eyes flicked back to the grave once her animosity was made clear.

Just gotta suck it up.

Cora approached the grave but kept a few feet of distance.

The blonde looked at her once more, her look lethal. "You have no business here. Leave."

"I just—"

"I said leave."

She was tempted to leave, but she stayed. "Is that your mother?"

Her eyes immediately narrowed.

The spirit beside her had one hand placed on hers, her head bowed in sadness.

"She's beside you—her hand on yours."

The blue spirit raised her head and regarded Cora.

That just infuriated the blonde even more. "How dare you?"

"You can see me." The spirit addressed her, pulling her hand away from her daughter's and rising to her feet.

"Yes."

She stepped forward, her arms resting by her sides.

"Yes, what?" The blond elf asked.

Cora kept her eyes on the spirit. "If there's something you wish for me to tell your daughter, I can."

The blonde got to her feet, her shoulders squared for a fight. "Walk away now, or I'll make sure that Queen Delwyn ejects you from our lands—as she should have done in the first place."

The spirit spoke. "Tell Peony that the brooch I gave her for her birthday looks lovely."

Cora's eyes shifted to the blond elf. "Peony, she says that the brooch you're wearing looks lovely...the one she got you for your birthday."

Her features immediately slackened as the revelation set in. Several breaths passed before she turned to the vacancy on the bench beside her, her fingers curling toward her palm. "Mama?" Her voice broke as a choked sob came forth.

The spirit moved to the bench beside her, her hand returning to hers.

"Her hand is on yours..."

Peony looked down at her hand on her thigh, her bottom lip trembling.

The spirit continued. "Tell my daughter that I miss her dearly...and it gives me great happiness to watch her visit me, beautiful flowers always in her hair."

Cora shared the information.

Peony started to cry, clenching the hand she couldn't feel. "Mom..."

CORA ACTED AS THE VESSEL BETWEEN MOTHER AND DAUGHTER, destroying the veil that separated the living from the dead. Peony seemed to forget that Cora was the one speaking because she never looked her way. She continued to stare right at the place where her mother sat, as if she could see her herself.

Her mother had died in the last war, never to return home after the final battle against King Lux. The musculature of her frame was slightly visible in the haze, and it was clear in the way she carried herself, like she was still covered in armor and weapons.

Peony wanted to know that her mother was okay, but all her mother wanted to discuss was her daughter and her life in Eden Star.

"Father never remarried..."

"Doesn't surprise me."

"He's still sad... I'm still sad."

"I know, sweetheart."

"Are you waiting for us?"

"I'm waiting for your father. You will have your own family someday, Peony. But of course, we will cross paths."

Peony wiped the tears away from her cheeks and gave a sniff. "Father still takes care of your birds."

"I knew he would. He hates that they wake him up every morning, but I know he loves them."

"He loves them because you love them."

She stared at her daughter for a while, her hand still on hers. "I'm sorry, Peony, but I have to go."

"No..."

"We will see each other again."

She nodded through her tears.

"*Rein-Lei-Vu.*"

"*Rein-Lei-Vu...*"

The blue spirit faded into the mist.

Peony took a deep breath the moment she felt her mother disappear.

These women were strangers, but the interaction affected Cora just as deeply as it did when Callon spoke to his *Sun-lei*. Her eyes were wet. Her chest hurt. It wasn't her place to linger and watch a woman grieve her mother's absence, so she stepped away.

"Wait."

Cora halted.

Peony walked up behind her with silent footsteps. She came into Cora's line of sight, with tears in her eyes that reflected the glow of the fireflies. "How did you do that?"

"Wish I knew."

Her eyes dropped for a moment. "Can you do that with other spirits?"

"Yes."

She took a moment then, her eyes still on the ground. "I haven't heard my mother's voice in...a very long time. But it came into my head so naturally because those were the exact words she would speak."

"I'm glad to hear that."

Peony lifted her eyes from the ground. "She was exactly the same...like she was in a good place."

"I think so too."

"Sorry I was so harsh earlier—"

"It's fine. I'm used to people hating me everywhere I go, so..." A quiet chuckle escaped her lips, a bitter and painful one.

"Would you...be willing to do that again?"

"Sure."

"I know it would mean a lot to my dad."

"Of course. I just have one condition..."

Her blue eyes narrowed.

"I don't want this to get back to the queen...so keep it to yourself." Cora tensed once she made the request. It was treasonous, to ask another elf to hide a secret this immense. But if Peony wanted to be connected to her mother again, she would agree.

Peony hesitated before she gave a nod. "I grant your request."

Cora stepped around Peony and walked away. "Come to my tree house if you need me. I'm usually around."

She stepped across the threshold of the tree house and peered inside to see Callon scraping the contents of his pot into a bowl at the dining table. A bird was perched on the windowsill, chirping as he turned his head left and right to get a peek. Like Callon knew he was there, he grabbed a piece of his dinner and tossed it, making it land right next to the bird.

The bird gobbled it up then took off.

"Looks like you have a pet."

Callon returned the pot to the stove before he regarded her, stern eyes in a stern face. Then he grabbed another bowl and split his dinner into two. "Barely heard you that time. You're getting better."

She took a seat at the table and pulled the bowl close. "One of Weila's recipes?"

Arms on the table with his head bowed, he spooned the food into his mouth. "Yes."

"She knew her way around the kitchen."

He chewed, his eyes out the window.

The mutual silence continued, the two of them eating together, no pressure to exchange words. Singing birds surrounded the house on all sides, growing louder as the sun set further and further.

"I made a friend...sorta."

Callon's eyes lifted to hers.

"Peony."

"Peony Mountain?"

"I don't know...the introduction wasn't that specific."

He took another bite. "What happened?"

She told him what had transpired at the Cemetery of Spirits.

Now his dinner was abandoned in front of him. His dark eyes were focused on her, serious and narrowed. "Her reaction?"

"Disbelief, obviously. But once her mother gave me details I would never know otherwise, everything changed. I told her I would continue to do it for her if she kept my secret from the queen."

"And her answer?"

She gave a nod.

His arms crossed on the table, his bowl set to the side, his eyes on the window again. "I would deceive Queen Delwyn for the opportunity to speak to my wife and son again. Others will feel the same. Your secret will spread among the elves—but it won't reach her ears for a long time. But by the time it does, it'll be too late."

"What if she just executes me?"

He gave a slight shake of his head. "The elves of Eden Star will stand in her way. If they lose you, they lose their loved ones too."

"I guess that's true."

"Peony will tell the others. The flame has been lit—and now the fire will spread." He turned back to her and studied her face. "There's pain in your eyes. Why?"

She held his gaze in static form, unsure what to share and what to hide. "I spoke to my father."

"Did his words provoke you?"

"No. I just...I wish he were still here."

He shifted his look away instantly, giving a slight nod of his head. "As do I, *Sor-lei*."

HER MIND PRESSED UP AGAINST THE HARD SURFACE WITH A grooved texture that felt like rigid scales on a muscular flank. Her open palm pressed against the dragon, feeling the rise and fall of his breathing lungs.

Pretty, you're back.

Hey, Flare. How are you?

You're always so sad when I speak to you. I don't like it, Pretty.

I'm sorry. I am happy to talk to you.

Does General Callon continue his tirade of coldness?

No, we're good now. Can you bring in Rush? I have something to tell you both.

Hold on.

Rush's voice emerged a moment later. **Everything alright, Cora?**

Yeah, I'm totally fine.

General Asshole came around?

She knew it was a joke, so she rolled her eyes. *Yes. But don't call him that.*

Come on, you know I'm only teasing.

I know. How are things with you?

Well, it's a bit complicated—

It's not complicated at all. We're lost. And he's the reason we're lost.

Don't act like you don't like eating those goats, alright?

The more I eat them, the more they attack us.

They're following us all through the mountains. We have to keep one person on guard all night. Not because of orcs. Not because of Shamans. But because of these goats that'll knock your teeth out.

I thought you had a map?

But it's not very detailed, and there're sooooo many mountains over here. It's like a needle in a haystack.

A needle on a mountainside.

Literally.

Are you guys going to turn back?

Nah. We'll figure it out. What did you need to tell us?

Well...I got our answer about the Shamans.

General Callon told you?

My father.

Based on the way you're talking, this sounds like bad news.

Because it is.

Alright. Lay it on us.

The Shamans are elves. Dark elves.

Silence.

Eden Star used to punish elves by cursing them... And I guess they turn into...whatever they are.

That's barbaric. And the elves are not barbaric.

He said it was a really long time ago. They're so ashamed of it that they've removed it from their history and lore. It's forbidden to speak of it.

Does that mean elves can use Death Magic? That would explain why you're capable of it.

I don't think they can. That black flower I told you about? That's what they used to make the curse.

So, the Shamans that exist today are elves from centuries ago.

Yes.

What does Ashe, King of Dragons, think about this?

I haven't told him.

Why is that?

Because if I do…it'll be over.

How have you been able to keep this from him? He would have witnessed the conversation.

My father told me it was only for me to know—so I blocked him out.

When was this?

This morning.

And when he questioned you, what did you say?

I'm still blocking him. He's pressed against my mind a couple times…

You never deny a king, Cora. Especially when he's trusted you with his mind, body, and soul.

I know…but I don't know what else to do.

You must tell him.

I still don't understand why you don't want to tell him.

Yes.

She sat up in bed, her arms crossed over her chest, the blankets around her waist. Whenever their voices were in her head, it was like they were in the same room, just a breath away. *Because if the Shamans never existed, King Lux would have been unable to force the dragons to fuse…*

Silence once more.

Shit.

A heavy weight of emptiness broke through his voice. *The elves have blamed us for centuries. They abandoned us to the dungeons. They stayed in their forest as we were tortured—all the while saying we deserved it.*

Cora closed her eyes to shield herself from the heartbreak in Flare's voice.

There is no word to describe that kind of cruelty. Not in Elvish. Not in Dragon. Not in Dwarvish. None.

I'm sorry...but I had to tell you.

Silence.

He's gone.

Maybe I shouldn't have said anything...or maybe said it better.

I would have told him anyway. And there was no good way to say it, Cora.

She tightened her arms across her chest.

You can't tell Ashe.

I can't lie to him...

I understand that's impossible for you to do. Believe me, I get it. But we both know what will happen when he knows the truth. Our only chance of securing this alliance is over. We need more than dwarves and elves to win this war. If we don't have dragons to meet their dragons in the skies, it'll be a massacre.

I know. But...

He'll leave Eden Star and return home—unless you force him into a fuse—

Don't even say that...

Cora, I know you never would. I'm just saying.

Well, don't ever say that again.

Rush turned silent.

What do I say?

You could say it's an elvish secret that you can't share with him.

Ashe would never accept that answer.

Then you need to lie to him.

Not telling him the truth is much different from outright lying.

Those are your two options, Cora. It doesn't matter which you pick—because both are a betrayal.

Ugh, I hate this.

I know. But if you never tell him, I don't see how he would ever figure it out.

He will—once we figure out why I can use Death Magic.

Tiberius didn't answer that?

No. We didn't talk about it. I was so stunned by what he told me that I didn't think about anything else.

Understandable.

I just can't believe this, you know?

It changes everything. Like our odds weren't poor enough...

Do you have any theories? About me?

Well, I'm even more confident that you aren't a Shaman. You haven't been cursed, and if you have, you would have been turned by now.

I guess that's true.

So at least we can rule that out.

But we aren't left with any other theories.

I'm totally stumped, Cora. I can't even think of anyone to ask.

What about Mathilda?

Just because she carries the flower in her shop doesn't mean she knows what the elves use it for. And even if she does know, that doesn't mean she can explain why you have the powers of a Shaman without the curse. The only person we could ask...would be a Shaman.

A shiver went down her spine, a vile and disgusting shiver.

But even if that was an option, I don't think it'd be a good one.

Yeah.

All we know is you have the power to take on the Shamans. And maybe...that's all that matters.

20

THE BURDEN OF THE VEIL

When Callon pursued her in battle, it was always a fight to the death.

He gave her his all—every time.

To wield her sword, block his hits, be aware of her footing, and project her mind to disarm his all at the same time...was exhausting. It was hard to concentrate on all things at the same time.

It made her drop her sword more than once.

"Again." Callon readopted his position.

You need to disarm his mind.

What do you think I've been doing? She pushed off the ground and grabbed her sword.

You're doing too much at once. Pick your battles, Cora.

When he's coming at me like a psychopath—

Not a psychopath. He's one of the greatest swordsmen, and you should feel honored that he's teaching you.

I do. I just... It's a lot, okay?

Too bad. You think General Noose won't be a lot?

I'll do the Skull Crusher if I have to.

How? You've never practiced.

I'm not going to kill a rabbit for the hell of it.

Then we need to hunt some Shamans.

Callon swiped his sword across the air, left and right, intimidating her from his stance a few feet away.

Not a psychopath, my ass...

Conserve your energy. Choose the moments that will have the most impact. Battles aren't won and lost in hours, not even in days sometimes. Your mind is just like the sword, the bow, the shield—it has its own purpose. Use it wisely.

Callon approached her, his sword ready to slice her head from her shoulders.

You can do this, Cora.

When they returned to Eden Star, Callon veered off the path toward his tree house. Cora continued on to hers, sore, with grass stains on her arms and neck.

I demand your truth.

Cora kept her eyes down, moving under the canopy of trees and taking advantage of the coolness of the shade. *I'm sorry, Ashe. I can't tell you.*

You must.

My father made me promise to keep it to myself.

Why?

I don't know...he just did.

But I'm Ashe, King of Dragons, the powerful being that shares your soul this very moment. We are one, Cora.

Her eyes remained on the ground as a heavy sigh filled her lungs. ***I know...***

Tell me.

I can't. I learned nothing about myself or my abilities, so it really doesn't matter anyway. It's of no use to us. Just some elvish lore.

Ashe turned quiet.

She approached the foot of her tree house and spotted Peony waiting there.

Who is that?

Peony. She's the one I helped in the cemetery.

And that man?

Must be her father.

Cora approached, visibly sweaty, all of her gear stuffed into her pack so no one would realize she trained with Callon deep in the woods. Her sword was wrapped in a bundle of bulky leaves to hide the outline of the blade. She was suddenly self-conscious of her appearance, her sweaty hair sticking to her scalp and the sides of her neck.

Peony stepped forward. "Cora, this is my father, Hyacinth."

Cora gave a short bow.

Peony did the same—as did her father.

Cora stilled at their actions, her eyes shifting back and forth between them quickly.

What is it?

No one has ever bowed to me before...

They may be the first, but they won't be the last.

Hyacinth was blond like his daughter, with the same blue eyes. But the rest of his features contained despair where hers contained beauty. He gave her a piercing stare, just the way Callon did in battle. "My *Per-lei* has told me of your abilities. It's no trick. It's no hallucination. The veil has truly been broken."

Cora nodded. "I'm happy to act as your vessel if you wish."

"Why?" His question exploded like a bomb from a cannon. "You're an outsider to Eden Star. Why would you offer your abilities to those who have vehemently opposed your existence in our forest?"

Didn't know that until now. "Because I've lost someone too. I know how that feels...outsider or not."

Hyacinth exchanged a look with his daughter before he turned back to Cora.

"Just let me put my stuff down, and we'll go."

Connecting two souls from across the grave was fulfilling—but also heartbreaking. There were always tears, always regret, always sorrow. The connection was sometimes more painful than the separation. It was the same experience she had with Callon—over and over again.

But it was her duty.

Without her, no one would ever have this opportunity. It was more than just a tool to gain favor with her people. It was also her moral obligation to provide closure to those who never had it.

Hyacinth's suspicions immediately evaporated once the conversation began. His *Sun-lei* said everything to confirm her authenticity, and his tears were immediate. His hand reached out repeatedly to where she was, like her spirit would solidify and they would touch once more.

The conversation drew to a close when she had to withdraw from the plane.

And just like Peony and Callon had, he begged her not to go.

He sobbed on the bench, his daughter beside him with her hand on his, the two of them grieving their loss together.

Cora silently excused herself and left the Cemetery of Spirits. She took her time moving through Eden Star as she proceeded to her tree house. The difference between the cemetery and the rest of the forest was striking. It was evening, but the sunlight still set the leaves aglow with a beautiful light. Fireflies were replaced by monarch butterflies and sparrows. The cemetery was silent, but the forest was loud with music from the songbirds. Visiting the spirits always left a weight in her heart that dragged her down to the earth, and it always required a night of sleep to pass. But the next time she went, it would happen once more.

She made dinner and ate alone at the table, her backpack and sword against the wall at her bedside. Slowly, the sun set further, the shadows elongating across her wooden floor.

I feel your sadness.

You always feel my sadness.

Because you're always sad.

The cemetery... It's just hard.

I understand, Cora. It's a heavy burden to carry, to be the vessel for someone's grief. To communicate through the veil and feel nothing would be impossible. You know how much Callon appreciates it, along with Peony and Hyacinth as well. What wouldn't you give to be able to speak to your father the way you do now?

I have no regrets about my actions. It just...takes a toll sometimes.

Someone approaches.

Cora turned to the door, recognizing Peony in the doorway, carrying a tray in her hands. "Just wanted to drop this off." She carried the tray to the table and set it beside Cora. "My family has a garden. We grow some of the less common items, like the blue turnips, sugar peas, purple cauliflower. Thought you might enjoy a casserole...as a thank-you."

Cora stared down at the dish, seeing the roasted vegetables in a sea of black rice. She'd never come across these things in the wild, and Callon never dropped them off either. It was a whole different menu for her to choose from. As much as she'd adopted her new lifestyle, eating the same things over and over got repetitive. "Damn, this looks good." Her meal had already been finished, but she didn't hesitate to grab her fork and dig in. The rice was naturally flavored from the rock salt and minerals, and the potatoes had such a distinct crunch that she'd never had before. "You made this?"

Peony brought her hands together as a smile moved on to her face. "I did."

Cora took another bite, talking with her mouth full. "This is, like, the best shit I've ever tasted."

Stop cussing.

Oh, right. "Sorry..."

Peony continued to smile. "I'm glad you like it."

Cora continued to eat because no amount of food would replace the energy she burned training with Callon every day. Her body was the tightest it'd ever been, but she was perpetually hungry.

"I also make a vanilla and chocolate swirl with raspberry sauce."

With her mouth full of food, she spoke. "Didyoubringit?"

This time, Peony gave a chuckle. "No. But I will next time."

"What else do you make?" Cora wiped her mouth, knowing she looked like a pig. "Take a seat."

Peony sat in the chair across from her, her posture perfect just like Callon's and every other elf Cora had ever seen. Her hands rested together on the table, her long blond hair interwoven with white flowers. She had a resemblance to the queen, especially in white, but there was much more kindness in her blue eyes. "Since we grow the less popular items, we keep our garden small, but our produce is very high quality because I sing to our crops every morning, from the moment their seed is planted into the soil."

"You sing to plants?"

She nodded.

"Does it work?"

"Yes."

"How?"

"Not sure. But they grow heartier, grow quicker. It's a commitment, but my mother used to do it before she passed away, so I took her place. My father comes out to hear me because I sound just like her…"

"That's beautiful." Cora set down her fork and spared the casserole before she consumed the whole thing. "I wish I could sing."

"How do you know you can't?"

"I don't know. I can just tell."

"Without proper training, you'll never know. You need to understand how to project your voice, to find that perfect pitch, to feel the vibrations of the world around you and match your voice to that resonance. Yes, some voices are better than others, but everyone has the ability to sing. Would you like me to teach you?"

"That's very nice of you, but I prefer the food."

She chuckled. "You sound like my father. He likes my cooking too."

"Psh, how could he not?"

Her chuckle faded to a smile, but within a few seconds, that faded too. "I apologize for the way I treated you before. Like everyone else, I didn't give you a chance because of my prejudice. That was wrong."

"Don't worry about it." Her eyes shifted to the window, the remaining light beginning to disappear. "I get it."

"There's never been a hybrid before now. It's shocking to the elves, even though they've had plenty of time to process it. We process time differently."

"Yeah, I've heard that before..." *Like a million times.*

"If you ever need anything from our garden, don't hesitate to ask. My father is in the market every morning."

"You would…let me take something?"

"Yes."

"In front of everyone?"

"After what you've done for us, there's nothing we wouldn't do for you, Cora."

Congratulations, Cora. You have a friend.

Yeah…I guess I do.

"Twilight has almost arrived." She rose from the chair. "I'll let you retire for the evening."

"Do you think you could show me your garden tomorrow?" The request left her voice like a tense arrow. It shot off spontaneously, without aim. While Callon filled a gaping hole that no one else ever had, she needed more than just him.

Peony turned back and gave a nod. "Of course. You're welcome—always."

Now.

Cora projected her mind to infect his.

Callon hesitated in his swing, a wince coming over his features.

Cora caught his sword with the edge of her blade and threw it down, trying to fling it out of his grasp.

His hand dropped, but his fingers remained tight on his sword. He maneuvered away, ducking under her swing, retreating backward as he fought against the agony burning in his mind.

Good.

The battle continued, Ashe instructing her to unleash her powers at just the right moment, to disarm him long enough to get the upper hand.

Very rarely could Cora actually get the sword out of his hand or her blade against his neck—but it did happen sometimes.

Callon channeled all of his rage into the battle, using it as energy to overcome the assaults that incapacitated his mind. Beads of sweat rolled down his temples and over his cheeks. His mouth was tight in a grimace, his hard jaw clenched like an angry fist.

His energy drained as the afternoon waned on, and by the end, he was an easier opponent to face. His physical endurance was stable as always, but his mind simply couldn't stay as sharp when the assaults chipped at his mental state.

She got the sword out of his hand.

She went in for the kill, ready to press the blade against his neck.

Beaten and exhausted, he should have surrendered, but he didn't. The sword was inaccessible because Cora stood directly over it, making sure he couldn't retrieve it.

His hands were up at his sides as he held his ground, ready to take her on with just his palms. His fair skin was red like a ripe tomato, and the rivers of sweat continued to drip down his face. But his shoulders remained strong, his eyes focused.

"Keep going?"

"Battles aren't only fought with swords."

"I don't want to hurt you—"

"I want to hurt you. Give me your best, Cora."

Fight him as if he wields a sword.

She jumped forward and swung her sword, aiming for his torso then his shoulder, missing every swing because he danced away quickly.

Don't let him get to his sword.

She blocked his path and continued her assault.

He ducked under her spin, spun into her, and slammed her hand down onto his thigh.

Her sword dropped.

Run!

He sprinted to the sword she'd dropped, but before he could grab it, she kicked it away and punched him in the back of the head.

He spun around and threw a fist.

It landed against her cheek, immediately giving her a headache.

There was no remorse in his eyes. With his palms tight into fists, he circled her, ignoring the swords.

You can't beat him physically. You must use your mind.

He rushed her, his fists flying.

She blocked each one with her forearms, grimacing because each hit would leave a bruise, even through her armor.

Now.

She pushed her mind, making him back away.

She rushed him, kicking him in the chest then dropping to the ground to kick out her leg and trip him.

He landed on his back.

She immediately crawled on top of him, assuming the fight would continue.

But he lay there, his eyes calm as if he'd just woken up from a midday nap. "Eye-gouge."

"What?"

"Unless you have a small blade on you to slit my throat, press your thumbs into my eyes. It'll permanently blind your opponent."

"That's...barbaric."

"It's not barbaric. It's war." His eyes turned angry, vicious. "It'll give you the opportunity to retrieve your sword and finish the job."

She'd been training for battle, but she'd never actually thought about the victories. For her to win, someone had to die. Repeatedly.

She stood up then helped him to his feet.

His sight was normal once again, and he examined her cheek with concern, his fingertips moving to her chin so he could examine it. "Are you okay, *Sor-lei*?"

She grinned. "You should look at yourself, *Tor-lei*."

He grinned back. "You've come a long way. I admire your dedication and resilience. I'm very proud."

Her heart clenched with both joy and guilt. "Without my powers, I wouldn't be able to hold my own."

"Doesn't matter. You do have them—and you should use them."

"I'm not hurting you, am I?"

"Headaches are a common side effect, but I've learned that a glass of wine is an excellent remedy."

"I didn't know you drank wine."

"I stopped after I lost my *Sun-lei*. She liked to enjoy dinner every night with a glass of wine. I detested the substance at first because it inhibited my abilities, but I grew to appreciate the dulling effect."

Cora watched his eyes light up when he spoke of her rather than plunging into a sea of gray. "I'll have to try it, then."

"Our vineyards are in the hillsides. Our wine is excellent. A lot better than the horse piss humans drink."

"I believe it."

He picked up both swords from the ground before he handed hers over. "Let's head back."

Together, they took the trail, side by side.

"Peony came by last night. Brought me a casserole from her garden."

Callon pulled his gaze away from the path and regarded her instead. "That was kind."

"I connected her father to her mother. She wanted to show her gratitude."

"Excellent, Cora." He faced ahead again.

"And this food…was unbelievable."

He glanced at her again.

"Not that your cooking isn't great."

He gave a slight smile before he faced forward once more. "Weila was the chef in the family. I take no offense to your words."

"She said she makes this vanilla-chocolate swirl with some kind of fruit sauce… I haven't stopped thinking about it."

"You've never shown passion for food before."

"Maybe it's because I'm starving all the time." She gave him a look of accusation. "Because we train every day, rain or shine, no excuses..."

"You're welcome."

"I'm complaining, if that wasn't clear."

"And you're a much better fighter, if that wasn't clear."

"Well, since I'm better, do you think we could lighten up—"

"No."

She gave a loud and exaggerated sigh.

"You don't fight. You're a *fighter*. So, you never pause your craft, because it's not a craft at all. It's who you are. The only time my training ceased was when I lost my family. You never know when your enemies will strike, when war will arrive on your doorstep. You must be ready—always."

"But I'm not a fighter—"

"If you want to defeat King Lux, you have to be."

She followed Peony's directions through Eden Star, ignored the sour looks on the way, and then arrived at the garden she'd described. There was a perfect break in the trees for the sun to flourish at midday, giving life to the produce that grew from the earth.

Peony was on her knees in the dirt.

But she wasn't alone.

There were two other elves there—one man and one woman.

The man had short blond hair and light-colored eyes. The sleeves of his tunic were pushed to his elbows as he squatted down and harvested carrots from the soil. He was muscular like Callon, like he was a soldier as well as a gardener. The woman was a brunette, her hair in a high ponytail, small flowers pinned behind her ear.

When Cora had thought it would just be her and Peony, all the fear vanished. But seeing other elves immediately brought on a wave of overwhelming intimidation. Sour looks had been cast her way on the entire journey, so now she would receive more.

Maybe I should just go.

No. This is your opportunity to grow your circle.

Did you see the way everyone dogged me on the way here?

Peony will vouch for you. Her heart is true.

Cora approached the garden and cleared her throat to announce her presence. "Wow, this is beautiful."

All three of them turned to regard her.

As she suspected, the two elves were guarded.

Peony was the only one who possessed any warmth. "Hello, Cora." She got to her feet and stripped off her gloves. "That's very nice of you to say. A lot of love and attention goes into this soil."

"I can tell."

The other elves rose to their feet but kept their distance.

Peony came closer. "We've got the turnips here next to the carrots, the cauliflower right here, and then our mushrooms are here. We grow our rice in a different place because this spot is just too shady for it."

"What about the vanilla and cocoa?"

"Just over here." She gestured to the trees at the end of the line, where the beans were visible on the limbs.

"Can you eat it raw?"

"It's edible, but…I don't recommend it." The male elf approached, so Peony made the introduction. "Cora, this is my friend Hawk. He helps me out sometimes."

Hawk regarded her with a simple nod.

Speak.

He didn't say anything.

You're the one who needs to be liked. Not the other way around.

"It's nice to meet you." She gave a slight bow.

There was a long pause of hesitation before he reciprocated.

Was that so hard?

When you're used to everyone hating you all the time, it's kinda hard to put yourself out there.

People won't stop hating you until you give them a reason to stop hating you.

"This is Lia."

Lia gave a silent bow.

"Hi." Cora did the same. "Peony brought me a casserole last night…it was one of the best things I've ever eaten."

"Then you haven't eaten well." Hawk had a deep voice filled with ancient tranquility. Peony seemed young in years, but he seemed old, despite his ageless appearance. "Because Peony thinks burning is the same thing as cooking."

Wow…what an asshole.

Peony grinned and cast him a furtive look.

After a moment, he smiled back.

Oh…it's a joke.

A poor one.

Elves don't joke.

Neither do dragons, but I know a bad joke when I see one.

"You want to help us?" Peony turned back to Cora.

"Sure," Cora said. "But I've never done this before."

"I'll teach you." She handed over her gloves. "Come on."

They gathered their harvest and carried it to the market, where it would be put on display the following morning. Then Peony invited them all to her tree house for dinner.

I just got an invitation to hang out!

Hang out?

You know, socialize.

What a terrible phrase...

Peony washed and prepared the vegetables while Lia took care of the cooking. There wasn't work for more than two people, so Cora sat at the table with Hawk, both of them enjoying the green tea Peony made.

Was hoping for some wine.

Maybe another time.

Hawk sat across from her, but his eyes remained on Peony most of the time, even when she faced the other way.

All Cora could do was stare at the elf across from her, unsure how to talk to him. **What should I say? Should I ask him a question?**

Just pretend he's me.

Pretending he's a dragon king is not going to work.

Then whomever you deem a friend. Perhaps Flare.

Flare didn't fit into that category. "Are you a gardener as well?"

He slowly turned back to regard her, showcasing intelligent eyes. "I serve in the army. That is my contribution to Eden Star."

"General Callon is my—"

Careful.

Oh, you're right. "Callon has been very kind to me since I arrived here."

Hawk regarded her with a solemn stare. "General Aldon is a strong leader who will protect the forest with his life—but General Callon will always be the true general to me. If he needed to depart our lands, I know that it was for a good reason. I do not need to question his motives or loyalty. I speak for most of us when I say this."

The throne is his to take.

But he doesn't want it, Ashe.

I don't care if he wants it. His duty is to his people—not himself.

He's given more than enough to his people.

It will never be enough until there's everlasting peace.

Is there such a thing as everlasting peace?

There was until the humans sailed to our lands.

Cora ignored Ashe. "He's a very honorable man. You served under him?"

"For a long time."

"So…the rest of the army was unhappy with the queen's decision?"

"Extremely. But she is our queen—and we must obey."

No, you don't.

How would you feel if the dragons didn't obey you?

They don't obey. A true leader doesn't give commands to be followed blindly. They lead by example, by inspiration. I asked for volunteers in this quest. If I expected any of them to obey, I would have commanded them all to join us. Subjects are entitled to free will. Entitled to opinions. Your queen is foolish for thinking otherwise.

"Since Callon has taken a vested interest in you, I will as well."

Cora blinked as she met his look. ***If it weren't for Callon, none of this would be possible.***

A quality of a king.

"He speaks highly of General Aldon. Said he recommended him as a replacement."

"I have no qualms about General Aldon. In the event of General Callon's passing, I knew he would be chosen. But General Callon has been our general for millennia, and since we experience time differently than you do, it'll take a very long time to come to terms with the loss."

"Do you think it's possible for him to get the position back?"

He gave a shake of his head. "Queen Delwyn will not go back on her decision—unless General Callon does something to regain her approval."

"What if General Aldon refused to lead?"

"Someone else would be selected."

"What if everyone refused to take the position?"

He cocked his head slightly. "You want him reinstated."

"Yes."

"Why?"

"Because...he left Eden Star to help me. If he hadn't, I would have died."

His eyebrows remained furrowed.

"It wasn't his fault. It was mine."

"General Callon left his post to help an outsider."

"I'm not an outsider." Her temper flared like the light from a shooting star. Peony and Lia both turned away from the counter to regard them both. "If he thinks I'm worth saving, then you should all think I'm worth saving."

"I never said otherwise."

"Then don't call me an outsider. I may only be half of you, but I'm still you nonetheless."

A slow smile moved on to his lips. "You misunderstood me. Or perhaps I misspoke. General Callon abandoned his post to help an outsider—and that makes you an outsider no more."

After a quiet dinner, Lia said goodnight and took the path in the opposite direction toward her tree house.

Cora and Hawk continued on the same path.

Hawk had the same posture as Callon, carrying himself like he wore heavy armor and his sword across his back. He kept a distance of several feet, his eyes straight ahead, the darkness of the forest lit by white candles at the foot of the trees.

"How long have you known Peony?"

"A couple of years. She brought flowers to the front line over twenty years ago. Each soldier was pinned with a white flower to protect us in battle. I fought alongside her mother—and you know how that ended."

"Was that with King Tiberius?"

"Yes. He also fell."

She looked straight ahead.

"She pinned it to my chest and moved on to the next soldier—but I never forgot her face. Perhaps I was just afraid, but her touch brought me comfort."

"You're afraid of battle?"

"Aren't we all?"

"I don't know… Callon doesn't seem to be."

"Well, he has nothing left to lose—because he already lost everything."

She turned to regard him, examine the side of his face. "Are you and Peony...together?"

"No."

"Oh, my mistake."

"No mistake, Cora. You perceive the truth."

"I...I don't understand."

He continued his pace down the earthy path, his voice and expression hiding any trace of pain. "I declared my love—but she didn't return it."

"Oh...I'm sorry."

"I hope in time she feels differently. In the meantime, her friendship is enough."

"You don't want to find someone who could return your feelings?"

"I have no interest."

"But if she doesn't feel the same way—"

"She made her feelings perfectly clear, and I respect her decision. I haven't pursued it or mentioned it again. But it's her company that I prefer above all others, and if that is under the condition of friendship, that's enough for me."

She let the conversation fade and looked ahead once more.

"My home is this way." He stopped at a fork in the road. "But I can escort you, if you like."

"Eden Star is pretty safe... I think I'll be okay."

Drop the sarcasm, Cora.

"I mean, that's very kind of you, but I know the way."

He gave a slight bow before he continued on the path to his home.

Looks like I made another friend.

Miracles do exist.

Oh, shut up.

21

GIRL TALK

CALLON STEPPED into her tree house, silent and swift like he was a spirit himself. His pack was on his back, his sword at his hip because he didn't have to conceal it the way she did. Even if he wasn't in the army anymore, no one would dare revoke his weapons.

She continued to pack her stuff at the dining table. "I'm almost ready."

"I arrive at sunrise every morning, so you should always be ready."

"Well, it's pretty hard to wake myself up in the *dark*."

Callon gave her his signature stern expression.

She continued to pack her lunch in the leaf container. "I met Hawk last night. Didn't get his last name."

"I know of whom you speak." He stood in the open area near her bed, arms by his sides, his gaze out the window.

"He spoke really highly of you."

Callon continued to stare.

"Said you're still the general…to him."

"A loyalty I don't deserve—but appreciate, nonetheless."

"He trusts that if you left Eden Star, it was for a good reason."

"That wasn't the case." He turned back to her. "As we both know."

"That's not true, Callon. If that hadn't happened, I wouldn't have met Ashe, and none of what I've accomplished would be possible."

He looked away again, dismissing the conversation.

"He also said that since you have a vested interest in me, he does too. So…your popularity is really helping me out around here."

"I'm glad."

She returned to her lunch, putting it away along with some extra berries for the red cardinal she'd befriended.

Callon turned to the doorway.

Cora did the same and followed his gaze.

Peony was there, along with Hawk and Lia. "I apologize, Cora. I didn't mean to intrude while you're entertaining."

"No, you're fine," Cora said quickly. "Callon is impossible to entertain."

Callon turned and gave her a stare.

Peony acknowledged him with a bow. "General Callon. *Mera-Nil-Weia*."

Callon reciprocated with a bow.

Lia did the same, bowing and saying those words. "*Mera-Nil-Weia*."

Hawk was the last, giving the deepest bow to his former commander. "*Mera-Nil-Weia*."

I wonder what that means.

Must be a gesture of respect. When a dragon wishes to honor me, they bring me a kill.

That's...touching.

Peony addressed Cora. "We were going to the market to have breakfast, but maybe you can join us another time."

More like never.

"She can join you now." Callon stepped aside and turned back to Cora. "I was just leaving." He gave her a curt nod then departed her tree house, moving silently down the vines even though his pack was full of supplies for a day's journey.

Cora abandoned her pack on the table. "Looks like I'm free."

They went to the café Callon had taken her to before, and while there were cold stares from every direction and a bit of hesitation from the waitress, Cora felt far more welcome than she ever had before.

They enjoyed their coffee and tea as they waited for their breakfast to arrive. Cora ordered blueberry pancakes and a vegetable crepe with cashew cheese melted on top. The café air wafted with an appetizing smell, orders passing by and being delivered to other elves at other tables.

Peony sat across from her. "I realize it's none of my business, but…are you and General Callon—"

"*No*. Yuck. Gross. Ew. No."

Peony gave a chuckle. "Alright, then."

"Besides, he's like… I don't even know how old he is. Like five thousand years old? I don't even know."

"Age is irrelevant when you live forever."

"Well, I'm in my twenties, so I'm pretty much a newborn to you guys," Cora said. "Gross."

Peony sipped her coffee and gave another chuckle.

"How old are you?" Cora asked. "I mean, you don't have to answer that. Didn't mean to be rude."

"You're fine," Peony said. "I'm less than a hundred. A child like you."

Cora shifted her gaze to Hawk. "I'm guessing you're a lot older than that."

He gave a slight nod. "A bit."

"I'm young like Peony," Lia said. "Just a bit older. We're the children of Eden Star."

"So, there are no actual children in the forest?" Cora asked. "You're the youngest elves?"

"Well, technically, you are," Peony said. "But yes. There have been no children for a while."

"I'm surprised," Cora said. "After all the lives that were lost in the wars…"

The waitress arrived and delivered the hot plates, but didn't depart before giving Cora another cold look.

When Cora looked at the deliciousness placed in front of her, it was as if that glare never happened. "Oh man, this shit looks goooooood."

They all stiffened.

Cora.

"Shit. I mean…" She slapped her own forehead. "Sorry."

Hawk was the first one to crack a smile.

The other two seemed amused as well and carried on with their breakfast.

Why is it so difficult for you not to speak crassly?

It's language. It's stupid to censor words because we deem them inappropriate.

It's called class, Cora. You clearly don't have it.

Because I'm real. What you see is what you get, alright?

Clearly.

"What you said to Callon, what does that mean?" She took a bite of her blueberry pancakes, and it took all her strength not to turn crass once again. The warm blueberries gushed in her mouth, the maple syrup so sweet in its freshness.

"*Mera-Nil-Weia*?" Peony asked. "May the beating heart of the forest protect yours. It's a sign of respect toward those who have earned the collective love of the elves as a whole. Very few have earned it."

I can't remember anyone saying it to the queen.

Quite telling.

"And *Rein-Lei-Vu?*" Cora asked.

Peony's eyes softened, like she knew where Cora had heard it. "I love you."

Lia was the first to go, and then Hawk followed shortly afterward. Just as Callon did, he was required to serve his rotation at the border for days at a time. That left her and Peony alone as they sipped their coffee with the dirty plates between them.

"If there's nothing romantic between you, what is your relationship?" Peony held the small cup of green tea between her hands, the steam rising toward her face because she'd recently received a refill.

Cora glanced at her coffee before she answered. "Queen Delwyn was very harsh toward me, and I think Callon took pity on me. He's taken me under his wing ever since. I know he lost his son, so I think it's just natural for him to be fatherly."

"That's how you see him? As a father?"

She nodded. "Yeah...I do."

"That's sweet."

"He's a good man. The best I know, really."

Peony gave a nod in agreement. "He's sacrificed everything for his people, and he keeps going. We acknowledge his sacrifice. My mother served under him and always said he was the greatest general that ever served in Eden Star. I've never met another warrior who has said otherwise."

"I hope he can get his position back."

"As do I. But I also understand if he doesn't want it." She looked down into her tea, a splash of almond milk swirling on the surface.

"So...Hawk is a pretty good-looking guy."

Peony raised her chin, distressed eyes locking on to hers.

"I asked him if you guys were together on the walk home last night."

"Oh..."

"He's just not your type or what?"

Peony's eyes dropped back to her tea. "Hawk is a suitable life partner. He's highly respected by the elves. He's a great swordsman on the battlefield, and he has a gentle kindness when he's home."

"Okay…so he is your type?"

"I think he would be a good husband and a good father, if we were given permission to do that, but we're better as friends."

"Is there someone else you're into?"

She lifted her chin, her eyes narrowed.

"Sorry," Cora said quickly. "I'm not trying to interrogate you. I haven't had girl talk in a really long time."

"Girl talk?"

"You know, when girls talk about the guys they're into."

She gave a slight nod in understanding. "No, there's no one else."

"Then what am I missing here?"

She set her tea aside and interlocked her fingers on the table. "Is girl talk confidential?"

"That's the foundation, yes."

"Alright." She looked away for a moment and cleared her throat. "My father has been very clear about this. He has no influence in the elf I choose for my *Wor-lei*, and if I choose to remain unmarried for my lifetime, that's an acceptable decision. But his one request was…that I do not choose someone who serves in the army."

"Why?"

Her eyes dropped. "Because he lost my mother...and his daughter should never know that sorrow."

"Oh..."

"My mother was one of the best. General Callon trained her himself. But she fell anyway, cut down by some monster. It was very difficult for us to retrieve her body, but my father made it happen because he couldn't go on and never feel her spirit again. I understand his request, and after seeing that kind of grief firsthand, I think it's a reasonable one."

Cora felt Callon's grief the moment she was in his presence. It was in his eyes...his sad eyes. His happiness had improved in recent weeks, either because he could speak to her when he wished, or his relationship with Cora filled the void that his family left behind. But that grief was permanent. Just better on some days...and worse on others. "Is that the only reason keeping you apart?"

After a quiet stare, Peony gave a nod.

"Well...if he dies in battle...won't you be sad anyway?"

"Yes, but that would be losing him as a friend rather than a *Wor-lei*. It will hurt much less."

"But won't it hurt more knowing you could have been more... but it never happened?"

Her stare shifted away.

"I know Callon wouldn't have chosen someone else...even if he'd known he would lose Weila."

Peony continued to look away.

"It's not my place to tell you what to do, to go against your father's wishes, not when we don't know each other that well. But if you have the opportunity to be together, even if it's going to end, I think you should take it. I know I would…" Firelight. Shadows. Embers. Starlight. Mist. A smile both boyish and arrogant. Big hands on her body. Kisses against her lips.

Peony grabbed her cup and pulled it close once more, her eyes still down. "What about you?"

The memories were shattered by the question. "What about me?"

"Do you have someone?"

Her eyes shifted away, unsure what words to speak, what to even think—especially with Ashe there. "I did. But…it didn't work out."

"I'm sorry."

"Yeah, it's been rough."

"I'm guessing this isn't an elf, then?"

She shook her head.

"Maybe you'll find someone here, when you're ready."

"I'm not really looking, so…"

"You have a long life to live, Cora. The heart aches for a long time. But it heals—eventually."

"Yeah…we'll see."

Guess what?

You think I have time for guessing games?

You have time to hang out with goats all day, so you tell me.

He gave a deep chuckle. You made some friends?

Yep.

Did you throw a rock at their head or...?

No, asshole.

Bribe them?

Didn't have to do that either.

Hmm...General Callon pulled some strings?

Shut up. I'm a very pleasant person.

The scar on the back of my head says otherwise.

She rolled her eyes as she sat up in bed, wishing he could see her do it. *Her name is Peony. I helped her and her father speak to her late mother, and then we kinda became friends. She introduced me to some other people she knows too.*

That's great, Cora.

Yeah, I really like them. I've never really had a girlfriend, so that's nice.

Not in your village?

They were too busy churning butter and making dinner for their husbands or whatever nonsense...

I'd like to watch you churn butter...

Shut up.

Wearing a little apron...things jiggling.

You're ridiculous.

He made a chuckle. You're on the right track. Keep it up, and pretty soon, you'll be the queen of that place.

Okay, that's a bit unrealistic.

You fused with Ashe, King of Dragons, and that was even more unrealistic. Come on. When they really know you, they're going to love you. You're right. You probably won't be queen, but you won't be an outsider either.

Maybe. Ashe and I think Callon should be on the throne.

He'd be as good a king as he was a general. But I doubt he'd ever be interested in that.

You're right.

He's a soldier. He wants to serve—not lead.

What's going on with you guys? I'm guessing you haven't found the dwarves because you would have told me.

We found a tunnel, went pretty deep into it, but then it was a dead end.

Are you sure? Maybe there was a secret doorway somewhere.

No, we're certain. And it was Flare's idea—so I'm giving him shit.

Is it really that hard to find these guys?

Have you been to the mountains?

Well, no.

Then you have no idea.

SHE LEFT EDEN STAR THROUGH THE SECRET PASSAGE AND emerged into the wildlands outside the forest.

Finally.

Sorry. I know it's been a while.

While you got to enjoy a feast at breakfast, my stomach growled for a bear.

Bear is Flare's favorite.

Bear is a staple in a dragon's diet.

They emerged into a clearing with ample space for them to unfuse.

Are you ready?

Maybe I should just lie on the ground for this.

You need to get used to this, Cora.

Fine.

Ashe unfused, separating his black body from hers.

Cora ended up on the ground—again. "Makes me sick every time." She opened her eyes and looked at jagged teeth and gray eyes. His breaths blew over her face. "But it's nice to see you in the scales. You're beautiful."

I know.

She gave a light chuckle. "Have fun. You know where to find me."

He gave her a slight nudge with his nostril. *You're beautiful too, Cora. On the inside as well as the outside.*

"Thanks…"

He walked away in search of his meal.

Cora sat up and dusted all the blades of grass off her clothes. It was an overcast afternoon, but spots of sunshine would break through and warm her skin. She crossed her legs and looked at the trees as she waited for Ashe to return.

Then she heard it.

A whine mixed with a growl.

It sounded like an angry horse trying to get her attention.

She turned to the sound and gasped when she saw him.

With black fur, gnarled teeth that extended outside of his jaw, and big black eyes with white in the center, he was exactly as she remembered.

And he still had the flower behind his ear.

"Honey, is that you?" She got to her feet and approached him with an outstretched hand. "I thought you fell. I'm so glad you're okay."

He hurried over, drool dripping down his sharp teeth to the grass.

"Okay, easy with those." She backed away so his teeth wouldn't rip through her clothes and flesh. "Thank you for helping us before. We might not have gotten away if it weren't for you."

Images flooded her mind—of herself. Of feeding him flowers, tucking one behind his ear, smiling at her, riding on the back of Flare in terror.

She placed her hand on his flank and ran her fingers through his fur.

He seemed to like it because he smiled—sorta. His eyes drooped a bit, and he twisted and turned his head so her fingers could get deep into his neck. Anytime she stopped petting him, he gave a snort and demanded she continue.

She chuckled. "Alright. That seems fair considering what you did for me." She petted him for a while, until he was finally satisfied. "So, what are you doing here? Just visiting? Where is home for you?"

An image came into her mind—a very disturbing one.

Dead trees with no leaves. Fog thick as smoke. Eternal darkness. The images were so fast that she barely captured their essence.

"That's home?"

He gave a nod.

"It's...nice."

He moved into her and nudged her with his horns.

"What?"

He did it again, along with a growl.

"What are you trying to tell me?"

His hooves pounded against the ground as he stomped backward, his eyes locking on to hers. His mind connected with hers, and a flood of images appeared.

A line of Shamans flying on steeds. More than just three or four. There were dozens, their features invisible under their cloaks. Under cover of darkness, they flew, over a dark ocean. The image changed to trees, thick and green trees with curling branches. An endless forest in sunshine.

The vision faded.

She tried to process what she'd just seen. "I...I don't understand what you're trying to tell me."

He gave another growl.

"Shamans...ocean...forest."

He dropped his head and nudged her in the side, careful to protect her from his teeth.

"Okay, a bunch of Shamans are flying across an ocean...toward a forest."

He pulled away and gave her a hard stare.

"Is...that forest Eden Star?"

He stared for a long time.

Cora hoped her assumption was wrong, that this was just a misunderstanding.

It wasn't—because he nodded.

Are you certain that's what he meant?

As certain as I can be given the circumstances.

Why would a steed loyal to the Shamans betray his master and tell you this?

Because I gave him a flower. She hiked back through the passage to return to Eden Star as quickly as possible.

A flower?

It's complicated.

He betrays his people because you gave him a flower...? That's not complicated. It's senseless.

I can't explain it, but we're basically friends. He gave me a ride to Rock Island and attacked the Steward of Easton's dragon so we could get away. I guess he must have come here from wherever they're from to warn me.

For a flower?

Just forget that part, okay? We're friends. End of story.

What do we do now?

I guess tell Callon.

Yes, that would be wise.

She returned to Eden Star and headed straight for his tree house. It was close to sunset, so he'd probably just made dinner. She ran up the vines and made it to his front door, but she saw that his home was empty. "Callon?"

He's not here.

She turned back around. ***Then where is he?***

Cemetery of Spirits.

You're right.

She left the tree house and headed to the other side of Eden Star, plunging into the mist, the sea of fireflies, the land of grief.

Callon was on the bench next to the graves of his family.

His head was bowed, his hands together, eyes closed.

Right beside him was the outline of a man. Muscular like his father, poised like his mother, his head bowed in mutual grief. His blue outline showed the same sharp jawline that Callon possessed. He had the same shoulders too, wide and muscular.

She didn't need to see his face to see their likeness.

She approached the bench, the news she came to share forgotten. "He's next to you."

Callon gave a small reaction, like he heard Cora even in his trance.

Turnion turned his head to regard her.

She met his look—at least where his eyes would be. "I'm Cora—your cousin."

He remained quiet.

Callon inhaled a slow and deep breath. "Not a day passes when I don't think of you. The loss of your mother has broken my spirit, but the loss of my son has broken my heart. I failed to protect you. I failed as a father. I failed as a husband. I failed…both of you." The tears came, rivers down his cheeks.

Cora looked away because it hurt too much.

Turnion remained quiet.

Callon cried quietly to himself before he wiped his face with the back of his forearm, giving a loud sniff before he brought himself to calm.

Turnion still didn't speak.

Callon waited, his quickening breath showing his impatience. "*Vin-lei.*"

Nothing.

"Why do you not come to me? Why do you not speak?"

Turnion was still, his eyes still on Cora.

Callon's voice came out as a whisper. "What have I done…?"

Turnion finally turned away from Cora, focusing his stare on his father. "A father should never have to outlive his son. But a son should never have to watch his father grieve his death. Your sorrow…is just too much for me."

Callon turned to look at his son, where he imagined he would be, his eyes red and wet.

"I don't want to feel your sorrow, *Kul-lei*."

Callon pressed his lips tightly together, forcing back the flood of tears that wanted to break through.

"I gave my life for my people. I died with honor, and I would die a million times to keep Eden Star safe from evil. I've found peace—and you need to find it as well. Honor me. But do not grieve me."

When he blinked, fresh tears came. "You're my son…"

"You will see me again, *Kul-lei*."

"You have no idea how much I miss you…"

"I do."

"I should have protected you."

"I was just as skilled with the sword as you—but it was my time. Do not carry this guilt. Do not carry this sorrow. I can't come to you and see you this way. I want to feel the presence of my father, the general, the strong man with hands that never shake. This…is too much for me. It breaks my heart to see you this way."

Callon inhaled a deep breath as he wiped away his tears with his palm.

"You suffer when I suffer—as I do with you."

He gave a nod.

"No more."

He took another breath before he gave a nod.

"*Rein-Lei-Vu, Kul-lei.*"

His entire body started to shake, his bottom lip trembling, the moisture on the surface of his eyes growing until the surface tension wasn't enough to keep them in place. "*Rein-Lei-Vu, Vin-lei...*"

Turnion faded away, his outline replaced by mist.

When he was gone, Callon let the tears come freely, his palms cupping his face.

Cora felt her own fall.

She moved to the seat beside him and placed her arm around his shoulders before her face rested against his arm. Her tears soaked the fabric of his shirt every time his chest heaved and he vibrated against her. "I'm sorry, *Tor-lei...*"

CALLON OPENED THE CABINETS AND GRABBED TWO CUPS FOR THE tea brewing on the stove. His eyes were bloodshot but dry as sand.

You need to tell him.

Now is not the right time, Ashe.

Cora, this is important.

He's grieving.

His son is dead. He will always grieve.

Callon carried the two mugs of tea to the table, and they sat together. His hands cupped the mug like he needed warmth on a cold day. His eyes remained on the liquid, even when he brought it to his lips for a drink.

"How are you?"

His eyes remained on the tea. "Unwell."

"Your son wants you to be happy."

"Which is impossible. The loss of a child…you don't recover from that."

"But you can make your peace with it."

He lifted his gaze.

"Your son wants a relationship with you. But your sadness brings him sadness. It's infectious—just like laughter and joy."

He gave an almost imperceptible nod.

"I know it's hard. I can't even imagine. But…I understand what he means. The people we love most…we never want them to hurt. Because when they hurt, so do we."

He took another drink.

"When you hurt, he hurts."

"Grief is like a disease. Once you have it, it's permanent. You manage it, and some days are worse than others. It's a lifelong illness that doesn't get better—just changes. But I will try to find peace with his death so I can continue my relationship with him beyond the grave."

She drank her tea, her eyes on her broken uncle across the table.

When his mug was empty, he pushed it away and looked out the window instead. "I'm glad to see that you're building relationships outside of the one we share. Not just to reach your goals, but for your own well-being. I know the elves have been unkind to you, but they are great people."

Now is the time.

"I know they are."

"And maybe you'll meet a partner as well."

Her eyes immediately dropped back to her tea.

"Callon, there's something I need to tell you." She lifted her gaze and met his.

His bloodshot eyes immediately turned serious. He was still and focused, his head slightly cocked.

"I wanted to tell you earlier today...but it wasn't the right time."

"What is it, Cora?"

"When I left Eden Star so Ashe could hunt, I saw the Shamans' steed. The one that flew us to Rock Island."

"And the significance of this?"

"I think he came to warn me."

"Of what?"

"He sent me images…of dozens of Shamans flying over the ocean toward a forest. When I asked him if that forest was this forest, he said yes."

"He said those words?"

"Well, no. He nodded at the question."

He sat forward, his arms moving to the table. "How do we know this isn't a trap?"

"I doubt he would have risked his life for us to get away just to trick me later."

"How are we really certain that's even what he meant?"

"Because he's not stupid. You respect all living things, but you're dismissing him like he's an imbecile."

"I don't think he's an imbecile. But he is a servant to the Shamans. He's not like the birds and butterflies in our forest. Surely you must see that."

Her eyes narrowed. "I see no difference."

"Cora—"

"You're being unfairly prejudiced. His soul is as pure as yours or mine. He's been enslaved by the Shamans to be a flying horse. That's not his fault, and it certainly doesn't attest to an allegiance to them."

Callon raised his palm. "For argument's sake, let's assume those were his intentions and his information is correct. The Shamans can come to our borders, but they can't breach them. The magic of the forest prevents them from doing so."

"Maybe they found a way around it."

"I doubt it."

"Just because something has worked in the past doesn't mean it'll work in the future. Don't be arrogant."

His eyebrows shot to the top of his head. "Arrogant—"

"Arrogance leads to complacency. That's how mistakes are made. People assume they have everything figured out until they realize that they don't."

"Even if you're right, what does it matter? Our army is always ready for an assault."

"Queen Delwyn needs to know."

"Whether the queen is aware of this information or not, her army is ready."

"She may be privy to information that you aren't. It's common sense to report information about a possible attack."

His hands came together on the table as he regarded her. "And how do we explain where we received this information?"

"Uh..."

"That you regularly use a secret passage you shouldn't know about so the King of Dragons can feed, and then you conversed with a steed of the enemy, and the reason you have a relationship with him is because he gave you a ride to Rock Island to free the man who slew King Tiberius? How do you think that will go?"

She rolled her eyes. "I don't know, alright? But she needs this information so she can be prepared."

"Eden Star is always prepared."

"So, the Shamans have staged an attack before?"

He stared.

"You assume they can't breach your lands, so are you prepared if they can?"

"There is no possibility of success."

"Then why are they coming here?"

"We don't know that for sure. Your little friend could be misinformed."

"Or he could be giving us a warning to ensure our survival and we're blowing it."

Callon bowed his head before he dragged his hands down his face. "Even if I told Queen Delwyn the truth, she would disregard everything and then exile us from Eden Star for breaking every single law of the land. It would accomplish nothing."

"Then who can you tell?"

His palms flattened against the surface. "I could relay my suspicions to General Aldon."

"Will he take you seriously?"

He continued to stare at his hands. "Yes."

"And he won't ask questions?"

"No, he won't question me."

"Will he tell Queen Delwyn?"

"Not if I ask him not to."

"How will you explain how you know this?"

He gave a shrug. "I won't. I don't need to explain myself. Something is coming—be ready for it. The order is straightforward."

"Okay," she said. "Sometimes I wish you were the king because you listen. Queen Delwyn never listens."

A heavy chuckle escaped his lips.

"What?"

"The only reason I listen, the only reason I betray my own people, is because of the love I have for you. It does not reflect my ideology. It does not reflect my loyalty to Eden Star. It is love that makes me foolish."

"Well, maybe being foolish is a good thing sometimes."

His eyes shifted out the window. "That still remains to be foreseen, *Sor-lei*."

22

HATCHLING

"Did you speak to General Aldon?" Cora walked behind him, doing her best to keep up. Her endurance and physicality were better than they'd ever been, but she still had to push herself hard to meet his pace. For every stride of his, there were two of hers. Sometimes three.

"Yes."

"And?"

"He accepted my warning."

"And that's it? We're done?"

"When it comes to war, he's the one in charge. It's in his hands now."

"What would you do? If you were still the general?"

"Double the guard on duty. Expand the perimeter. Plant scouts farther into the wildlands."

"You think he'll do those things?"

"Yes."

"He told you this?"

"No." He halted in his tracks and turned back to regard her. "He still lives in my shadow, and he'll continue to live in my shadow until his service equals mine. It's in his best interest to heed my warnings in case it truly comes to pass." He faced forward again and continued his hike.

"I hope I'm wrong…"

"Don't worry about the safety of Eden Star. It's not your job."

"Doesn't mean I don't care—because I do."

They reached their secret glade they used for training and dropped their packs and unsheathed their swords.

"Have you acted as a vessel to anyone new?" He tested the swing of his sword with his warm-up.

"No one has asked."

"I'm sure they will soon. Be prepared when they do."

She held her sword at the ready, knowing he would strike when she least expected it.

"Switch hands."

"Sorry?"

"You're going to use your left hand today."

"Uh, why?"

"What will you do if your right arm is broken in combat?"

She stared at her arm, like she could see the broken bones through the skin.

"That's why, Cora."

"Can you fight with your left hand?"

He tossed the blade to the other hand and spun it around just as fluidly.

"Okay...no need to show off."

"So, what happens if I do break an arm?" They were on their way back to Eden Star, her in the rear while he took the lead.

"It hurts."

She rolled her eyes. "I meant, do you have a healer? Do you use magic?"

"Both. We have a healer who uses magic."

"You just have one healer?"

"Yes."

"So, it's just one guy healing a bunch of people in battle?"

"It's a very complicated task and requires thorough training. Not just anyone can be a healer. Magic is used to map out the body and then heal it properly, but if you do it improperly, you could cause more damage instead. Or worse, kill them. It's a skill of the mind. It requires no touching. A healer uses the body's natural processes to heal itself."

"Wow…that's really cool."

"But you should avoid breaking your arm because he can fix ailments, but not remove pain."

"Why not?"

"Pain is a notification from our mind that something is wrong. If you turn that off, it might turn off other things as well, such as automatic processes like breathing, producing urine, things of that nature."

"Sounds like you know a bit about it."

"I know some basics—just in case I need them in battle."

"You think you could teach me?"

"No. We don't have time for that."

They returned to the heart of the forest, the tree houses in the canopies, other elves walking by on their outdoor stroll.

"Would you like to visit the cemetery?"

"No." He halted on the path, his tree house in the opposite direction. "I need some time before I return. Some meditation. Some grief counseling."

"I didn't know they offered that."

"I've never tried it. But now I realize I might need it." His hand moved to her shoulder, and he gave her a squeeze. "You did well today."

"I got my ass kicked. What are you talking about?"

He chuckled. "But you tried. You didn't complain. You just did your best. The Cora I first met would have been a smartass until she got her way."

She rolled her eyes.

He smiled wider. "See you tomorrow, *Sor-lei.*"

"Bye, *Tor-lei.*"

She stood beside Peony at the counter in her tree house.

"Layer the nuts in between the turnips and the cauliflower. It gives it a nice crunch." Peony added one layer then the next, showing Cora how to make the casserole she was so fond of. "The almond crème keeps everything together, so you drizzle that on top and it provides a nice cohesiveness."

"Not too hard."

"Nope." She put it in the oven and set the timer. "Now we wait."

"Torture." Cora took a seat at the dining table.

Peony chuckled and poured more tea into their cups. "How's your week been?"

She'd waited for an attack that never came. As the forest remained quiet and peaceful, she wondered if the information had been false or misinterpreted. Either way, it was a relief that nothing had come to pass. "I helped Helda speak to her sister at the cemetery."

"Oh, that's nice. Helda misses her so much."

"Yeah."

"That has to be rough for you, huh?" She sat across from Cora and brought the steaming cup to her lips. "Having to be a part of this emotional journey."

"It is, but I'm happy to do it."

"If only there were someone in the cemetery for you, you'd be able to enjoy your abilities as well."

Cora drank her tea and licked her lips. "I'm going to make this casserole for Callon. I think he'll really enjoy it."

"I'm sure he will," she said. "It's sweet that he's taken you under his wing."

"Yeah, he's a good guy."

"The entire forest was grief-stricken at Turnion's passing. He was so much like his father—dedicated to his people."

"I know."

"Has Callon spoken to him?"

She nodded. "He has."

"Good." Her eyes softened. "I'm sure that has brought him immense peace."

"I think it's brought them both peace."

"Cora, it won't take long for your abilities to become an open secret. Everyone has lost someone, and everyone will want the opportunity to speak to them—on an ongoing basis."

"That's what I'm hoping for. Everyone contributes to Eden Star in some way. They're soldiers, gardeners, scholars, something. This is how I can become a valuable member of society."

"Master of Spirits."

"That's quite the title."

"I think it's perfect. And it's a great way for you to have a meaningful impact."

"Yeah."

"But I fear Queen Delwyn will be upset when she learns of your secret—unless she wants to use it herself."

Doubtful. "It would be selfish for her to take this away from her people. It has brought so much peace."

"I agree. But I also understand why it would be cause for concern. There's never been anyone in our society with your unique abilities. She's already suspicious of you, and that suspicion will probably grow."

"Yeah...she's not my biggest fan."

"You'll just have to change her mind, then."

Hawk crossed the threshold. "I can smell that casserole all the way from my post at the border."

Peony gave a smile. "It's quite fragrant, isn't it?" She retrieved another mug from the cabinet and filled it with the freshly brewed tea.

Hawk took the seat beside her empty chair and gave a subtle nod to Cora.

"How are things out there?" Cora asked.

"Unremarkable—as always." He was stiff in his seat, not using the support of the chair to cushion his back. He still wore his armor with his bow slung across his back. After a long rotation in the forest, the first thing he wanted to do was come to Peony rather than go to his private accommodations.

"You're an archer?"

"Among other things—but it's my specialty."

"I'm pretty good with the bow myself."

"Is that a challenge? Come to the training grounds, and we'll see whose aim is true."

"Training grounds? I didn't even know we had that."

"Because it's for the army. But I might be able to get you in."

Peony removed the casserole from the oven and set it in the center of the table.

Once she was near, his eyes were on her, glancing at her repeatedly. "How's your garden, Peony?"

"Coming along nicely." She served the casserole onto plates. "Thanks to you and Lia."

Cora watched Hawk stare at Peony, giving her a look Cora had never received herself.

Peony looked at her again. "And of course, Cora as well."

Now it felt like she didn't belong, not when their two energies combined to ignite flames of a shooting star. Their bodies never came into contact and their eyes barely did either, but the connection between them was undeniable.

She'll change her mind—eventually.

I hope so.

THE BLUE DRAGON SOARED OVER THE TWILIGHT SKY AND released a stream of fire, burning the soldiers and cannons on the ground. Everyone caught fire, and the blood-curdling screams added to the cacophony of war.

Her eyes smarted from the heat of the flames.

Obsidian swooped around then headed straight her way.

She unsheathed her sword.

Obsidian's eyes narrowed at her form on the ground, and when his toothy jaws opened wide, a circle of fire was in the back of his throat, deep in his chest cavity.

She pushed her mind forward—though she felt nothing but a solid wall.

The heat came next.

The smell burned her nostrils.

She was on fire, smelling her own flesh burn.

CORA!

She jerked up in bed and opened her eyes.

Run.

Red-hot flames set her tree house ablaze. The vines that once grew through her window had been charred to ash. Half of the roof had caved in, falling on the opposite side away from her bed. Smoke drew into her lungs with every breath and made her eyes water until she could barely breathe. ***What's happening?*** She pushed out of bed and landed on the floor.

The rest of the roof caved in at that moment and fell onto the bed where she'd lain just moments ago.

Crawl.

On her hands and knees, she maneuvered across the ground and headed to the doorway.

Grab your sword.

It was next to the wall, so she grabbed it along with her pack, coughing the entire way.

Most of the vines of the stairway had been burned away, so her escape plan was severed. ***Did someone set my house on fire?***

Survive now. Questions later.

How do I get down?

The tree house collapsed further, now a squashed pancake of fire.

Jump on that tree and climb down.

I'm not a monkey!

Do it!

When she looked past her own tragedy, she realized her tree house wasn't the only one set ablaze.

The fire was everywhere. She pushed her mind outward, getting to the invisible front door. ***Flare? Rush? Are you there?***

No response.

Cora, we need to go.

She tried again. ***Rush?***

They can't help us, Cora. We're on our own.

She took a short running jump and hit the trunk with her chest. Her fingers and nails dug into the bark to secure her weight above the ground. She gave a scream, all of her fingers in pain.

She made the long descent to the forest floor and fell to her knees.

The tree that once housed her home was completely consumed. Red-orange flames engulfed the entire thing, turning it into fuel so it could grow bigger and larger. Everything that had once been hers would be turned into a pile of ash on the forest floor.

The foundation of the trunk grew weak—and then it collapsed altogether. It cracked smack in the middle, and the flames soared to the floor, the tree house coming apart during the descent.

Screams pierced the night from all directions. She'd never heard them before but knew exactly what it was—the screams of elves.

Put on your armor.

Callon!

Armor, Cora.

She threw down her pack and donned everything as quickly as possible, securing it in place before her bow was slung over her back and her sword secured at her hip. Her empty pack was left at the base of the tree.

She ran down the path, watching screaming elves flee in the opposite direction she was going. In their chaos, one bumped into her but shoved off and kept going. One elf was lit up with flames and collapsed feet away. The screams stopped as the flesh continued to melt off the bone.

Cora looked away and nearly retched.

Callon can take care of himself, Cora.

We both know I'm the first thing he's going to run to—and I don't want him to die searching for me. She sprinted as fast as she could, her lungs finally able to breathe now that smoke from her burned tree house was out of her body.

When she reached his tree house, she stopped.

It was consumed in flames, about to collapse any second. "No..."

He escaped, Cora.

"Callon!" She cupped her mouth with both hands and yelled into the night. "Callon!" *Ashe, there's room here. Let's unfuse, and you can fly away. No one will even notice.*

Silence.

This is bad, and I'm probably going to die. And if I die...so do you.

Silence.

Come on! I don't have time to wait around.

I will not leave you.

What? Why? The burning trees lit up the forest, the screams echoing from every direction. The world was just shadows and flame, the enemy invisible but everywhere. The most serene place in Anastille had become a bonfire of wood and bones.

Because you're my hatchling.

She could no longer see the destruction of the forest. Now all she could see was a majestic black dragon, its head hung low so he could meet her gaze. Dark eyes bored into her, his snout close enough to give her shoulder a bump. *Ashe...*

We are one. His mind fused with hers, giving her a jolt of energy, sight that could penetrate the darkness. Her mind felt weightless, her thoughts sharp as the tip of an arrow. *Now let's find him.*

Just when she ran forward, Callon's tree house collapsed, the trunk turning to ash and losing its stability. Cora sprinted away, missing the embers that popped into the night and floated like fireflies. The heat seared her skin, even through her armor, and her lungs got a breath of smoke.

Run in the direction of your home. He will be somewhere along the way.

Her dragon sight could pierce the darkness when her elven eyes couldn't—and she saw them.

Dark cloaks. They billowed behind them as they moved, as if the creatures floated across the forest floor. Long, bony fingers were visible, fire in their palms. Like shadows that moved with the changing sun, their presence stretching in different places. They moved all over, torturing one elf then lighting up the tree next to the corpse.

Now she could hear them too.

Click-click-click. Cliiiiicck.

"Callon!" She sprinted ahead and maneuvered through the trees, ignoring the clicks that haunted her from every direction. Every click was followed by the scream of a terrified elf. But when the screams stopped, that was even worse because that meant…

She stopped when she spotted him on the ground.

He was easy to see—because he was clad in the armor of a general.

His sword by his side.

The Shaman stood over him—torturing him.

Callon writhed, on his back, his entire body shaking as his skull started to cave.

With speed she never could have produced on her own, her feet hit the ground like she had wings to take flight, her body gliding through the air like the feathers of a bird. She crashed right into the Shaman, hitting a stack of pillows rather than a solid being, and tackled him to the ground. One hand went deeper into his body than the other, as if he were twisted like a staircase, as if he were ethereal rather than physical.

He made a scream she'd never heard before, the howl of a wolf but with the shriek of a fox. It was so loud that it masked the ongoing destruction inside Eden Star. It drowned out the pleas for help, the thuds of the trunks as they hit the earth.

He was back on his feet instantaneously, his crouched body turned toward her, thin, dead branches for fingers.

He raised his palm.

Her mind projected forward, and as if her fingers had a grip on his head, she snapped his neck, making his body collapse to the ground. Within a heartbeat, she'd crushed his skull from the inside out, plunging him into the eternal darkness of nothing.

He didn't even have time to scream.

"Callon?" She was on her knees at his side, trying to help him up.

His breaths were ragged, and his features were tight in a permanent wince. His stern eyes were closed, and he groaned, his hand immediately moving to his temple like he had the worst headache of his life.

She gave him a second to recover—while the forest continued to burn around them. She scanned the area around them, screaming elves running away from their torturers, suddenly dropping dead when the Shaman behind them did their magic. It was a bloodbath—just without the blood.

When he had the strength, he grabbed his sword from the ground and pushed to his feet, staggering slightly.

She threw his arm over her shoulder and supported him.

He pushed her away. "I have to protect the queen."

"You're in no condition to fight—"

"I will not let these monsters take my forest." He turned on her, his eyes back to their serious hostility. Eyes wide-open and full of unspeakable rage, he looked maniacal. "You need to run, Cora. Take the secret passage out of the forest."

"This is my forest too, Callon. I'm not letting it burn."

He threw his arm down in frustration, his orders not being followed with perfect obedience. "I can't protect you—"

"But I can protect *you*."

His dark eyes reflected the firelight behind her, shifting back and forth quickly.

"We do this together."

After a long stare, he gave a subtle nod. "Let's go, *Sor-lei*."

QUEEN DELWYN STOOD ERECT AS THOSE WHO DIED TO PROTECT her lay at her feet.

Melian was facedown on the stairs, the blood from her slit throat a pool on the steps below. General Aldon's eyes were lifeless, staring up at the stars that he couldn't see, even if he were alive, because they were blocked by the smoke. Other elves who gave their lives to protect her lay slain at her feet.

Click.

Click.

Cliiiiiicccck.

The Shamans surrounded her on all sides, their cloaks dragging behind them as they crouched and glided through the air. They circled her, like a murder of crows waiting to peck out her eyes once the time was right.

Her gown was stained with blood from those who had bled to keep her heart beating, but she held herself like her white gown was as pure as a flower that still flourished on its stem. Her crown remained perfectly straight on her head, her posture as confident as ever. The only cue to her demise was the fire in her eyes.

In the black armor of the king, General Noose stood before her with his sword at his side, the mirth in his eyes as well on his lips. "We will burn this forest until there's nothing left. Then we will build our castles and our keeps. Our homes. Our brothels. Our farmlands. Elves, once immortal, will be forgotten. Shall I keep you alive long enough to see the last elf slain? Or should I grant you mercy and do the honors now?"

Queen Delwyn held his gaze with an unflinching stare. Bright green like the forest surrounding them, her eyes were the only light in the dark place. There was no one left to protect her, but she carried herself like an army was at her back, arrows trained on her enemies.

A deep chuckle escaped his throat. "I could take you prisoner and have my fun with you. An elf…that would be a first." He raised his sword slightly, pointing the tip at her feet. "But I've always been an impatient man—"

Callon broke through the trees and sprinted to the bottom of the stairs. When he got to General Noose, his sword flashed with the surrounding firelight and the greenness of the queen's eyes. He struck down General Noose's sword, putting his body between him and his queen.

General Noose's sword dropped momentarily as he backed away.

Queen Delwyn flinched at his sudden appearance, taking a step back up the stairs to get away from the fight. "Callon, flee. Save who you can."

Callon kept his position, his sword held at the ready. His angry eyes burned into General Noose's, and he gripped the pommel of his blade so tightly that it stretched the fabric of his gloves. He was still, his eyes unblinking, ready to drive his enemy out of Eden Star.

Click. Click. Click.

Cliiiiiiick.

Click.

General Noose let his sword hang at his side, a large grin across his big mouth. "General Callon. I'm glad you're here. You deserve an honorable death. I'm happy to oblige." Without warning, his sword slashed with the speed of the wind, meeting Callon's with a distinct clank that rang throughout the forest.

The men engaged in battle, delivering a flurry of hits and strikes. They circled each other, dodging left and right, ducking under the swipes and jumping over the blade as it swung at their feet. They moved with the speed of shooting stars, everything happening so quickly that it was hard to know if it happened at all.

Callon met his might—but only barely. His battle became a defensive one, blocking the flurry of hits that came his way rather than striking on his own. He became Cora in her training, unable to participate as a worthy opponent.

He's too weak to win this fight.

A Shaman raised his palm toward Callon.

Cora's reaction was instantaneous, bringing him to a collapse. Her mind caved in his skull, killing him before he could move against her uncle.

The swordfight continued, both fighters oblivious to the deceased Shaman that blended into the darkness.

General Noose pushed Callon back, struck down his sword so it landed on the grass, and brought him to his knees in front of the queen.

No.

Callon winced, like the pain in his mind was just too much to carry on. He was not the inferior fighter, but the torture his mind endured had severed the connection between his thoughts and his body. He couldn't hold the sword as he did before. Couldn't execute a lifetime of training.

The mirth burned in General Noose's eyes as well as his mouth. His grin of victory was grotesque, as if slaying his enemy was the greatest pleasure he'd ever known. General Noose raised his sword and prepared to swipe Callon's head clean from his shoulders.

But then he gave an involuntary jerk and backed away, his hand clutching his temple.

Callon didn't waste the opportunity and dove for his fallen sword.

General Noose growled as he looked at the sea of Shamans, surveying them in the circle, lines of tension on his face as his temples throbbed. "What is this game?"

Click.

Click. Click.

Cliiiiiick.

General Noose gathered his bearings and came for Callon once more, his eyes full of even greater blood lust.

Callon raised his sword to deflect the attack rushing down on him. But his grasp on the pommel was weak, his shoulders heavy, his body slow. He knew he would be slain, but he carried on anyway.

But Cora got there first.

She took his place and shoved him back, her body blocking his, her brilliant sword meeting the steel of the empire.

Callon fell onto his back at the foot of the stairs. "Cora!"

The General's sword met the fire of her scales, a thud different from steel on steel. It was steel on earth, a quiet thud rather than a clank of metal. He shoved her sword with his as he stepped back, his wide eyes staring with incredulity that quickly turned into glee.

"Cora, no." Callon tried to push himself to his feet but collapsed back on the stairs. Too weak to get to his feet, he was helpless to interfere. "Please. I beg you. Run." His voice broke with the emotional plea of a father, desperate to protect the one thing he had left. "Don't do this..." His eyes filled with a thin film of moisture, of heartbreak, of frustrated tears.

General Noose flicked his sword around his wrist as the grin spread. "If the little girl wants to play, let her play." He extended his hand and gave a dramatic bow before he righted himself again.

Cora gripped her sword with both hands, moving her feet the way she'd been taught, waiting for the unexpected attack she'd been trained to anticipate. The blade was weightless in her hands. Strength from an outside source flooded into her body. The darkness was as easy to pierce as daylight. She was aware of everything, from the sweat that dripped down his temple to the shine of saliva on his front teeth.

Focus, Cora. He may have the strength of a man—but you have the strength of a dragon.

Not just any dragon—but the King of Dragons.

Yes.

General Noose rushed her, his sword swinging with the speed of Callon's on his best day.

She was ready for it, her red sword blocking his hit along with the next and the next. Their swords danced together in a series of blows, each hit meeting the block of the other. His armor was made of steel, so she aimed her attacks at his wrists and neck. She barely needed to take a breath because she was so calm, her mind so focused there was no panic, no palpitations to her heart.

General Noose withdrew. "Not bad—for a little girl."

Callon pushed to his feet again. Instead of being the most respectable swordsman in Anastille, he was now an old man, a man who didn't move the way he once did. But he tried anyway—to no avail. "Cora!"

The General was done playing with his food and came at her hard, ready to end this right now and for good.

Now.

She pushed out her mind, hitting him like a shot from a cannon.

He gave a loud groan and fell back, his features showing the agony that writhed inside his skull.

Kill him.

She pushed her mind out again, to crush his skull the way she did with the Shamans. The fight would end quickly, and King Lux would lose his greatest pawn. It wouldn't just be a victory for Eden Star, but for the continent.

Click. Cliiiiick. Click.

The Shamans' minds formed a protective wall around the General's, protecting the final layer before his skull could be compromised.

She continued to push—but she was exhausted by the action. It was an element of surprise she hadn't expected, a strength she couldn't defeat. She was powerless, and if she kept going, she feared her own mind would be incapacitated.

Stop.

She pulled away.

General Noose recovered and came at her again, this time with a scowl.

His hits were harder, fueled by venomous rage, pushing her back with the strength of a bull. Every strike possessed the power of all his muscles, of all the strength of a man three times her size. He came down on her like storm clouds, unleashing hail and thunder. He was a volcano, his lava about to drown her in fire.

Cora met his hits, never giving up an opening for him to slice her head off her shoulders. Now her breaths became labored, her thoughts strained, even with Ashe's help. Without their union, she would have no help to prevail. She would have been defeated at the first blow.

Now.

She pushed again, compromising him a second time. His sword lost its momentum, and he faltered just long enough to give Cora an opening. She went for the break in his armor, between his vambraces and his gloves.

Her sword sliced over his wrist, deep into the flesh.

He stumbled back and gave a growl as he felt the bite of his injury. His eyes went down to his hand, the blood dripping over his gloves and to the grass below him. One drop splashed on his boot. He raised his arm and watched himself bleed before his eyes flicked back to hers. His breaths became heavy, his eyes menacing.

"Who's the little girl now—*bitch*."

His nostrils flared as he righted himself, blood still dripping everywhere. His sword switched hands because the open wound made his grip too slippery. His heavy breaths deepened. The rage in his eyes was lethal. "Two can play this game."

What does that mean?

Focus, Cora.

The assault happened, hitting her mind from all sides, like blades dragging along the sides of her skull. They all shot through the bone, trying to get in, to break it down from the inside. Her body buckled and she winced, Callon's screams now blurry whispers in the background. "CORA!"

Click.

Cliiiiiccccck.

General Noose came for her once again. "Let's see who's the bitch now."

This is all I have, Cora.

She got another rush of energy, just a bit more to increase her focus, another involuntary jolt to her body.

But now, I must retreat to save my strength. I know you will defeat him, Hatchling.

Her sword met Noose's, the ringing in her ears, the gnawing in her stomach. Her eyes closed as she held his offense, using a greater sense than sight. She held back the weight of a mountain with the strength of a dragon, her power coming from the union of two souls. It was a blistering headache, agony. The pain was overwhelming. She gave a scream then sliced his wrist once again, digging her blade deep.

This time, he screamed as he fell back. "Arrrrggggghh!"

Cliiiiicccck.

Her eyes opened, and she regripped her sword, seeing General Noose bleed from both hands. Despite her pain, she couldn't wipe away the victorious smirk across her face.

"Cora!" Callon continued to scream. "Run!"

The Shamans rushed in, the strength of their spell increasing with proximity. There were six of them, all of their palms raised, doing their dirty work so General Noose could slice her head clean from her shoulders.

She pushed through the pain and projected her mind around her. The assault came from various directions in front of her, some sources stronger than others. With all the might they could muster, they struck to kill, to buckle her knees from underneath her and make her eyes empty forever.

She pushed herself harder than ever before, invading all minds at once, infecting every single skull.

The torture on her mind ceased.

The six Shamans collapsed on the ground—all dead. With a unifying thud, they were no more. Just corpses on the ground. More dead than they were before.

General Noose hung back, his sword falling to his side. His eyes surveyed the dead before him. Six bodies in cloaks surrounded him, the allies that were supposed to be invincible. Then his eyes turned to her. Now, there was no gloat. No grin. No taunt. Nothing.

She breathed through the agony, the ringing now faint in her ears. The pain lingered, but it was a fraction of what it'd been before. Her adrenaline masked the rest of it. Her victory straightened her spine, darkened her eyes, made her step forward with a confidence she'd never possessed before.

All General Noose could do was stare.

She flicked her sword around her wrist before she took her offensive stance once again. She challenged him with her gaze, ready to end this fight for good. She'd taken out two of his wrists, and now she would go for his neck next.

But General Noose stepped back.

The remaining Shamans did the same, backtracking away from her.

She wouldn't let him leave this forest with his life. Not after what he'd done to Eden Star. After what he'd done to the trees, her people, even her queen. She pushed her mind out to General Noose, determined to make him a corpse like the pile of cloaks next to him.

But she couldn't.

Her mind couldn't even reach that far away. There was a barrier, not in front of him, but in front of her own mind.

She had nothing left. She'd exhausted all the strength and energy Ashe had provided, had depleted her own reserves long ago. She could feel the fatigue in her muscles as well as her mind. If she hadn't expended it all on the Shamans, perhaps she would be able to take him out now. But she also might be dead if she hadn't.

General Noose gave her a final hard look. He sized her up differently, as more than just an equal, but an actual threat. His sword remained at his side as he backed away and joined the ranks of the soldiers he'd brought with him. He kept his eyes on her until he was far enough away. Only when he was at the line of the trees did he turn his back on her—and retreat.

23

INTO THE MOUNTAIN

"Oh yeah, this is the place." Bridge examined the stone doorway with his arms crossed over his chest.

"We thought that last time," Rush said. "And the time before that...and the time before that."

"Look." Bridge walked to the wall then dragged his hands over the stone, removing the centuries of dust. "Those are runes. Dwarven runes."

About time.

Hey, you slowed us down too.

Not as much as you.

I didn't see you complaining when you ate all those goats.

Ugh. I'm sick of goat. I want a grizzly.

Well, I don't think they have grizzlies in here, so you're shit out of luck.

"This is great and everything," Zane said. "But how do we open the door? There's not a doorknob anywhere."

"What does the map tell us?" Liam asked.

Rush unfolded the map and took a look. "Not much. There's an X, and next to it the word *Push*."

"Push?" Bridge asked incredulously. "We're supposed to push solid stone?" He pressed his palms against the stone and gave a hard push. "Yeah, that's not going anywhere."

"Perhaps Flare could push it?" Liam asked.

Always looking for an excuse…

Can't blame him.

"Flare won't fit in here."

I'm far too massive and beautiful.

I don't think beauty is the deciding factor here.

"Wait." Lilac moved to one corner and peered up at the ceiling. "Doesn't it look like it curves?"

"Curves?" Zane joined her. "What do you mean by that?"

"Like this isn't straight." She pressed her palms against the wall and dragged it down.

Bridge examined the other side, looking down at the ground. "Actually, I think I see a little crack…"

Rush kneeled beside him, seeing the hole that indicated there was empty space somewhere.

It's a ball.

Sorry?

A big ball.

Seriously, no idea what you're saying.

An enormous boulder is blocking the entrance.

Ohh...

Took you long enough.

"Flare says it's a boulder."

"And we're supposed to push it out of the way." Bridge straightened then pressed his palms against the stone once more. "Which would be totally fine...if it didn't weigh as much as a mountain. How are we going to move this thing?"

"Together?" Rush asked. "I can use some of Flare's strength too."

"This doesn't make sense," Liam said. "Dwarves may be stocky and strong, but they're much smaller than an average human. It would take dozens of dwarves every time they wanted to go come and go. It's just not practical."

"If their goal was to make it as difficult as possible to reach them, then I say they succeeded." Lilac pressed her hands against the door with one leg in front of the other. "A little help here?"

They all lined up against the boulder and pushed.

It moved one inch. Then two.

Bridge gave a loud grunt. "You think those goats could help us?"

Rush pushed his shoulder into the rock, keeping the slow momentum going. "Wouldn't that be nice..."

The rock finally rolled away, finding a curved groove in the ground that guided its path against a different wall. It gave a loud rumble before it went still.

They all took a moment to regain their breath, bent at the knees, panting, wiping the sweat from their foreheads.

Bridge straightened. "Now what?"

Rush stepped into the long tunnel, which grew darker the farther he looked down. Torches lined the walls, but they were absent of flame. "I guess we go say hello?"

The hallway was endless.

On and on it went, branching off in different directions, the passages dark unless they held up a torch to chase away the shadows. Instead of veering off in any direction, they continued to go straight so they would always know the way back.

"I'm so glad I'm not a dwarf." Bridge held the torch as he walked beside Rush. "Could you imagine doing this every time you come home?"

"I don't think the dwarves do much coming and going. We were on that mountainside for nearly a month and didn't spot a single one."

"Well, they can't grow their crops underground, so they've got to leave for food."

"Unless they exist off a diet rich in goat legs."

Bridge chuckled. "And goat milk."

"That's gross."

"It wasn't so bad. Nice to have a little cream in my coffee."

Rush stuck out his tongue as he gave a grimace.

"So...have any idea what you're going to say when we finally find them?"

"I thought you were doing the talking."

Bridge rolled his eyes. "This was all your idea, man."

"I don't know. I hope the words come to me."

"Wish Flare could do it."

"You and me both."

I heard that.

Because you never know when to mind your own business.

"What's that up ahead?" Bridge took the lead, carrying the torch over to the spot concealed by darkness.

"What is it?"

"A slide...I think." Bridge kneeled and shone the torchlight on the passageway in the rock.

"A slide?" Lilac stuck her head inside and tried to peer into the passageway. "It does look like a slide. But I can't see where it goes."

Bridge carried the torch farther, revealing a dead end. "Huh. Looks like we're out of road."

"Maybe this is where they drop supplies to storage," Rush said. "So they don't have to carry it all the way."

"That means the main entrance is through one of the side tunnels," Zane said. "Should we go back?"

"Bad idea," Liam said. "We'll just get lost—which is the point."

"Well, this could lead to a pit of lava," Zane said. "A death trap."

"You guys are ridiculous." Lilac sat at the edge and dangled her legs. "I'll go."

"Whoa." Bridge grabbed her wrist. "Let's rear the horse for a second. One person should go and give the all clear to the rest. That makes sense, right?"

"Are you volunteering?" Lilac asked.

Bridge shrugged. "It's better me than you..."

Lilac gave him a gentle pat on the cheek. "You're a sweet brother sometimes. But it's fine. I'll go ahead."

"No—"

Lilac jumped down and disappeared on the slide. "Woo-hoo!"

"If she dies, then I'm going to die," Bridge said. "Just so I can yell at her in the afterlife."

Rush kneeled at the hole in the rock, listening to her slide farther away until there was silence.

They all squeezed closer to the entrance, straining to hear any sign of life.

Rush ducked his head inside and called out. "Lilac? You okay?"

Her distant voice came back. "Imahsors!"

"What?"

She yelled a little louder, but her words were still incoherent. "Imahsoooorrrs!"

"She sounds fine," Zane said as he stepped onto the slide. "Let's go for it." He pushed himself forward, and he disappeared into the dark tunnel. One by one, they went, Rush taking the rear.

Rush carried the torch, keeping it away from his face so he could light the path as they descended deeper into the mountain.

Flare's mind became smaller, his presence retreating the deeper underground he went.

It'll be okay, Flare.

You don't understand.

We'll get out of here as quickly as possible.

The slide ended, and he landed in a pool of cold water. The torch was extinguished once it was submerged, and he choked down a rush of liquid straight into his lungs. He broke the surface and coughed until his lungs were clear, finding the edge of the rock to hold on to. "That was fun..." Soaking wet, he pulled himself out of the water, getting to his hands and knees on the stone slab. "Everyone okay?"

He pushed his wet hair out of his face and watched the water leak out of his pants and boots. There was still a gulp of water lodged in his throat, so he spat it out onto the wet surface. "Guys?" He looked up, seeing everyone ignoring him.

He got to his feet, his weight and pack considerably heavier now that he was carrying pounds of ice-cold water. He pushed his hair out of his face once again then stilled. "Shit..."

The cavern was aglow with green stones in the corners, providing light throughout the ground and up the rigid edges of the inverted rock crevasses. The stones were along the walls, lighting up the inside of the mountain all the way to the very top of the cavern. It was a dim glow, but enough to see the horrifying details.

A sea of bodies hung from posts, sometimes several on a single rope. They were full skeletons now, flesh and hair decomposed long ago. There was no breeze in the cavern, so they hung there idly, for eternity.

There were at least a hundred—if not more.

With bones too thick to belong to a lithe elf and skeletons too short to be human, there was only one conclusion to draw.

They were dwarves.

Bridge surveyed the area with his hands on his hips. "Yep. This is bad. Really bad."

"Can we go back through the slide?" Lilac walked to the edge of the pool and peered up to the stone arch that delivered them there. "Maybe we could build something—"

"You want to crawl all the way back up there?" Bridge asked incredulously. "It's a slide for a reason, Lilac. You can't go back."

She flipped back around. "So, you just want to chill in this dwarf graveyard?"

Liam approached the closest cluster of corpses with narrowed eyes. "Decomposition this far underground would be very slow. This must have happened years ago. Many years ago."

"New plan," Lilac said. "We get outta here as quickly as possible."

Bridge rounded on her. "You think?"

This is bad, Rush. And I can't help you.

"Let's just calm down, alright?" Rush turned back to them. "I admit this is a pretty gruesome sight, but we're making a lot of assumptions right now when we have no idea what happened."

"Oh, you're right." Bridge joined Liam next to the closest skeletons. "This was probably a birthday party."

Rush rolled his eyes.

Bridge rounded back on him. "The dwarves were overrun and annihilated by some psychopaths—clearly."

"Or perhaps these dwarves disobeyed their king, so they were very publicly executed," Rush said.

Bridge moved his hands to his hips and gave him a stare.

"Or maybe there was a famine, so they took their own lives instead of starving," Rush said.

Bridge continued to stare him down, as did the others.

"Okay." Rush rolled his eyes again. "Fine. They were probably defeated in a conquest…"

"But by whom?" Bridge asked. "Who would do this? It wasn't men because you would have known about this."

"Well, my father didn't tell me *everything*. But you're probably right."

"And it wasn't the elves," Bridge said.

Rush examined the remains with his head cocked. "The goats, maybe?"

"Rush." Lilac gave him a smack in the arm. "This is serious."

He's never serious.

You're back, then?

If you aren't going to take this seriously, then I need to.

Rush grabbed pieces of his clothes and wrung them out in his hands, releasing as much moisture as possible so his garments wouldn't feel so heavy—and cold. "I think the plan is pretty simple. We need to find a way out of here—and not be seen."

"I have a feeling that's not going to work very well." Bridge started to pace, his fingers interlocked at the nape of his neck. "We have no weapons—"

"Here." Rush cut down the closest dwarf and let the bones smack against the stone. The dwarf's sword was still secured at his waist, so Rush removed the belt and handed it over.

Bridge didn't take it. "One, that's disgusting. And two, that's not a blade. That's a dagger."

Rush forced it into his hands. "It's sharp and pointy, isn't it?" He cut down other corpses, brittle bones breaking apart when they hit the rock at their feet. They harvested the weapons they could find.

"I found a note." Lilac unrolled it. "But it's in Dwarvish...can't read it."

Liam took it out of her hands. "My Bargora, we are overrun. The rock won't hold. I will meet my end with honor defending our mountain. I don't regret my death, but I regret leaving you and Rulan. I love you both." Liam rolled the note back into place and slipped it into his pocket.

Lilac released a deep sigh. "Man..."

Bridge looked at the pile of bones on the ground. "What happened here?"

Rush stepped over the corpses and headed to the archway in the cavern, large pieces of rock on either side where their assailants had broken through. "I have a feeling we're about to find out."

24

FAZURKS

I can't reach her.

The rock must be too thick. Or we're too deep underground.

I will try again later, but I think you're right.

I told her not to worry if that happens.

She'll worry anyway.

The glow of the green stones illuminated their path through the mountain. Caves branched in different directions, their destinations unknown. Stairs led them either up or deeper underground. The large caverns contained workshops or dining halls, all ransacked. There were bodies along the way, all dwarves.

The storerooms still had dried fruits and nuts along with water and preserved ale, so they were able to stock up on a few things and rest before they continued forward. Conversations were limited, all of them doing their best to stay as quiet as possible.

"I'm starting to wonder if there's anyone here." Lilac came to Rush's side in the lead.

"You really want to take that chance?" His sword was sheathed at his side, but he kept his hand close in case he needed it. His armor was minimal, so a battle ax to his shoulder could be deadly.

"I'm so lost right now. I don't even know the way we came."

"Me neither."

"You have no idea where we're going?"

"Do I look like a dwarf to you?"

Her eyes sharpened like arrows.

"The exit has to be near the surface, so the higher we go, the greater our chances."

"I guess that's true."

"I don't want to be dramatic or anything, but I really don't want to die in a cave."

"You think any of us do?" Bridge asked her from behind.

"Sorry, Lilac," Rush said. "I don't think anyone gets to choose that…"

"Well, I'd prefer it to at least be in battle," she said. "That's what we're working toward, right? All of that is lost if we die here…where no one will ever find us."

"Enough with the death talk, Lilac," Bridge said. "Rush, I think we should call it a night…or a day. Whatever it is."

Scaffolding was mounted against the wall, high up the rock so they could access hundreds of feet in the air. There were pickaxes abandoned on the walkway, as if they had been digging for something before the onslaught happened. They'd had no idea an enemy marched on their mountain until they were already inside. Rush turned around. "I want to get out of here as quickly as possible."

"I'm with you," Bridge said. "But I don't want to be attacked when we're exhausted either, especially when we have no idea what we're up against."

"Not to be a wimp or anything," Lilac said. "But I'm tired too."

They're right. You need to keep your strength. Some of these caverns are big enough for me to fit, but if we cross paths with the enemy at the wrong place, I won't be able to burn them for you.

"Alright." Rush moved forward again. "Let's find a good spot."

They walked awhile longer before they found a decent hiding place, a small but deep cut into the cavern wall. It was a tight fit, but if anyone passed through the cave, they probably wouldn't even know they were there.

They opened their bedrolls and lay side by side, their packs as pillows.

Bridge sighed. "I miss grass…"

"I miss straw," Lilac said.

"I'll take this over the galleon any day," Zane said. "At least it doesn't move."

Rush sat up with his back to the wall, his sword across his thighs, eyes on the opening.

"Rush, you should sleep," Bridge said. "You're the only one of us that knows how to fight."

"Excuse me?" Lilac asked.

"Don't pull that," Bridge said. "If you knew how to fight, Rush wouldn't have been captured at Rock Island. Pickpocketing and stabbing people between the ribs with a little dagger does not compare to what Rush can do with a sword."

"It's fine," Rush said. "I'll wake you up when I get tired."

Someone approaches.

Rush stiffened, his hand gripping the hilt of his blade.

Bridge caught on, his eyebrows furrowed.

Rush pressed a forefinger to his lips.

Everyone stilled in place.

The footfalls started in the distance.

They grew louder.

And louder.

When they were near, Rush could distinguish the details. Whatever it was, it was heavy, massive, with feet with enough heft to shake the rock with every step.

Sounds like an orc.

Too heavy for an orc.

Rush focused on the crevasse in the rock and spotted the black hide of an enormous creature. Seven or eight feet tall, with long black hair that covered the back of its neck, it had arms that bulged with muscles and shoulders that were broader than any man's. The view only lasted a split second, and Rush absorbed as many details as he could.

It is an orc.

I've never seen an orc that looks like that. Is he alone?

Why?

Just answer the question.

No. You answer the question.

I'm gonna take him down.

Why?

Because he knows the way out of this place.

The footsteps started to quiet as the enormous orc moved past the opening.

Too dangerous.

It's a lot more dangerous than wandering around this place with those *things* lurking around.

You have no idea what you're up against.

I'll just sneak up behind him and shank him. Done.

The footsteps stopped.

The orc sucked in a deep breath.

A loud sniff.

He smells you.

Of course he does...

Quick. Before he alerts the others.

Rush pushed through the crevasse to get back onto the path, his sword gripped at his side.

The orc had already turned around, his enormous black eyes narrowed on Rush. A behemoth, every breath expanded his bare chest, the muscles of his torso, his ribs, his chest all moving together like plates of armor. He carried no weapon—because his body was the weapon.

His breaths were audible as quiet growls, his shoulders rising and falling with the movement of his lungs. His black lips pulled back as if to smile, but a second row of teeth emerged, pushing over his jaw and protruding out.

Oh, just lovely...

He's going to scream.

If I miss, all I have is my bow—

Then don't miss!

The orc bent forward and inhaled a deep breath to give his shout.

Now!

Rush threw the sword—impaling him right in the throat.

The orc staggered back before he fell to the stone floor with a thud.

How am I supposed to question him now?

You wouldn't have been able to question him while he feasted on your flesh either.

Rush ran over and looked down at the impaled orc. **Uh, he's still alive.** Vicious black eyes stared up at him, narrowed and menacing.

He must be paralyzed because he's not reaching for you.

Damn, that was a pretty good shot.

Rush.

Rush kneeled down. "Tell me the way out of here, and I'll end you."

"What in the...?" Bridge came over but kept his distance. "What is that thing?"

"I think it's an orc," Liam said. "But I've never seen an orc like this before."

"Look at his teeth!" Lilac pointed at his face. "He's like a dragon."

What did she just say?

"Guys, keep it down, alright?" Rush said. "More might be coming." He turned back to the orc. "We got a deal or what?"

The dark stare continued.

He can't speak because of the blade.

What if I pull it out and he screams?

That's a real possibility.

This place is a maze. We'll never figure it out without some help.

It's risky, but I understand.

"I'm gonna pull this out. If you scream, I'll smash your skull with this rock until it's ground beef, alright?" He propped up the rock with his palm. "Here we go." He grabbed the sword by the hilt and tugged it out.

Blood started to pool at his throat.

"Tell me the way out of the mountain."

He stared, his large eyes shifting back and forth, and then he opened his mouth and released a blood-curdling scream.

"You asshole." Rush grabbed the rock and smashed it down on his face.

No blood! They'll see.

Rush grabbed the orc's thick head and snapped his neck.

Hide!

"Help me." Rush hooked his arms under his shoulders.

"Help you what?" Bridge asked. "We've got to run!"

"I don't have time to explain." Rush tried to drag him, but he was too massive. "Just do it!"

Loud screams came from the opposite way.

Quickly!

They all grabbed a body part and pushed him through the crevasse, getting him into the darkness and out of the path.

A sea of footsteps approached.

What if they smell us?

They'll probably keep going until they find this guy.

And if not?

Then we're dinner.

The footsteps echoed in the cave, the sound so loud none of them could hear themselves breathe. The green glow was vanquished when the black bodies obscured all the light. Growls and roars accompanied their footfalls—as if the orcs were marching to war.

They all stayed still, an enormous corpse on top of all of them.

The blackness passed and the footfalls faded.

That was close.

What do we do now?

We gotta move.

I'm sure they left Fazurks behind.

Fazurks?

It means The Big Ugly.

We know there's no exit the way we came, and if we don't leave this cave, they'll find us on the way back. They didn't pay attention now, but they'll definitely be combing every inch of this place on their return.

True.

"Pack up your things. We're leaving."

"What about the orc?" Bridged asked.

"Leave the Fazurk," Rush said.

"Fazurk?" Bridge asked. "Did you just make that up?"

"Flare did," Rush said. "It means The Big Ugly in dragon."

Lilac gave a nod in appreciation. "Hit the nail right on the head."

THE CAVES BECAME BIGGER, EXPANDING AS THEY INCHED CLOSER to the surface.

The elevation is changing—slowly.

That slide must have taken us all the way to the bottom.

Should have gone a different way.

And end up right in their den? No. We shouldn't have come in the first place.

There was no way to know, Rush.

My stupidity is going to get everyone killed.

We've survived worse.

Uh, no, we haven't. We could always fly away, but now that's not an option for us. You're doing great down here, by the way.

I have to.

Rush knew they were about to head into trouble when the orcs' voices started to reach their ears. So deep it didn't seem real, they were vile, accompanied by growls between words. It was hard to make out what they were saying, but they seemed to speak a common tongue.

They approached the entrance to an enormous cavern, flames visible in a huge fireplace. Their silhouettes were distinct shadows, cast against the wall in a distorted proportion.

Rush kneeled behind the rock and watched.

"What are you thinking?" Bridge came to his side.

"I've been out of good ideas since the moment we decided to come here."

"You think this is what Mathilda meant?"

Rush slowly turned his head to regard him, the truth hitting him like a woman's palm against his cheek. "I hate witches."

"I wonder why she didn't tell you."

"Because her warning was enough—and she did say there was nothing but death here."

"But still..."

"She doesn't care whether I live or die. Clearly."

"She seemed to care when she gave Cora those dragon tears."

"I think that was for Cora—not me." He looked into the cavern again, distinguishing long tables and a roast turning on the spit over the fire. There were mugs on the counter, probably filled with the ale they stole from the dwarves.

There were only two options. To step into the cavern with the Fazurks or to take the cave to the left of it.

"Should we sneak past them?" Just when Bridge asked the question, two Fazurks left the cavern and disappeared into the cave that would be their escape plan. Another Fazurk passed in the opposite direction. "Alright…maybe sneaking isn't going to work."

"This must be their settlement—next to the entrance. Flare says our elevation is much higher than when we started, so I think we started at the bottom and are near the top."

"Maybe. Or maybe we're just in the middle…"

"Don't even say that, man."

"The area is big enough for Flare. He can move right to the entrance and set the entire cavern ablaze. Like fish in a barrel."

"True."

"I think that's a pretty good plan."

"Except one thing…"

"What?"

"The rest will know we're here—and we have to run *through* them."

"But at least we won't be chased from behind."

"I suppose..."

"I think it's worth a try. We don't have any other options."

Rush sagged against the rock. "I'm sorry I got you into this."

"You didn't get me into anything, Rush. I wanted to be here."

"Well, I'm about to get you and your sister killed. We're going to be the next roast over that fire."

"Even if that's true, we chose to be here. It's not your fault, Rush."

He bowed his head.

Bridge gave him a clap on the shoulder. "Did you really make it all the way here just to die?"

"Seems that way."

"No. We're going to figure it out. We always do."

Rush?

Hmm?

There's someone here.

Rush immediately turned around to check the rear. "If there was a Fazurk behind me, I think I'd know."

No. Not behind.

Then in front of us? Because I see them come and go.

Not a Fazurk.

There's someone else here?

Yes. They're pressing against my mind.

Is it Cora?

No. Her mind feels different.

Push back.

Every time I try, they retreat. They are trying to feel my mind without being felt in return.

Maybe try talking to them?

I will.

"What's going on?" Bridge asked, recognizing the look on Rush's face.

"He says there's somebody here—and not a Fazurk."

"Really?" Bridge asked. "Can they help us?"

"I don't know. It's clear they don't trust Flare because every time Flare pushes back, they retreat. They are trying to feel us out."

"Well…I think this is good news."

"At least we know we aren't alone."

"Hold on a sec." Bridge dropped his gaze. "That whole talking with your minds thing…isn't that something only dragons can do? Well, except for Cora."

"Yes."

"So, does that mean...there's a dragon here?"

"It's possible. But I doubt it."

"Why?"

"Because I never knew these Fazurks existed until now. They must have breached the mountain from the north, a place inaccessible to Anastille except by flight. So, if they exist... what else could exist? We've only scratched the surface. Plus, dragons don't live underground."

"Oh, that's right."

"I don't know whether they're friend or foe...and I wouldn't make any assumptions."

I INTRODUCED MYSELF—BUT I WAS MET WITH SILENCE.

Not sure if that was a good idea or not...but it is what it is.

Why would it be a bad idea?

Because our enemy could know exactly who's inside their mountain.

Whoops.

We're probably going to die anyway, so I guess it doesn't really matter. "Alright, you guys ready for this?"

All equipped with swords, they stayed in the rear, doing their best not to look like cornered rabbits.

"Just stay behind me."

They snuck past the large cavern where the Fazurks waited for their meat to finish its roast over the fire and entered the tunnel just to the left. It was a long cave with a curve at the end, and there was noticeable light coming around the bend.

"Sunlight?" Bridge whispered.

"Probably firelight." Rush took the lead with his sword gripped at his side, sticking to the wall toward the inner curve. He crept closer and closer and poked his head around the side. It was quite the view, a large cavern that extended far above his sight in the cave. A wooden bridge crossed a chasm, scaffolding was all along the walls, large stone bowls with enormous fires all along the bridges and the walls. But what he noticed was the light shining down from above.

Sunlight.

You see that?

Yep.

So close.

Fazurks marched everywhere, from one side of the bridge to the other, all throughout the cavern that led to the opening somewhere at the top of the mountain.

If the opening is large enough, I can fly us out.

I doubt it's big enough, Flare. It's probably an opening they created themselves.

I can still burn as many of them as I can.

But if you burn the bridges, we'll never escape.

So, you intend to run all the way there?

You got a better idea?

Guess not.

"What's the plan here?" Lilac joined the circle, the only one looking reasonable with a dwarf-sized sword in her hand.

Rush gave a shrug. "Run."

"That's your brilliant plan?" Lilac asked. "Run?"

Liam glanced behind him. "I hear footsteps."

Now the adrenaline kicked in because this was really about to happen, and some of them wouldn't make it to the top—or any of them. "There's sunlight, so there's got to be an opening somewhere. We run across the bridge and make our way to the top."

"With a bunch of Fazurks chasing us?" Zane asked.

"If there's room, Flare will emerge and burn them while you escape," Rush said.

Bridge shifted his gaze to his sister. "You don't leave my side, alright?"

"Oh, come on," she said. "You're just as useless as I am."

Liam turned back to the group. "They're gonna hear us any minute. It's now or never."

"This is suicide," Zane said. "But at least it'll be a good story... if anyone lives to tell it."

Bridge turned to Rush, his eyes sad, his smile forced.

Rush ignored his look and started to run.

Flare fused their minds deeper together, an electrifying connection that allowed Rush to see the landscape better than with his sight alone. He could see behind him, on the side past his regular peripheral vision. The entire cave was mapped out.

Guide me.

Across the bridge.

Roooooaaaaaar!

One by one, the Fazurks released their howls, erupting all around them in a violent protest. The sounds echoed in the cavern, back and forth against the walls like a bouncing ball, amplifying the sound until anything else could scarcely be heard.

Left.

Rush made it across the bridge and turned away from the Fazurks coming from the other directions. He lost his footing running so fast but pushed himself upright again, his palms covered in dust from the floor.

Climb up this scaffold.

I can go straight.

Do it!

"Climb up." He grabbed Lilac first and tossed her up so she could grab the bar. "Go."

Hold them back.

Rush unsheathed his sword with a burst of energy, the power of the dragon in his veins. The Fazurks were two feet taller, several times bigger in size, and had teeth that could cut through his bones. But he swung his blade with the strength of ten men and sliced the head clean from its shoulders.

The Fazurks stopped.

Their teeth broke through their jaws a moment later, along with their screams.

I will tell you when to run.

The first rushed at him, coming at him with bare hands and claws.

Rush sidestepped the attack, swiped the blade clean through both wrists, and then kicked him aside. The Fazurk tumbled over the edge, screaming as he fell to the ground below. **I wouldn't be able to do this without you.**

I wouldn't be free without you.

Rush stabbed the next one through the stomach and then kicked the one that came for him, teeth first. Another head was sliced off the shoulders, the heavy body collapsing a moment later.

Dozens more came for him.

Run.

Rush sprinted to the scaffolding and jumped as high as he could, reaching far higher than he would as just a man, and pulled himself up as quickly as he could.

Lilac and Bridge pushed a boulder over the edge and smashed the Fazurks hot on his tail.

Thanks, guys.

He reached the top and grabbed on to Liam's and Zane's hands, who yanked him to the top of the scaffolding.

Push the scaffolding down.

Rush sliced through the rope that bound it to the wall, the Fazurks climbing up the wood like spiders up a wall. Together, they all pushed, making it topple over and smash the Fazurks beneath it.

Right.

"Let's go." Rush took the lead again, running along the wall to the next scaffold against the mountain.

Below them, a sea of Fazurks appeared, pouring out of the cavern from where they emerged, this time with swords.

Rush helped each one up the scaffolding and looked behind them, seeing them crawling up the walls with their bare hands. When he looked at the ceiling, he realized how far they had to go—and there were more Fazurks on the way. **Man, that's a long way.**

I will get you there. Now, climb.

Rush took up the rear, climbing up the wooden beams until his friends pulled him over the edge. The ropes were slashed, and they toppled it over like the other. "We gotta slow 'em down. Push the rocks over the edge."

They worked together to push them over the edge, to smash the Fazurks down below and slow their pace just a bit. They smashed the first group of Fazurks then rolled over the next edge, getting a whole other layer below.

Keep going.

They ran to the other side of the canyon, where the next scaffold was positioned.

Rush.

"Come on, go." He stitched his fingers together and took Lilac's boot so he could shove her up to grip the bar. **What?**

They are coming from the top.

Rush looked to the opening in the ceiling, catching glimpses of blue sky between enormous black bodies. They were flooding in from up top, like water from a faucet filling a basin. **That's the only way out of here...**

I know.

"Rush, come on." Bridge hung over the edge, his arm hanging down.

What are we going to do?

I don't know.

Rush started the climb, moving slower this time because there was no point. Whether they went up or down, their demise was guaranteed. **I can't let them die. We have to figure out a way.**

There's no room for me to fly or perch. And even if I could breathe fire, there's too many.

Rush let Bridge pull him over, and he climbed to his feet.

They immediately sprinted to the other scaffold, oblivious to Fazurks pouring in from the surface.

Rush remained, listening to the sound of thousands of footsteps from the top and down below. The roars of the beasts, the sound of victory before their teeth sank into their flesh. His life had been long, too long, so death wasn't a hard pill to swallow. But the death of those he cared about…would never fit down his throat.

Wait.

You have an idea?

Tell them to stop climbing.

Rush sprinted to the other side of the cavern, getting to Liam before he climbed up. "Hold on. Guys, come back down."

"What?" Bridge asked. "Why?"

"Just do it!" **What's your plan?**

Go straight.

Go straight where? There's nothing but rock.

Do what I say.

He moved to the cliff face, seeing nothing but solid rock. It was so smooth, there was nothing to even grab on to. No way to climb. **Flare, what am I supposed—**

Start knocking.

What?

They are coming.

Who?

Knock.

He started to pound his fists into the rock.

More.

"Guys, come on."

"Rush, is this a joke?" Bridge grabbed him by the shoulder.

Rush twisted out of his hold and kept pounding. "I don't have time to explain. Knock—as loudly as possible."

They all moved to the wall and started to pound their fists.

Louder.

"Louder!"

Lilac slammed the hilt of her sword into the wall, and the others did the same to protect their hands. Rush slammed his palms into the rock over and over, the sound of their enemy growing louder against their backs.

Rush stopped to turn around, seeing the Fazurks sprinting at them like ants out of a hill. "We're out of time."

No, we aren't.

The wall vibrated and shifted, forming a sliding door that revealed a dark passageway. There was no sign of a secret door in the rock, just a flat surface, camouflaged so well that it would fool anyone.

Now, go.

25

TALC

The door shut behind them and locked into place.

The Fazurks screamed on the other side, their fists pounding against the solid rock that now separated them. The roars were still audible, just muffled. It took Rush a moment for his eyes to adjust to the darkness since Flare had withdrawn his abilities. "What just happened?"

"Follow me." A deep voice pierced the darkness. His outline became visible, several feet shorter than Rush and several inches thicker around the waist and thighs. He turned down the dark passageway, his footsteps leading the way.

Bridge reached for Rush's arm in the darkness. "Is that a dwarf?"

"Yeah, I think so." **You asked them to help us?**

No.

So, you're saying they just offered?

Yes.

That was awfully nice of them…

Rush was the first one behind the dwarf, the passage so narrow and short that he had to crouch to get through most of it. His palms slid against the stone walls on either side of him for direction, so he wouldn't accidentally bump face-first into a solid wall. "What's your name?"

"Durir."

"Thank you, Durir."

"It wasn't me who saved ye."

"Where are you taking us?"

"To the last Stronghold in the mountain."

Well, it sounds like we aren't prisoners.

Even if we were, dwarven imprisonment would be preferable to a Fazurk meal.

No kidding. That was close. I thought we were done for.

We've survived worse.

Why do people keep saying that? No, I'm pretty sure that was the biggest close call we've ever had.

Ashe, King of Dragons, seemed intent on burning you to death.

That guy is all talk.

Grrrr.

Respectfully, of course.

After maneuvering through the dark passageways, they finally came to a large cavern similar to all the ones they'd already seen, illuminated by the green stones that provided a glow to all the corners. It was a storeroom, with racks of bottles and canned foods, preserved meats and other items.

Durir stepped aside until they all filed out before he gripped the handles jutting out of the rock, slowly rolling it into place and sealing the passageway. The rock thudded against the other wall, dust filtering from the ceiling, and then everything went still.

Rush stared at the sealed passageway. "Am I the only one in shock right now?"

"Nope." Bridge spun in a circle as he examined the contents of the room.

"I think the shock will hit me later," Lilac said. "I felt so stupid knocking on that dumb wall...guess it wasn't so stupid after all."

Rush moved to Durir. "We saw all the bodies in the caves... We feared the worst. It's a relief to know we were wrong."

"Yer weren't wrong." In the light, his features were so distinct, with bushy eyebrows and a beard as thick as a rug. A pudgy face squished together with fat cheeks and full lips, it was exactly as Rush remembered from a very long time ago.

"What do you mean?"

Durir nodded to the next passageway and continued forward.

Rush followed, the rest of the gang behind him.

They emerged into another large cavern, a throne at the top of a rock slab. Wooden benches filled the room, most of them empty, with the exception of a few dwarves that enjoyed a pint in solitude.

Durir continued, showing them a room full of bunk beds, some of them occupied, and then a large underground lake with a waterfall at the rear. That was where most of the dwarves were congregated, their feet in the water or their bodies floating. "This is all we have left." He guided them back to the first room, the one with the throne, which was now occupied.

The throne wasn't taken by a king, but a queen. With thick red hair, blue eyes, and a stocky figure like all the other dwarves, she sat on the chair carved out of rock, runes etched into the surface.

Her presence wasn't majestic or intimidating, not the way it was when he was in the presence of his own father, with Ashe, King of Dragons, or the elven kings throughout history. This ruler was as empty as the dark cave they'd just crawled through.

Her blue eyes barely acknowledged them, like they weren't even there.

Durir came to her side. "Megora, Queen of the Stronghold."

She turned her gaze away. "I am no queen. A queen has to be alive—and I'm not sure what I am anymore."

Is this who you spoke to?

No. It was a man.

Rush stepped forward. "My name is Rush—"

"I know your name, Rush Hawkehelm. You're a man who requires no introduction."

"Hope that's a good thing..."

She turned back, eyes still cold.

Or maybe not. "What happened here?"

"The son of a king should be able to figure it out."

You told them who I was?

Yes—both of us. They didn't ask any questions.

I'm so confused right now.

Megora continued. "They came from the north, invaded our mountain like the plague, infested it like rats in the sewers of Anastille. Our mountain has never been breached in our history. We were unprepared. They came, slaughtered us. All we could do was save the few nearest us. We closed off the Stronghold, where we stand now, and have remained ever since."

Rush bowed his head. "I'm sorry..."

"Our king made the hard decision—and has since lost his mind to madness. I have taken his place despite my dissent. We're no longer a kingdom—so there is no need for a ruler. We've remained here for years, living off what we have left in our storerooms, but for what reason, I do not know. Whether we perish now or later, what difference does it make?"

Silence crippled Rush as well as everyone else. The caves where they stood were haunted by the ghosts of the many dwarves that died so the few could live. "Have you tried to escape?"

"There's only one way out of this place—as ye've seen yourself."

"And the Fazurks have taken it over..."

Her eyes narrowed.

"That's what we call them," Rush said quickly.

Her head turned, and her gaze glossed over. "We're outnumbered a hundred to one. To attempt an escape is a promise of death."

"Why did you save us? You risked your position."

Her hands remained on the arms of the throne, her short nails dark from the dirt that slipped underneath them. "Whether they know we're here or not, they can't reach us."

You thought that last time.

"And if they could, it doesn't matter. We're doomed anyway."

Rush studied her composure, seeing the lifelessness in every part of her body, not just her eyes. "You didn't answer my question."

She turned her attention back to him.

"Why did you save us?"

I feel them again.

Here?

Yes. They are close.

Queen Megora studied his countenance. "Our world is underground, far away from the bickering of men and elves. You came to our shores and destroyed Anastille, and while we've remained unaffected by your conquest, it doesn't mean you're welcome in the Stronghold."

No surprise there...

"If you were anyone else, we would have left you to your fate. But you deserved to be spared."

"I did?" Rush asked. "Why?"

She rose to her feet, still short despite the slab of rock that elevated her above the others. With her eyes on Rush, she came closer, taking the stairs one step at a time, regarding him like she knew him from an older time. "Because you saved Talc—my dragon."

Queen Megora sat across from Rush at the table, pints of ale and canned food on the surface so everyone could eat. A fire was lit in the hearth, bringing warmth to the dark cave. "When Flare shared his identity, she asked me to spare ye. The answer was no, of course. But then she shared her memories with me, the night when you came to the dungeon and freed three dragons."

Rush hadn't touched his ale or the food they offered. His hands remained on the table, and he stared at the cracks in the wood, the veins of the tree that was now long dead. With heavy breaths, he remembered that night vividly.

At least one escaped.

Yeah.

Queen Megora studied him with intelligent eyes in heavyset cheeks. "Are ye alright?"

Rush gave a nod. "Just…a bit emotional. After I released them, pandemonium broke out. King Lux deployed his entire arsenal to retrieve them, and I feared what would happen once they were recaptured. I knew they would be worse off… and that's consumed my nights as well as my days."

The blades in her eyes noticeably dulled.

"To know that at least one escaped is a huge relief. How did you find her?"

"She crashed into the mountain—a broken wing."

Shamans.

I will burn them all.

"She didn't want to come into the mountain, but she had no choice. The plan was to heal her broken wing then let her fly farther north. But then the Fazurks came…and we had no choice but to fuse."

"So…this assault just happened?" Rush asked.

Queen Megora gave a nod.

"What do you know about the Fazurks?"

"They are orcs—but not a kind we can identify."

"They must be from the north. But how did they pass through the mountains?"

Her blue eyes took on a vacancy. "That's unknown. There are no paths through the solid rock. There's no way over or beneath. We know they're from the Shadow Lands, but we don't know how they passed through."

"The Shadows Lands?"

"It's what we call the north."

"Why do you call it that? Have you been there?"

"Everything we know has been passed down through the generations. But no living dwarf has passed the border in thousands of years, so it could just be folklore at this point." Her ale was untouched, her bushy hair pulled back into a braid down her back. "Sunshine doesn't penetrate the clouds. It's a cold and dark place. It's not a land inhabited by civilized beings, but by *things* that live in the dark."

Rush grabbed his mug and took a deep drink. "Sounds like the perfect place for those Fazurks."

"The Big Ugly..." Megora released a quiet chuckle. "Aptly named."

Have you spoken to Talc?

Not yet.

"Why have the Fazurks penetrated the border now?" It was a question more to himself than Queen Megora. "Because crossing the border would be more work than it's worth…unless they had a reason."

"There was no time to ask questions, Rush. We were too busy running for our lives."

"How did they break in to the mountain?"

"By sheer numbers. Broke it down and passed right through."

Rush reached into his pocket and withdrew the folded piece of paper he'd found on the corpse of a fallen dwarf. "I found this. You can return it to the rightful recipient…if they're still alive."

Her eyes scanned it quickly before she folded it once again. "Bargora is no longer with us. But Rulan survives. I'll be sure to give this to him."

Rush nodded.

"What did you see?"

He kept his eyes down.

"What did they do to my people?"

He still couldn't lift his eyes. "They fought to their last breath…and there were no survivors."

The queen continued to pierce her stare into him, her pale face slowly filling with a flush that turned her cheeks red. Not rosy pink. But blood red.

"Are you the king's daughter?"

"No. The royal line perished in the assault. I was elected by my people—which is the first time it's ever happened in our history."

"How many of you remain?"

"One thousand and twenty-three." Unlike most queens, she wasn't covered in diamonds and elegance. There were no distinguishing characteristics that elevated her status whatsoever. But the passion for her people gave her a distinct quality that separated her visage from all the rest.

"And how many perished?"

"Seven thousand and eighty-four."

"Perhaps there are still survivors somewhere in the mountain. The cave system is extensive, and I suspect we only traversed a very small part of the territory."

"Even if that's true, we'll never know. We are not only separated by rock, but by beasts that roam our halls and claim it as their own. When their storage supplies deplete, they will perish—just like us."

"Then you need to escape."

"One thousand against ten thousand?" Her eyebrow arched high up her face, her deep voice taking a note of incredulity.

"I didn't say fight them. I said escape."

"The only way out of here is through that same passage from which ye arrived."

"Then how did you get all this stuff in here?"

"A cavern. A cavern that we destroyed to keep them out."

She must escape. Not just for our sake—but for Talc's.

"Talc can't stay underground. Captivity has poisoned the mind of your king. It's snuffed out all your hope as well. Imagine how he must feel—a creature of the sky."

Her eyes immediately dropped.

"She can't stay here."

"Then where would she go?" she asked. "The second she's outside the mountain, she'll be hunted."

"I know a place where she'll be safe."

"Where?"

Rush kept her gaze as well as his silence.

Her stare demanded answers, but she didn't press with her words. "We have a few Durgin, but not enough for us to get away. And certainly not enough for us to defeat them."

"Durgin?"

"Warriors."

Talc will fuse with Bridge, and we'll get her out of here when we depart.

That could work. "When we escape, we'll take Talc with us. She'll fuse with one of us and then unfuse once it's safe."

"Escape?"

"We can't stay here, Queen Megora."

"Ye'll have to. Because we can't open the passageway again. They'll be waiting for it."

Flare's mind instantly changed, becoming bigger, thicker, like a rattlesnake uncoiling its body. The click from his throat was audible, like his lungs were about to light a fire that would consume them all.

"We aren't staying here." Rush bored his gaze into hers, the anger swelling under his skin, the rage tinting his eyes red. "We're on a mission that can't be halted."

"I can't risk what we have left."

"You just said this isn't living—just waiting for death."

"But it is still living. I have women and children in here. I already risked our safety by saving ye from the Fazurks, so yer request is full of entitlement and insensitivity. Be grateful that your lungs still draw breath."

I will burn each dwarf, one by one, until she changes her mind.

Calm down.

I will not. I will not stay here. I will not be a captive once again. I will not dwell underground without seeing the sky. I will not succumb to this torture—

Flare, I will get us out of here. I promise.

His mind pressed to every corner of their consciousness, trying to break free from the anxiety, the fear, the desperation. The distress transferred from his mind to Rush's, along with all the terror, the pain, the memories.

I know you're scared.

Silence.

It's okay to be scared.

Silence.

But I will get you out of here. You will see the sky once again. You will feel the wind beneath your wings. Your scales will shine in the sun once more. I will not stop until I make it happen. Just give me some time.

26

THE SACRIFICE OF THE DURGIN

THEY LAY down on their cots and settled in for the night, having some privacy in a secluded cave off the main path. Their bellies were filled with fresh food for the first time since they'd arrived in the mountains, and the ale gave a nice numbing effect behind the eyes and in the stomach.

Bridge leaned up against the wall beside him. "I know she's just trying to protect her people and all that, but what's the point? Unless they know someone is coming to save them, they're just going to die anyway. They may as well try to get out of here, and if they don't, allow us to leave."

Flare was still pressing against Rush's mind, but he was distant, just as he was when he was asleep. But he definitely wasn't asleep now. A barrier divided their minds, giving Flare both the solitude and silence he needed. The only time they were separated was in sleep, and a lot of the time, they chose to sleep at the same time. So, this separation was difficult, especially when he knew his dragon suffered. "I agree."

"So, what are we going to do? Because dying in this mountain is not how my story ends."

"It's no secret that everybody hates me. But Talc convinced Megora to save me."

"Yeah. What's your point?"

"I think she can convince Megora to let us go."

"Yeah, you're probably right," he said. "So, let's do it. What are you waiting for?"

"Flare."

"What about him?"

"He's…inaccessible right now."

"Why? Did you piss him off?"

His eyes narrowed. "No. But thanks."

"Then what's going on?"

"He's really worked up. Dragons aren't meant to be underground, and he's not handling it well."

"He handled it up until this point."

"But then Megora said she wouldn't let us go…and that sent him over the edge."

Bridge gave a slow nod. "Gotcha."

"So, when he comes around, I'll talk to Talc."

"What do you know about Talc?"

"Honestly, nothing. But she saved me, so that's a good sign."

"Yeah."

Everyone else got into their cots and pulled the blankets to their shoulders. There was little warmth underground, and the longer they were away from the sun, the more their limbs started to frost.

"Did you try to talk to Cora?" Bridge asked before he took a drink from his canteen.

"Still can't reach her..."

"Too bad. Because we could really use Callon's help right now."

Rush folded his arms over his chest as he crossed his ankles, his back propped up by the cave wall. "Hmm, that's not a bad idea."

"What?" Bridge twisted the cap onto the bottle then stowed it in his pack.

"If the elves helped us with the Fazurks, we could free the dwarves."

"But what's the point of that?" He pulled his jacket out of his bag and put it on, the dampness in the air from the nearby waterfall bringing him a chill. "There's only a thousand dwarves left. They aren't ideal allies anymore."

"But these mountains are huge. There could be others."

"Wouldn't they have helped us if they were there?"

"Why? They have no obligation, unlike Talc."

Bridge gave a slight nod. "It's a lot to ask of the elves. They come to fight for a chance there *could* be more dwarves? And let's not forget, they despise you."

"But they don't despise Cora."

He gave a shrug. "It's still a long shot."

"If we help the dwarves now, and there are more, they'll be our allies later. It's called public relations. The dwarves have no investment in the happenings of Anastille, so we need to secure an alliance in some way. This is the way to do that."

"Rush, it's a long shot. A *really* long shot."

"But if I could make it work, we could accomplish exactly what we came here for."

It took Flare a day to come back to Rush.

They spent that time in the cave, keeping to themselves. Most of the dwarves didn't seem to be aware of their presence at all, but that would probably change once word spread that Queen Megora had granted asylum to a human.

I have an idea.

I hope it's a good one.

We talk to Talc—and ask her to convince the queen. She convinced her to save us in the first place.

Yes. That does make sense.

So, patch me through.

Hold on. I need to gain her permission first.

Alright.

A couple minutes later, Flare returned. *I'll connect you. But I must warn you, she's feisty.*

And you aren't?

Flare ignored the taunt and connected their minds. *Talc, here's Rush.*

It was no different from speaking to Cora, but it felt like an entirely new experience. When he spoke with Ashe, it was a constant discomfort. It wasn't a natural feeling, not the way it was with Flare and Cora. It felt like an intrusion, like he was somewhere he didn't belong. **Thank you for saving us from the Fazurks.**

<u>*A scale for a scale.*</u> Her voice was just as powerful as Flare's, just distinctly feminine. <u>*My debt is repaid.*</u>

Thank you, nonetheless.

<u>*You saved a few of my brethren, but this doesn't forgive your cruelty. We are enemies as far as I'm concerned.*</u>

"Damn, you weren't kidding." **I know this doesn't mean much to you—**

<u>*Then don't speak it.*</u>

I just want you to understand that I'm committed to freeing every dragon enslaved by my father.

And what of the ones that have already died?

Rush sighed.

The ones that died in their cages? The ones that were killed for refusing to be a pet?

His mind shut down, as if wounded by a blade between the ribs.

Talc, I understand how difficult this is for you. There was a time in my life when I hated Rush as much as you do. But he's a good man—on my honor.

Perhaps we have different standards of good—and yours is very low.

Or I've just witnessed his character in a way no one else ever has. It doesn't matter where you start, but where you end up. He's risking his life to free all the dragons in captivity. He's prepared to kill his father if he refuses to surrender. He's our ally.

Talc ignored his words. *What do you want from me?*

To thank you. And also ask for your help.

My debt is repaid. I owe you nothing—not even this conversation.

We need to get out of this mountain, and I'm sure you wish for that as well.

And go where? There's no place in Anastille for free dragons. My scales will shine in the sun—and those demons will spot me from a mile away. I was too weak to fight when I escaped, but I'm weak still.

We have a place for you. A place where you'll be free.

No such place exists.

It does. Ashe, King of Dragons, lives.

Silence.

He's on a hidden island far out in the sea. The surviving free dragons live there—in peace. I will take you there at the first opportunity.

The silence continued.

I speak the truth, Talc.

If free dragons survive, why are you here?

Because I have to save the ones that remain behind. It's our duty. You've suffered enough, so you deserve to live in peace, if that's what you wish. But we can't accomplish that if we're stuck underground. You must convince Queen Megora to let us go.

And how will I escape?

You'll fuse with one of our men.

Her voice deepened, injecting venom into the air. *Never.*

Talc—

I'll fuse with a dwarf. Even an elf. But never a human. Humans are Shamans that don't hide their face.

Not all humans are that way. You can trust us.

I trust you—but not him.

There is no other way to get you out of here. I give you my word that Bridge will allow you to unfuse whenever you wish. He's not like the men you're used to. I know that's hard to understand after thousands of years of captivity. But the world is changing. Men are changing. We're not the only ones who want King Lux off the throne. It's also elves. It's also men.

Silence.

The other option is to leave you here—under the mountain. We can reunite you with your people, on a beautiful island that's far away from everyone and everything, and you can be free once more. But we can't do that unless you come with us.

What if he won't allow me to unfuse?

Then I'll eat him.

Silence.

You have my word, Talc.

After a long stretch of silence, her voice emerged. *If I escape with you, I may be forced into a fuse. I may die in the attempt to flee. But if I stay here…I'll die under a mountain…and not even leave behind my bones.*

I agree.

Do you have a plan?

Yes—but I need your help.

What do you wish of me?

You must convince Megora to let us go. If that passage is the only way out of this place, we must take it.

That is a terrible plan. You didn't make it out the first time. Why would you escape the second time?

We'll figure it out.

There're too many, Flare. And now they are watching. Without help, you'll have no chance.

Perhaps you can convince her of that as well—to help us.

Unlikely. She already spared you because of me. I can't convince her to make another sacrifice—at least not without something in return.

I need you to try.

Silence.

Our lives depend on it.

Another stretch of silence passed. *I will do my best.*

RUSH RUBBED THE TOWEL OVER HIS HAIR TO GET THE WATER OUT of the strands, tugging it back and forth to get the scalp to dry. They sat together at the edge of the dark pool, the rest of the dwarves clearing out the moment they approached the lake created by the waterfall in the rear. Rush shook out the towel to dispel the drops before he rolled it up to return to his pack.

"I miss bathing." Bridge did the same with his towel, wringing it in his hands so the moisture dripped onto the rock. "I had my own bathroom...until you came along."

"And I had my own castle—get over it."

Flare interrupted the conversation. *Queen Megora wishes to speak with us.*

Did Talc convince her?

That was all she told me. Let's go.

Rush closed his pack and left it at Bridge's side. "Gotta go. Megora wants a word."

"Don't be a smartass, alright?" Bridge said. "Because we all want to get out of this black-widow paradise."

"Got it." Rush left the cavern and returned to the room with the throne, finding the dwarf at one of the wooden tables with a pint of ale in front of her. Rush had never witnessed this level of casualness with anyone, not his father or the rulers of Eden Star. "Don't like the throne?"

Her eyes looked over the edge of the mug as she took a drink. "It's a rock. Very hard. And very cold."

Rush took a seat on the bench across from her, his pint already waiting for him.

Her hand remained on the handle of her drink as she stared. "Your request is denied."

Smoke poured from Flare's nostrils, the fire in his stomach as well as his belly. Rush could feel it rather than see it, feel the rage his dragon struggled to contain. "Why?"

"Because of the reasons I already gave."

"Your dragon wishes to be free—and you deny her?"

Her intelligent eyes narrowed. "That's not what I said—"

"Talc wishes to be free, and you're not allowing it. That's what I'm hearing."

The anger burned like a fire that had just received an extra log. Anger turned to rage. Embers turned to flames. "She won't make it out of here. None of ye will."

"We have a chance—if you help us."

"Help you? How?"

"If you give some of your fighters, it'll give us a distraction long enough to escape."

"You expect me to sacrifice the Durgin I have left? I've always known men are selfish and entitled, but this reaches new heights."

"Megora, men, elves, and dwarves all have the same beliefs. Some will die so others will live."

"You aren't one of us." Blue eyes flicked back and forth, cheeks red with the strain of her anger. "I will not sacrifice my people for you."

"No one knows the dwarves are compromised. No one is coming to save you, Megora. Your people will die of starvation or cannibalism, waiting for aid that will never come. But if you help us escape, I can help you escape later."

The beer was neglected entirely, put off to the side.

"Talc and Flare alone can extinguish them from the skies."

"What about the ones deep underground? You can't help us."

"No. But I can send people who can."

"Who?" Her arms rested on the table, and she leaned forward. "Men don't care about anyone but themselves. They will not come."

"I will ask the elves."

"The elves?" She sat back slightly, the word like poison on her tongue. "They're just as reclusive as men, and they have no reason to help us."

"They're preparing to take on King Lux. They need as many allies as they can get for the war about to ensue. Help me escape, and I will return with the elves to liberate you, to cleanse the invaders from the mountain you call home. In exchange, you will fight with us."

"That's two favors for the price of one—I know my math."

"Bringing an army to rid the plague that's infested your mountain is more than the equivalent of two favors. You know numbers, but I know what those numbers are worth."

Megora turned quiet, her long nails tapping against the wooden table between them. "I've lived under this mountain for a long time, indifferent to the happenings of Anastille, but

I'm not stupid. The elves hate men as much as they hate dragons. And you're telling me General Rush can just march into their forest and call for aid?"

"Well, it wouldn't happen like that. I have a powerful ally among the elves. She can make it happen."

"But there's no guarantee."

"Nothing in life is guaranteed. But I promise you, I will do everything I can to make this happen."

"And if the elves deny your request?"

Rush gave a shrug. "I'll figure out another way. Flare and I can do a lot of damage just from the air. Lure them aboveground and torch them to smithereens."

Her eyes were a striking blue but seemed to be covered with a permanent film of dust. Dirt from the rocks. Grime from the mold adhered to the surfaces. Slightly green from the stones that illuminated the caves. "I'm putting our fate into your hands, Rush. Do you understand that?"

"I do."

"You're asking me to trust you, when the entirety of human history has proven how untrustworthy you are."

"I'm not like them—anymore."

"I can ask the few Durgin we have to sacrifice themselves in the hope that you return with the forces we need to save the rest of us. But do you understand the weight of that request? I'm asking my men to literally die for yours."

"Either a few die now, or you all die later. Not to sound heartless, but that's your reality. I'm sorry."

After a heavy stare with sagged shoulders, she gave a nod. "I will grant your request."

Told you.

Flare released a sigh of relief.

"When can we leave?"

"I must speak to the Durgin first. I will not order anyone to their deaths. It must be voluntary."

"I understand."

"But it shouldn't take long to receive the answer."

"You'll need to unfuse from Talc so she can refuse with Bridge. Is there a cavern large enough for us to do that?"

A long stare ensued. "Talc will not be going with you."

Grrrrrrrr.

Rush sized up his opponent, realizing her presence was far bigger than her height. "We already established that she can't stay here."

"It's the only leverage I have. If you don't find a way to free us, then you don't free Talc either. Consider it motivation."

"I don't need motivation. You already have my word."

"Not good enough. If you truly intend to free us, then Talc staying behind a little longer shouldn't matter."

She is cunning.

I have a different c-word in mind.

But she's strategic. She knows the dragons are our priority. We will fight much harder for her than any of the dwarves. I'm angry—but I also respect her wisdom.

"We have a deal, General Rush?" Her eyes studied his face, as if she was aware of the conversation going on inside his mind, because she had her own conversation occurring at the exact same time.

"It's just Rush." He swallowed the disappointment and pushed on. "And yes, we have a deal."

"Am I the only one who doesn't think that's vile?" Lilac leaned against the wall, one arm propped on her knee. A meager dinner was in front of her, stale bread, assorted cheeses, and a pint of ale—a traditional Dwarven feast. "How is she any different from King Lux?"

"I agree." Bridge was against the opposite wall, his fingers tearing the hard bread apart so it was easier to chew on.

"I don't like it either," Rush said. "But it is different."

Liam cocked his eyebrow in disbelief. "How?"

"A ruler will do anything for her people." Rush gave a shrug. "And that's exactly what she's doing."

"If the positions were switched, you wouldn't do such a thing." Bridge got a piece into his mouth, slowly chewing because the chunk was so stiff.

"I'd like to think so…" His eyes dropped. "But we know my track record. And Talc doesn't seem to feel oppressed. When we spoke with her, she seemed content with the fuse. It still appears consensual, in a complicated way."

"So, how's this going to happen?" Lilac said. "Some poor dwarves run out there and get eaten while we book it?"

Bridge's fat cheeks stilled for a moment, disgust moving across his face.

Rush kept his eyes down in shame. "Yeah, I guess. It's voluntary, so there may be no dwarves at all. If that's the case, then—"

"Rush." Queen Megora approached, stepping into their enclave, her petite frame casting a long shadow on the wall from the lantern behind her. Her red hair was clipped back, her boots were scuffed and worn, her jacket wrinkled from the constant dampness in the air. But she still had the presence of authority.

Rush pushed off the wall so he could get to his feet, abandoning the meal that he hadn't touched.

Her blue eyes focused on his face, hot with open hostility. "You have five Durgin."

Sheer surprise moved into his expression—because he hadn't even expected one. "Five? That's—"

"An incredible sacrifice. I explained that if we free you, you will return with forces to eradicate the parasites that have infected our mountain, which will give the dwarves another chance to reclaim our home. These dwarves lost their families in the conquest—and welcome death."

Speechless, Rush stood there, unable to offer remorse or gratitude.

"The exodus will ensue at nightfall."

"We're doing this tonight?" Rush asked in surprise.

"Yes."

"You know night and day when you're in here?" There were no cracks in the rock, nor hints of sunlight anywhere in the Stronghold. It was perpetual twilight, a gentle glow that mirrored starlight coming from the rocks stuck to the caverns like moss on a tree.

"With fire, the Durgin will run into the mountain, and like the dogs they are, the invaders will follow. That will be your opportunity to escape."

"We'll be going against the herd. I don't see how it'll be possible for us to escape."

"Because you'll climb."

"Up the scaffolding?"

"No. Straight up the wall."

"Like spiders?" His eyebrows jumped up on his face.

She wore no hint of amusement. "Dwarves are excellent climbers."

"You're going to have to give us a few pointers, then."

Queen Megora turned to the dwarves standing behind her. After she gave a nod, they came forward and presented apparatuses. They appeared to be metal vambraces but were only solid on the posterior side. Three distinct circles were fused to the metal, and inside those circles were three bright green spots, plump like pillows. The second piece looked like a metal shoe, with the green pillows on the heel of the foot as well as the toe. "Climbers. We've used them for centuries to scale the inside of caverns as we continue building our infrastructure. A dwarf has never fallen in our history—not with these."

Rush took one and examined it, eyeing the green material inside the ring. "What is this?"

Bridge pressed it into the wall beside him, and when he let it go, it hung there. "Neat." He grabbed it to tug it down, and his hand slipped because the hold was so strong. "Whoa…" He tried again, using both hands to yank it off, but nothing worked. "I can see why no one has ever fallen…"

Queen Megora's stocky arms remained at her sides as she watched Bridge with a look that was borderline bored. "Twist."

"What?" Bridge turned back to her.

"Twist. The sponge will release."

Bridge did as she instructed, and effortlessly, it came free with a quiet pop.

Rush tested it out himself against the wall, hearing the popping noise over and over.

Fascinating.

"Did you find these sponges in the Stronghold?" Rush asked.

"Yes," Queen Megora said. "They can only be found deep underground, near sources of water. They're long-lasting and highly durable. I suggest you spend the day practicing." The longer her stare lingered, the colder it became. "This sacrifice can't be in vain. It's the first time my people have felt hope—and you'd better not take that away."

27

BLOOD, FLESH, AND BONE

THE ROCK WAS STILL in place, blocking the path to the tunnel that led to the outside cavern. The torches on the walls were lit, giving the place greater illumination than it'd ever had before. The color of the rock was distinct now, along with the shine of moisture that clung to all the surfaces. Rush's heart would normally be pounding like a drum, like it always did when he was on the precipice of something big. But this time, it was still like a shallow river. This time, it was lifeless, like this very mountain.

The Durgin were lined up near the opening, dressed in the thick armor of the dwarves, an image of their mountain as a crest on their chests. Axes were over their backs, along with swords. Little blades protruded from their belts. Their helmets were solid metal, covering so much of their face, it was unclear how they could see anything besides what was directly in front of them. They were about to march to their deaths, but they were so still and calm that it seemed like they had other plans. They didn't breathe heavily. There wasn't a drop of fear in their eyes.

I've never known anyone so brave.

Nor have I.

Other dwarves stood at the entrance to the cavern, silently saying goodbye to the Durgin that would die now so they could live later.

Queen Megora walked up to each one and spoke to them in Dwarvish. It seemed to be a saying because she said the same words to each and every one of them. Her hand went to each of their shoulders as she passed, letting it linger for a few seconds before she continued forward.

I feel like shit.

As do I.

We shouldn't have come here.

We had to come, Rush. We're the villains now—but we will return as heroes.

The rock was rolled to the side—and the pathway was revealed.

The Durgin held up their torches, and as the rest of the dwarves broke out into a somber song, Queen Megora lit each one.

One by one, they stepped into the passage.

Instantly, Rush's words came out, audible over the song, just before the last Durgin left. "Thank you…"

Slowly, a Durgin turned and regarded Rush, the torch held high over his head. Eye contact ensued, dark eyes hidden beneath bushy eyebrows. It lasted for seconds, a contact so powerful that it went deeper than flesh. "Save my people. Save the Stronghold. That is the only gratitude I need." He followed behind the others and disappeared inside the passage.

Durir stayed at the entrance and watched them move down to the other end, one hand on the handle of the rock, prepared to roll it back into place if the Fazurks managed to get inside.

They all waited—the song filling the cavern.

Rush felt the weight of the Climbers on both of his arms, even in his feet despite the fact that they were against the earth. His ears focused hard to listen over the song, to hear the rock rolling back into place at the end of the passage.

Durir must have gotten a signal from the other end because he ushered Rush and the others forward.

We will be one for this.

Yeah, I need it.

The song stopped, and the dwarves stared.

In heavy silence, they filed into the passage. When Rush passed Queen Megora, they shared a look.

A long look.

Crouched down, Rush entered the passage first, followed by the others. The burning torch the dwarf held illuminated the end of the passage and guided them forward. When Rush made it there, he felt it.

The drumming of his heart.

The dwarf grabbed the handle and prepared to roll it aside. "Take the wall directly to the side of this entrance. When you can't go any farther, there will be a path that can take you to the opening."

Rush nodded.

The dwarf rolled the rock to the side and revealed the dark cavern.

Like a horde of spiders, the Fazurks sprinted to the cave that led deeper into the mountain, their roars and cries shaking the walls of the mountain. There was a torch down below—where one dwarf had already perished.

Rush swallowed.

We don't have time for this, Rush.

Rush hopped out of the passageway and waited for everyone else to be free. "Start climbing."

The rock rolled back into place, sealing the surface like the door hadn't been there in the first place.

Everyone pressed their Climbers to the wall and began to go, twisting their limbs every time they needed to pull free from the surface.

Rush remained behind, giving them a head start so he could guard the rear. The Fazurks continued to run into the cave like dogs chasing a thrown stick. Their animalistic instincts were too much and overcame their logic. They could have checked the entrance they had previously discovered, but the blood lust was just too much.

Rush didn't even need to linger, but he watched them pour inside, all murderous and vile.

We will kill them all.

Yes.

But not tonight. Hurry.

Rush jumped high onto the wall, caught himself with the Climbers, and used his connection with Flare to scale the mountain at a speed no other man could replicate. He caught up to the group then passed them. Like ants on the wall, they were unnoticeable, blending into the darkness, the popping noises masked by the shouts of blood lust from down below.

It was a challenging climb, and by the time they reached the top level, they were out of breath, their palms sticky, their shirts sticking to the sweat on their backs. One by one, they collapsed on the path and caught their breaths.

Rush removed the Climbers from his body and quickly stowed them in his pack. His eyes were on the opening on the other side of the cavern, Fazurks still running inside, far fewer than before.

Why are so many outside the mountain?

No idea.

We didn't see any on our journey here—just a bunch of goats.

Those assholes…don't remind me. "Guys, up. We gotta keep going."

Their gear was stowed, and they were on their feet once more.

"What are we going to do?" Bridge asked. "We can't sneak past them. I mean, there's too many."

"All I have to do is get outside," Rush said. "Flare can burn them all."

"What about the Shamans?" Bridge asked. "They'll see."

They will see.

Ugh. I feel like every day has been the worst day of my life lately. "We don't have a choice. I run out, they chase me, I burn them to ash. When they're distracted, make a run for it."

"How will we find one another again?" Bridge asked.

"Make a fire. I'll see you from the sky."

Bridge dragged the back of his wrist over his forehead, catching all the sweat that beaded on his face from the climb. "I don't have a better idea, so let's do it."

Rush took the lead, sticking to the wall as he approached the entrance, the Fazurks too distracted by the chaos below to peer into the shadows. When he was close, he crouched down, hidden behind an outcropping of rock. **Ready?**

I've always liked charred meat.

Fury

Rush stared at the path, waiting for a distinct break between the Fazurks so he could sprint to the surface. They continued to pour inside, usually in groups of a dozen.

In three seconds.

Rush righted himself, and when the last Fazurk in the group passed, he sprinted.

He ran up the path and breached the surface, the nighttime sky greeting him like an old friend. The stars filled the wide expanse of darkness, twinkling lights in the eternal space. Fresh air hit him, a cleanse to his lungs.

Flare inhaled a slow and deep breath, the tension ebbing away.

The oncoming Fazurks roared.

Take it away.

Rush felt his body change, felt the wings explode out of his back, the talons erupt through his fingertips. Rage ripped through him. Vengeance. Blood lust. Mania. The ground disappeared, and the stars became brighter as they reached for the sky. The air whipped under his wings, the breeze soothed his scales, and the freedom made the fire in his lungs explode.

Flare whipped around and glided over the entrance as the jet of smoldering fire escaped his open mouth. A stream of deep red flames illuminated the night as it scorched the earth and everything that stood there a moment ago.

Burn.

Flare steadied himself in place and continued to release the flames from his lungs, burning the entire line of Fazurks, scorching all the ones that inhabited the surface. Then he flew to the entrance of the cave and burned that too. Fish in a barrel, there was nowhere for them to go. Their hides caught fire, and the screams that pierced the night could be heard from every corner of Anastille.

The scaffolding caught fire and toppled over. Bodies collapsed but remained on fire. What was once the bottom of a cavern was now a lake of fire.

Okay, that's enough.

It is never enough. I'm a dragon—and I burn.

Let's not forget that Shamans have undoubtedly seen this spectacle and they're headed this way now.

I will not change back.

Flare.

No.

If I could give you more time, I would. If we could stay in this form the whole time, that would be far more beneficial than me running everywhere. But they'll see you. Come on, Flare.

Grrrrrrrr.

When I can, I'll give you all the time you want.

Flare glided to the bottom then hit the earth.

Trust me, I'm so over running everywhere and getting into fights with mountain goats.

Flare released his hold, and they changed back, Rush back in control. Corpses burned around him, the light so bright it was a beacon to anyone who was awake at that time of night. **Just gotta find the others.**

They can't be far.

Rush navigated around the dead. When his boot caught fire, he shook it off and extinguished it. "Bridge!" He cupped his mouth and called into the night. There was no call in return, so he climbed up one of the rocks to get a better view. **Where are they?** He stuck his fingers into his mouth and whistled, not seeing a bonfire in their vicinity. The sky was smoky with bits of hot ash flying everywhere, so visibility was poor. **You didn't burn them too, did you?**

Silence.

Flare?

His hair prickled, standing on end along the back of his neck and his forearms.

Then the sky went dark—for just a moment.

The stars were blocked by something massive.

Shit. He slid down the rock back to the earth and caught himself on his palms.

Thud.

With his back to the rock, he remained crouched down, his ribs the drum and his heart the pedal. With his breath held, he waited. He waited for the announcement that he dreaded. He waited for the emotional onslaught.

"Doubt my parenting skills—but I did not raise my son to hide like a coward." Deep like the very center of the lake, his voice was full of the long years he lived, of someone who had lived long enough to see regimes rise and fall over many lifetimes.

With his eyes closed, a sigh escaped Rush.

"You're the son of a king." His voice became louder as he drew closer. "Show your face."

He shook his head as he seethed through his clenched teeth. "A king? More like a tyrant."

Rush, I'm here.

He straightened his body and stepped out from behind the rock, the landscape still ablaze from the damage Flare had caused. The smell of burning Fazurks gave the air a repugnant stench—perfect for the occasion. Stars that were once visible were now veiled by a sky of smoke.

In his full black armor with his cape blowing in the breeze behind him stood King Lux. The blue eyes were identical. The hard line of his jaw uncanny. The same blood that pumped through his heart pumped in Rush's. Intelligent eyes shifted back and forth as he regarded his son from the distance, specs of ash floating in the air around him. "No need to flatter me, son." A smile broke through the intensity of his stare—packed with arrogance.

We have no armor. We can't fight him.

I don't think I have a choice.

Flee.

A temporary solution. Very temporary.

King Lux stepped forward, his boots audible against the stone. His sword remained sheathed, but his hand dangled close, ready to draw. "This madness ends now. Return, and I will grant you mercy."

Rush gave a slight shake of his head. "Nah, I'm good."

His eyes narrowed instantly, his hand giving a slight flinch toward the pommel of his sword. "You may be my son, but my patience is limited."

"So is mine—and I lost my patience for you a long time ago."

His eyes narrowed even further, his smile gone as well as the arrogance. "You served me for thousands of years. You kept peace in Anastille. You were a general who made your king proud. And you were a son who made his father proud."

"Killing innocent people and enslaving an innocent race makes you proud? Those are your requirements?"

He took another step, his boot crunching into the dirt.

"I hope you hate me, then—because I hate you."

His stoic face remained impassive, as if he didn't hear a word. "You plot to overthrow me? You have no chance—"

"Really? Because you look pretty scared right now. Searching the skies for me. Leaving High Castle and doing the grunt work yourself because everyone else has failed to catch me. You must feel threatened to get off your ass like this."

His fingers gripped the pommel, and he withdrew the sword from the scabbard, the blue scales singing against the steel as it emerged. "A father should never outlive his son. Nor should he have to execute him."

"You know, there's a third option…"

His blue sword hung at his side, his fingers squeezing the handle through his black gloves.

"I'm just as guilty as you are. I've committed atrocities I can never take back. No amount of remorse will pay for the blood I've spilled. But we can end this now. We can release the dragons and give them the freedom they deserve. We can start over."

"If dragons were fit to rule, they wouldn't have handed me the throne. If dragons were meant to be anything more than servants, they wouldn't have handed me the keys to their kingdom."

"You've been fused with Obsidian all this time—and you feel *nothing* for him?"

The king's eyes remained fixed in place—empty inside.

"Then you must feel nothing for me too."

"The only reason you're alive is because I allow it."

Rush released a drawn-out sigh. "That's sweet, Dad…"

He moved forward again, the distance between them starting to close. "I can't allow this to continue. Surrender."

"You're the one who needs to surrender."

His fingers gripped the pommel noticeably tighter. "I've fought to wound—never to kill. But that's about to change."

"Yeah, me too."

Careful.

Rush bottled his temper. "We don't have to fight to kill—if you just let this go."

His deep voice rumbled. "Perhaps you haven't thought this all the way through. Because if we release our dragons, we die."

"And we will die as father and son—in peace."

He gave a subtle shake of his head. "I deserve to live forever. I took that immortality and claimed it as my own. I won't give it up—not for anyone."

"Really? Because I think it's overrated."

"You just don't know how to live."

"I didn't know how to live—but now, I do." He unsheathed his sword from his scabbard, stepped forward, and dragged the tip across the dirt, drawing a distinct line in the sand. "The line is officially drawn. Your call. We can fight each other to the death—or you can salvage what's left of this torn relationship."

"Our relationship has nothing to do with this—"

"It has *everything* to do with it. I'm your son—and I've pledged my life to fixing all of your destruction. Free dragons are extinct. The elves are isolated in their forest. The dwarves have been overrun by monsters. Everything that made this world pure has been destroyed—by us." He slammed his hand into his chest. "If you feel *anything* for me, if family means a damn thing to you, you will join me."

A long stare ensued.

"No man can be this evil." He threw his arm down. "Come on, do the right thing here."

"I already am." He moved forward, taking several steps as he approached the line that separated them. "You're too naïve to understand what your king has accomplished, what your father has done for his family. Our world was on fire, and I saved us from ruin. The only reason you're alive, in more ways than one, is because of me." His boot stepped on the line and dragged across, dissolving it back into the dirt. "I found us a new home. I saved our race from extinction. I've secured enough power that no one could ever oppose us again. You think I'm evil? If I surrendered our power, someone else would take it, and they would do the exact same thing. That's the nature of this world. That's the nature of all beings—from elves to dwarves. I watched our world burn behind us as we sailed away, and as long as I'm living, no one can ever take anything from us again. I will live forever. I will rule Anastille forever. No one will change that." Once the dirt had been returned to what it was, he stepped back. "You're the one who will join me. You've forgotten who you are. You've forgotten *what* you are. Because you're just like me—blood, flesh, and bone."

Rush gave a shake of his head, all the blood draining from his heart and dumping into his stomach. There was no chance of reconciliation. There was no chance that they would coexist peacefully. Someone had to die. And even if it wasn't him, it was still the outcome he didn't want.

He changed the grip on his sword. "I had a similar phase when I was young. Tired of living in the shade of my father's mighty oak, I became difficult. Disobedient. Headstrong. Insubordinate. That shared experience is the only reason my blade points at the ground rather than at your throat. I need to enlighten you. Your cause is hopeless. The dwarves are no more. And neither is Eden Star."

The drumming in Rush's chest stopped. His pulse went still. Everything went still.

His eyes shifted left and right, reading the words that King Lux projected on his face. "General Noose and the Shamans have taken Eden Star. Your only allies are now my prisoners. As I said before, you have no chance."

Rush held his sword at his side, except his grip was weak. Despair. Betrayal. Fury. He felt it all at once.

Pretty.

No...

He lies.

Talk to her.

I can't do two things at once. I need to be here with you.

"You lost, Rush."

"I don't believe you. You can't breach the magic of their forest."

"I can when I know another way inside." The arrogant smile was back, coupled with despicable joy in his gaze.

Shit.

How does he know?

Like he'd ever tell.

A growl escaped Flare's throat. *He must burn.*

Yes.

King Lux straightened his shoulders as his smile slowly faded. "I will slay my own son—if I must."

Rush felt new life enter his lungs. The world became clear. His vision expanded, seeing the entire topography of his surroundings, even behind his back where his eyes couldn't see. Adrenaline pumped into his heart. Strength filled his muscles.

Now he noticed his father's features in greater detail, the subtle lines in the corners of his eyes from sun exposure, the enormous muscles of his shoulders and arms. The fuse had frozen him in time, making him just ten years older than Rush in bodily form. The man looked more like a brother than a father, but Rush didn't have the heart for either. His eyes swore an oath to deliver on his threat—and take his life.

I want him dead. But we must flee.

There's nowhere to go.

He'll kill us both.

Not if I kill him first.

You have no armor.

I don't need it.

Rush—

His hand squeezed his sword so tightly he nearly yanked a tendon out of his hand. **I end this now—and it's over for good.**

And if he ends us, it's also over for good.

King Lux lunged, swinging his sword with the speed of the wind.

I'm sorry, Rush. Flare came into being, launched into the sky, and beat his wings harder than he ever had.

Obsidian came into being instantly, as if King Lux already knew what would happen.

There's nowhere to go!

You're outmatched, Rush. At least I have my scales.

Obsidian is nearly twice your size.

And I'm twice his speed.

I can take him on the ground.

You are thinking with fury—not logic.

Flare flapped his wings and maneuvered, flying as fast as he could toward the Shadow Lands.

Where are you going?

Hiding in the smoke.

The wind had carried the smoke north, the only cover they had.

Obsidian was fast to follow, appearing in the smoke, his massive jaws opening wide then closing right on his tail.

Roooooooooaaaaaar! Flare kicked him in the face with an enormous foot and got his tail free.

Go!

Flare beat his wings and maneuvered out of the way, diving down into the mist then jerking hard to the right.

He's not messing around this time.

Neither am I. Flare dived then flew back up, never staying in the same position for long, using the smoke cloud as cover. Without sun or starlight, his scales didn't reflect, and that shielded his red color a bit.

Cliiiiiiick. Click. Click.

We've got company.

I can handle them.

And Obsidian? We have to figure out an escape plan.

The Shadow Lands?

I don't know anything about that place.

Neither does he.

A Shaman on a steed appeared in the smoke, headed right toward them, his open palm showing the fireball he was about to launch.

Move, move, move!

Flare dived again then soared fast, breaking through the edge of the cloud and emerging on the other side.

Obsidian was there, flying in place, his open mouth giving a direct view of the fire coming down the pipe.

He's corralling us like sheep.

I'm no sheep. He darted to the right and returned to the cloud, a Shaman whooshing by right across his face. *But he is.* He flew out the opposite side of the smoke and returned to the clean air, the surface of the mountain still ablaze with the corpses as fuel.

What's your plan?

Another Shaman emerged in hot pursuit.

That's Shadow.

How can you tell?

I just can.

The two Shamans were on their tail, and the fireballs began to launch. Flaming orbs of heat passed by in the darkness, the warmth passing across his scales like the force of the sun.

They surrounded him in opposite directions, launching across the sky, almost hitting Flare a couple times.

Your plan sucks, Flare.

Just trust me. He continued to dodge the fire, flying low then high, outmaneuvering their throws like he knew exactly when they would launch.

Obsidian's above you.

Yes. I see him.

Obsidian beat his wings as he remained in place, and then his throat opened to launch his stream of fire.

If you don't do something right now, we're toast. No pun intended.

Whether intended or not intended, now isn't the time for one. Flare dropped down and flew directly beneath the blue dragon, dodging the line of fire and coming back up on the rear. Obsidian began to turn to face his assailant, but his bulky body slowed his movements. Flare seized the opportunity—and bit down on his tail.

Roooooooooaaaaaaar!

That's your brilliant plan?

No. Flare dodged out of the way again and went straight for a Shaman. His talons reached out, and he yanked the Shaman right off his steed, biting into his hand before the fire could form in his palm. *This is.*

Shadow launched his fireball to free his comrade.

Flare released the Shaman and let him fall to the ground, his steed nowhere in sight.

Flare dropped too, missing the burning fireball by just a few inches.

The fire soared overhead—and hit Obsidian directly in the wing.

Rooooooooaaaaaaar!

Who's the sheep now? Baaaaaa!

The enormous blue dragon toppled from the sky, unable to carry his massive weight with a broken wing, and he plummeted into the darkness.

Flare...that was badass.

Yes, I know. But we still have to deal with Shadow.

What about the others?

We'll come back for them. Flare pounded his wings and took off, headed away from the Stronghold and to the valley.

Wait.

Yes?

He's wounded...

Flare kept going.

I can kill him.

Perhaps. But not with Shadow in the skies.

Take out Shadow. Then we do this.

Are you sure—

Yes.

Flare continued to fly, deliberating in his mind.

This is our chance, Flare.

You don't have armor—

I don't need armor! Bastard took Eden Star. Took Cora…

Flare continued to fly, but then he dropped down and turned around. *This means we must kill Ashe's brother…*

He'll understand…it's necessary.

They entered the smoke once more, surrounded by a gray mist that was harsh on the lungs as well as the eyes.

Where are you, Shadow?

Rush absorbed the landscape, his heart about to burst with adrenaline. The only break in the silence was the flap of Flare's wings in between his moments of glide. Minutes passed, and there was no sign of him.

Rush spotted him first. **He's behind you. Right on your tail.**

Flare whipped around in a flash, pulling his wings flush against his body, and spun around to smack his enormous tail into the cloaked figure. Shaman and steed both gave a shriek before they were launched into the darkness.

Nice shot.

Flare dropped out of the cloud of smoke and opened his wings to catch his fall above the surface, eyes scanning for the enormous blue dragon with blood splashed on the rocks. Most of the fire had been quenched when all the flesh had been consumed, so the majority of them were pyres of smoke. But fires still burned in isolated camps. It lit the landscape—and there was no large blue dragon.

Both scanned the area, eyes piercing the darkness for the shine of blue scales. Their eyes lifted to the skies in the direction of High Castle, searching for the dark silhouette as he retreated.

There was nothing.

He's changed into his human form so we can't find him. Flare landed on the ground, his talons digging into the earth. Smoke and ash blew in the breeze, rising up with the flakes of embers.

Rush came forth, marching forward as he pulled the sword out of his scabbard. He gripped it by the pommel and held it at the ready, prepared to slice the blade across his father's throat and watch him drown in his own blood. "And I'm the coward?" He shouted into the smoke, into the darkness, spit flying from his mouth. "Show your goddamn face so I can kill you! Come on!" He advanced through the rocky terrain, his eyes scanning his surroundings, gripping his sword so tightly his knuckles burned. "Fight me!"

Rush.

"Slay your son!" Angry tears poured down his face, the veins in his temple trying to burst through the flesh that kept them in place. "*Do it!*"

A gentle hand dropped onto his shoulder, strong fingers gripping him through his shirt.

Rush kept his eyes straight ahead, sucking the smoke into his lungs with every deep breath he took, his fingers loosening their grip on the sword. His eyes remained wet—from the anger, from the smoke, from it all.

Another hand moved to his other shoulder, just as gentle.

Rush dropped the sword on the ground.

Bridge squeezed his shoulder once again. "Come on…let's go."

28

UNKINGLY

Their silhouettes disappeared into the trees, but chaos ensued around her. The smoke in the air was so heavy that every breath drawn caused tired eyes to water, caused her seared throat to cough. Her sword lowered to her side, red like the flames that claimed Eden Star, and her fingers barely clung to the hilt. Her eyes remained on the place where General Noose had vanished, waiting for him to return even though she knew he was gone.

"Cora." Callon's strong hand gripped her shoulder and forced her in his direction, so she could see the wildness in his eyes. His forehead was still tense with wrinkles, incapacitated by the mental torture he'd endured before she'd intervened. One shoulder dropped lower than the other, and he carried himself as if physically wounded by a blade. But he had enough energy to scar her with his look. "It is my responsibility to protect the queen—not yours. You were supposed to stay hidden." Spit flew from his mouth, he was so livid, rage stabbing her face with every look and every word. "How dare you—"

"I'm okay, Callon." Her hand went to his shoulder, her touch gentle instead of angry like his.

His eyes flicked back and forth.

"I'm right here. Still here."

The anger immediately receded back into his body. His fingers went limp at the same time.

"You trained me well, *Tor-lei*."

His eyes softened in a brand-new way, a way that had never happened before. An involuntary breath took him, the kind that made his eyes water, and not from the smoke. His fingers gripped her shoulder again, and he pulled her into an embrace. His arm locked around her back, and his other hand cupped the back of her head. His breathing grew heavy as he held her, squeezing her like he never wanted to let her go.

"I'm okay…" With her cheek against his chest, she rubbed his back.

He continued to hold her, embrace her longer than he ever had before. "*Rein-Lei-Vu, Sor-lei*. It means—"

"I know what it means." Her eyes watered more—and not from the smoke. "*Rein-Lei-Vu*…"

He held her a moment longer before he pulled away and looked her over with eyes that had regained their command and hardness. But a slight smile formed on his lips. "Between you and me…that was pretty *badass*."

A sudden laugh escaped her chest, his words completely unexpected.

"Callon." The Queen's harsh command destroyed the warmth of their moment, dunking them back into the harsh abyss. Eden Star was still aflame. The dead were at their feet. The forest cried in pain.

Callon straightened himself before he faced her, hiding any sign of weakness or fatigue. "What are your orders, Your Majesty?" His sword was in his scabbard, his bow across his back, his arms rigid at his sides.

"Aldon has fulfilled his oath. I reinstate you as General of Eden Star. Secure the perimeter. Get the wounded to the infirmary. Heal the forest before we lose any more of it. Those are your orders—now, go."

If he's doing everything, what is she doing? She is unkingly.

You're back.

I knew you would prevail, Hatchling.

Callon secured his hands behind his back as he addressed her. "I will take the position—but temporarily. When Eden Star has returned to its former peace, a new general will be elected."

Her eyes widened immediately, her reaction forming quicker than she could sheathe it. "It wasn't a request—but an order."

She rules with fear, subjugation, and intimidation. We have a term for this. Wuzurk. In your tongue—tyrant.

Callon remained with his hands behind his back, looking up at the queen as she stood on the blood-soaked stairs. "Now is not the time for deliberation. Eden Star burns, and our people need us."

"Then go—and don't make me ask a third time."

Wow...okay. Is King Lux looking to be set up? Because I think I met his match.

Unkingly.

Callon gave a slight bow then turned away.

The Queen's gaze shifted to her. Her green eyes were red like the fire that consumed the trees, and the anger burst forth with more strength than the volcanic eruption that took the Land of Ashes.

Bitch, don't look at me like that. I just saved Eden Star.

With her eyes still on Cora, she spoke. "And, General Callon?"

He halted, his face tightening into a look of annoyance. He quickly concealed it before he turned around to face her once more.

After a long stare, she dragged her sight off Cora to look at Callon. "We will speak of this later."

CALLON TOOK THE LEAD, RUNNING BACK THE WAY THEY'D COME to the heart of the forest, where the market had once been, where the remains of the tree houses were now debris and ash on the ground. Infernos continued to consume the forest, fire now replacing serenity. Dead elves littered the ground, their open eyes reflecting the flames in the sky. "The enemy is gone. Put out the fires. Help the wounded."

Hysteria subsided significantly once Callon appeared in his elven armor and gave out his orders. A group of elves ran to the base of one tree, and with their palms directly on the smoldering wood, they closed their eyes and focused.

Callon joined them, reaching his hand above their heads to plant his palm against the bark. With his eyes closed, he did as they did.

Cora watched the canopy, and slowly, there was new growth. New bark replaced the charred pieces. New branches emerged to replace the ones on fire. Everything that the flame touched was ejected by the tree, dropped to the forest floor, where it could continue in an isolated burn until it was out of fuel.

Without instruction, she didn't know what to do, but she joined the group, her palm moving between bodies to find a surface she could reach. She closed her eyes and pushed her mind out, feeling the consciousness of the tree that burned alive. The touch used to be met with serenity, with the sound of water moving through the roots into the heart of the tree, with the breeze through the leaves.

But now, it screamed.

She'd performed the Skull Crusher on the Shamans, but their death was so swift she didn't feel it.

But this was a slow and painful death—and she felt it all.

She urged the tree to grow, guided water from the earth into the roots, pushed it through the branches. Buds grew on the limbs then quickly became flowers and leaves. Branches fell around them, like a snake shedding its skin to make way for the new one.

Then the screaming stopped.

The elves pulled away.

Cora looked up the bark into the branches, seeing that the tree didn't look the way it once had, that the limbs were too immature for the age of the trunk, that the branches were uneven on the two sides of the tree, because one side had been set aflame, while the other hadn't. It would take a long time for it to grow naturally, to look the way it once had.

She was disgusted.

Callon launched into action and rounded up the elves he came across, telling some to work on the next tree, while he asked others to get the wounded off the ground so a burning branch wouldn't crush them.

"Cora!"

She turned around and spotted the bright blond hair and blue eyes. Her hair wasn't in a perfect braid with flowers interwoven through the strands. Now, it was a mess—and her eyes were red and blotchy. "Are you okay?" Cora ran to her friend and, without thinking, wrapped her arms around her in an embrace.

Peony immediately reciprocated without hesitation. "Yes, I'm fine. You?"

"I'm good." Cora pulled away, the flames still rampant with destruction. "Your dad?"

"He's helping the wounded."

"Lia?"

"I haven't seen her..."

"Hawk?"

The question made her eyes shine even more, the thin film of moisture more noticeable. "He's on duty at the front..."

"I'm sure he's fine." She blurted out the words without taking a moment to really consider them, whether she actually believed them or just wanted to make her friend feel better. But it was what she would want to hear from someone else.

Peony gave a nod, her eyes still sad.

Callon ran up to Cora. "I need to head to the front. Put out the fires with the others—that's your best contribution."

"Okay," Cora said with a nod.

His hand went to her arm, and he pulled her close. "Keep your sword with you." He spoke close to her ear, so Peony couldn't hear.

"Why?"

Without giving an answer, he dropped her arm and departed.

Night turned into day. Day turned into night.

Over and over.

There was no sleep for anyone, not when the forest remained a blaze. Elves worked together to save every tree they could, but unfortunately, some of them couldn't be spared. They fell—turned into ash.

Once the fires were out, the dead were carried to the cemetery. The corpses were lined up on the dirt while the graves were dug and the headstones engraved. The wounded were carried to the healer, Voronwe.

His building was in the northern part of Eden Star, away from the center as well as the market. It was built to accommodate several dozen elves—but not hundreds. Cora and Peony carried an unconscious man through the door, his arms over their shoulders, his feet dragging behind.

There was nowhere else to put him besides the floor, so that's where they laid him, straight on the wood.

Voronwe focused on a patient on his table, his hands joined together and pressed against his chest.

"I'm going to see if there's news about Hawk…" Peony left, her hair oily and matted against her scalp after several days of hard labor, of heat from the searing flames, and not bathing or sleeping.

"Alright." Cora continued to watch Voronwe, an elf with silver hair but a youthful face. With his eyes closed, he slid his hand across his patient, feeling the bones against the skin. He seemed to have found what he sought because there was an audible crack.

The patient was motionless—too deep under to wake.

Voronwe moved his hands to another place, eyes still closed, fixing entrails that he couldn't see.

Cora watched.

The patient's visage slowly changed, from a dull gray to a flushed cream. Breaths became deeper and more natural. The tension in the face slowly faded. Blood flow had been restored with his mind.

All of the wounded had been collected, the fires had been extinguished, so it was the right time for her to rest. But she remained, fascinated by what this elf could do with just his mind. She could take life away—but he could give it.

When he was done, he whispered in Elvish under his breath then removed his hands. As if he'd known Cora had been there the entire time, he turned to regard her. Light-colored eyes examined her face, as if he could see past her flesh to everything underneath.

"Can I help?"

"Are you a healer?"

She shook her head.

"Then no." He moved to the next patient.

She wandered to the rejuvenated patient on the table, an elf she didn't recognize. She wasn't even sure if she was the one who had brought him in—because there had been so many. She stared at his chest, as if she could see what had been broken and what had been fixed. "When we put out the fires, I directed the water into the roots, forced the buds to grow, helped the tree shed old bark and replace it with new bark. Is that…what you're doing?"

"The simplification is insulting." His hand touched his patient, his eyes open and focused on his actions. "A tree is a one-dimensional being. It operates in a linear fashion. Elves are much more complicated. Bone. Cartilage. Blood. Tissue. Organs. There's so much more."

"Is that why there's only one healer?"

"Yes." His hands glided over, mapping out the body in his mind. "It took a very long time for me to reach this status. It's about exploring the body with just your thoughts, understanding normal, functioning anatomy, distinguishing a variant that's still normal, and deciding if something needs to be altered—and if it's the right thing to be altered. Change one thing—change the whole body. It takes experience, much experience."

"Yes, that does sound complicated."

"Tell me…did General Callon drive the Shamans from Eden Star?" He looked up as his hands continued to move, his eyes settling on her.

Cora swallowed, her wrapped sword stuffed into her pack. "Actually, it was me…"

"You?" His eyes dropped, looking her over.

"Yes."

CORA!

Her head exploded with his loud voice.

Cora, are you there? Cora?

"Please excuse me." She left the building and returned to the forest, stepping off the path and into the tree line. *I'm here. Are you guys okay?*

Rush's voice came next, his voice bursting through a solid door and breaking it into pieces. **Are you alright? Has Eden Star been taken?**

Wait...how do you know about that?

So, it's true...

General Noose and the Shamans invaded our forest, but they are gone now. For the last few days, we've been putting out the fires and healing the wounded. But a lot of elves have fallen.

But you're okay?

Yes, I'm fine.

Rush released a heavy sigh of relief.

What a relief, Pretty.

What about you guys? I tried to reach you, but you were gone.

We were in the Stronghold. *Really* **long story. You have time to talk?**

All the wounded had been delivered to the healer, the dead had been taken to the Cemetery of Spirits, and the fires had been quenched. There was no place she could go because her home had been destroyed. She hadn't slept in days. *I'll get back to you in an hour. Just have to find somewhere first.*

THESE THINGS ARE BIG AND UGLY. I MEAN, REALLY UGLY. THEY infiltrated the Stronghold like ants overrunning a neighboring anthill. I could take on a couple myself, but not forever. But she sacrificed her Durgin so we were able to escape.

Durgin? She sat in the shade of a tree near the river, the same place she and Callon had lunch after their training sessions.

Dwarven warriors.

That's so sad.

Yeah, it sucked. But there was no other way. We were able to escape, and now I need to return with an army to flush out those Fazurks from the Stronghold. The remaining dwarves will have their mountain once again, and Talc will be released to us.

How many dwarves are left?

Maybe a thousand. But we hope there are more hidden somewhere in the mountain. It's a really big place, so you never know.

I hope so too. It'll be hard for them to defend their mountain in the future with such low numbers.

True.

And the Fazurks are from the Shadow Lands?

They gotta be.

I would never eat one—too hideous.

How would they get through the rock? I thought it was solid?

Maybe they climbed? I don't know—but these guys aren't from Anastille.

Just...why now?

Psh, no idea. It could be any reason. Maybe their food source has become scarce so they're searching elsewhere. Or maybe someone told them to climb the rock and invade the Stronghold... I don't think we'll ever know.

They smell too.

Okay...not relevant.

Pretty doesn't smell.

She was exhausted, dirty, and overwhelmed. But she gave a chuckle. *I miss you guys. I get used to our separation when we're apart, but then when we talk...I'm not sure how I ever did.*

Rush gave a long pause before an answer. Same here.

So, what happened next? How did you know Eden Star was under attack?

When I breached the surface, Flare took over and burned them.

They smell even worse when they're on fire.

Rush ignored him. **We knew the fires would attract the Shamans, but we didn't have a choice.**

The Shamans told you?

Well, the Shamans weren't the only ones that came.

Oh... Cora pictured the blue dragon from her dreams, a dragon she'd never seen in person, only through the thoughts she shared with Ashe. *What happened?*

Rush didn't speak.

You don't have to talk about it if you don't want to.

Words were shared. So were threats. We battled in the skies—and Obsidian fell.

For good?

No. He changed into his human form—and disappeared in the smoke.

Coward.

He told us that he had taken Eden Star.

That was a lie—because we prevailed.

General Callon protected his people once again. Is he alright?

Yeah, he's fine. But it wasn't him...

Both Rush and Flare stayed quiet.

The gentle sound of the stream beside her was replaced by the flames of the inferno. Sunshine was drowned in the blackness. Music from songbirds was replaced by the screams of dying elves. *I was asleep when it happened. Ashe woke me up, and if he hadn't, the smoke would have a moment later. My tree house was on fire, and if I hadn't jumped, I would have gone down with it.* She swallowed, replaying a moment that seemed to occur an eternity ago. *I searched for Callon first. I heard the clicks of the monsters just as I heard the screams of those they killed. When I found him, a Shaman was there—performing the Skull Crusher. Without thinking, I just did it...I killed him.*

She closed her eyes, remembering the way he could barely stand. *He insisted I take the secret passage out of Eden Star to safety while he protected Queen Delwyn. I refused to leave his side, so we went together. There were a dozen Shamans. General Aldon was dead. The Queen's guard Melian was slain too. There were other elves on the stairs, elves who died trying to protect her. She was the last one standing. General Noose was about to slay her, but Callon got there first—*

Too weak to fight, his blade fell. Ashe's deep voice emerged, kingly in its authority, exuding power that could be felt by each of their minds. *The effects of the Skull Crusher had dwindled his mind. But Cora's fiery blade met General Noose's before he could be slain. My strength became hers, our minds became one, and with unbridled power, Cora killed six Shamans at once, all the while holding her own against one of the best swordsmen in Anastille. Outmatched, General Noose and his monsters retreated from Eden Star.* The pride in his voice was unmistakable. *My hatchling prevailed.*

Ashe, King of Dragons. It is a pleasure to hear your voice once again.

It is mine as well.

Cora remained quiet, silenced by the story her dragon had just told.

After a heavy silence, Rush spoke. **Attagirl.**

All the tension in her face left when the smile formed.

Wish I could have been there to watch you kick his ass.

I didn't really kick his ass—

You defeated him in battle, and he retreated. Same thing, Hatchling.

Callon has trained you well. Must be proud.

Yeah...he is. But it was Ashe too. Without my abilities, I wouldn't have stood a chance, so Ashe helped me learn how to utilize my skills.

You're the only reason Eden Star still stands. If you didn't have any friends before, you'll definitely have them now.

I don't know...the queen looked ticked.

Maybe she always looks that way.

No. I could tell by the way she spoke to Callon that she's not happy.

Wuzurk.

Translation?

Flare spoke. *Tyrant.*

Callon told me to keep my sword with me, so I think he anticipates an issue.

You literally saved all of Eden Star...and she *still* doesn't like you?

Ashe's deep voice rumbled. *Wuzurk.*

Well, this puts a damper on our plans.

What plans?

I told Queen Megora that I would return with an army to eradicate the Fazurks for good. Was hoping the elves could be that army.

Cora shook her head as she watched the water drip through the cracks in the rocks of the riverbed. *Yeah...that's not going to happen.*

You've gotta have some friends by now. I thought that was the plan?

Yes, I have some. But not a lot.

Well, what is some?

Like three...

Wow...that's bad.

Look, it's hard to make friends when everyone already has this preconceived notion of who you are.

Yeah...been there, done that.

Cora dropped her gaze, the guilt instant.

When everyone knows that you're the one who saved the forest, everything will change, regardless how the queen feels about it. I'm not worried about it.

True. Ashe spoke. *You will earn the favor of every elf that lives.*

Even if that's true, I doubt I'll be able to convince Queen Delwyn to send her army to the Stronghold.

You can if Eden Star wants more allies. They already have the dragons, and now they'll have the dwarves. Unless…you haven't spoken to her about that either.

The right time has failed to present itself.

You still haven't asked her? What have you guys been doing all this time?

Look, she hates me. Would you ask someone who hates you for a favor? That would be like me asking a Shaman if he wants to have brunch.

Rush gave a chuckle. **Sorry, I pictured that in my head…**

His deep voice broke through the laughter, serious as a cloudy sky. *Our plan was to earn the affection of the elves through her communion with the dead. It's been a slow process because we can't simply announce her abilities without attracting the ire of the queen. But now that Cora has defended Eden Star, it should be much easier to accomplish this. She's proven her loyalty to the elves, as have I. It's also abundantly clear that King Lux has his destructive gaze on the forest. They have no choice—they must fight.*

And they'll need allies to do that.

Exactly.

Cora, I'm sorry for everything that Eden Star has lost—but this definitely worked out in our favor.

You're right.

We'll head to Eden Star. It'll take us a few weeks to get there with all the obstacles in our way. Hopefully, the elves will be ready to return to the Stronghold with us by the time we arrive.

Alright, we'll get to work.

29
_____

THE QUEEN OF CORRUPTION

The perimeter of Eden Star was untouched.

There was no disturbance in the brush or the wildlife, no sign there had been any struggle to breach. When Callon checked the secret passageway, there were no signs of entry there either. The watchmen were unharmed, completely bypassed, and the enemy had headed straight for the civilians.

It was a relief that his men had been unhurt—but it had cost the lives of those unable to defend themselves. The days were long, and the nights were longer. There was no time to sleep, not when he was responsible for the entire elven army.

"General Callon."

With his arms by his sides, he stood on the balcony of the tree house, a perfect view of the terrain outside Eden Star. The blue skies were empty, the lands were quiet, and there were no signs of assault from ahead. "Yes?" He pivoted slightly to meet the soldier's eyes.

"Queen Delwyn wishes to speak with you."

He held his gaze for a moment before he left the balcony. "Fangorn, you're my sword and bow in my absence."

He gave a slight nod. "Yes, General."

Callon departed the tree house and returned to Eden Star, heartbroken when the music wasn't as serene as it once had been. The songbirds were quiet. The butterflies absent. Resilient as ever, the forest continued on—but it wasn't the same.

He was tempted to deviate from the path, to check on Cora, but it would take far too long to locate her now that her home had been destroyed in the fire. His home was gone too—along with all his possessions. Weila's recipes. Turnion's watercolor portrait. All those heirlooms—burned.

The pathway through the market was different, all the carts and shops destroyed. Elves worked to rebuild, carrying the natural wood they scavenged throughout the forest. The Queen's residence remained, one of the few things that had escaped the fire. But the steps were stained with the blood of those who died to protect her.

He stopped, examining the place where he'd fallen, where his sword had dropped because he'd been bested in battle. The damage to his mind had severed his connection to his body—and he'd become too weak to fight.

The shame was potent.

But the pride for his *Sor-lei*—indescribable.

Fury

He rose up the steps and entered the fortress where her throne stood at the top.

She was there, seated with her legs crossed, the crown of flowers perfectly placed on her elegant head. Her blond hair was in wavy curls, spread out across her shoulders, shining like the summer sun. She would be a beautiful sight to behold —if it weren't for the scowl on her hard mouth.

Decorated in his queen's armor with his sword on his belt, he held her gaze and waited for instruction.

Ferocious eyes met his.

"The perimeter is secure. The only soldiers that we lost were the ones stationed deeper inside the forest. After a thorough investigation of our borders, I'm unable to determine the enemy's point of entry."

Her fingers drummed against the wood, her long nails giving a distinct tap every time they made contact. "Ask Cora—I'm sure she knows."

The foul accusation was like fire down his throat—and straight into his belly. "She is the reason Eden Star still stands."

"Irrelevant when she's the reason they marched on this forest in the first place. We've lost hundreds of elves—because of her. That girl is a poison. She's soaked into the roots and rotted the trees. She's destroyed Eden Star—"

"You draw breath because she took up her sword and defended you." He stepped forward as he breathed heavily, his hand instinctively needing his sword as if battle had crossed the threshold. "You are her queen—and she protected you."

"I wasn't the one she cared about."

"Because of her courage and strength, the two of us speak this very moment. General Noose would have burned this forest to the ground—and done unspeakable things to you afterward. Cora is the daughter of a king, and she has proven her loyalty. The fact that you're still unable to see past your own insecurities makes the fit of that crown questionable."

The tapping of her fingers stopped when she rose to her feet, her white dress no longer stained with splashes of red blood. "I told you this would happen. I told you that our enemies would hunt her here. I would have exiled her from this forest, but you blackmailed me."

"A queen can't be blackmailed—not when she lives a truthful life. If you didn't wish to conceal the truth and lie to your own people, then I would have been powerless to interfere with your rule."

Her eyes were as narrow as the tip of an arrow. "As long as she remains here, we're unsafe. A target has been placed on Eden Star—and we must move it. Our forest has never been breached, and yet, the first time it occurs happens to be when that girl is here. That speaks volumes."

"We've always been at war with King Lux and the empire. This isn't new."

"But that war has never been at our doorstep. I knew she was death the first time I saw her—and I continue to believe it. We still don't know how our enemy broke through the magic of our forest, and that's not a coincidence. She had something to do with it—"

"Lies. This is a spun tale to get what you want."

"Lies? I watched her kill six Shamans at once—with Death Magic. The magic of the forest must have eroded over time. Because she's one of them."

Callon stepped forward. "She is *not* one of them."

"Then explain."

His eyes shifted back and forth. "Spies reside within Eden Star."

Queen Delwyn stared like she couldn't entertain his suggestion whatsoever. "I understand your biological affection, but it is misplaced—she is not one of us."

"She is."

"She is what the empire wants. When we hand her over, his focus on Eden Star will end. He'll get what he wants, and we will have peace."

"*Peace?*" Callon moved up the first stair, unable to restrain his steps. "The only peace King Lux will accept is when all the free races of this world are annihilated or subjugated. You're a fool to believe otherwise. I can't explain Cora's abilities, but I can explain her heart. We are her people—and she will bleed for us. It would be wise to appreciate the asset that she is because her abilities are the greatest weapon we have against the empire. He wants to destroy her so she can't be used against him—and you would be obliging that desire. Cora is our greatest potential for destroying King Lux and the empire for good. Our other crusades failed, but now we have a real chance. She can destroy the Shamans. She can wield a sword with the strength of a man. She can unite the most unlikely allies imaginable. Be worthy of the crown upon your brow—and do the right thing for us all."

A stare as cold as winter ensued, greener than the forest around them. "It seems that you've forgotten who leads Eden Star. It is I, Queen Delwyn, not General Callon. You will carry out my commands without question because I decide what is best for us all."

"Move against Cora, and I will tell everyone who she really is."

Her hard face remained in place—subtly livid. "Then I will have to move against you as well."

His jaw hardened as he clenched his teeth tightly together. "My mind was broken, but I still came for you. I knew my sword couldn't defeat his, but I defended you anyway. I laid down my life for yours without regret."

"Because that is your place—to serve me."

"It is to serve an honorable ruler. But that is not you."

She lowered herself back onto the throne, her hands gripping the edges. "You have served me faithfully these last twenty years. Served Tiberius for a century before that. I would take no pleasure in strife with you. So, stay out of my way, and there will be no strife."

"General Callon." An elf stopped his direction and gave a deep bow.

Callon continued on his way, his eyes scanning the forest in search of Cora.

Another elf stopped and gave a bow. "General Callon. Thank you for your service. Eden Star blooms because of you."

"Not because of me." He halted and stared at the elf he didn't recognize. "It was Cora. She defeated General Noose in battle and killed the Shamans. If it weren't for her, I'd be dead like all the rest."

The elf straightened and met Callon's look, bewildered. "Shamans can't be killed—"

"Not anymore." He continued, moving to the location where her tree house had once been. There was still debris on the forest floor, but most of the burned wood and ash had been discarded.

He went to his tree house next, but there was nothing left at all.

The tree didn't survive.

What was once his home was now grass with pieces of ash caught between the blades. The home where his wife gave birth to his son no longer existed. The place where they cooked their meals and sipped tea at the dining table was gone. His home—the most special place in the world—had passed on. "*Sun-lei...*"

"Callon."

He turned at the sound of his name. "Cora, are you alright?"

"I'm fine. Just exhausted from all the cleanup." She turned her backpack around and opened the top to stick her hand inside.

"Let's go. We need to talk."

"Hold on… I have something for you." She pulled out the green book, tattered and worn, one corner of all the pages blackened from fire. "I was looking through the debris of your house, and I found this."

He stared at the book that he'd left on the kitchen counter, his wife's elegant handwriting scribbled along the pages, all of her favorite recipes jotted down in one place. His breaths grew heavy as he stared.

"It's a bit scuffed up and some pages are missing…but I thought you'd still want it." She placed it in his hand.

He squeezed it between his fingers, the greatest possession that his wife had left behind. "Thank you…"

"I found this too." She pulled out a picture frame with a painting inside. "Half of it is missing so it's just part of his face, but I thought it was better than not having it at all."

Callon took the picture, seeing half of his son's face in his uniform. Like always, his heart turned into a fist and gave a squeeze. The loss never got easier, but sometimes his acceptance of the loss did.

"That was all I could find. I looked through everything before I let them take anything away. It seems like the fire got everything else. I'm sorry…"

"No." He looked at both of the pieces in his hands, the two things he would have saved if he'd had the opportunity. "These are the only things that I care about anyway."

30

NOT A MOMENT LONGER

THEY STEPPED into the clearing where they had their training, where Cora had slept every night since the attack to stay out of everyone's way in Eden Star. The stream was as quiet and serene as ever, like a fiery assault had never taken place.

"What is it?" She dropped her heavy pack, her mobile home. It was weighed down by her armor and her wrapped sword. It gave a distinct thud when it hit the grass. "Did you see anything at the border?"

"Did you tell anyone of the secret passage?" He barked out the question, his eyes strained as they focused on her face.

"No."

"Are you certain?"

"Yes. Why?"

He studied her face a moment longer before the hostility waned. "Just had to make sure."

"You think…that's how they got in?"

"I have no idea how they got in." He was still in his armor, working day and night for the past few days. His eyes weren't as bright as they normally were, like he'd never had the option to sleep since the fires started. "We combed the border thoroughly and saw no signs of penetration."

"Was there any sign of entry at the secret passage?"

He shook his head. "This mystery perplexes me."

"Well, they had to get in somehow."

"My best guess at the moment…the enemy resides in Eden Star."

"What? That's not possible…"

"Our forest is massive. I told you that the great majority of the population resides in the heart of the forest. But there are others that live deep in the woods, hundreds of miles in the trees." He looked away, his gaze piercing the tree line as if he could see someone watching them that very moment.

She followed his gaze, as if she could see it too. "But why would they do that?"

"For elves, age isn't a measurement of years lived. It's a measurement of insanity."

"What does that mean?"

He turned back to her. "The Spirit Ceremony allows an elf to pass from this life with dignity, to give a proper goodbye before eternal rest. As a child, it's hard to understand the desire, but when you're older, you'll feel that yearning. But the few that never do…lose their minds. They retreat into the trees, never to be seen again."

Her eyes flicked back. "That doesn't explain the betrayal."

"Their madness explains it."

"Have you told the queen this?"

"Your question brings me to the purpose of this conversation." He approached the stream and bent down to splash the water against his face, to let the cold drops cleanse the sweat that had accumulated over several days. "I informed her of my theory, but all she cares about is you."

This woman fails to surprise me.

"You've got to be kidding me."

Let me burn her. We've wasted enough time with diplomacy.

Callon returned to her, drops falling from his chin. "I wish I were."

"I saved her ass."

"I know."

"Not to toot my own horn or anything, but this forest is still here because of me."

"I know that too."

"So, what does she think? That I brought General Noose and the Shamans into Eden Star and then…fought them? That literally makes no sense. I know she's a bitch, but she's not a stupid one."

"I agree. It's just an excuse."

"She's doing all this because she thinks her husband had an affair? It bothers her *that* much?"

"You're a threat to her power. That is the issue."

She threw her arms down. "Could I just volunteer myself to be queen and take her throne? Does it even work like that?"

"Tiberius was the greatest king that ever lived. If the people knew that his daughter was among us, then yes, it's possible they'd want you to lead instead of Queen Delwyn. Her reign has been unremarkable up until this point, but now that the border has been breached, people will question her ability."

"She needs to chill because I'm not interested. Maybe if I tell her that, she'll calm down. And I should tell her that Tiberius was literally poisoned into infidelity. Maybe that will help too."

"Far too risky."

"I think leaving her rampage unchecked is more risky."

"That would require you to reveal that you can speak to those who are no longer with us. That's something that should be concealed as long as possible." The sun dried his face, his skin back to its natural state, his usual shadow now a thick beard because he hadn't shaved in days. The dark color matched the pupil of his eyes.

"My crew is on the way here. They went to the Stronghold to initiate an alliance with the dwarves, but I guess it was overrun by these hideous orcs. There's a clan of surviving dwarves trapped underground, but without aid, they'll never escape."

Callon watched her.

"And they have a dragon..."

"I don't like where this is going, *Sor-lei*."

"Rush made an agreement with the queen. They'll return with an army to rid the mountain of the Fazurks. In return, they'll release the dragon and pledge their alliance to the elves for the upcoming war."

He gave a slight shake of his head. "Cora, that will never happen."

"Well, I assumed that the queen would like me after I saved her...stupid me."

"Tell them to turn around. They're wasting their time."

He's right. You have no leverage with the queen now.

"What's our next move?"

He turned back to the water. "Her threat was very clear. We stay together at all times."

"What about when you're at the front?"

"Then you come with me."

"We don't have homes. Where will we sleep?"

"Here."

Hatchling, we came here to request an alliance with the queen. This endeavor has failed.

We can't give up, Ashe. "What does she want with me? To exile me?"

Callon kept his eyes on the brook. "To hand you over to King Lux."

It was one of the rare times she was speechless.

"I made it very clear that will never happen. She makes a move, and I tell the elves who you really are. She may be the leader of Eden Star, but I'm the leader of our army, as I've been for thousands of years. My political power rivals hers—and I will destroy her if necessary."

I've never heard him speak this way.

Neither have I.

Then this is serious—very serious.

Rush?

He's asleep, Pretty.

I really need to talk to him.

Alright.

Rush came into the conversation, his thoughts clear like he'd been wide awake. **Everything alright?**

We've got a problem.

What's going on?

You know how Ashe said I killed all the Shamans, blah, blah?

That's not how I would describe it, but yeah. What's your point? Blah, blah.

Now isn't the time for jokes.

You started it.

I was just trying to save time.

Well, that worked out great.

Get on with it, Pretty.

Basically, the queen doesn't peg me as the hero of Eden Star. She thinks I'm responsible for everything.

By what logic?

Callon says it's just an excuse to get rid of me.

I should bite her in half and put one piece in the ocean and the other in a volcano.

I can't ask for her help with the dwarves. It would be totally pointless.

Then the dragon alliance is out of the question.

Yep.

Are you in danger right now? We're hustling to get to you.

She wants to hand me over to King Lux.

Cunt.

Grrrrrrr.

But I have Callon, so I'll be fine.

I never imagined there would be a ruler more corrupt than my own father.

Tell me about it.

We're never going to make an alliance while she sits on the throne. We don't have enough people as it is, and the elves are one of the few formidable foes against King Lux. We need them.

I know.

So, she has to go.

You want me to stage a coup?

I want Callon to take her place. That would fix all of our problems. And he's a far better leader for the elves anyway.

He said he wasn't interested.

I have a feeling he's changed his mind about that. If she really tries to hand you over to the enemy for her own selfish interests, she's a corrupt ruler. And if she successfully throws away the greatest weapon Eden Star has, she's a stupid one. He serves the leader on the throne, but his loyalty is to Eden Star. If his duty requires him to take on the role, trust me, he will.

Maybe. So, what do we do about the dwarves?

Do you think your three friends would volunteer?

Only one is a soldier, and I doubt he would leave his post for this. We're friends, but we aren't that close.

What about Callon?

I can ask...but it's really not the best time.

You're forgetting something, Hatchling. You're a decent swordsman —and you're fused with Ashe, King of Dragons—

Swordswoman.

We can handle a few gophers in a hole.

But that wasn't the deal. We came for the queen—and that didn't work out.

It hasn't worked out yet, but it shall.

Are you sure?

We are one, Hatchling.

Cora became Callon's shadow.

Wherever he went, she was close behind. When she joined him at the border, the soldiers never questioned her presence. She lingered in the background, watching Callon issue orders and receive hearty obedience in response. His subordinates didn't just regard him with respect, but something much deeper.

He has the blood of kings.

I know he does.

Twilight descended, and Callon withdrew into his office in one of the tree houses. There was a desk covered with maps and notes. He sat with upright posture, made notes with a quill, and then stared at the parchment with a hard gaze.

Cora hardly ever spoke so she wouldn't distract him.

A soldier entered, a bow over his back. Blond hair. Blue eyes. It was Hawk. "General Callon, the west has no activity."

He kept his eyes on the paper and gave a subtle nod.

Hawk regarded her with a stare before he stepped out.

She followed him. "I'm glad to see that you're alright."

He turned around and stood tall, his armor the same as Callon's, just without the flower medals. "Unfortunately, Eden Star suffered the casualties. Not us."

"Peony has been worried about you."

"I received her note today."

"Good."

"I'm glad that she and her father are well. I did lose a few friends, however."

"I know... It's terrible."

His hands moved behind his back. "General Callon told us that it was you who saved Eden Star—not him."

She met his gaze.

"You have a powerful mind. I can feel it when you draw near. Thank you for using it to our benefit—rather than our detriment."

"I would give my life to protect this forest."

"You've already proven that." He gave a subtle nod then stepped away.

"Do you think this will change anything?"

He halted but didn't turn around.

"Between you and Peony…?"

He remained quiet for several long seconds. "We've taken our immortality for granted. I hope she realizes that."

When Callon's rotation ended, they headed back to Eden Star. Between the enormous trees, the air smelled like pine and morning dew. Wild flowers brushed against their legs as they passed, vegetation overgrown in the grass and meadows.

"Have you fully recovered?"

Callon was completely equipped for war, the plates of his armor fitting over his chest and shoulders like a second skin. His shield was hooked to his back, along with his bow and a large quiver of arrows. His long sword was always at his belt, just inches from his hand.

"Your mind, I mean."

He continued forward, his gaze straight ahead. "It took several days. I've been well ever since."

"I was worried."

"The effects were temporary—like a very bad headache that takes time to resolve."

"I'm glad I got there when I did."

"The torture had gone on for minutes. If it hadn't, I would have defeated General Noose swiftly."

"Minutes?"

"Yes."

"But…that's not possible. I mean, it is. But only for me."

He halted, careful not to step directly on a bundle of orange flowers. "I've pondered this extensively over the last week. The Skull Crusher is lethal to anyone who comes into contact with it, even just for a few seconds. That's why we lost so many elves that night. It wasn't the fires. It wasn't the fear. It was the Death Magic." He turned his face to regard her. "I trained you to prevail by using your mind. Your lack of experience and strength are compensated by your unique abilities. But I didn't just train you—you trained me as well."

She gave a slight nod.

"I'm not immune to the Skull Crusher, but I can survive it longer than most."

"I think you're right. It makes sense."

He continued forward again, moving past the enormous trunks of the trees. Most of the sky was impossible to discern because the canopy was too thick, but rays of sunshine struck the forest floor and brightened the petals of the flowers.

When they passed the final copse of trees and entered the heart of the forest, a row of soldiers blocked further progression into Eden Star. Twelve soldiers in full armor were in a straight line like a fence.

Queen Delwyn was right in the middle.

Shit.

Do not fear. She doesn't know who she's dealing with.

You can't burn them, Ashe. Then we'd be no different than the Shamans.

It wasn't me that I was referring to.

Callon instinctively stepped in front of Cora.

Queen Delwyn stared, eyes without remorse. "Step aside, General Callon. We will go through you if we must."

He slowly withdrew his blade from his scabbard, metal dragging against metal, the sound audible and sharp. His hand spun the blade around his wrist before he stabbed it deep into the earth, marking the line that shouldn't be crossed. "The war with the empire has reigned for thousands of years. But it's different now. Eden Star has never been breached, but our forest burned, our people were murdered, and our serenity was forever changed. This is only the beginning. King Lux has revealed his agenda—to rid this earth of us forever." With arms by his sides, he remained in front of his sword, blocking Cora from view. "When my sword fell, Cora defended Eden Star with hers. She killed the Shamans with her mind. General Noose's conquest would have been easy if it weren't for Cora. She saved us all—and she pledged her alliance to us. If King Lux wants her, it's because she's a threat. It's because she's the one person on this earth who can defeat those monsters. To hand over a weapon so powerful is inconceivable."

In her white dress with flowers in her hair, the queen stood with her hands together at her belly, flanked by fully armed soldiers on either side. There was a slight smile, as if his emotional plea was a mere joke. "She wields a blade of dragon scales. Any friend of Eden Star wouldn't wield such a weapon."

"The blade she wields is irrelevant. It's who she wields it for that matters."

I can't let Callon die for me.

He will prevail, Hatchling.

"She is Eden Star's savior—and should be treated as such. She should be treated with respect...because she's the daughter of a king."

The smile vanished, and her beautiful face turned tense.

"The daughter of King Tiberius—Cora Riverglade. My *Sor-lei*."

The men who flanked the queen all turned their gaze on Cora, trying to see her past Callon's frame.

"I've served as the General of Eden Star for thousands of years. It has cost me everything I hold dear. My wife. My son. My brother. There is no sacrifice I wouldn't make for my people. My loyalty is unquestioned. If Cora were a true threat to Eden Star, the tip of my own blade would impale her throat. But she is no threat to Eden Star or its people. In fact, she's the best thing that's come into this forest in a millennium. I would lay down my life to protect hers the way I would with Eden Star. I can vouch for her—and my word is my truth. You've trusted me to lead us into battle. You've trusted me to protect our forest. You've trusted me for thousands of years. Trust me now."

The queen's steady gaze pierced his, shallow like the shoreline, the hatred visible from the surface to the bedrock. "Your judgment has been clouded by your misplaced affection. There is no proof—"

"She wears Tiberius's ring. And even if she didn't, she possesses the same kindness in her eyes that he did. Their likeness is easy to see—if you ignore the human traits and focus on the elven."

"Whether it's true or not, it does not matter. She's an enemy to Eden Star—and will be handed over to King Lux. With her gone, there will be no more attacks on our forest. There will be lasting peace."

Callon remained rigidly in place, tall and strong, ready to take on twelve soldiers with his bare hands. "King Lux isn't interested in war. He's interested in complete domination. Once he has it, there will be peace—in death."

"My decision has been made." The crown upon her head bloomed with white daisies, of a purity that didn't exist in her heart. Her eyes were the brightest green, but the darkness in her heart had turned them gray. "Take her."

Cora reached for her sword.

No.

She dropped her hand.

Wait.

As if a command hadn't been given, the soldiers remained still. They looked to General Callon—as if they expected him to give an order.

"I said, take her." She looked from side to side, waiting for the first elf to step forward.

"I won't slay my own men." He didn't reach for his sword lodged in the dirt. "So, they'll have to kill me if they want her."

"That's no problem." She gave a subtle nod, instructing her men to serve out the execution.

Nobody moved.

His rule has always triumphed over hers. Now will be no different.

Queen Delwyn's eyes moved from side to side, waiting for her men to carry out the sentence. Not a single sword had been drawn. It was as if she hadn't spoken at all. She grabbed the soldier to her right and shoved him forward. "Now."

He stumbled slightly before he regained his footing, his white-blond hair pinned back with metal clips that resembled flowers. He gave a glance over his shoulder before he looked at General Callon, the man he followed into battle.

Callon held his position, looking his soldier in the eye.

The soldier stepped forward and reached for the sword in the dirt.

Cora's hand immediately went to her hilt.

It took both hands for him to tug the sword out of the ground, the tip compacted with a layer of dirt. He eyed it for a moment before he turned it around, grabbing it by the blade, and offered it to its owner.

Callon took it without pulling his gaze away from his. "Thank you, Rylan."

Told you.

Rylan gave a bow before he backed away and returned to the line of men—this time far away from the queen.

Queen Delwyn's face was identical to the angry look the poisonous frogs wore. Her lips smashed hard together, and her eyes narrowed to slits. A slight tremor overtook her body, her fingers curling into fists.

Callon held her gaze, but when no words were forthcoming, he addressed the men. "Inform all of Eden Star that King Tiberius lives on—in his daughter. Cora Riverglade is the savior of this forest, and she is one of us."

The soldiers scattered, venturing in different directions to spread the news throughout the forest.

Queen Delwyn never took her eyes off his.

Now they were all that remained, the atmosphere so hostile that the songbirds and their music had relocated elsewhere. There was no sunshine in the shade of the trees. No joy amid the rage in her eyes.

She stepped forward, her bare feet silent against the grass.

General Callon inserted his blade back on to his hip.

She stopped just inches from him, her eyes shifting back and forth between his. "You will live long enough to regret this—and not a moment longer."

31

STUNNING SCALES

Cora walked beside Callon, still speechless.

He led the way like he knew exactly where they were going—even though neither one of them had a place to call home.

The soldiers must have been quick to spread their news because most of the elves she passed regarded her with intense stares, scrutinizing her features for signs of similarity to their fallen king. Their eyes dropped to her hands, too—to the ring on her thumb.

Callon left the center of Eden Star and hit the weather-beaten path they took to their private glade, where they practiced in secret, prepared her for the battles to come.

She stepped closer to his side. "You should come with me."

He kept his eyes on the path.

"Can you?"

He gave her a side look.

"After what the queen said, maybe it's not best for you to stay here."

"I'm unafraid."

"Can you come anyway?"

He halted on the trek and regarded her.

"I don't think this rescue is going to be as simple as I hope…"

He glanced back the way they'd come, as if he could see Eden Star through the dense trees.

"Need all the help we can get."

He continued to stare into the forest. "Cora." After several breaths, he turned back to her. "As much as I want to protect you, I can't abandon Eden Star. It was different the first time, but now that our forest has been breached, I can't leave. My people are actively at war now—and I must lead them."

She gave a nod in understanding. "I didn't ask because I need your protection. You know I can handle myself. But I am worried about leaving you behind…"

"My connection with the elves is much stronger than hers. You don't need to worry."

"But the last thing she said—"

"She will be off the throne before she can make good on her word."

"What do you mean?"

He gave her his full stare now, a strong jaw that matched the strength in his eyes. "I'm going to remove her from power—and take her place."

Yes.

A jolt of lightning moved into her heart, and her eyes widened as a result. "You are?"

"She's given me no choice. Not only has she lied to her people to preserve her image, but now her decisions are actively hurting the elves she swore to protect. Her corruption goes deep—and I think there's more beneath the surface."

Spoken like a true king.

"I've never wanted the crown. Still don't. But as the General of Eden Star, it is my sworn duty to protect the forest and its inhabitants, to make any and all sacrifices to ensure its immortality. I know the crown should be handed to you next, but you're just as unfit to rule as the queen. You're a child—and not just in our eyes."

"It's not my cup of tea anyway…"

"When King Lux is defeated and peace returns to this land, I will step down. A new regime will step in—and a new legacy will be born."

"I think that's a great idea. Except the last part. Whether we're at war or peace, you're the rightful king."

His eyes shifted back and forth as he regarded her.

"How will you achieve this?"

"That, I don't know. But I do know that she won't expect it."

"I don't think anyone will…"

Pretty?

Cora lay on her cot in the meadow, a few feet away from where Callon slept. It was a clear night, and the starlight was almost too bright to sleep. *Hey, Flare. How are things?*

We're getting close to the forest. Had to take a couple detours, but we made it.

I can't wait to see you.

Me too, Pretty. Here's Rush.

You're still in one piece, right?

Yes. But it's a long story…

Blah, blah?

She gave a quiet chuckle out loud.

Callon turned in his pack to regard her, stirred at the sound.

"Sorry…"

He gave an annoyed look and rolled on his side to face the other way.

The queen ordered her men to take me away, but when Callon refused to step down, the soldiers backed off. Instead, Callon ordered them to tell every elf in the forest that I'm Cora River-glade...daughter of Tiberius.

General Badass...

I know.

Did you ask him to help us?

He said he can't leave Eden Star, not after it was attacked.

That's fair.

He also said that he's going to overthrow the queen...and take her place.

Whaaaaaat? Okay, that's it. He's officially General Badass from now on.

She gave another chuckle but kept it within her mind this time. *I couldn't believe it.*

It's the right move for his people—so I can.

I'm a little worried about leaving him here alone. I can't even talk to him...

He's the last person you need to worry about.

You're probably right.

Based on my calculations, we'll arrive tomorrow afternoon. Ready?

Yes.

We'll meet you at the same place. How are the shitheads anyway?

Shitheads?

The little frogs I dropped off.

She rolled her eyes. *They're good. Getting really big. About half the size of an adult.*

Man, that's still enormous.

They're a lot more subdued in the forest because they know they're safe here.

You think that's another reason General Noose invaded the forest? To get rid of the last of them?

It hadn't crossed her mind. *Maybe. But that doesn't matter anymore...now that they know what I'm capable of.*

Wait until they find out about Ashe. He gave a chuckle. *Man, I'd give anything to see my father's face...*

The fireflies lit up the shrouded mist in the cemetery, providing a solid screen that provided a barrier of privacy for anyone else visiting the spirits of their loved ones. The stone bench was cold to the touch, even through the fabric of her pants.

"I was able to fight him off until he retreated with the Shamans. Queen Delwyn was unharmed, and Callon recovered. We put out the fires, but most people lost their homes. A lot of people perished. We still don't know how they got in..."

The wisps of blue smoke that outlined his presence floated in the air, the line permanent but also ethereal. "I felt the disturbance. I knew something terrible had befallen Eden Star."

"The forest will recover...and we'll rebuild."

"It's a great relief to know my queen and brother are both well."

"Yes."

"And it brings me honor to know that my daughter was the savior of this beautiful place." There were no features in his countenance, but his stare was present, hot on her face. "I'm grateful that my brother has been such a presence in your life. Without him, victory would have been impossible."

"He's the greatest person I've ever known."

"I can only imagine how grateful Queen Delwyn is."

"Actually...she accused me of being responsible."

His stare ensued.

"Said I was the reason they entered Eden Star. Decided to turn me over to King Lux. It would have happened...if Callon hadn't intervened. There's no doubt of her corruption at this point. Callon intends to remove her from power and take the throne for himself."

The silence passed on indefinitely, like he was too overwhelmed to form a response.

Cora feared she'd offended him—and he would disappear.

"You seem to be describing a different man—because my brother would never do such a thing. But if he has…it's for good reason. He's not susceptible to temptation. There's no ego to feed. His stomach doesn't gnaw for power. Every action he takes is for the good of his people—so this must be right for Eden Star."

"It is."

"This is a hard truth to accept. I shared my life with Delwyn in every intimate way imaginable. But now I sort through the memories of the past, wondering what I was so naïve to miss."

"I'm sorry…"

"I'm the one who should be sorry—and ashamed."

"Love makes us overlook things sometimes…"

The silence returned, hanging there like the mist.

"I'm leaving Eden Star. Not sure when I'll return."

"Where do your travels take you?"

"To the Stronghold. The dwarves need our help—and they have a dragon."

"A dragon fused with a dwarf? Unheard of."

"We want to free the dragon and forge an alliance between them and the elves."

"How can an alliance be forged when the Queen of Eden Star has no interest?"

"I'm hoping that Callon has claimed the throne by the time I return."

"His ascension may be swift. He's unanimously loved by every elf in Eden Star. There is no elf in our history that has served his people greater than he has. He will be a great king. Far better than I was."

"They still love you—even though you're gone."

He turned quiet again.

"I think that's why they tolerate Delwyn. Out of respect for you."

The outline of his head turned away.

"I'm not sure when we'll speak again…so I wanted to say goodbye."

After a while, he turned back to her again. "Please be careful, Cora. I don't want this to be our last conversation—with the veil between us. I would much rather you speak to me while alive than while dead."

"I'll be okay. I'm not alone."

"I know your dragon will keep you safe. Have you told him what I revealed to you?"

"No. He asked a few times, but I told him it was elven folklore. It hurt to lie to him. I still feel terrible about it."

"With a connection as profound as that, it goes against nature to deceive and conceal. It's not a door that you open and close. The door doesn't exist at all."

Another jolt moved into her heart, stopping it for a few seconds before it continued on. Her eyes penetrated the mist, desperate to see a face that no longer existed. "You speak about this like…you know exactly how it feels."

Silence.

Her heart drummed like the sound of war, loud in her ears, strong in her temples.

His head turned away, regarding his own grave. "Because I do."

Her lungs sucked in the air instinctively, her nostrils flaring as her blood demanded a dump of oxygen. A million words came to her mind, but somehow, she couldn't get them into her mouth and on her tongue.

"It was a short while…but it was the most intense connection I've ever felt. There is no relationship more intimate than one that is fused. My spirit has found peace on this side of the veil, but the heartbreak has never stopped. Even now, I share every thought like she can still hear it."

"You…you were fused with a dragon?"

He nodded. "The plan was to destroy the Steward of Easton in his castle before moving on High Castle. When we camped for the night, I took my evening walk alone. That was when I came upon her—and her stunning scales. Alone. Scared. Injured. With King Lux scouring every inch of Anastille, she had nowhere to go, especially with broken wings. She trusted me when she didn't have reason to. And we fused."

Cora took a breath, speechless.

"Our time together was short. Just for a year. I took her to Eden Star, and she was overwhelmed by the beauty of the trees. With her large size, she could never experience the forest the way I could. I gave her things she couldn't find herself. She did the same for me. Our friendship deepened. It turned into something more—familial."

"What happened to her?"

He dropped his chin as he sucked in a deep and painful breath. "I was killed—and so was she."

They took the secret passage out of Eden Star.

The rocky crevasses on either side of them blocked the sunlight from heating their already warm skin. Roots grew in the cracks. And even in the shade, flowers still bloomed. Water trickled down from a waterfall that couldn't be seen.

Now that Callon was the general once more, he was always in his armor, ready for a battle that could arrive on his doorstep in the middle of the night.

"Callon?"

His eyes remained ahead as he escorted her out of the forest. "Yes?"

"There's something I need to tell you."

They passed through the rocks and entered the meadow on the other side, the wild flowers swaying in the subtle breeze.

The trunks of the trees in the forest were beautiful, but the wide-open view was special in its own way. "I'm listening."

"My father shared something with me. He told me I could share it with you."

He took a few steps in the meadow before he stopped to regard her.

She held his gaze, the sun beating down on them both now that the mountain was behind them. "When he died…he was fused with a dragon."

There was no reaction—at least, not at first. It took several moments for his roots to soak up the drops of truth, to process the words he'd just heard.

"He came across her in the countryside. She was injured, so he fused to keep her safe. They remained that way for a year—until he was killed."

His stare hardened—visibly angry.

"That's too much of a coincidence, right? The fact that he was fused…and I have these abilities."

"Tiberius Riverglade, King of Eden Star, would never betray his people. He would never harbor the enemy within our borders. He would never conceal such a secret from us all—let alone me."

"Callon—"

"You misunderstood him." He continued his walk, this time his stride quicker.

She watched him go.

Give him time.

I don't understand. He knows I'm fused with you—

It's a different kind of betrayal, Hatchling. His own brother harbored this secret—and never shared it.

Probably because he knew he would react this way.

Because of my decision, he lost the people he loves most. For his own brother to fuse with his enemy, it's a different kind of betrayal. He needs time—so let's give it to him.

Now that the border of Eden Star was being monitored on a grander scale, they had to venture farther away from the tree line to avoid detection. The trek was spent in silence—at Callon's request.

They moved through a copse of trees and reached the other side.

When she saw them, her heart sprouted wings and flew with the strength of a dragon. They sat together on a gathering of boulders, shaded by a lone tree. Rush stood on a rock, one leg hiked higher than the other as he faced the other way, keeping a lookout.

Callon halted at the last tree—as if he refused to go any farther. His eyes drilled into Rush's backside with the same wild anger with which he regarded General Noose. His hand reached for the pommel of his sword, but after a heavy breath, his hand returned to his side. When his emotions were gathered, he turned to Cora. Now that she was about to depart, the anger he'd been harboring faded. The tension released from his face. "I know you're strong. I know Ashe will protect you. But please be careful, *Sor-lei*."

Her eyes softened as she gave a nod.

"You're all I have—and I can't lose you."

"I can't lose you either…"

He embraced her with both arms, hugging her tightly as he rested his chin on her head. "Return as soon as you can."

"I will." With her cheek pressed to his chest, she closed her eyes. "*Rein-Lei-Vu*."

His hand cupped the back of her head. "*Rein-Lei-Vu*…" When he pulled away, he pressed a kiss to her forehead, his hand still supporting her neck. Her body suddenly went cold when his affection was taken away, when he turned and returned the way they'd come. He didn't look back.

She watched him go until he disappeared into the trees.

The weight of her heart pulled her entire body to the earth. Her eyes blinked several times to dispel the moisture that built up on her bottom lid. When tears escaped, she wiped them with her fingers and marched forward. "I'm here…"

Bridge and the others came over to greet her, exchanging hugs and pleasantries.

Rush walked over but lingered, giving everyone else an opportunity to stay hello first. When the group parted, he stepped forward, wearing his handsome smirk. "You okay?"

"I'm fine. I just hate saying goodbye."

"It's not goodbye. It's see-you-later."

She nodded.

He kept his distance, his arms by his sides, eyes on hers.

She watched him in return, her heart aching for a whole new reason. "I'm really happy to see you…"

The smirk faded, his eyes giving away his emotion. "Is that for me or Flare?"

She moved into his chest and wrapped her arms around him, her face fitting against his chest just the way it used to.

His arms reciprocated in a flash, cupping her petite size with his big hands, bringing her so close there wasn't a breath between them. His chin rested on her head, and he gave a deep exhale.

Her hands instantly remembered his body, remembered every aspect of his physique. It was like stepping into her home, the most comfortable place in the world. Fire chased away the mist. Affection chased away the loneliness. "You."

32

ONE THING IN COMMON

THE CAMPFIRE GLOWED JUST LONG ENOUGH to cook the meat. A rabbit was split five ways—and Cora subsisted on the food she'd packed. The flames were snuffed out before darkness arrived, but there was still a red-orange glow in the embers.

Everyone retired to sleep in their bedrolls. Cora took the first watch because she wasn't tired, but Rush remained across from her, his handsome face fatigued by the constant travels across Anastille.

Rush sat on the ground with his back to the rock, his arms resting on his knees. "So, Hawk loves Peony, and Peony loves Hawk, but since she's afraid he's gonna die, she's like 'Nah, I'll pass'?"

"I wouldn't put it like that, but pretty much."

"Well, that sounds kinda dumb."

"I know. I hope the attack on Eden Star changes her opinion."

"It's nice that you made some friends. What did you bribe them with?"

She narrowed her eyes in a playful way.

He gave a chuckle. "You know I kid."

"There's also Lia too, but I'm not as close with her as the other two."

"How did everyone react when your lineage was revealed?"

"Honestly, I don't know. Callon and I stayed away from Eden Star after our confrontation with the queen. But the people loved Tiberius so much that I suspect it will improve my social standing significantly."

"I'm sure it will get the queen off your back."

"I don't know… She's vile. I'm worried what she'll do to Callon."

"She can't touch him. He's been protecting Eden Star far longer than she's been queen. The elves know that."

"I know, but…you should have seen her face. She's tried to get rid of me so many times, and Callon has always prevented it. I'm more than just a thorn in her side. I'm her biggest vulnerability."

"Because she thinks you want to be queen? That's ironic because you have no interest in the crown, and now Callon is going for it—and he's a much bigger threat."

"Yeah, it is ironic." Her eyes dropped to the fire, the gentle glow growing fainter.

"There must be more to the story."

Her eyes lifted up again.

"Maybe she does hate you. Maybe she is humiliated by her husband's infidelity. But to sacrifice all her integrity to hide this secret...doesn't make sense. She's hiding something else."

"Tiberius said she hasn't come to visit him since he died."

"Suspicious, isn't it?"

"A bit."

His eyes dropped and looked her over, examining the strong but durable armor Callon had provided her. "You look cute in that, by the way."

She instinctively looked down at herself. "Thanks. I thought I could use it for what's to come. And I'd rather wear it than carry it in my pack the entire way."

After he looked her over, his eyes settled on her face, the stare so focused he didn't blink.

She met his look and gave a swallow.

"It's nice to have these conversations while I can see your face." Crickets were loud in the meadow around them. An occasional hoot split the night. The sky was cloudless to expose a full moon, the light piercing the darkness. His hands together around his knees, Rush's eyes glowed as he examined her, a subtle smile on his lips. "We've been apart for so long... it's hard to believe you're really here."

"I know..."

"I have to warn you, being a fugitive isn't nearly as comfy as having a private tree house in a magical forest. Your back is gonna ache from sleeping on the ground. There's going to be a spider in your bedroll from time to time. And the food...pretty terrible."

She gave a smile. "I don't mind any of that—as long as we're together."

He didn't hold her gaze with as much intensity as before. Now his eyes softened, like a flower that began to wilt.

"There's something I need to tell you."

The stare continued.

"When I was talking to my father, he told me he was fused with a dragon."

The look of longing disappeared when his eyebrows jumped up his face. "King Tiberius of Eden Star? An elf?"

"Yes."

"Whoa...what? When?"

"A year before he—" her eyes dropped "—he died."

Rush digested the implication of her words with a hard jaw, with a look of loathing. His eyes shifted away for a few seconds before his focus returned. "Where did he find a dragon?"

"He said they were about to challenge the Steward of Easton, and he found her hidden in the forest with two broken wings.

I guess she was scared and had nowhere to go, so she trusted him to fuse."

Rush dropped his gaze to the fire, his eyebrows scrunched together. "I don't know how that would be possible."

"He wouldn't lie."

"I'm not saying he is. I just don't understand how there could have been a dragon just sitting in the forest."

"Well, she had two broken wings, so she was obviously being hunted."

When Rush looked away again, a whole new look of pain on his face, she knew he'd figured it out.

"What?"

He gave a quick shake of his head. "I don't want to say..."

"Rush."

He ignored her look.

"You can tell me anything."

"It's not that. I just don't think you want to know."

"I probably don't...but you still need to tell me."

After a breath, his eyes reconnected with hers. "My father tortured dragons at random, to keep them in compliance. So, he would force some of them to flee... for us to chase them. To give them that small hope of freedom just so we could take it away...and mutilate them in the process."

She inhaled a slow and deep breath, every bit of air painful in her lungs.

"I never did that…just to be clear."

Not that she'd needed more of a reason to kill King Lux, but now she had another. It hurt even more now that she was fused with Ashe, the dragon that had become more than a friend, more than an ally.

"He was at the right place at the right time… Good for her."

"Yeah. He took her to Eden Star, and I guess she loved it. They were really close…from the way he described it. The way he talked about their relationship, it was like he was talking about my relationship with Ashe. Your relationship with Flare."

"I suspect the fuse is the reason he's so partial to this cause. The elves hate dragons so much, I wouldn't be surprised if they would have just left her there to die. None of them would have offered the fuse. And none of them would have defended her either."

"You're right."

"That relationship gave him a perspective that no one else has. You guys are strangers, but it looks like you have at least one thing in common. A unique, profound thing in common. My father and I are both fused, but his relationship with his dragon is vastly different from mine…as we both know."

"Yeah, you're right."

"Did he say anything else? What happened to her?"

She couldn't meet his gaze as she answered his question. "She passed away…when he did."

Whatever his reaction was, she didn't know because she couldn't see his face.

Silence continued, long and weighty.

She lifted her chin and looked at his visage—and had never seen it so pale. It was the exact color of the moon, like all the blood had been sucked from his flesh by leeches. "Rush—"

"One less dragon, because of me."

"Look—"

"You can't make me feel better, so don't try." He left the campfire and walked into the darkness. His silhouette was visible, but only for a few seconds. He blended in with the night, his footsteps silent, until he was no more.

They avoided common paths and trails and stuck to the brush as much as possible. It caused several detours, adding days to their journey. They were just as vulnerable in the daylight as the darkness, so there was no good time to move across Anastille. They just did it—and hoped for the best.

This is taking too long.

Well, we can't fly.

We could. I blend into the darkness better than any other dragon.

And the others?

They can meet us there.

We stay together.

That wouldn't be a problem—if the company weren't so unpleasant.

Ashe, he feels terrible—

He could feel worse, and it wouldn't make a difference. A lifetime of repentance and remorse doesn't even scratch the surface. He slays dragons. He kills kings. That's who he was—and still is.

Cora knew her dragon well enough to know that nothing would assuage his anger. She let the conversation die, waited for a change in the tide to dispel his foul mood. Rush was in the lead, so she quickened her pace to catch up. They hadn't spoken since last night, and judging from the distance he kept between them, he still didn't want to. "Whatever happened with the goats?"

Rush turned at the question, his high eyebrows showing his surprise. "We didn't run into them on the way out. If we had, probably wouldn't have made it."

"You think we'll run into them again?"

"Unfortunately."

"Come on, goats are cute. I want to see them."

"These are not ordinary goats. These are the kinda goats that will knock you flat on the ground."

She rolled her eyes. "The only animal you like is your dragon."

"When did I ever say I like him?"

She gave him a hard nudge in the side.

His short wince was quickly replaced by that smirk along with his deep chuckle. "I'm getting an earful right now."

"Good."

He rubbed the tender spot as he continued to walk, and once it subsided, his arm dropped to his side. "How'd you sleep? Probably miss your bed made of flowers or whatever."

"Wasn't so bad."

"I'm not sure what I'm looking forward to more. Defeating my father and freeing all the dragons or having a bed again."

"The second one, probably."

"You know me so well." He turned his attention forward, leading the group through the trees and taking cover from the skies. The Stronghold was visible on a clear day, but so was the distance they had to cover to get there. "So, I've been doing some thinking—"

"Wow, that's a first."

Now he nudged her in the side. "Ha-ha. Blah-blah."

"Careful...I'll throw a rock at your head."

He chuckled and kept going. "I've felt a target on the back of my head all day."

"I'll save it for the...what do you call them?"

"Fazurks. Or the Big Uglies. Terms are interchangeable."

"Not gonna lie. I'm relieved I have Ashe for this."

"If you didn't, I wouldn't even entertain this idea."

"Come on, I handled General Noose on my own."

"You're right." He gave a nod in agreement. "Wish I hadn't missed it...but also hope it never happens again."

"So, what were you thinking about? Must have been important since you do it so rarely."

"Wow, just gonna keep 'em coming, huh?"

"Like I said, I missed you."

His eyes softened the way they did long ago, in a different time, in different circumstances. His gaze lingered like smoke hovering over the flames. "Your father was fused with a dragon when he conceived you. Perhaps that explains your abilities."

Ashe's powerful voice intruded. *He's right.*

"But what does that explain, exactly?" she asked. "That...I'm part dragon?"

Yes.

"Yes." Rush continued his pace even though his entire focus was on the conversation between them. "When you're fused, you're one. So, if you were conceived under those circumstances, perhaps parts of the dragon were transferred to you."

"That doesn't explain why other people fused with dragons don't sire children with the same abilities. What about you?"

"My father wasn't fused before I was born. Come to think of it, no one has been fused and had children. Families were born a long time ago, and now that they're immortal, there's no reason to continue reproducing. My father is very picky about whom he allows to fuse with one of his dragons. Most of the time, they're temporary fusions. He doesn't grant immortality to just anyone."

"That's why they continue to serve him—because everyone wants to live forever."

He nodded. "And he has a small inventory, so he has to be deliberate in his decisions. General Noose was promised a dragon for his loyal service, so that's why we're seeing him everywhere we go."

"He almost took Eden Star...and would have received a dragon if he had."

"But it didn't happen—because of you."

I MUST FEED.

We're out in the open right now.

But my scales are as dark as night—and the blanket of clouds conceals the stars.

What does that matter?

My body won't block out the stars, so you can't see me pass.

Oh...gotcha. "Rush?"

"Yes?" He examined the field and the distance before he turned back.

"Ashe is hungry."

I don't need his permission.

"And a bit grouchy…"

Rush took another scan of the surroundings before he regarded her. "It's not ideal, but we need him to be strong for the Stronghold. Tell him to be careful since he doesn't know the terrain well."

I DO NOT TAKE ORDERS FROM YOU.

Cora winced at the scream in her head.

Rush must have noticed it because he dismissed himself.

"Alright, let's do this." She stepped farther into the stalks of grass, away from everyone else so she'd have ample room to make the separation. She pulled her mind away and felt his mind mirror it, their souls coming apart. Then the world shook as she lost her footing, swaying until she hit the ground.

Ashe opened his wings and took flight.

A large hand moved to her shoulder. "You alright?"

She pushed herself up, getting to her knees and then her feet. "Yeah. I'm just not used to it yet."

Rush looked into the sky where Ashe had been—and saw no sign of him. "He really is invisible."

"Yeah."

"That's going to be a big help in the future." He withdrew his touch and stepped back. "You'll get used to the mechanics."

"Got any tips?"

He chewed the inside of his lip as he considered. "It's been so long that I don't even remember what it feels like…"

"Oh, that makes sense. I used to get really sick. At least that doesn't happen anymore."

They returned to the main campground, where everyone else was settled in their cots. But no one was asleep—because Ashe took their full attention.

Liam continued to stare into the darkness, hopeful for a glimpse. "I hope to see his scales in the light of day."

"How big is he?" Lilac asked.

"Freakin' humongous," Bridge said. "He's nearly twice the size of Flare."

"What's he like?" Lilac turned to Cora, who took a seat beside her.

"Majestic. Wise. Glorious," Cora answered. "And a bit stubborn…"

"He can't be *that* stubborn," Bridge said. "He's here, right?"

Cora gave a nod.

"Since we're all awake, let's talk about the plan," Rush said. "We're still a few days out, but we should figure out what we're going to do when we arrive."

"Wait…you don't know what we're doing?" Zane asked. "That's the plan?"

"Come on, I never have a plan," Rush said. "And we do just fine."

"We were almost trapped underground forever," Lilac said. "I don't think that constitutes fine—"

"*Almost*," Rush said. "I got us out of there, didn't I?"

Lilac rolled her eyes.

"I think we've got to lure as many of the Fazurks out of the tunnels as possible," Rush said. "Burn them to a crisp. Do it over and over."

"But how are we going to get them out of the tunnels?" Cora asked.

"That...I don't know." Rush sat with his arms on his knees. "Maybe good ol'-fashioned bait?"

Bridge narrowed his eyes on Rush. "I hope that means you're volunteering..."

"Cora and I can't do it," Rush said. "We're the ones with the dragons."

"Of course..." Bridge shook his head. "Look how that worked out."

"What about water?" Cora asked.

Rush stared at her, perplexed. "Water?"

"What do you mean by that?" Lilac asked.

"I've never been there before, so this could be a total miss, but could we flood the mountain?" Cora asked. "Is there a lake nearby or something?"

"Hmm...that's an idea." Bridge looked at Rush. "Flush 'em out. They gotta have a water system of some kind."

"But I don't know where it is or how it works," Rush said. "And I don't know how to drain it either. Plus, if there are surviving dwarves down there, it could drown them too. That's a good idea, but I don't think it'll work. Let's stick with the bait idea."

"Do you think they'll be stupid enough to fall for that, though?" Zane asked.

"Yes," Rush said quickly. "They're a bunch of idiots."

"What do we do about the Shamans and Obsidian?" Bridge asked. "When they see the commotion on the mountain, they're going to come back."

"The Shamans won't be a problem this time." Rush turned to Cora. "Because we've got this superpower right here." He gave her a wink.

Heat flushed her cheeks as if she'd submerged herself in the hot springs.

"And I hope Obsidian does come—because it's two-on-one this time." Rush held up two fingers.

"That might be a problem..." Cora was relieved that Ashe was on the hunt so he couldn't hear this conversation. "Since Obsidian is Ashe's brother."

"Ashe has already said he'll do what's necessary," Rush said. "Back on Mist Isle."

"But it's one thing to say that and another to actually do it..." She understood his mind better than anyone else—except Diamond. She felt his raw emotions, knew his responses to circumstances without sharing a thought. To feel that anguish with him...would be terrible.

"I suspect that once Obsidian sees Ashe, he won't be able to move against him," Rush said. "He's been fused with my father for a long time, so perhaps his mind is too far gone at this point, but it's a possibility."

"True," Cora said.

"But then my father will know that free dragons still exist... somewhere." Rush dropped his head. "We would lose that element of surprise."

"And he would search everywhere for that island," Cora said. "We can't let that happen."

"You're right," Rush said. "So, if Obsidian comes...you'll have to hide."

Cora nodded. "Got it."

33

BAAAAAAHHH

I SEE the way she looks at you.

Rush stopped at the edge of the tree line, examining the landscape for a passing army, for a dragon in the sky, a tiny black dot far into the distance.

She misses you.

Look, I've finally gotten to a decent place about the whole thing...so don't yank me backward.

I'm just saying.

Well, don't.

Just wanted you to know that you aren't alone in your heartbreak.

Rush shaded his eyes as he studied the surroundings at the base of the mountains. They couldn't scale the mountain in the dark, so they had to go first thing in the morning, even though that left them exposed. **I doubt they're there. Probably assume we wouldn't return.**

Probably.

Bridge walked up as he spoke to Cora. "Sailing the seas on a pirate ship sounds cool and everything, but it *sucked*. I was so sick the entire time. And then we almost died a couple times —and I can't swim."

"Why were you on a ship if you can't swim?"

Rush turned to her. "Thank you."

Bridge rolled his eyes. "I don't live in a port city and I'm nowhere near a lake, so when would I learn?"

"Everyone else here learned," Rush said.

"Well, I guess my mom was too busy dealing with the monster-spawn that is my sister." He propped his hands on his hips and looked at the looming mountain.

Lilac gave him a slug in the stomach as she passed. "We're climbing that thing again?"

Bridge leaned over, holding his stomach as he labored through the pain.

"Yep," Rush said. "And we gotta do it fast."

"I've never climbed anything before," Cora said.

"Stay in front of me," Rush said. "I'll catch you if you fall."

Lilac's eyes shifted back and forth between them, her gaze narrowed.

Rush caught the look and stared back. Before she could make a comment, he took a step forward. "Coast is clear, so let's get to it." He started at a jog, moving across the stalks of grass and to the base of the rocks. He boosted Cora up then went behind her.

She climbed to the top of the boulder then looked down. "So, where are the goats?"

Rush pulled his heavy body to the top and got to his feet. "You'll smell them before you see them."

Cora crinkled her nose in disgust.

Rush couldn't keep the grin off his face because she somehow looked cute no matter what she did with her expression. "Come on, let's keep going."

IT WAS AN ALL-DAY TREK TO THE HIGHEST PART OF THE mountain. They were miles from the entrance to the Stronghold, purposely keeping their distance from the Fazurks that were crawling around the entrance.

When they were this high up, a fire was out of the question, and the higher elevation brought a chill across their shoulders. They were a bit closer to the stars, so now they were a little bigger, a little brighter. Everyone was lying in their cots to get some sleep on the solid stone, while Rush sat with his arms on his knees.

The stars are really bright up here.

His eyes shifted as he looked into the darkness, hearing her voice in his mind.

Brightness entered the night when there was a streak across the sky. He noticed it but didn't really focus on it.

Wow, a shooting star. That's cool.

Can't sleep?

Hard to go from flowers to this.

I can imagine.

You never seem to sleep.

I'll sleep when I'm dead.

I'm really not tired, so I can take over.

It's fine. Really.

Heavy silence passed for a while. ***There's something on your mind.***

My father.

Because of what happened here?

Yep.

I'm sorry.

Yeah…it's…whatever. Doesn't matter.

I have Dorian and Callon…and you don't have anybody. But just know that you always have me, Rush.

He almost said something back, but he kept it lodged deep in his throat, where it died.

At first light, they maneuvered over the rocky mountains and approached the entrance to the Stronghold. From the top of the world, they had clear views of Anastille, of Polox in the distance, even Cora's village.

In the other direction were the Shadow Lands.

Covered by heavy cloud bank, the world was still a mystery to the naked eye.

"Smell that?" Bridge called from the back.

Rush inhaled the pungent smell with his nose, recognizing it right away. "Great...they smell even worse."

Now I'm hungry.

That's disgusting.

Men smell worse—in my opinion.

Thanks...

"*Baaaaaahhh.*"

Rush's hand reached out and snatched Cora by the arm, stopping her before she could go any farther. "Whoa, hold on."

The goat appeared on one of the rocks, white with brown spots, his horns pointing straight out.

Cora stared at him before she gave Rush an incredulous look. "You're scared...of that?"

"Not *scared*," Rush said quickly. "Just learned my lesson."

"*Baaaaaahhh.*" He wiggled his little tail.

"Shit, he's calling for the others," Bridge said. "What do we do?"

"You guys are ridiculous." Cora yanked her arm out of Rush's grasp and approached the goat. "He's like two feet tall."

"Cora, be careful," Rush said. "I'm serious. He'll buck you off the mountain."

She gave him a glare over her shoulder. "I'll take my chances, alright?" She stuck out her hand, took a knee, and then watched the goat smell her. "Hey, honey. You're so cute." The goat quickly became acquainted with her, so she petted her hand over his head and down his back.

He closed his eyes and dropped his head, rubbing his horns into her body.

Cora chuckled as she massaged his scalp. "Ah...this is the sweet spot, huh?"

Rush glanced at Bridge.

Bridge glanced back, eyes still wide. "Elves..."

Everyone loves Pretty.

I'll say. "Hey...I have an idea."

"What?" Bridge asked. "Buck it off the mountain while we still have a chance?"

"We need bait, right?" Rush moved closer to his friend, no longer concerned about Cora's safety. "We put some bells on this guy and make him run into the Stronghold. All the Fazurks will come out to play."

Bridge cupped his chin. "Not a bad idea—"

"That's barbaric." Cora abandoned the goat when she heard what they said, and now her eyes were worse than the storms on the sea. "We aren't doing that."

Bridge dropped his arms. "It's better than one of us going in—"

"We'll find another way." Her gaze was still lethal, the suggestion enough to make her blood boil. "We aren't sending a baby goat to his death."

Bridge glanced at Rush again. "Elves..."

"Oh, trust me," Rush said. "I already know."

When they approached the entrance, they crouched down behind an array of boulders to examine the Fazurks. They came and went, some leaving the Stronghold and taking a trail toward the Shadow Lands. Others entered through the hole in the mountain, carrying kills they intended to roast over the fire. The Stronghold had been entirely claimed by these beasts, as if the dwarves had never been there in the first place.

"What now?" Bridge asked, squatting beside him.

"I don't know." Rush tried to count them, but there were too many. "Burning them will be easy, but the second I take flight, I'll be visible from leagues around."

"Can you burn them from the ground?" Bridge asked.

"Sure," Rush said. "But I leave myself pretty vulnerable."

"Not if you have another dragon." Cora joined their conversation, her long hair in a high ponytail off her face, her black elven armor depicting flowers on the surface. The material was durable, so it moved and breathed with her, preserving her femininity while also showcasing her strength. "I can cover you."

"You're even bigger than I am," Rush said. "A lot more visible."

Cora gave a shrug. "I don't think there's any way to do this without that risk. We just have to be quick. Might have to retreat a couple times then return."

"That won't work," Rush said. "Once they figure out that we're here for a reason, they won't leave. We'll have to abandon the dwarves and Talc. We need to do this in one go."

Cora gave a slow nod. "No pressure at all…"

"Wait." Bridge was between them, so he turned to Cora. "You can talk to, like, any dragon, right?"

"It's more complicated than that," Cora said. "But pretty much."

Rush leaned forward and watched his friend. "Where are you going with this, Bridge?"

"Couldn't you talk to Queen Megora?" Bridge asked. "You know, through Talc?"

"I mean, I guess," Cora said. "But why would I?"

"Couldn't we ask her for some pointers?" Bridge asked. "Maybe she can tell us how to get these guys out of the mountain."

Rush couldn't stop himself from narrowing his eyes on his friend's face. "That's actually pretty smart…"

"Why are you surprised? I'm a scholar." Bridge turned back to him. "So, obviously, I'm intelligent."

"With half the stuff that comes out of your mouth…" Rush shook his head. "I don't think so."

Bridge threw an elbow into his side.

Rush gave a grunt as he dropped his head. "Okay, I deserved that."

"So, let's get rid of these guys on the surface before we go further." Cora looked at Rush. "Ready?"

He continued to rub his sensitive ribs, wearing a slight wince. "Yeah, let's get to it."

The second Flare emerged, the Fazurks took notice.

Enormous, with blood-red scales and a toothy smile, he opened his impressive jaws and let out a stream of lava-hot fire. The flames matched his exterior color, creating an inferno of searing heat.

The Fazurks directly in front of him lit up like matches, burning from head to toe, their mighty roars becoming painful screams. Their knees quickly gave out, and they collapsed, now burning firewood.

His talons in the earth, he turned his head left to right, burning the stampede that came from different directions. *This is fun.*

Yeah, kinda is.

Too bad they taste like bat.

You know what they taste like?

I took a bite last time…terrible.

Wow, there's a lot of them.

Their group increased in size from the north, so many that a single jet of fire couldn't catch them all and guard the other side at the same time. *We could use some help—*

Already on it. The enormous black dragon appeared on the collection of boulders beside him, scales the color of darkness, the muscles in the shoulders as big as the ones in the thighs. Ashe opened his throat and let the fire stream out, red-hot, but a slightly different hue, with spots of yellow.

The Fazurks were engulfed in flames.

Everything is so much easier when you're a dragon.

It really is.

Ashe marched to the entrance of the Stronghold, igniting every foe in his path, knocking the bodies aside with his massive talons when they got in the way. The hole was far too small for him to fit, but it wasn't too small for his mouth. He sealed his mouth over the entrance and released the flame. *That oughta do it.*

Rush took care of the rest of the line until there wasn't a Fazurk left standing. **That has to be most of them. If there's more, then they pop out babies like rabbits.**

Ashe continued to blow his fire into the hole, but he pulled back and took a look. *The ants are gone.*

"Rush!" Bridge ran out from his hiding place in the rocks, his arm pointed at the sky. "Shamans!"

Cora, hide.

Ashe instantly transformed back into Cora, who collapsed on her knees once she was back in her body. She pushed herself forward, getting back on her feet and moving forward. *Do you think they saw me?*

I'm not sure. You were on the other side of the rocky outcropping, so I think we're safe.

Rush came forth as he transitioned, tall on his feet.

"What are you doing?" Bridge came to his side, sweat gleaming on his forehead. "They're headed right for us."

Rush gave him a pat on the shoulder. "Trust me."

The details of the two Shamans came into focus, their cloaks billowing in the wind, their monstrous steeds jet black like Ashe. Fireballs formed in their palms, throbbing with energy they conjured from their abilities.

Rush nodded toward Cora.

Bridge followed his gaze and watched.

They hovered feet away, reining in their steeds to halt in the sky. Their prey didn't run and scream, and they were clearly bewildered by the sight.

Cora closed her eyes—and they fell.

Just like that.

The Shamans collapsed off their steeds, fell hundreds of feet, and then disappeared over the horizon of the mountain.

The surviving steeds took off, darting back the way they came.

Rush grinned. "Attagirl."

Bridge turned back to Rush, wearing an incredulous look. "Did that just happen?"

"Yep." He crossed his arms over his chest as he looked at the other dots in the distance, other Shamans that had seen the fire explode from his snout. They halted their steeds then turned around, retreating. "Ba-ha-ha-ha!"

"Uh...why are you laughing?" Bridge watched the sky before he turned back to Rush, eyebrows raised.

"Because it's hilarious. These guys have been up my ass this whole time, and then bam, they're gone." He snapped his fingers. "Like that." He dusted off his hands. "*Poof.*" He gave another laugh. "Man, I'm going to really enjoy this."

Fury

They moved through the entrance of the Stronghold, immediately surrounded by rocky caverns, smoke from the fires, and dead carcasses that littered the ground. The scaffolding had collapsed from the inferno, so there was no way to get down except to climb.

Once they were far enough down to give adequate space, they transitioned into their dragons. Flare carried everyone to the bottom, while Ashe never volunteered. He landed at the bottom of the cavern, looking into the passageway that led deeper underground.

Flare looked up at the solid wall where the dwarves were hidden. *The wall hasn't been breached. They're safe.*

Can you feel Talc?

Yes.

Can you talk to her?

I'll try.

Flare is trying to talk to Talc right now.

Alright. We'll keep an eye on the passageway. Whenever Ashe saw a group of Fazurks emerge around the corner, he released another stream of fire.

Flare returned. *I can feel her mind, but the barrier is too thick for us to speak. Dragons aren't meant to be underground.*

While they spoke with their minds, everyone else took a seat and waited, watching the dragons do the work. Lilac took out an apple and peeled the skin with a knife. Bridge unrolled a map and took a look. Liam leaned against one of the rocks as if he might take a nap.

Pretty, try. I'll take your place.

Flare took over the passage, blowing fire at the monsters that continued to come even though they knew full well what the outcome would be.

Okay, hold on.

Ashe walked to where Flare had been standing, his eyes finding the same location in the rock.

Besides, this is more fun. Flare opened his throat and released a stream of fire over and over, watching their bodies burn at the opposite end.

Rush waited, but he was too eager for news to keep quiet. **Can you hear her?**

Yes. We're talking.

What is she saying?

I can't do two things at once, so give me a minute.

Rush let Flare take over while his mind wandered elsewhere, waiting for Cora to return with the news he hoped to hear.

Why are you so anxious?

Because we need to get out of here as quickly as possible.

Why?

I'd rather not continue the last conversation I had with my father.

He's injured.

I'm sure he's healed by now. And I doubt he'll come alone this time.

Okay, I'm back.

What did she say?

Queen Megora said there's some kind of filtration system farther inside. It allows them to circulate the air, get rid of the mold and moisture, and draw in fresh air from the outside.

How does that help us?

Because if we turn it on and blow our fire, the flames should reach every single part of the mountain.

Awesome. That's a great idea!

So, she's going to walk me through it. Give me directions until I find it.

Wait…back up. *You* aren't going in there.

I'm the only one who can talk to her. It has to be me.

Tell her to come out.

She said she won't until the Fazurks are gone.

Coward.

Rush.

Sorry. Not sorry.

They left their dragon forms and returned to their two feet once more.

Rush gave everyone a quick rundown of the plan, which required them all to stay behind. "I'm going to escort Cora to the lever for the filtration system."

"But that leaves us with no dragons," Bridge said.

"There's no other way," Rush said. "I'm the only one who can match them in battle. If she goes in there alone, she'll be ripped to pieces."

"*Eh-hem*." Cora stared, her eyes narrowed.

"Cora, these things are huge. Trust me."

The hostility reigned. "It makes more sense for you to cover the tunnel—"

"No." He pulled his sword out of the scabbard and marched to the entrance of the cavern. "We don't have time to argue about this. They're coming, so we need to be quick. Let's go."

Cora jogged to his side, and the two of them entered the tunnel. She withdrew her red blade and carried it, her fingers tight around the pommel. Their footsteps were loud in the cave, their breaths heavy too.

They switched their conversations to their minds so their voices wouldn't give away their presence. **How far in is it?**

When we get to the next opening, there will be a hall to the left.

You've got to be kidding me…

What?

Last time I was there, it was full of Fazurks.

Maybe there won't be as many this time— They rounded the corner and saw an army of them emerge out of the tunnel on the other side. This time, they had weapons—and shields. *Oh boy.*

Go to the lever. I'll handle these guys.

How?

Just go.

She took off at a run, turning left and entering the hall.

The Fazurks raised their swords, released a roar, and charged.

Allow me. Flare came forth, fitting into the cavern with just a few inches to spare, and charred them into blackened meat.

Cora, are you alright?

I'm fine. Just...having...a hard time...getting there.

Why are you talking like that?

Because I'm hauling ass!

More fire. Flare stepped over the fiery carcasses and stuck his head deeper into the tunnel from which they'd come, burning them to smithereens. *Okay, that should buy us enough time.*

Rush came forth and reached for his sword and sprinted into the hall. Tables were turned over. Pints full of ale were on their sides, with shiny pools on the floor. Fazurks were on the far side, chasing after Cora, who was running on top of all the cabinets to get to the lever in the corner.

Rush climbed onto one of the tables and let out a loud whistle. "Idiots, over here."

They all turned to regard him, their teeth pushing out of their jaws, serrated like saws.

"Who's a good boy?" He clicked his tongue and patted his thighs. "Come on. Come get it."

Their attention off Cora, they came forward, their growls turning into roars.

Rush withdrew his blade and spun it around his wrist. "Step right up. Who will be the first to lose their head?" **Go!**

Cora continued her run and dropped down onto the floor. The lever was in the corner, made of a thick rope. Both hands gripped it tightly, and she used her whole body to pull down, to make the hard mechanisms turn.

When the sound of the wind was audible, Rush knew it'd been done. **Run. I'll be right behind you.** The Fazurks came for him all at once, climbing up the table or reaching for his legs. He slashed his sword across a couple throats, kicked one Fazurk in the head, and then stabbed his blade into the spine of another. His eyes were no longer on Cora, just focused on his own survival.

He quickly became overrun, far too many for him to handle in tight quarters. They were climbing up the table on all sides, from in front and behind, reaching for his legs and swiping at him with their claws. Even with Flare supplying his focus, there were just too many. He was outnumbered.

"Rush!" Cora called from the entrance of the hall, the Fazurks oblivious to her because he was the meatier prize.

He kicked another one out of the way and spun his sword, slicing two throats in one go.

More climbed onto the table, suffocating him from all sides.

Cora, run!

"No!"

Rush took a fist to the face, the momentum hitting him so hard he lost concentration for just a second. Another Fazurk moved in, teeth sharp and glistening. Everything became a blur for a short while, the roars fading as if they were far away.

The face came closer, so many teeth in his mouth.

Rush! Focus.

Rush stabbed his blade into the Fazurk, right through the torso. He collapsed.

He spun around to intercept the next one, but he collapsed—for no reason at all.

A hand gripped his arm and gave him a tug. "Come on."

They jumped off the table and landed on shaky legs but kept running. When they rounded the corner to return the way they came, their speed dropped—because they were going against the wind.

Push it.

With a force strong enough to make their boots slide over the rock, the filtration system was as powerful as a storm. With every step they took, their bodies slid back a few inches, their cheeks stretched back. They kept their mouths closed. Otherwise, they couldn't breathe with the wind slapping them in the face. They pressed on, but with difficulty.

They're close behind you—drafting.

Rush grabbed her wrist and shoved her forward, keeping his body between her and the Fazurks. He could hear their roars for just a split second before the wind carried it away. He turned around, pulled out his sword, and stabbed the two closest on their heels.

Rush!

Keep going. I'll hold them back.

Use the wall.

He sliced another and watched it collapse. The pile of bodies became an obstacle for the others, slowing them down a bit. They had a greater chance of escape than they had a second ago. **What?**

Look at me.

He sheathed his sword and turned around, tears streaking down his face from the unforgiving bite of the wind.

She motioned for him to join her, her back flat against the wall. ***It's a lot easier when you hug the wall.***

Instead of going straight against the wind, he went diagonally, feeling an instant relief once he was right up against the wall like Cora. **Smart idea.**

Thanks.

With their backs against the wall, they slid sideways, inching closer to the entrance.

The gang stood in front of the opening, their hair swirling because the wind was coming from a hole in the ceiling that had opened once she'd pulled the lever. Bridge extended his hand and pulled Cora in first. Lilac got Rush.

"Hurry up," Bridge said. "They're following you."

Rush became Flare as everyone else backed up to get out of his way.

The Fazurks looked like the undead, popping out of the ground and walking with a slow gait, their arms outstretched.

"They look so ridiculous right now," Bridge said with a snigger.

Flare inhaled a deep breath, compressed the air in his lungs, and then released an explosion of fire that was immediately sucked up by the wind, traveling down the tunnel with the speed of a flood.

The Fazurks were knocked down and rolled back with the fire, disappearing.

Flare continued to release the flames, only stopping to take a breath and recharge his lungs. Then more fire came, swept away by the tunnel wind. *I will not stop—until every last one is dead.*

"No way anyone survived that." Lilac dusted off the ash that had sprinkled her jacket in the chaos.

"Maybe a few stragglers," Bridge said. "But not enough to do any real damage."

"But the Stronghold must be utterly destroyed." Liam looked back through the tunnel, which was still warm after the fire was gone. "They'll have to completely rebuild."

"It's better to start over than never to start at all," Zane said.

"Guys." Cora pointed to the rock wall. "Look."

The rock had rolled aside—and revealed a dark passageway.

They all remained quiet, staring intently at the place where the surviving dwarves would emerge.

With her long hair, Queen Megora emerged first, her eyes wide, taking in the scene of destruction before her. She gazed at the destroyed scaffolding, the burned corpses scattered across the floor, and then met their looks.

All Rush could see was pain—the pain at the devastation of their home.

Durgin filed out behind her, armed to the teeth, ready to defend their queen.

Rush stepped forward. "I know it's not the way you remember, but at least it's yours again."

The Durgin lowered their axes as they stood on either side of the queen, seeing the smoke rising up to the hole in the ceiling, seeing the place they hadn't seen in months, a place they'd thought they would never see again.

It took some time for Queen Megora to compose herself, to swallow the sorrow and find the strength to carry on. "We must seal the entryway before they return. Hurry." The Durgin were the first to follow those orders, and as more dwarves came out of the passageway, it was clear that they'd come prepared for the job.

Every dwarf that remained in the Stronghold responded to the command, rushing over to seal the gaping hole in the ceiling that the Fazurks had somehow created.

"How are they going to do that...?" Lilac's eyes watched them cross the cavern to the hole and get to work. "And more importantly, how are *we* going to get out?"

Cora turned to Rush. "I didn't think of that."

"There'll be another way," Rush said. "And it'll be easy to find now that we actually have directions."

Minutes later, Queen Megora arrived at the bottom of the cavern, her commanding presence making up for her petite size. She had to look up to meet each of their gazes, like a child looking up to a parent. Few Durgin came with her, holding their axes at the ready. Her eyes settled on Rush the longest. "You fulfilled your promise—and swiftly."

Rush gave a nod. "I hope this is a dawn of a new relationship between men and dwarves—as well as dwarves and elves."

Her eyes shifted to Cora's, examining her for a great length of time. "The Queen of Eden Star is not only half elven, but also fused with a dragon. Much has changed since the last time we ventured aboveground."

"Oh…I'm not the queen." Cora dropped her gaze momentarily. "But I represent Eden Star."

Queen Megora examined her once again. "Are you the General of Eden Star?"

"No," Cora answered. "Callon Riverglade is still in charge. But I'm…Cora Riverglade. Tiberius's daughter."

Rush felt his eyes flick away entirely on their own, focusing on the queen and nothing else.

"Then I'm still in the presence of royalty. Thank you for coming to our aid." Queen Megora gave her a slight bow before she regarded Rush once more. "When Talc insisted that I spare you, I almost denied her. There's no human life worth saving, not when they've shown us who they really are. But I'm glad that she convinced me—because I was wrong. Most men are evil—but perhaps not all."

Rush gave a nod. "Thanks…that means a lot."

"If not for you, the dwarves would have passed from this life forever. Our lineages, our traditions, our hoards—all gone. We will come to your aid whenever you need it. But first, we need to rebuild our caves. We need to search for survivors and pray we aren't all that's left of the Stronghold."

"Can we help with that?" Rush could hear the dwarves hammering behind him, sealing the open rock that had allowed the Fazurks to pour in like a waterfall. But then those noises fell silent—as if they were finished.

A stain of hostility used to be smeared across her face, but now she regarded him with kindness, with a gaze of respect that hadn't been there previously. "We can take it from here. You've done enough—"

Thud.

The Queen's eyes widened slightly at the sound.

The chatter ceased. No one moved, as if a single breath would give away their location.

Rooooooooaaaar!

Obsidian.

Rush turned around to regard the hole that had once been there, completely sealed with rock as if it'd never been broken in the first place. "Will that hold?" His voice emerged as an unnecessary whisper.

The queen's tone echoed his. "If it's been given time to dry."

"And has it?" he asked.

"Yes, but barely."

Thud.

Rocks and sand sprinkled down from the ceiling under the weight.

Rush's eyes found Cora's. "He brought backup this time..."

Thud.

A lot of backup.

More sand fell from the ceiling, little rocks landing like drops of rain.

"You have another way out of here?" Rush asked, turning back to the queen.

"Several." Her eyes were up on the ceiling too. "Assuming the Fazurks haven't destroyed them."

"Then let's get out of here." Rush grabbed his friends and directed them toward the tunnel that had recently been full of fire. "Just in case that ceiling doesn't hold."

Almost everything in the tunnels was burned to ash.

Anything made of metal survived, but the cabinets, the tables, the sleeping bunks were all destroyed. Now there was a permanent aroma of smoke in the air. The ventilation system would have to be on for a straight week for that stench to leave.

"I wish you could have seen us in all our glory." Queen Megora escorted them through the endless passages, still knowing the way even though she'd been trapped for the last few months. Her Durgin remained at her side, armed and armored, as if they were still not to be trusted. "Not when it was invaded by rats. Not when it was burned to a crisp."

"It will be glorious once again," Cora said. "And then, we'll be able to see it."

"I hope so." She led the way for hours, taking them through the long tunnels that branched in various directions, knowing exactly when to turn left and when to turn right. No one stopped for breaks—because the adrenaline was still too strong.

They eventually returned to the cave system they'd seen at the start of their journey.

"I remember this place." Bridge pressed his palm against the wall to feel the texture of the stone. "We were too scared to go left or right, so we just went straight."

"I remember," Lilac said. "That slide was pretty fun…"

"That's the supply chute," Queen Megora said. "For nonperishable storage items."

"Where do you get your supplies?" Rush asked.

"We pay private merchants to deliver our goods rather than venture out on our own," Queen Megora said. "Anastille is such an unsafe place. I would never send dwarves out there unless I had no other choice."

"Then how do you know Mathilda?"

The queen continued her graceful walk forward, her long hair in a thick and bushy braid. Nearly half the height of Rush, he could see right over her head without a compromise to the view. "Ah, the witch. I haven't seen or heard from her in a long time."

Rush waited for the answer to his question, and when it didn't come, he pressed further. "How do you know her?"

"She's come to our mountains to barter. Sell us items that were quite useful. But then asked for some of our dwarven goods, like our Durgin Glue, our Climbers, and Sun Orbs. They only grow in the Stronghold, and that's where they are to remain. She didn't like that decision. Never saw her again after that."

Rush exchanged a quick look with Cora beside him.

That's all she cares about—collecting things.

Seems that way.

They finally arrived at the entrance, the enormous rock exactly where they had left it. The Durgin worked together to roll it away, to reveal the cave and then the view beyond. It was twilight now, just enough sunlight to see the world beyond.

Queen Megora faced Rush. "This is where we part. We're in no place for war at the moment. Our mountain needs to heal first. We all do. But when we're ready, we'll join you in your war against King Lux."

"You have some time to do that," Rush said. "Because we've got a lot of other things to take care of first. How will I contact you again?"

"This entrance here." She reached into her pocket and pulled out a piece of parchment with a sharpened piece of rock. After she planted it against the wall, she sketched out the directions to the Great Hall. "Here you are."

Rush folded it and tucked it into his pocket. "Yes…directions."

"Take care on your journeys." She gave a slight nod to everyone, except Cora. She received a bow, a custom of her people. Then Queen Megora turned to depart. All their matters had been settled, and it was time to part ways.

"Whoa, hold on." Rush moved forward, his hand raised. "Aren't you forgetting something?" He waited for her to give a laugh at her carelessness, to say that the events of the day had distracted her mind.

Queen Megora turned back around. "No." The answer was hard as stone. Final.

"Uh, Talc?" Rush said. "You agreed to release her."

I don't like this, Rush.

I don't either.

Her hands moved behind her back, and she regarded him, now cold. "By keeping Talc, I can be in communication with Cora even from a distance. That is the best strategy to prepare for war."

Cora locked her eyes on Rush, the anger in her gaze.

Rush forced himself to breathe instead of losing his temper, from declaring war and slaying the Durgin that guarded her. "Dragons can't stay underground. It's unnatural."

Queen Megora kept her regal pose, as if she were addressing subjects rather than allies. "Well, she's handled it quite well—"

Cora withdrew her sword in a flash. "Hand over Talc, or I'll slit your goddamn throat where you stand."

Rush glanced at her, his eyebrows raised. **Damn.**

Queen Megora immediately stepped back so her Durgin could move forward and dissolve the threat.

But they didn't.

Their axes dropped to the floor, they fell to their knees, and they winced with closed eyes, their hands gripping their skulls. Their screams bounced off the walls and echoed down the chamber, probably all the way back to the Great Hall.

Queen Megora stared at her in horror. "What are you—"

Cora gripped her sword with two hands, prepared to strike. "Release Talc, or they die."

Their screams grew louder.

"Alright." She threw her arms down, but the torture continued. "I said, alright!"

Cora released the spell and lowered her sword.

The Durgin came to, but they still winced, the pain in their minds lingering and leaving them incapacitated.

Now Queen Megora stared at Cora with wide eyes, taking a step back to put even more distance between them.

Cora moved forward, closing the gap between them, getting right in her face.

Man, she's so hot.

If she were a dragon, her flames would burn hotter than the sun.

Cora sheathed her sword as she kept her eyes locked on the queen. "Cross a dragon, you cross me. You'd do well to remember that."

Obsidian and the others must have departed because there were no signs of enormous dragons in the area. Their bodies didn't block out the stars as they passed, and Flare and Ashe didn't feel the presence of another dragon in their vicinity.

Queen Megora took her distance then unfused.

A green dragon emerged, her scales difficult to see in just starlight.

Just like Cora, the queen collapsed, her Durgin rushing to her to help her upright.

Talc stretched her neck then gazed at the nighttime sky, her dark eyes reflecting the bright heavens. Her wings opened and closed several times, and then she tested her legs, dug her claws into the rocks, and marked the surface with her enormous talons.

She's beautiful.

She really is.

She was about the same size as Flare and just as ferocious.

Queen Megora approached the dragon to place her palm against her scales. "Please take care of her."

Talc turned to look down at her—and issued a low and long growl.

She immediately backed away with her Durgin and returned to the entrance of the tunnel.

Connect me.

Hold on.

Rush stepped forward. **You're beautiful, Talc. I can only imagine how beautiful your scales will look in the sunlight.**

I can't imagine at all. Because I've been a prisoner to men—and then to dwarves.

I'm sorry that you had to go through that. But it's almost over.

She looked up at the skies again.

I wish I could give you more time, but you're too visible, even in the dark. It's time to fuse—

No.

Talc, you can't roam Anastille as a dragon. They'll see you within seconds.

I've only been in dragon form for seconds, and you already want me to submit to someone else.

Not submit. It's to keep you safe—and it's temporary.

She released a quiet growl.

Bridge is a good guy. I promise you.

Which one is he?

Rush patted him on the shoulder.

Talc turned to regard him, her eyes narrowed.

Bridge gave a hesitant wave. "Hi...nice to meet you."

What kind of name is Bridge? She looked at Rush again. *Does he build bridges?*

Uh, no. He's a scholar.

Talc turned her head and settled her gaze on Cora. *I want the elf.*

She's unavailable.

I want her.

She's already fused with Ashe.

Ashe, King of Dragons, is here?

Yes.

I still want her.

Rush released a sigh. "She wants you."

"Me?" Cora asked. "But I have Ashe."

"I know...but that's what she wants."

Cora regarded Talc. "I'm flattered by the request, but I have Ashe. I'm the only one he'll fuse with."

She released a growl.

"You saw what I did with Queen Megora," Cora said. "Trust me, if Bridge gives you trouble, we won't allow it—not that he would. You've got two dragons on your side."

Talc looked at the stars once again. *Wish I could fly again...*

You will. Rush felt the heartbreak in his chest, a pain he understood like he experienced it himself. **Soon enough.**

34

JUST YOU

"Wow...this is weird." Bridge swayed on the spot, as if he was suddenly too heavy to be supported by his legs. "Oh geez, she's loud. Really loud." He planted his palm on his forehead, giving a grimace. "I feel sick."

"You always feel sick." Rush supported his friend, giving him a pat on the back. "Just give it a second."

He bent over at the waist, catching his breath like he'd run across Anastille and back.

Lilac rolled her eyes. "Pathetic."

Let's do what I taught you.

You taught me a lot of things.

Connect all our minds.

As in, all three dragons?

Yes.

Wow, that's a lot. She focused her mind and brought them all together. *Talc?*

Her feminine voice was distinctly different from Flare's and Ashe's, and it had a lot more punch. <u>Yes, I'm here. Fused with a man whose mother decided to name him after the most unremarkable man-made structure in existence. Even Moat would have been preferable…</u>

Flare released a chuckle. *He's one of the good ones, Talc.*

<u>I don't care if he is. He's unworthy of my mind.</u>

Ashe's deep voice came forth. *No man is worthy of our minds. But it's a necessary sacrifice for what we're trying to achieve—freedom for all dragons. We're lucky enough that some humans challenge the Wuzurk that sits on the throne, that they believe we deserve to roam the land that belongs to us.*

<u>Ashe, King of Dragons. It is an honor to feel your mind again.</u>

And yours as well.

<u>I'm sorry…this is super weird. Who's talking?</u>

You'll get used to it, Bridge.

Soon, it'll feel so second nature that you'll wonder how it wasn't always like this.

<u>I guess I'll have to take your word for it…</u>

"What's the plan now?" Lilac took a seat on one of the boulders, her legs crossed, the hilt of her dagger sticking out of her pocket. "I can't wait to get off this mountain and sleep on some grass again."

"We could return to the Hideaway and wait for Captain Hurricane," Liam said. "He could ferry us back to Mist Isle."

"We do have three dragons…" Zane took a seat beside Lilac on the rock. "Couldn't we lure him out into the open and ambush him?"

The emptiness of Rush's gaze passed when he came back to the conversation. "You heard all those thuds. He's searching for me with a whole fleet. He means business. I say we return to Mathilda and question her again. She'll probably be a lot more receptive to Cora."

"Actually…there's something I wanted to ask." Cora crossed her arms over her chest, a bit cold with the sun gone and the hard breeze at this elevation. "My village is on the way. Could we stop by?"

"Did you forget something at home or…?" Lilac cocked an eyebrow.

Rush studied her face, understanding her intentions without having to ask. "Let's do it."

"Thank you." Cora gave a subtle nod. "Dorian knows a lot more than he told me…and I want to know what it is."

"YOU RECOGNIZE IT?" RUSH WALKED BESIDE HER IN THE LEAD, the sun at their backs.

The hills led to a lake, the water still, the bank untouched as if man had never set foot there. "Yep. The first time you saw me naked."

He grinned. "Yep. A memory I still hold very dear in my heart."

She gave a chuckle as she continued her pace. "I bet you do."

He waggled his eyebrows.

"But for the record, that never would have happened if I'd known who you really were."

"I did turn around, you know."

"After you stared for a good five seconds."

He gave another grin, handsome and playful. "I'm a man, alright? If there are tits…I'm gonna look."

She gave him a playful smack.

He gave another chuckle. "Ah, good memories."

"It's crazy to think that's how all of this started…"

"It's like it was meant to happen, huh?" He grinned down at her as he walked beside her, his eyes playful but also deep.

"Yeah, does seem that way."

They stopped to hydrate and refill their canteens. After a short break, they continued up the hills until they spotted the village down below. Only a few hundred people lived there, so there was no fence around the exterior, farmlands around the perimeter.

This is where you grew up?

Yep.

It doesn't suit you.

It never suited me. "So, I guess I'll go in while you guys wait here."

Rush dropped his bow and shield along with his pack. He left his sword on his hip. "I'll go with you."

"I'll be fine on my own—"

"I'm coming with you."

"What about the others?"

"Now that we've got Talc, we can keep in contact." He moved forward. "Come on, I didn't make the best first impression on Dorian. Showed way too much teeth for a first encounter."

"You would have made a worse impression as you."

He rolled his eyes. "Ha."

Lilac shifted her gaze between them. "You guys are the weirdest couple I've ever seen. All you do is tease each other back and forth, but I haven't even seen you hold hands."

Cora studied Lilac before she turned her gaze on Rush.

His charming smile was long gone, along with the playfulness in his eyes. "Come on, let's get going." He moved down the hill for the village, not waiting to see if Cora was beside him or not.

Cora stared at Lilac for a few seconds before she went after him.

As if nothing had happened, Rush kept his eyes straight ahead, focused on their objective.

She stared at the side of his face.

He never met her look.

"So, you told her?"

He released an angry sigh. "No."

"Really? Because it seems like she knows full well—"

"I didn't tell her." He halted, giving her his hostile stare.

"If that's true, why does she think we're a couple? You told Bridge, and he told her—"

"That's not what happened either."

"Really? Because it seems like you were bragging about everything that happened on that island..." She marched ahead, wishing he wouldn't follow this time.

I warned you, Cora.

Stay out of this. She threw up her mind, shutting him out.

Rush snatched her by the arm and yanked her back. "I would never do that. You know that. Come on, you *know* me." He slammed his hand into his chest, making a distinct thump against his hardness. "You know how I feel about you—"

"Then why won't you just tell me why she knows? If there's nothing to hide, then you would just tell me. But you do have something to hide...from me." Her eyes shifted back and forth as they bored into his, angry that she was left in the dark by the one person she shared everything with. When she didn't get an answer, she twisted out his grasp and marched on.

"Alright, I'll tell you." He came after her, matching her stride again. "She came on to me, so I told her there was someone else. I never said who that someone else was, but she figured out it was you."

Her stride slowed, as well as the adrenaline in her heart.

"I didn't tell you because...I didn't want to make things weird between you guys."

Cora stopped altogether and faced him. "She and I both deserve more credit than that. You're a gorgeous man, and I don't blame her for going for it. I would have done the same thing."

His cocky smile didn't move on to his face, and his eyes retained their seriousness. He inhaled a deep breath and let it slowly leave his lungs, his jaw still tight. "I didn't tell anyone what happened between us. That was just for us. Bridge asked a couple questions because he knows how I feel about you, so I told him you turned me down." He drew another slow breath, a pause before he continued. "But for the sake of full transparency...Lilac and I did have a thing in the past. It was a few years ago. Just physical. Didn't mean anything to me."

She tried not to picture them together, to let the monster of jealousy raise its ugly head. "I don't blame her for still wanting you... I would too."

His eyes gave a slight look of relief.

She dropped her gaze, her heart aching the way it used to. "I'm sorry that I got so upset…"

"I'm sorry that I didn't give you more credit."

"I don't even care if you told anyone. I just… You said you wouldn't, so I felt betrayed."

"I would never share something that personal with anyone—not even Bridge. Yes, I've talked about the women who come and go once in a while, but I respect you too much to make that a point of conversation. Even if we were still together…I still wouldn't talk about it. That time together…meant the world to me."

She dropped her gaze again because the sincerity in his beautiful eyes was just too much. "It meant the world to me too…" After a breath, she lifted her gaze, having the courage to meet the stare that filled her dreams. Blue eyes, both hard and soft, penetrated deep into her soul, read her soul like words on a page, played like music from the harp. "It's been really hard for me."

He swallowed, his eyes dropping momentarily. "Yeah…it's been hard for me too."

"I normally talk to you about everything…but I can't do that now. Not with Ashe. Callon. Anyone, really. I've been so busy in Eden Star that it's helped me not to think about it, but during those quiet times…it gets to me."

He gave a long nod. "It gets to me too…all the time."

She stared into his eyes and saw the same pain that she felt in her heart. Some things were better left unsaid, but they somehow came pouring out when she least expected it. Everything had been sealed behind her heart, but it came flooding out like water through a broken dam. "I want to be the bigger person and say you should be with her if that's what you want, but...I don't think I could handle seeing you with someone else. At least, not right now."

His eyes narrowed on her face, a twinge of surprise in the corners. "I don't want her."

Her breaths grew heavy; her entire body grew heavy.

"Just you."

The butcher's shop was still on the corner. Chickens that escaped their coops were in the middle of the road, trying to escape one of the dogs that came sniffing around. It was broad daylight, so people were out and about, and it didn't take them long to notice Cora and the armed man beside her.

"People like to stare, huh?" Rush gave a wave.

"Nothing has changed around here..."

A group of girls stood on the porch of a house, most of them holding babies and toddlers in their arms, watching Cora go by.

Rush waved to them too.

One of the girls smiled and waved back enthusiastically.

"Stop flirting."

"Not flirting. Being sarcastic."

"Well, you're a really good-looking guy, so you're giving them false hope."

"You've said that like five times since this morning." He grinned. "It's been a great day."

She approached the house where she grew up, the blue shutters, the windows slightly covered by the white curtains. The front door was made of deep mahogany, a dark wood with a thickness that made it impenetrable to the blade of an ax. After a breath, she knocked.

"Nice place."

"Dorian built it himself."

"Now it's even nicer."

Footsteps sounded before the door swung open. She didn't expect Dorian to be home, but she'd wanted to try first before she went to the shop and was seen by even more people. His look was instantly annoyed, as if he expected a solicitor of some kind. Then it was full of shock, like he couldn't believe his own eyes. "Cora…?"

Her eyes immediately watered at the sight of him, of his sun-weathered face, his blue eyes that contrasted against his graying hair. His skin was like leather from being outside so much, but he was still lean and strong.

She moved into his chest and gripped him tightly.

He gripped her back, his chin on her shoulder, his arms holding her like a father who didn't want to let go of a child. "Sweetheart..." He pulled her inside and ignored Rush as if he wasn't standing there.

When she pulled away, she saw that the house was exactly as she remembered it, the same blue couches and coffee table, the staircase with the paintings on the walls. It smelled the same. It felt the same. It was no longer home, but it still felt like the home that she remembered. "I'm sorry to drop by like this—"

"Never be sorry." He squeezed her arms. "You're always welcome here. Always."

She smiled before she turned to Rush. "Dorian, this is Rush... my friend."

Rush extended his hand. "It's a pleasure to meet you, sir."

Dorian took his hand. "Likewise. But none of that sir stuff..."

"Of course." Rush cleared his throat.

Dorian opened the swinging door that led to the kitchen. "Come on. I'll make us something to eat, and we'll catch up."

"It's been mayhem since I left." Cora left her mug on the counter, most of the tea already sitting in her belly. "So much has happened. That was a really rough draft, but basically the gist of the whole thing..."

Rush looked down into his mug, tilting it from side to side but not taking a drink.

Dorian sat across from Cora and glanced at Rush. "Can I get you something else?"

"Maybe something stronger…if you're offering." He set the mug aside.

He chuckled then grabbed a decanter of amber liquid. "All yours."

Rush poured his tea into Cora's mug before he filled his with the strong stuff. "You're too kind."

Dorian returned to his seat. "That's one tall tale. You stabbed a Shaman and fled for safety…and ended up in the company of the general of the empire, three dragons, and a couple scholars." He poured himself a glass of scotch after Rush was finished with the bottle. "I want to say I'm surprised…but the most unlikely things have always followed you wherever you go."

"Yeah, it seems that way." She stared into her mug.

Rush threw his head back and took a drink. "Yes… That's the stuff."

"I'm glad that you stopped by," Dorian said. "It's almost been a year."

Cora's eyes lifted to meet his. "What…really?"

He nodded. "Yes."

Her eyes dropped back to her tea, not realizing she had spent so much time in both Eden Star and Mist Isle. Everything had happened in a blink of an eye, so it felt so much shorter than that.

Rush nudged her in the side. "Looks like our one-year anniversary is coming up."

Dorian shifted his eyes between them.

Cora laughed off the joke. "Well...there's also something I wanted to ask you."

With his cup between his hands on the table, Dorian watched her with relaxed shoulders, as if he expected to field questions about the town.

"The night I was left at the gate... What happened?"

Once the subject had been broached, his carefree gaze immediately intensified into something more. Lines formed on his face. Eye contact was severed when he looked away. The distress was like blobs of bold ink from a quill onto the page.

"And please don't tell me you don't remember...because I know you do."

His gaze was focused out the back window, as if expecting someone to pass by. "When you left, some of the king's men came to interrogate me and your brothers. I told them you were abandoned in the village, and the only reason I took care of you was because I took pity on you. I must have been convincing because they left without provocation—and have never returned."

"Good."

"I hope they don't realize you've returned…and come back after you're gone."

"We'll be careful," she said quickly. "I would never want to put any of you at risk."

He nodded. "Good. Because it's also in the best interest of everything you're fighting for."

Ashe's voice returned, connecting with her mind now that the barrier was gone. *He's a man of secrets.*

"What do you mean by that?" Cora whispered, looking at him in a whole new light.

Dorian dropped his gaze into his scotch. "When I was young, naïve, optimistic…whatever you want to call it…" There was no inflection of affection in his voice, no joy in his eyes. Everything about him was different. "I joined an alliance of mercenaries who wanted to overthrow King Lux. We all had our reasons…the untimely death of my father was mine. It was about revenge more than anything else."

At least these are good secrets.

"Common sense eventually prevailed. I would either die young for this hopeless endeavor, or I could live a long and fulfilling life away from the Empire. I chose the latter. I disassociated myself from the cause and settled down with a family instead. I haven't regretted the choice—especially since they're all dead now."

"Then who dropped me off at the gate? They left my father's ring—which has protected me since the moment I stepped into Eden Star."

He looked Cora in the eye, giving a slight shake of his head. "I don't know who it was, Cora. But they knew who *I* was. They left you there with a note asking me to take you in because you would die otherwise. My job was to give you a simple life in a small village, to keep you away from the outside world. That would have been much easier...if you weren't so headstrong." He gave a slight chuckle, his eyes gazing over with memory. "If I had been asked this before, I would have said no. But once I saw you...I couldn't. I took you in and raised you as my own—and I still have no regrets."

"So...when you saw the ring, you knew who I was?"

"I knew it was an elvish ring, but I knew nothing of your parentage. The older you grew, the more obvious your features became. But since no one here knows what an elf even looks like, they never became suspicious—thankfully."

"This group of mercenaries...you said they're gone?"

"Yes."

"How do you know?"

"Because I saw their bodies outside of Polox when I returned for goods."

"Oh...I'm sorry."

"I am too. It could have been me..."

"You don't think...this alliance still lives on?"

"Unlikely."

Rush interjected. "But it must—because they came to you after the fact."

Dorian gave a hesitant nod. "Yes, I suppose you're right. I left the organization long before that, so someone must have kept tabs on me. But if they dropped off Cora, it must have been because they were compromised in some way."

That's true.

"Why didn't you tell me all of this when I asked?" Cora said.

"Because I wanted you to have a normal life." He stared at her. "I wanted you to stay here where you'd be safe. The last thing I wanted you to do was chase elves in Eden Star...and pose questions to the wrong people. But in the end, it didn't matter, I guess."

Rush took over. "Dorian, we're in desperate need of allies right now. The dwarves need to rebuild, and the elves are complicated. If some kind of resistance still lives on, we need to find them. Is there anything you can tell us? Anything at all? A name, location, a place to start our search?"

Dorian kept his eyes on Cora. "I admire what you're doing. Really, I do. You remind me of myself. Optimistic. Doing the right thing, even if it's the hard thing. But the last thing I want is for something to happen to you, Cora. He's too powerful, and he has spies in the most unlikely places. Tread carefully."

"I'm aware of the risks, Dorian. But even if it claims my life, it would still be worth it."

He dropped his gaze, her words too much to even contemplate.

"Dorian." Rush's deep voice brought him back to attention. "There has to be something you can tell us."

His eyes remained down for a long time, and after a deep breath that made his shoulders rise then fall, he lifted his gaze. "I don't know who she was. I don't know her name. I don't even know her face. But I do know this...she was a witch."

After a long goodbye, they departed the village and headed up the hill.

The visit with her guardian was too short, and too much of their conversation had been about important matters. She didn't ask about his shop. She didn't even ask about her brothers—who were all out of the house at the time. "Do you think it was Mathilda?"

"Wouldn't put it past her. And Polox isn't too far from here."

"True."

"She's definitely acquainted with this resistance group. I wasn't worthy of the knowledge, but I'm sure you will be. Maybe she has the answers to both of our questions."

"Yeah..."

"What is it?"

"I'm worried about Callon."

Rush slowed down his pace and regarded her. "Your guardian just dropped this revelation, and...that's what's on your mind?"

She stopped their progress altogether, her hands on her hips. "The outcome of this war will be determined by Callon's success in this matter. We need the elves—and whoever sits on that throne dictates our actions."

"You want to go back and help him overthrow Delwyn? I'm sure Lilac can sneak behind her and push her down the stairs..."

She didn't laugh. "The only reason we've made it this far is because we can stay in communication no matter where we are in the world. If I could stay in communication with Callon, it would be instrumental."

Once he followed her train of thought, his eyes narrowed. "Talc."

"I feel terrible for even suggesting it because it seems like I just want to use her...but it would make a huge difference. No matter the leagues that separate us, we could coordinate. That's something King Lux would never anticipate."

Rush shifted his weight then ran his fingers through his hair. "It makes a lot of sense."

"Doesn't it?"

"But I already told her we would take her to Mist Isle to be free. That was the only way I could get her to convince Queen Megora to let us go."

"Well, I'm sure Queen Megora's hesitation changed her attitude about that."

"Good point."

"She'll say no at first, but I'm sure we can convince her."

"So, we do this now or after?"

"Now. If we could get Talc and Callon to fuse, we could head to Mathilda next...and hopefully that materializes into the next thing. In any case, Callon isn't going to take charge of Eden Star overnight, and the dwarves are overcome right now. We need more people. We should look for those people and keep our connection with Eden Star at the same time. General Noose could return..."

"I agree."

"And if she won't fuse with Callon, I could let him fuse with Ashe—"

No.

Ashe—

I have no qualms about his character. He's a good man. But you're the one I agreed to join, and I will not be bound to anyone else in this manner. You're my hatchling.

"Never mind..."

Rush gave a smile. "I knew how that was going to go down."

"Alright. Then let's work on Talc and head back to Eden Star in the meantime."

35

RETURN TO EDEN STAR

"I'm soooo tired of going back and forth." Bridge dropped his pack and took a seat near the campfire. They stopped under a canopy of three trees, the copse so dense it would be difficult to spot the flames from the sky. "My legs have not looked this thick since I was a kid who played outside all day."

Lilac skinned and gutted the deer before putting it on the spit over the fire. The juice splashed into the flames and sizzled, and the smell of roasting meat filled the campsite.

Rush sat beside Cora, his eyes on the side of her face. "Is this okay?"

She'd made a dinner out of what she could find, wild nuts and berries, some cauliflower. "I'm fine. Don't worry about it."

When the meat was finished cooking, it was split among the five of them, and they ate in silence.

Cora took the opportunity to speak with Talc. *Ashe, will you help me?*

You're asking me to convince a dragon to fuse.

I wouldn't do it unless I thought it was necessary. Surely you must agree that having a connection to Eden Star is vital to win this war.

I do. But this goes against everything I stand for.

Me too, Ashe.

As if he were in his dragon form beside her, he took a long breath and let it out slowly. *Alright.*

Thank you. She pressed her mind to Talc's and felt the connection instantly. **How are you?**

<u>Every breath I draw is much lighter than the breaths I took under the mountain. The weight of the rocks pressed on my chest and lungs. It was a slow suffocation. But now I see trees. I see sky. I see plains.</u>

I'm glad you're feeling better.

<u>You forced Queen Megora's hand—thank you.</u>

Of course.

<u>Being stuck under the mountain had taken its toll on her as well. I became a crutch for her—as she did for me. But she was more reluctant to let that go than I was. I know it wasn't just the temptation of my power, but her affection for me as well.</u>

I hope you're right.

<u>I'm eager to get to Mist Isle, to open my wings and feel the wind against my scales.</u>

I can imagine.

<u>*Your powers are extraordinary. How did they come to be?*</u>

Honestly, I don't know. Still trying to figure that out.

<u>*And your ability to communicate—how?*</u>

I think I'm part dragon...as crazy as that sounds.

<u>*Your mind does feel like one of a dragon. When I first felt it, that was exactly what I assumed.*</u>

Not the first time I've heard that. How are things with Bridge?

<u>*He's a puny human.*</u>

She gave a chuckle. *He just has a sensitive stomach.*

<u>*Puny.*</u>

She stared at the fire while everyone ate, doing her best to block out the sounds of masticating, teeth ripping into flesh. *Talc, there's something I need to ask you. And before you get upset, I want you to hear me out.*

Her voice had been gentle a moment ago, but now it had a bite. <u>*This sounds perverse—and I don't like it.*</u>

I want you to understand that we will take you to Mist Isle if that's what you wish, but I do have a favor to ask.

<u>*Yes?*</u>

My uncle is the General of Eden Star. His name is Callon. We've been trying to secure an alliance with the elves for the great war to come. Only problem is, Queen Delwyn is very difficult. Callon is trying to rectify this.

And what does this have to do with me?

We have other obligations in Anastille that require us to be away from Eden Star. But we need to remain in contact in order to orchestrate this war. The only way to do that—

No.

I thought you might say that—

Then how dare you ask?

Look, I wouldn't ask if it weren't important.

I was told that I could be free on Mist Isle—

And that's still true, Talc. This would only happen if it was voluntary. No one would ever force you to do anything you don't want to.

Then take me to Mist Isle. This conversation is over.

At least give me the opportunity to make you want to do this, Talc.

There's nothing you can say that will make me want to fuse with an elf instead of going to the last retreat of free dragons. I've been a prisoner for thousands of years. I've paid my dues. Now it's my time to be free.

Mist Isle is the final home for the dragons. If it's gone...there is nowhere else.

Silence.

You can go to Mist Isle and enjoy it as long as you can. But if we don't win this...you won't be free for long. He'll sail to the shores and repeat history. But you have an opportunity to help us win.

You have an opportunity to turn the tide. Having you in Eden Star can alter the course of history.

Silence.

The fuse isn't permanent. You're free to leave it whenever you wish.

So you say...

I can vouch for Callon. He's the most virtuous person I've ever known. Honestly, sometimes his integrity is annoying...

Cora, what is your favorite thing to do?

Sorry?

Something you do every day that you couldn't live without.

Uh...be with the people I love.

Something rudimentary.

Eating? I guess I love to eat.

Well, what if that were taken from you? Something so trivial, something so normal, something that's part of the human experience? That's how I feel when I can't fly. I haven't been able to fly for a very long time.

I understand that, Talc. Really, I do. But that freedom at Mist Isle is temporary. Freedom is not guaranteed unless you fight for it. Please, help us fight for it. Whenever we no longer need the communication, you're free to go. You can choose to stay and fight, or you can flee to Mist Isle.

My answer has been given.

Ashe, a little help here?

She has changed hands three times now. Barely had a moment to catch her breath.

I understand that. But you know we need to make this work.

After a long stretch of silence, he projected his mind to them both, his voice powerful but also gentle. *Talc, I understand your hesitance—*

It is not hesitance. It is a concrete refusal.

It was not that long ago that I took your stance. Cora asked me to fuse to pursue this mission. Not only did I refuse, but the question itself was a grievance. I am King of Dragons. How dare she even consider making the request? It goes against everything I believe in, for our majestic minds to be connected with anyone beneath us.

Yet, here you are.

Because Cora was right. I have a family on Mist Isle, a Zuhurk and two hatchlings. They'll never truly be safe because time passes so quickly for immortals, and before I take my next breath, a fleet of ships will come to our island. Elves and dwarves will fall—and we'll be all that's left in the world. We won't survive the siege. The ones that refuse will die, and the ones that are weak will be subjugated once more.

She has the mind of a dragon. She can trap you in a fuse forever— and you'll never see your family again.

That possibility does not concern me.

Why?

Because we are one.

Silence.

What started as a mere partnership deepened into something more. She is my hatchling—even if she doesn't have scales or wings. That was the original purpose of the fuse, to have a connection so deep that the trust is unquestioned. It's the first time I've experienced it. King Lux and his men are evil—but not all men are.

Silence.

I understand what I'm asking you—but I must ask anyway.

<u>*It is a lot to ask.*</u>

I know that. You were a prisoner to King Lux, and then you fused with a dwarf to survive. You've never been your own. You've never been a dragon. You've always been part of something else. You deserve more. But the dragons that remain in captivity deserve more too. The free dragons at Mist Isle deserve more than a small island. They deserve their rightful home—Anastille.

Silence.

You aren't obligated to have a deeper connection with Callon. It can be about the task—nothing more. If you ever need to reach out, Cora and I will always be available for you.

The connection with Talc severed—and she was gone.

That went well...

You need to understand. She thought she was going straight to Mist Isle to open her wings.

She still can. We aren't taking that away from her.

But she knows it would be wrong to make that choice.

They moved across Anastille, taking the route that Rush had laid out through his travels. The journey used to be a straight line, but now it was filled with detours to take cover in forests and between hills.

Rush stopped to take a drink from his canteen before he wiped his mouth with the back of his forearm. Sweat gleamed on his forehead, and the cords in his neck popped from the exertion of the long day. "I realized something." He screwed the lid back into place before he continued forward.

"What?" Cora kept his pace despite the heavy armor on her body, the supplies bouncing around in her pack.

"Even if you get Talc to go for it, Callon never will."

"I'll talk him into it."

"I don't know, Cora. This isn't the same thing as accepting Ashe or not slaying me every time he sees me. You're asking him to fuse with a dragon. This is a big deal."

"He'll do it for me."

"Cora, he *hates* dragons."

"He's come a long way. I'll make it happen."

"It sounds like Talc isn't on board either…"

She'd kept her mind closed for several days, so Cora had given her space. "I think she'll come around."

THEY CROSSED THE DESERT AT NIGHTFALL.

Talc came forth and inhaled a large breath, her wings extending and giving a good stretch.

Flare took Lilac and Liam on his back.

Talc took Zane.

Together, they crossed the desert, close to the ground, racing over the sand and cacti to reach the other side. Several hours later, they landed on the soft grass and turned back into their two-legged forms.

That felt nice.

Cora resisted the urge to pester her once more, deciding to let her enjoy her moment of freedom without provocation.

They made a camp early in the morning so they could rest, and after the long trek across the desert, the dragons needed to feed. All three dragons dispersed, getting their kills in the grassy valleys that were hidden behind the mountains.

Everyone lay in their cots and went to sleep.

Cora stayed awake to keep watch.

Rush was asleep while Flare hunted, so he wasn't available for conversation.

The last time she'd come this way, she'd passed through these very trees. Deeper into the forest they'd gone until they'd approached the border of Eden Star. That was where she'd received her first kiss—and she still remembered it like it was yesterday.

How are things out there?

I just finished a bear. Ashe's voice was as strong as it was when they were a single entity. It was like he was right beside her—within her soul. *But I need another.*

It's been a while since you hunted.

A long while.

Can you see Talc?

Yes. I'm keeping her close in case.

You think she'd take off?

No. Grow reckless, perhaps.

You think you could talk to her again…since she's in a good mood.

I would hate to spoil the moment.

I understand. I just feel like your words mean a lot more to her than mine.

I'm Ashe, King of Dragons. Of course they do.

Then…you think you could try? Dragon-to-dragon?

I suppose. Just let me eat another bear first.

The dragons returned and re-fused with their counterparts.

How did it go?

She was more receptive—but still resistant.

I was hoping to get her on board before we talk to Callon.

I don't think that's likely.

We can't stall either... We have to keep moving.

They stayed on the outskirts of the forest and traveled to the last location where they'd met. It was on the verge of the open plains, with a wide view of the valleys between the hillsides. Everything on this side of the desert was lush and untouched—wild.

"Wait here," Cora said. "I'll get him."

Before she could leave, Rush grabbed her by the arm. "Be careful, alright?"

"I'll be fine, Rush." She slipped out of his hold then left them behind.

The secret passageway was as deserted as ever, and she passed through without interference. The music of the forest fell on her ears the moment she was within the perimeter, and the serenity it provided was soothing. It was as if she'd never been gone. She hadn't missed Eden Star on her journey, but now that she was reacquainted with the forest, she couldn't fathom how she'd left in the first place.

The trees started to thin as she moved closer to the heart of the forest. Elves were present on the trails through the trees, their arms full of the items they'd grabbed at the market. Some of the tree houses had been rebuilt, and the fact that people carried produce and flowers suggested that normalcy had returned during her weeks away.

She took the path to Callon's old tree house, hoping that it'd been rebuilt and he currently occupied it. The more elves who passed, the more they recognized her, giving her a hard stare as if to discern the features that were similar to their fallen king. Not a word was spoken to her. There was no sheathed hostility like before. They just seemed entranced.

When she looked up at the tree that had once housed Callon's home, she saw a brand-new tree house. Constructed of different types of trees, it was multicolored, from pine to birch, an array of options because natural lumber became scarce when they had so much to rebuild. The vines that grew over the outside and into the windows were slender and small, young saplings that had just come from the seed.

"Yes." She took the vine stairway to the open front door, seeing a brand-new place that looked nothing like it used to. It didn't feel the same either, all that history gone. The walls were bare of artwork. There was no sense of ownership. "Callon?" She stepped farther inside, hoping he would emerge from the hallway or kitchen.

She was greeted with silence.

She stepped into the kitchen to search for clues—and found the green notebook on the counter.

We'll wait for his return.

There was fresh produce in the basket, so she took a seat and helped herself.

Hours later, he returned, in the middle of the afternoon.

Dressed in his armor and medals, his sword at his hip and his shield across his back, he was the formidable foe that any enemy should fear. His dark eyes complemented the durable metal on his body—strong and unforgiving.

It didn't take long for him to realize he wasn't alone. He stopped on the threshold of the living room, his dark green eyes piercing her face with scrutiny. Hostility waned, and the affection shone through, like sunlight breaking through the winter clouds. "*Sor-lei.*"

She left her chair and embraced him. "I like your new place."

He gave her a squeeze before he let her go. "What happened with the dwarves?"

"We got rid of the orcs. Everyone is okay."

"Good." He gave a nod. "It's good to have you back."

"Any luck with you-know-who?"

He gave a slight shake of his head. "Still working on it."

"I figured it would take longer than a few weeks to overthrow a dictator."

"Might be quicker with you around. Now that the elves know who you are, they've been asking for you."

It's nice not to be hated—for once. "Actually, I have to leave Eden Star again. But I needed to talk to you first."

He stepped closer. "Everything alright?"

"Yes," she said quickly. "Everything is fine. But…we need to have this conversation outside the forest. Can we go now?"

He studied her for a long moment before he gave a subtle nod. "I just finished my rotation."

"Perfect timing." She headed to the front door but stopped when she saw Turnion's painting leaning against the wall. Half the canvas was missing, but his son's full presence was somehow captured. "Found a place for it yet?"

He lifted it off the ground and stared at it for a long moment. "Not yet. Still looking for the perfect spot."

They left through the secret passageway and ventured across the wildlands.

"I will speak with your friends—except for him."

Cora didn't have to hide her look of disappointment because they were both focused on the trek ahead. "He's part of this, Callon."

"I don't care."

"You don't have to like him, but you have to tolerate him—"

"I have to do no such thing." He halted in his tracks, his look menacing. "Those are my terms. Take them or leave them."

Do it.

He needs to let this go—

Remember what you're about to ask him to do. We need his spirits to be light, not burdened by the weight of his brother's murder—and his brother's murderer.

"Alright..." Cora kept going, and Callon quickly followed. ***Rush?***

I'm here.

Callon and I will be there shortly. But...he wants you gone.

No surprise there.

I'm sorry...

It's fine. Don't be. I'll leave now.

I'll get him to come around. Now just isn't the time.

You're right.

They arrived at the group minutes later, Rush absent.

Callon was shorter than everyone there, armed for battle, distinguished in his gear but also in his presence. His eyes flicked across them, as if sizing them up for battle. He greeted them wordlessly—with a hard stare.

"So, here's the deal..."

Callon turned his stare on her.

"We stopped by my old village, and my guardian said a witch dropped me off at the gate when I was a newborn. He was part of a resistance against King Lux, which has since fizzled out. But we think we have a promising lead."

"What do you ask of me?" His arms moved behind his back as he stared down at his niece. In Rush's absence, he was calm and subdued, the first time he'd been that way among her friends.

"Look, I know it's a lot to ask—"

"I will do anything I can to help you. But like I said, I can't leave Eden Star. I can't leave my people when they're vulnerable."

"It's not that..." She gave a slight shake of her head.

"Then what is it?" he asked. "What have you brought me out here to discuss? What conversation is inappropriate for Eden Star?"

"It's not really the conversation per se..."

His eyes flashed like the reflection of a swinging blade. "Speak."

He won't receive this request well, regardless of how it's worded. Just tell him.

"We want to move ahead and secure more allies. I don't know what that will entail, how long I'll be gone, where we'll end up...and we'll have no contact with one another. If General Noose returns to your borders, I won't even know about it. So, we need a way to stay connected."

"And how can that be accomplished?"

I haven't agreed to this.

Cora ignored her. "I told you we saved a dragon…"

The confusion in his gaze suggested that he hadn't drawn the right conclusion. Not yet anyway. But it came, like a large wave growing larger before it finally broke on the shore. The anger was instantaneous, like steam from the spout of a black kettle.

"Before you say no—"

"My answer is not no—it's *never*."

"Callon—"

"Your entire reason for getting wrapped up in this is to free the dragons. Yet, here you stand, doing the exact opposite."

"That's not what's happening—"

"I've tolerated Ashe in Eden Star because I wasn't given a choice—"

"And he's the reason we're all still alive right now. Without his strength, I wouldn't have bested General Noose. I wouldn't have killed as many Shamans as I have. Like it or not, we need the dragons—and they need us."

His jaw clenched, his eyes full of menace. "Be that as it may, I'm not left with the obligation."

"You're the only one I trust."

"Doesn't matter."

"It'll allow us to communicate with each other."

"*Doesn't matter.*"

"She'll give you abilities that you didn't have before, strength that—"

"None of which I *need*." He stepped closer, sizing her up as a real opponent. "My sword and shield are more than enough. I've survived so many battles and served so many kings because I'm the master of my craft. There's nothing a dragon could give that I don't already possess."

"What if you need my help—"

"The General of Eden Star doesn't need the service of a *child*." His eyes were full of smoke, the fire somewhere deep inside. "It is my duty to protect you—not the other way around."

Cora, this is going worse than I expected.

Callon turned on his heel and departed.

"Callon."

He continued like her words were carried on the wind.

"What if I need you?"

He halted in mid-step.

"We'll be leagues apart. Even oceans. How will you protect me if you can't hear my call? How will you live every day, not knowing whether I live or die?"

He didn't turn around, his breathing heavy.

"I understand you don't want to do this... I get it. I'm so sorry that I have to ask this of you when I've already asked you for so much. I know it goes against everything you believe. Trust me, I do. But...unless I stay here while everyone continues on without me, there is no other way." She inhaled a deep breath. "You say that King Tiberius is the greatest king to ever rule Eden Star…and he was fused."

After a lifetime of silence, he turned around, his face even more pissed off.

"Please."

He chewed the inside of his cheek, something he'd never done before.

"We'll have the ability to coordinate from all across the continent. King Lux doesn't have that ability—and it's the reason we'll defeat him. It's the greatest tool a general can have—"

"Silence."

Cora winced as she sucked in a breath.

"My wife and son are dead because of *them*."

"Callon…"

"You've never asked me for a request harder to grant. I'd give my life for yours. I'd turn my back on my own people to keep you safe. I would betray my own queen based on your word alone. But this…" He shook his head, his jaw clenched.

"I know all of this and asked you anyway—because I had to."

He turned away, his eyes squinting in the sunlight. He examined the world, the breeze moving through the deep green cape at his back.

Give him a moment.

Cora waited, her chest aching with the tension.

After a loud breath, he turned back to her. "I have conditions."

She gulped down a breath of air in disbelief.

He held up a finger. "It's for communication purposes only. We exchange information pertinent to this cause. There will be no relationship. I do not wish to be connected with this being the way you're connected with Ashe."

She gave a nod.

He held up a second finger. "The instant this purpose is fulfilled, we unfuse. Immediately."

She nodded again.

He held up a third finger. "Under no circumstances will I fight while being fused. I'm the General of Eden Star—down to my bones. I will not raise my sword for my people while being intimately connected with anyone that isn't elvish. I do not need the strength of a dragon to defeat my enemies. I'm perfectly capable of slaying kings on my own."

"Alright."

He dropped his hand to his side, but the rage continued in his eyes, storm clouds passing across the surface, full of promise of a very cold winter.

Talc?

Silence.

Ashe, can you talk to her? I just need—

Bridge collapsed on the ground as the dragon came forth, scales as green as the evergreens around them. A thud vibrated the earth as her talons hit the soil, her enormous tail half the height of the trees in the center of Eden Star. Golden eyes stared at Callon down below, her mouth parted to show her rows of teeth.

Callon was up close to a fire-breathing dragon, but he didn't even blink. Like she was an opponent he could easily handle alone, he stared at her without a touch of fear. His eyes were squinting in the sun, making the lines of tension more prominent.

I agree to fuse.

Bridge was still on the ground, his sister there to support him. "So glad that's over..."

What changed your mind?

Talc kept her gaze fixated on Callon. *Because he's only doing this for one reason—to win this war. There is no personal interest. No temptation. No desire. It's a sacrifice—as it is for me.*

Cora's eyes moved back to Callon. "Talc, this is Callon, General of Eden Star. Callon, this is Talc."

The most he could do was give her a subtle nod. "We'll do what we must—then go our separate ways."

She stepped forward.

"She's ready."

Callon held his ground as she came to him, still unafraid even though anyone else would shrink back and recoil. She stood over him, her long neck bringing her face close to his, her nostrils flaring to smell him.

"Put your hand on her chest."

Callon swallowed his look of disgust as best as he could—and then obeyed.

For a few seconds, nothing happened.

Then a flash of movement, of light.

Callon remained behind, still as a rock, like a dragon hadn't been sucked into his body for the first time. His eyes dropped for a moment as he processed the transition, but then his chin rose again, strong and proud, and the anger was back on his face.

She stared, somehow seeing the green dragon deep under his skin, seeing her soul inside him.

After a final stare, Callon turned away—and returned to Eden Star.

MESSAGE FROM THE AUTHOR

Thank you so much for reading Fury!

I wrote the attack on Eden Star three different times, and when Cora takes on General Noose, I was writing and just muttering, "ohmygodohmygod," the entire time I was writing it. And then the scene with Rush and his father at the Stronghold...that was painful to write.

I've been listening to Chevelle while writing this, and "The Red" is the perfect song for that scene. The ash in the air, the ferocity between the characters, so much tension. And then the end when Callon fuses...did anyone see that coming???

Anyway, I'd really like to know what you thought of this installment, so if you post a review, I will read it.

The final book in the series releases April 25th, so the wait isn't much longer!

You can preorder **Slay** now.

You can also sign up for my newsletter to be the first to know about Slay's release:

https://mailchi.mp/57fc055f4215/fuse-series

Thanks for reading,

E. L. Todd

FINDER'S REWARD

I realize I'm a bit biased when I say this, but I really believe this story has the potential for an adaptation to TV or Film. (Could you imagine Flare with his glorious scales as they shine in the sunlight right on the screen? Oh, he'd be so pleased.) So I'm offering a reward to anyone who can get this into the hands of a Hollywood producer. 10% if it's sold to a studio. This doesn't include optioning, which is the period of time when they have the rights to shop around and pitch to studios. I know it's a looooong shot, but a lot of people are reading this series and it's receiving strong reviews. I think Rush, Flare, and Cora have a chance.

Thanks so much for helping me make this dream a reality!

You can email me here:

<u>hartwickpublishing@gmail.com</u>

Subject: Finder's Reward.

I get a lot of emails so I don't wanna miss it by mistake.

Printed in Great Britain
by Amazon